INCARNATE
THE THIRD ENTITY

RUSSELL MARCUM JR

KUDOS FOR INCARNATE

"The pacing is expertly handled, with Jake's battles against both earthly and supernatural forces heightening the suspense at every turn and bringing some genuinely unexpected twists ... a compelling and thought-provoking read for fans of Christian Thrillers."

– K.C. Finn, Readers Favorite

"This book is a unique perspective on God/Religion, it is powerful and captivating."

– Deb Ramos, AuthorsXP

"*Incarnate* ... merges the suspense of a crime thriller with the weighty themes of Christian theology ... "

– Chanticleer Book Reviews

"Incarnate is a well-imagined and skillfully written thriller with believable characters."

– Divine Zape, Readers Favorite

"What makes this story truly exceptional is how it weaves the supernatural with the gritty reality of Jake's world ... The battles he faced, both human and otherworldly, kept me turning the pages late into the night ... recommended for anyone looking for a story that challenges the mind and touches the heart."

– Lilly's Reviews, Literary Titan

"Tackling towering existential matters and exploring the foundations of Christianity through a unique and creative lens, Russell Marcum Jr. boldly delivers in his new novel, Incarnate: The Third Entity, a powerful novel of redemption and revelation."

– Self-Publishing Review

Published and printed in the USA.

Indie Pub Press

ISBN -13: 978-1-964559-43-8

This book is dedicated to my favorite nieces and nephews: Brodie, Sydnie, Kylie, Robin, and Roger.

Waylon Jennings's songs on YouTube
"You Ask Me To" and "Dream On"

"Divine revelation is perfect and, therefore, it is not subject to continual and indefinite progress in order to correspond with the progress of human reason … "

(Excerpt from 1864 *Syllabus of Errors* of Pope Pius IX)
– Carl Sagan, *Pale Blue Dot*

"Many felt that Copernicus and Galileo were up to no good and erosive of the social order. Indeed any challenge, from any source, to the literal truth of the Bible might have such consequences. We can readily see how science began to make people nervous. Instead of criticizing those who perpetuated the myths, public rancor was directed at those who discredited them."

– Carl Sagan, *Pale Blue Dot*

CHAPTER 1

William Jacob "Jake" McCallum paced uneasily on the patio at the back of his brother's house, waiting for Walker Davidson, his wife Donna, and their three kids. He had a bad feeling about their impending visit, partly because of Walker's new, reticent behavior toward him but mostly because he dreaded having to say goodbye to Sarah.

Jake was a deputy sheriff in Beecham County, West Virginia, for nearly ten years. He worked directly with the new sheriff and chief deputy on drug investigations. They invited federal authorities into Beecham County to help them clean up the drugs, but six months ago, those federal authorities turned on them and indicted the sheriff in an illegal coal sale sting. Then, they investigated the Sheriff's Department and indicted Jake for mail fraud connected to his duties as President of the Beecham County Deputy Sheriff's Association.

Legal fees and joblessness forced Jake to burn through his savings quickly. He was left broke, without any income, and unable to keep his apartment. He was barely hanging onto a car that would soon be repossessed. Walker and Donna had offered to help, but their three children left them with very little in the way of discretionary funds. Fortunately, Nick, Jake's older brother by six years, was more settled and better equipped to lend a helping hand. Nick generously took Jake in, stood up for him, and stood beside him in federal court as he was tried, convicted, and sentenced to federal prison.

Jake became friends with Walker during the year and a half between his high school graduation and his stint in the U.S. Army. Walker was twelve years old, and Jake was seventeen. They became nearly inseparable for two summers, riding his brother's horses, camping, hunting, fishing, and sometimes just running through the mountains in wild abandonment. Jake experienced a second childhood. His brother's house became an unofficial "base of operations" for Walker and him, and he turned eighteen at the end of that first summer.

At the end of the second summer, still unsure of what he wanted to do with his life, Jake joined the Army. Three years later, when he was released from service, he returned home with a somber, more serious maturity than when he left. Just six months short of the end of his enlistment period, he met, fell in love, and then traumatically lost his one and only true love.

Jake served in the military police while in the Army, so when he returned home, he took a job with the Sheriff's Department. Walker became his most frequent visitor, and their friendship morphed into something more akin to a father-son relationship. Their literal age difference was the same, but a profound sadness had aged Jake, making him more mature, and helping Walker brought some meaning to his life.

When Walker finished high school, he took a job in a welding shop, and six months later, with Jake's help, he married Donna, his high school sweetheart. Although they had a close relationship, Jake was surprised when Walker returned from his honeymoon and shared intimate details of his wedding night. Jake always knew Walker and Donna were good kids, but he was surprised when Walker confided in him that they had both been virgins. Reminded of his own experience and moved by Walker's willingness to share, Jake opened up for the first time and shared details of his and Sarah's own ill-fated "wedding night."

Jake met Sarah almost ten years ago during the last year of his three-year hitch in the Army. He was stationed in South Korea for that final year, and after having been in-country for only six months, he felt an irresistible urge to go home. He had thirty days of accrued leave and decided that finishing his tour of duty would be much easier if he went home for a month. He'd seen enough of the world and had found nothing more desirable than the mountains of West Virginia.

He started that thirty-day leave by flying into San Francisco International Airport, where he had a six-hour layover. He was walking through the crowded concourse when Sarah literally swept him off his feet. She had dropped some travel brochures and was squatting to pick them up. Jake didn't see her, fell over her, and both ended up sprawled on the floor.

As he helped her up, Jake immediately beheld the most beautiful girl he'd ever seen. Her dazzling blue eyes were set perfectly in her oval face, and she had a light olive complexion. She was barely five feet tall, petite, and had long, shiny black hair. Her eyes reminded him of the eyes of Melissa Sue Anderson, a girl who grew up on the old TV show *Little House on the Prairie.* Jake liked watching old movies and old TV shows. He also listened to old country music. He often thought he'd been born a few decades too late, but not today. Today, he was sure he'd been born to be in this exact place at this precise moment.

You're beautiful, he thought as he stared into those eyes. Then, much to his amazement, he realized he had spoken those words aloud. To cover his embarrassment, other words spewed from his mouth without first being screened by his brain. He would later look back on that encounter and realize that speaking directly from the heart, unfiltered by the mind, was what love was all about. It had indeed been love at first sight.

Jake wore his usual civilian attire: baggy blue jeans, a white T-shirt, and a long-tailed top shirt left unbuttoned and untucked. She wore a tan dress a shade darker than her skin yet light enough to emphasize her eyes and hair. The dress was tight enough to reveal glimpses of her shapely body but loose enough to understate her natural beauty.

He didn't make it home on that trip. He cashed in the remainder of his airline tickets, collected his duffle bag, and took a room at the cheapest motel near the airport.

It was a whirlwind romance that lasted only five days. They spent their days together, but he spent his nights alone in his motel room, watching old movies on the motel's nearly-worn-out DVD player. When his actions threatened to become too amorous, she candidly informed him that she was a virgin and intended to stay that way until her wedding night.

On the fourth day, he took her to a fancy restaurant and proposed marriage. She said yes, but as soon as the exhilaration of the moment passed, they faced the seemingly impossible task of planning their future. He had the next three weeks free but would then have to report back to South Korea to complete his military obligation. She was four months short of her eighteenth birthday, and she was positive her father would never give her permission to marry before she was eighteen.

She spoke as candidly about her home situation as she had about her lack of sexual experience. "Mom died of cancer three years ago, and she had been a faithful church member," she said. "Dad hadn't been a religious man, but he'd been a good man so long as he was under her influence. He took Mom's death hard and seemed to rebel against God. He became an alcoholic and barely held on to his job as a police officer with the San Francisco Police Department. He forbade me to have anything to do with the church, refused to let me invite friends to the house, and absolutely forbade boyfriends. He even disabled the telephone when he went to work so boys couldn't call."

She explained she was planning to run away from home on the day she turned eighteen. She had been scouting the bus station, the train station, and the airport for possible destinations. That was what she'd been doing when Jake tripped over her at the airport. Fortunately, so far, her father hadn't placed her under house arrest. Her days were pretty much her own, but she had a curfew. She had to be in the house before her father got home from work or before dark, whichever came first.

Jake was initially unsettled to learn she was only seventeen and on spring break from her last year in high school, but they finally agreed on an acceptable, totally honorable plan. They talked for the rest of the evening and all the fifth day, fine-tuning that plan. He would leave immediately to return to South Korea to finish his military obligation and cash in the rest of his unused leave. On the day of his ETS from the Army, he would return to the same room at the same motel, and she would meet him there. At that time, he would be free of the Army, and she would be legally emancipated from her father. They would ride a bus to West Virginia, stopping in Las Vegas to get married.

His flight back to South Korea would leave at ten o'clock the next morning. Sarah left him at the motel, promising to return in time to share breakfast before his departure. That night, he was half-heartedly watching a movie and fretting over how he could make it through nearly seven months without her when he heard a soft rap at the door. He was cinching his bathrobe as he opened the door. It was Sarah.

"I slipped out of the house," Sarah said. She looked at him as if her whole world depended on his answer. She asked, "Do you love me enough to do something for me?"

It was raining, and thunder reverberated in the distance. Her black hair was plastered to her head and around her beautiful face. Her clothes clung to her shapely body like they had been painted on. Shaking off the temporary paralysis that this sudden vision of loveliness instilled in him, Jake stepped forward, put his arms around her, and pulled her inside. He closed the door and kissed her cool, rain-dampened face.

"I really love you," he assured her.

"Will you do something for me?" she asked again.

He could only guess something might have happened between her and her father. He didn't know what she might ask: fight her father, desert the Army to run away with her, or some other darker chore. He couldn't guess what it might be, but whatever it was, he knew he couldn't refuse her.

He said, "I do love you, and I'll do anything you ask me to." It was a sentiment expressed in an old Waylon Jennings song.

He put his arms around her again, but she pushed back from him to look into his eyes.

"Will you marry me right now?" she asked.

"Anything you ask," he reiterated.

She pulled a DVD from her purse.

"This is the video of my mother's wedding ceremony," she said. "If we recite our own vows while we watch it, we can make it our ceremony. This can be our wedding night."

Jake was lost in her liquid blue eyes, drowning without a struggle, being pulled below the surface of love where two souls became one. He felt helplessly intoxicated by her beauty. Standing in front of the TV, the ceremony was a blur, but after their vows were made, every touch, every smell, and every bit of sensory input was indelibly etched into his psyche. Their bodies – hers chilled from the rain and his warmed from the bed – came together like warm and cold weather fronts, creating a storm of passion that rivaled the thunderstorm raging outside the window.

Back when he was in middle school, Jake once heard a high school girl on the school bus declare, "Sex without love is like masturbation." His experiences with sex caused him to dismiss that sage advice, but Sarah became the living personification of that wisdom. With her, he reached heights of passion he never knew existed.

Jake boarded his plane the following day on an emotional high, not knowing that in three short weeks, his reason for living would be taken from him. While waiting in Seoul, South Korea, for a scheduled helicopter flight that would take him to his unit near the DMZ, Jake ran into his unit's Company Clerk. Instead of waiting for the chopper, he caught a ride in the Company Jeep. The helicopter on which he was supposed to be riding went down, and the U.S. Army, in one of its notorious SNAFUs, declared that Jake was killed in the crash.

He contacted his family and rectified the mistake, but how could he be certain Sarah knew he was alive and well? How could he be sure she hadn't heard the erroneous report, or if she had, that she'd seen the correction? He couldn't bear the thought that she might believe him dead, and their rendezvous canceled. He had her mailing address, but he was reluctant to use it. She'd only given it to him in case of an emergency.

He had to know, so he wrote her a letter. He was in misery for two weeks until he finally got a response from San Francisco. He expected the letter he received to be from Sarah, but it was from her father's attorney instead. It rocked his world and proved he'd never known true misery.

The letter informed him that the attorney represented Sarah's father. According to the letter, Sarah ran away from home and was found the next day, involved in a fatal accident near the airport. An autopsy revealed she'd been raped. Based on Jake's own admissions in his letter, criminal charges of statutory rape and contributing to the delinquency of a minor would be filed, as well as a wrongful death lawsuit.

Jake was nearly undone. The loss of Sarah, combined with the obscenity of what her father planned to do to him, was almost more than he could bear. It was the first time in his life he'd ever wanted to die. Several times, he'd stood on a sidewalk contemplating stepping out in front of a fast-moving truck. The fact that he never took those last few fatal steps was as much a mystery to him as why neither the military nor the civilian authorities came for him.

After the initial shock eased and the pain of loss became at least tolerable, he began dreading every day, sure that this would be the day he would be arrested and dishonorably discharged from the service. As the days turned into weeks, the fear turned into guilt, and he began hoping each day that this would be the day that punishment would bring some degree of relief. He had started to accept his culpability in her death. After all, he *had* placed her in harm's way. She wouldn't have been involved in that accident without being with him at the airport.

Virtually in a daze, he completed his tour of duty, and while being released from military service, he looked over his shoulder for the escort that would take him to San Francisco. But nobody showed up. He had to change planes in San Francisco and expected to be intercepted there by Sarah's father and other police officers, but nobody showed up there either.

There was no layover in San Francisco this time, and he went directly from his arrival gate to his departure gate. He boarded his flight to Dallas, Texas, without a problem. From Dallas, he went to Atlanta, Georgia, and then to Charleston, West Virginia. He went home, expecting the authorities to await him, but nobody except family and friends were there.

Life was what happened while you waited for something to happen, so Jake signed up for unemployment and went through the motions of looking for a job. Two months passed without a word from San Francisco, and he saw an advertisement for employment with the Beecham County Sheriff's Department. A Civil Service examination was scheduled, but what grabbed his attention was that applicants were required to pass a criminal background investigation. Jake took the test and waited.

Two deputy sheriffs came knocking on his door a month and a half later. Seeing them, he felt a sense of relief at the prospect of being punished. He was expecting they'd come after they did the criminal background check, but he was astonished when they announced the purpose of their visit. They notified him that he'd successfully passed everything. They didn't come to arrest him. They'd been sent to offer him a job as a deputy sheriff.

RUSSELL MARCUM JR.

Jake took the job with the Sheriff's Department. When Walker and Donna had their first child, Jake stood shoulder to shoulder with the proud father as the nurse placed the baby girl in the nursery window. Walker had already seen her, but he said he wanted to show her to his best friend. Ordinarily, Jake found newborn babies unappealing, but he couldn't deny the beauty of this one. He'd expected a scrunched-up little body, wrinkles, and no hair, but this baby was an exception.

"You're beautiful," Jake whispered as he stared at her through the window.

She was the living embodiment of perfection. Her features were smooth, her arms and legs were straight, her light olive complexion was unmarred, and her crowning glory was the sparse golden hair fanned out around her head like a halo. Except for the color of her hair, she was the spitting image of Sarah. She had dazzling blue eyes, flawless body symmetry, and natural beauty.

Jake glanced at Walker, and his good friend was looking at him with a big, broad smile on his face.

"What's her name?" Jake asked.

Theatrically clearing his throat, Walker rhetorically asked, "Remember telling me about that girl in San Francisco?" Then, he said, "I told Donna about it; she thought it was the most romantic thing she'd ever heard. She said that if we ever had a girl, she wanted to name her Sarah."

"Sarah?" Jake said, relishing the name as he looked at her. Then he whispered, "My Sarah."

Sarah set the pattern for Jake's possessive claim on Walker's children. In his younger days, Walker had been a constant presence around Jake's house, but after the children were born, Jake became a constant presence around Walker's house. Except for several failed relationships, his work and Walker's kids had become Jake's whole world. He was proud that Walker granted him privileges usually reserved for grandparents.

Two years after Sarah came into the world, Walker's second child was born, and a year and a half after that, his third child. Both babies were boys, Walker Jr. and Mark, and Jake had been present for each new birth. His joy increased with each new addition to Walker's family, but little Sarah had already become the light of his life. When Sarah uttered her first sounds, Jake was there. When those first sounds slowly evolved into recognizable words, Jake realized she had been trying to say his name even before she could talk.

Jake's reverie was interrupted by the scrunch of tires on the gravel road. He walked to the patio's edge, looked down at the road, and saw Walker's car turn into the driveway. He parked in the wide spot in the curve and got out. Jake instantly noticed that Walker's body language was weird. He looked like he was walking to the gallows instead of visiting a friend.

Walker was carrying one-year-old Mark, Donna was holding the hand of three-year-old Walker Jr., and five-year-old Sarah was bringing up the rear, looking at her feet in the unstable gravel. Jake greeted Walker and Donna, hugging each of the boys in turn. He kneeled to receive Sarah, but when she looked up at him, she wheeled around and ran back down the driveway. Jake looked at Walker, but Walker just shrugged a shoulder to indicate he didn't know what she was doing.

"Where're you going?" Jake called after her.

"Forgot something!" Sarah called back over her shoulder.

"Watch where you're going!" Donna nearly screamed and, giving voice to her primary concern, added, "Slow down before you fall."

Walker shepherded Donna and the boys into the kitchen, where Jake's brother Nick, his sister-in-law Jenny, and his nephew Jimmy were preparing a snack for the kids. Nick and Jenny treated Walker and Donna like they were part of Jake's family, and they happily welcomed the kids with open arms. Walker came back out to wait for Sarah with Jake.

The tiny blonde in a floral sundress and pink shoes came back up the driveway carrying something in both hands. It appeared to be heavy. When she got to the patio and put her burden down, Jake scooped her up and wrapped her in his arms.

"Hi, baby," he said as he kissed her cheeks.

"For you," Sarah said, indicating the Kroger bag she'd put down.

"What's that?"

"I heard Mommy say you need money for a lawyer," Sarah said.

She had always been very precocious and often used grown-up words and complex ideas. Jake let her stand on the edge of the patio while he quickly looked in the Kroger bag. It contained her piggy bank. He set it aside, wrapped his arms around her again, and pulled her onto his knee as he sat down.

Sarah said, "I know you'll come when I need you," her tone holding a strange mixture of prophecy, question, and statement. Then she whispered, "I love you."

"I know," Jake whispered back, a game they often played.

From behind them, Walker cleared his throat and said, "I need to talk to you, Jake."

Jake kissed Sarah again and said, "Honey, you better go in and get some cake and cookies before the boys eat it all up."

Jake started to set her down, but she turned, threw her arms around his neck, and hugged him fiercely. Strong emotions passed between them, and Jake's eyes filled with tears. He hadn't told her he would soon have to go away to prison for a long time, but she seemed to know this wasn't an ordinary goodbye.

Before she let go of him, Sarah mysteriously whispered, "You'll win. I know you will."

After Sarah went into the house, Jake picked up the bag with the piggy bank and said, "Let's walk down to your car."

Jake quickly decided on the only thing he could do with the piggy bank. He went down the driveway to the back of Walker's car and waited for him.

"Do me a favor with this," Jake said, indicating the piggy bank he was holding. "I can't keep her money, but I can't hurt her feelings by not accepting it. Put this in the trunk and cash in the coins when you get time. Buy her a new piggy bank and put the paper money in it."

Walker opened the trunk without saying a word. He then hid the piggy bank under a blanket, still without speaking.

"So, what's up?" Jake finally asked.

Walker closed the trunk, looked down, and toed the gravel. Finally, he blurted out, "I don't want you coming around my house anymore."

Jake was stunned. It was a sucker punch to the heart.

"What in the hell are you talking about?" Jake asked, spitting out each word as though to get a bad taste out of his mouth.

"People have been calling and telling me they've seen you at my house when I'm not home," Walker said. Either gaining confidence or driven by a flash of anger, Walker continued, "They tell me you've slept with Donna."

"What's the matter with you?" Jake snapped. "What people? Who have you been talking to?" When Walker didn't answer, Jake continued. "If you recall, me coming around your house while you were working was your idea. After Sarah was born, you asked me to help Donna out when you were working. Remember when I was parked at the Courthouse holding Sarah while Donna was shopping and paying bills? I let Sarah stand in my lap and hold on to the steering wheel. One of the older ladies who works in the Sheriff's Tax Office came out of the Courthouse and stopped to say hello. She said, 'Oh, I bet you're proud of that one.' I knew what she must've thought, but I just said, 'Yes, ma'am, I sure am.' I told you about that when it happened, and you laughed."

Walker didn't say anything, and he wasn't laughing now. He turned, opened the front passenger door, and sat down. He dropped his keys while trying to use one to open the glovebox.

Jake didn't wait to see what Walker was doing; he just started up the driveway in disgust. He'd been fired from his job, convicted of mail fraud in federal court, and sentenced to fifteen months in federal prison. He expected the conviction would cause him to lose friends, but Walker was one friend he thought he would never lose. Two weeks ago, he was playing with the kids in the living room when Walker came home from work. Nothing seemed to have changed at that time.

Jake heard the car door slam when Walker got out and started following him up the driveway.

Walker inscrutably said, "I wish I didn't know now what I didn't know then."

Jake was at a loss for words. This accusation had utterly blindsided him. Standing before the sliding glass door, he just shook his head as he slid it open. He hesitated in the doorway, turned, and said, "Take good care of my kids."

"Then, you admit they could be your kids," Walker said.

Jake was dumbfounded. He was no longer trusted like a blood relative with unfettered access to Walker's wife and kids. He had never cursed Walker before, but right now, hurt welled up inside him, and words like heck, darn, and shucks just couldn't accurately express his feelings.

"Go to hell, you crazy son-of-a-bitch," Jake retorted as he was turning away, and as he was closing the sliding glass door, he added, "Asshole!"

Jake walked through the house without stopping in the kitchen. It felt like the end of the world. He didn't want to talk to anybody. The evasions and cold shoulders he'd gotten from other friends and co-workers were nothing compared to this mind-numbing betrayal. He continued through the house and out the front door. He walked off the front porch and down the bank to the road. He turned left and headed toward the barn. A small part of him hoped Walker would follow and apologize, but his overwhelming emotion was that he couldn't stand the sight of him right now.

CHAPTER 2

W hile the old Pastor was concluding his sermon from the pulpit, Eli turned and whispered to his father, "I can't do this anymore, Dad. I tried to be content to just sit and listen, but the Pastor preached those same old, tired contradictions that he was preaching back before I left home. The last time I felt like this, I ran off to the Navy. I don't want to leave again, but I think I'd be happier at another church."

Eli Cavenaugh grew up in Manchester, Kentucky's First Free Will Baptist Church. His father had been an assistant Pastor in the church for as long as Eli could remember. At the age of twelve, he had gone to the altar, but instead of his faith growing as he got older, the contradictions between creation and evolution created a schism in his mind. He felt compelled to leave the church but was also reluctant to incur his father's disapproval and disappointment, so instead of leaving the church back then, he left home and joined the U.S. Navy.

He spent four years in the Navy without going home, and then he spent the next year traveling around the country. He met his true love in Detroit, Michigan, married her, got a job in a car factory, and settled in the suburbs. He joined a small community church where he found a new perspective on the Bible that changed his life. His first child was born a year after his marriage, and two years later, his second child was born.

After being laid off from his job in Detroit, his nightly dreams became fixated on Kentucky, and although he hadn't talked to his parents in nearly ten years, he picked up the phone. In a week, Eli, his wife, and their two children were packed in a U-Haul and headed for Kentucky. They were greeted with open arms when they entered his parents' house.

Eli settled into the house his father found for him, accepted a job at his father's furniture store, and returned to his father's church. Nothing seemed to have changed except for some new faces. The same people were conducting the same services. A pleasant month passed without incident, and Eli wondered how he could have ever left this place.

However, all that changed tonight when Pastor Thurman Cromwell took to the pulpit. The circumstances of his leaving came back with a vengeance. Thurman cockily strolled into the pulpit, and although he was nearly eighty and suffering the infirmities of age, he demonstrated that he was still very much in control of the church. Eli sat through the sermon, disagreeing with almost everything the Pastor said.

When the service ended, Eli's father suggested, "Let's go in the back and use one of the classrooms."

Now, confronting his father, Eli dreaded the disapproval that would come, but his father surprised him.

"With God, all things are possible," his father said calmly and reasonably. "Can't you just take it on faith?"

"All things are possible," Eli agreed, "and it's possible to accept contradictions if you have faith, but what good is the Bible if you must have faith before the Bible can inspire faith? If evolution is more self-consistent than the Bible and not contradicted by reason, which is more likely to be embraced? Pope Pius IX put the Bible in a catch-22, requiring an unshakable faith in the old interpretations of the Bible that don't make any sense now. It would help if the Church admitted that Popes are not infallible."

When his father looked nonplussed, Eli said, "In 1864, Pope Pius IX declared that divine revelation is perfect and not subject to change to correspond with progress and reason."

"Okay," his father said as he leaned back, steepling his hands under his chin. "You want to leave this church, and you want me to agree. Tell me how you would preach creation."

Eli started with Adam and Eve's childlessness in the garden, affirming the axiom that the price of immortality is sterility. Obviously, what can't age can't reproduce, necessitating Adam and Eve's loss of immortality. He concluded by describing the role of the Gentiles outside of the garden.

"That sounds reasonable, and I don't think anybody would go to Hell for believing that the cavemen were the Gentiles," his father offered. "Unfortunately, however, you've forgotten the event that makes cavemen irrelevant."

Eli smiled. "I didn't forget the flood, Dad." He said, "It's important to understand why the flood occurred. The good news for the Jews was that they were God's chosen people. The bad news was that God set a higher, unattainable standard of conduct for them, thus the need for Jesus. Clearly, the flood punished God's chosen people without destroying the Gentiles. Just as the waters of the Red Sea were held back for the passage of the Jews, the waters of the flood were held back to shield the lands of the Gentiles. In Genesis 10:5, the Bible establishes that the Gentiles continued to exist in their own lands in just the third generation of Noah's family after the flood."

Eli summed up his position on Creation, crossed his arms, and waited. When no response was forthcoming, he said, "I can't submit to the out-of-date teaching anymore, Dad. Do I have your blessing to find another church?"

After briefly deliberating on it, his father said, "No." Then he calmly added, "I think you should become a preacher."

"But, but…," Eli stammered, shocked. He collected himself and said, "I've never considered preaching, but even if I could preach, what about Pastor Cromwell? He'd have a heart attack if I got up before the church and said what I've said here."

"I can't say I totally agree with Thurman's dogmatic resistance to change," his father said, "because I've seen the decline of the Church. Something must be done so that the Bible can return the Church to its former glory. Seek ye first the kingdom of God, and all other things will be added unto you. Either Thurman will see the light, or you'll find a path around him."

*****

Just over a year later, amid a mixed reaction loosely defined by age, Eli stepped down from the pulpit after having preached his first sermon. The younger crowd was enthusiastic, and the older folks were polite and respectful, but the elderly, including the Pastor, were downright cold. Eli was almost out the door when one of the deacons caught up with him.

"Pastor Cromwell would like to see you in his office," the Deacon said. "I'll catch your dad and send him in."

Cromwell wasn't known for polite invitations. He was better known for assuming an archaic degree of authority that hadn't existed in the Church for more than a century.

"Wait," Eli said as the Deacon turned to leave. "I'd appreciate it if you don't tell Dad. This is something I need to handle on my own."

Eli didn't want to become a source of division in the church. An insoluble problem between himself and the Pastor could hurt the church, but the same problem between his father and the Pastor could destroy it.

As soon as Eli entered the office, the Pastor commanded, "Sit!"

The Pastor was sitting on the edge of his chair, leaning forward with his elbows propped on the massive desk, his hands fisted under his chin.

Eli was determined not to lose his temper. "Excuse me?" he said, unmoving.

"Please," the Pastor said, somewhat moderating his tone and indicating the chair.

As soon as Eli sat down, Pastor Cromwell lowered his hands to the desk, pushed himself to his feet, and leaned forward to tower over Eli as much as the big desk allowed.

"That was blasphemy," the Pastor declared with unconcealed anger. "I will not allow that preaching in my church. You're a heretic, and I should have you arrested and banned from the church. You'll never preach again. I demand you apologize to me and then apologize to the church."

The Pastor was turning red and working himself into a rage. Eli became concerned that the old man might work himself into a heart attack. He resisted the urge to stand.

"I'm not Galileo," Eli said in his most reasonable tone, "and you don't have the authority to have me arrested or banned. I know the Board of Trustees must approve everything in this church."

"I could refuse to let you preach again," the Pastor said with less bluster but still angry.

"That could be taken before the Board, too," Eli said, letting the implied threat of a confrontation between the Pastor and the Board of Trustees hang in the air. He knew the Pastor knew that his father was an influential member of the Board.

The Pastor sank back in his chair, having obviously realized he couldn't carry out the threats he'd made. He stared at the ceiling for a long time. When he arrived at a decision, he opened his desk drawer and withdrew a folder.

"What if you stay in the church but promise to do any preaching elsewhere?" the Pastor said, reluctantly offering a compromise. "They need a preacher up at the prison camp," he concluded, handing the folder to Eli.

Either Thurman will see the light, or you'll find a path around him. His father had been right on both counts.

"That could work," Eli said, secretly ecstatic, taking the folder and eagerly accepting the proffered compromise.

He hadn't told anybody about his recurring dreams over the past few months involving the prison camp and his growing conviction that a fantastic truth was about to be revealed to him. In his dreams, he interacted with an inmate in that prison camp who was intimately connected to that truth. Now, it appeared that the dreams had been prophetic. He was excited about the opportunity to preach, but more than that, he was relieved he would have access to the prison camp without going there as an inmate.

CHAPTER 3

The world was waking up from its long winter nap. Foliage was turning green everywhere, dappled with splashes of color from wildflowers, blossoming trees, and flowering bushes. Jake was deep in thought, oblivious to the beauty of nature that was busy renewing itself all around him. It was the evening after Walker's visit, and Jake sat alone on the front porch, ostensibly enjoying the early spring weather, but his calm outward demeanor was masking an inner turmoil.

Twilight's last gleaming, Jake thought, watching what he expected to be his last sunset. The last rays of the sun were shining through the trees on the ridgetops as shadows darkened under the trees in the valley. Twilight came early and lingered longer in the mountains and hollows of West Virginia, and Jake's thoughts turned gloomier than the dimming light around him.

His world was turned upside down when he was prosecuted for mail fraud. In just two days, he was required to report to the Manchester Federal Prison Camp in Manchester, Kentucky, to begin serving a fifteen-month prison sentence. But his legal woes weren't what brought Jake to the breaking point. The desertion by his best friend this morning brought him more grief than even the prospect of going to prison. Because of Walker's accusation, his relationship with Sarah was effectively terminated. He'd lost his apartment, his job, and his friends. Now that he lost his Sarah for a second time, he had no reason to live. He hated that his brother would have to deal with the aftermath, but he couldn't help what would happen after he was dead.

When Jake learned that the federal authorities he invited into this majority-Democrat county had an agenda of their own, he confronted the FBI agent. He bluntly asked, "Why are you people investigating my sheriff?" The agent had just as bluntly replied, "It's not our choice. Our orders come from Washington. We've been ordered to investigate political corruption."

Jake informed the sheriff about that conversation with the FBI agent and acknowledged that if the investigation wasn't politically motivated, then someone in the government might be protecting the drug dealers. Either the drug dealers became the incidental beneficiaries of a political power grab by the Republicans, or they were getting intentional help. The sheriff became incensed by the duplicity of the federal authorities, and he adamantly declared, "Either we get them, or they get us." As it turned out, Jake had to admit, *they got us.*

The Sheriff was ultimately removed from office by an FBI sting that used the sheriff's closest friends to entrap him. The sting involved the illegal sale of a stockpile of coal that never physically existed. It was a crime wholly manufactured by the federal authorities. The Chief Deputy was a novice politician as well as a rookie cop who was easily intimidated by the FBI. He capitulated and confessed to every dirty deed he'd ever done, starting in his childhood. The federal authorities attempted to use the Chief Deputy to entrap Jake, but that failed. They had to settle for using the BCDSA's charitable Bingo games against him.

Jake was president of the Beecham County Deputy Sheriff's Association, and he was ultimately convicted of mail fraud for filing paperwork that omitted payments made to the other deputies for working Bingo games. It was made a federal crime based entirely upon the fact that the forms were sent through the U.S. mail. Jake was sure the federal authorities targeted him because his drug investigations were becoming productive. They knew that a criminal conviction against himself would end his investigations and destroy his credibility.

When he was indicted, Jake sought help from Nick, his older brother. His brother's support was unconditional.

"Don't you want to know what I was indicted for?" Jake had asked his brother.

"Does it really matter?" Nick responded. "I've known you all your life. Even if you killed somebody, I know you would have been justified."

Jake was deeply moved by his brother's declaration of trust and support, particularly considering the commandment against killing and the fact that his brother was the pastor of a little church. Nick had been at his side through every court appearance. Even after his antagonistic speech at his sentencing, or maybe because of that speech, Nick continued to be his staunchest ally.

Jake dreamed every night, and while he was sitting alone, his thoughts eventually turned to those dreams. During what little sleep he managed to get the previous night, his dream tormented him with everything he'd lost. It affirmed that he had nothing for which to live, notwithstanding what a loud voice said just before he awoke. *"Your life is about to become as strange as a Dean Koontz novel,"* the voice declared.

"Mind if I join you?"

Jake jumped as he was abruptly jerked out of his thoughts. He hadn't heard his brother come out of the house.

"Sorry," Nick said. "I didn't mean to startle you. I just thought you might want some company."

"It's okay," Jake said. "I was just thinking about something. I thought you and Jenny were watching a movie."

"We were, but it went off about a half hour ago. She's in the kitchen, and Jimmy's in the shower getting ready for bed."

Jake looked around, amazed that he hadn't noticed the darkness beyond the lights of the house.

Nick sat down, and Jenny came out with a cup of coffee, trailed by their two dogs, a brown boxer and a black rottweiler. Jenny got the dogs when they were pups, and in tribute to the old *Rocky* movies, she named them Rocky and Apollo. Jake teased her that she should have named them Rocky and Bullwinkle because of the rottweiler's goofy antics.

Jake hadn't known what to do with his life, but Nicolas McCallum seemed to have always known he wanted to be a preacher. After high school, Nick got his electrician's certification and took a one-year Bible course. He became an electrician in the coal mines and eventually became the pastor of a little church. He married Jenny and bought this house on 255 acres. The property included some bottomland and one mountainside. Their fourteen-year-old son, Jimmy, was born here.

"Want some coffee, Jake?" Jenny asked, turning to go back into the house.

"No, thanks," Jake said. "Don't need anything to help me not sleep."

Jenny just grinned. She opened the door but hesitated, looking toward the sound from the road. The pavement ended on the other side of a little hill, and depending on their speed, cars could make a lot of noise when they transitioned from asphalt to gravel.

"Seems to be more traffic in the hollow lately," Jenny remarked before going back into the house.

It was a dead-end hollow with only two other houses above the McCallums'. There usually wasn't much traffic because the family in the first house above them was away most of the time visiting relatives, and the residents of the last house were an elderly couple who got infrequent visitors.

Nick seemed to know Jake's thoughts were in a dark place. He sipped his coffee and said, "Everything happens for a reason. Even the bad things work toward the glory of God."

Jake didn't respond, but after a few minutes of silence, he asked, "You ever think about nonexistence?"

Nick hesitated and seemed to be carefully considering his words before he answered. "Sooner or later," he said, "everybody comes face to face with their own mortality. I've had a few close calls and several occasions to …"

"No," Jake interrupted. "I don't mean death. I mean absolute nonexistence: no people, stars, or even space. I get a weird feeling when I try to visualize it. I think nonexistence must be impossible. No matter how microscopic you shrink matter before a big bang, there's still something there. That would mean that something had to have always existed."

Jake considered himself an agnostic, concluding that Evolution and Creation had identical drawbacks. Both required a high degree of faith in something that couldn't be proven. But, it seemed to him that believing in an Omnipotent Being was more reasonable than thinking that nonliving chemicals came together to create living cells that just accidentally evolved into such a clear delineation between flora and fauna. If there were rules governing which cell was plant and which was animal, then who made those rules? And if there were no rules, what would keep those cells from creating more freaks than a mad scientist's laboratory?

"You know I believe God always existed," Nick said. Always unable to resist an opportunity to encourage Jake toward faith, he added, "But it sounds like you're seeking the truth, and that gives me hope." When Jake didn't respond, Nick asked, "You want to talk about what happened with Walker?"

"For some stupid reason, Walker thinks I slept with Donna," Jake said, his anger tinging his words.

"Did you?" Nick asked matter-of-factly with neither judgment nor accusation in his tone.

"No," Jake said.

"Did you tell Walker that?"

The question surprised Jake. It suggested that Nick might have talked to Walker.

"No," Jake said, "because he didn't ask – he just accused. Walker had already decided I was guilty, so whatever I said wouldn't matter. He said he didn't want me coming around his house anymore." After a few moments, Jake asked, "Why? Did Walker say something to you?"

"He just said somebody called him and told him some things they shouldn't know. I reminded him that you have enemies who might be spreading lies. When I pressed him on it, he would only say that you didn't deny it."

"He didn't ask me anything," Jake repeated with finality.

Their conversation returned to the nature of existence versus nonexistence, and they talked until Nick got up and announced that he needed to get ready for work. He worked the midnight to eight shift, and he chose that shift so that he could arrange his sleep schedule around his church duties.

"I'm going to lie down and read for a while," Jake said. "Have a good night, and don't work too hard."

"N-O God, no peace," Nick said. "K-N-O-W God, know peace," he added, spelling the words no and know and grinning broadly. "I'll see you in the morning. I'm taking tomorrow night off, so like on Fridays, I'll just sleep for a few hours when I get home. Maybe we'll have a cookout or something."

Nick had arranged to take tomorrow night off so that he could drive Jake to Kentucky the following day. On Fridays, he usually slept only a few hours so he could sleep again when nighttime came, and that's what he would do tomorrow.

Jake said goodnight to everybody and retired to his bedroom. The décor of the bedroom was what Jake thought of as barely managed chaos, but he made a conscious effort to have as little impact on it as possible. When he moved into his brother's house more than a month ago, Jimmy graciously gave him his bedroom and took the guest bedroom next to his parents to afford Jake some measure of privacy.

Jake got comfortable in bed, cleared his mind, and began reading one of his old Dean Koontz novels. He collected Koontz's works and reread them from time to time. Twenty minutes later, he heard Nick leaving for work. After a couple hours, he was nearly a quarter of the way through the novel when his eyes began to burn. He laid the book on his chest and closed his eyes. Without realizing it, he slipped into a dream world.

"I now pronounce you man and wife. You may kiss the bride," the preacher said on the video.

They turned to each other and kissed passionately.

Sarah gently pulled away. She turned the DVD player off and then the TV. Without saying a word, she undressed, toweled off, pulled down the covers, and slid into bed.

Jake shed his bathrobe and waited. Sarah slid over and held the cover back invitingly. Jake quickly took his underwear off, slid in, and wrapped his arms around her. His bed-warmed body met her rain-cooled skin in an orgy of rapturous sensations. Eventually, he entered her. They rocked in the natural motion that was the primitive dance of life, and when they simultaneously climaxed, he emptied his seed into her.

Jake breathed in her essence as he held her, but the sound of barking dogs suddenly intruded. Something must be wrong, Jake thought. There shouldn't be any dogs in this motel. He rolled away from her, lay on his back, and listened to the silence. Suddenly, the dogs came back.

He woke up as the dogs ran past his bedroom door, and when they got a little farther away, they started barking again. He quickly remembered where he was and knew what was happening. When the dogs heard something outside, they ran repeatedly from the front to the back door until somebody came to investigate. He started to get up but hesitated when he heard his nephew's voice. He saw it was still dark outside, and when he looked at the clock, he saw that it was a few minutes after six.

"I see taillights going up the hollow," Jimmy said.

Jimmy said it loudly enough that Jake could hear him, but Jake was sure he must be responding to a question coming from his mother's bedroom. Since it was near the time when Jenny and Jimmy usually got up anyway, Jake laid back down. He listened for several minutes to ensure it was nothing more than a passing car. When he heard no unusual activity, he relaxed and began thinking about the dream. He was surprised when he felt a wetness in his crotch. Thirty-two years old, and here he was, having a wet dream like a teenager.

He wanted to get up and shower but didn't want to face Jenny and Jimmy. He didn't usually get up before they left for work and school, and he didn't want to change that today. He didn't want them to remember him as being deceitful or give them any reason to feel guilty that they hadn't recognized his intent and tried to stop him. He couldn't help but lie to his brother, and he only hoped that Nick would forgive him.

He would have asked to hold Sarah in his arms again if he'd been given one wish. But he'd been given so much more than that. He lived again the most momentous hours of his life. He took it as a good omen and an affirmation of the rightness of what he planned to do today.

He didn't expect to fall back to sleep, but when he closed his eyes to better focus on Sarah and savor the love the dream had reinvigorated, he entered a dream world again.

He stood on a precipice that divided creation from the unformed void, looking upon the lights of the physical universe, beholding creation from a bird's-eye view. He saw the galaxies in all their splendor, dancing to an ancient rhythm like exalting music translated into its optical equivalent. Knowing that Sarah was no longer in any physical world, he turned his back to the lights and faced the void.

"Sarah?" he cried into the void.

Gradually, the intensity of his stare was rewarded with the soft, radiant glow of ethereal beings who seemed to move in and out of his range of vision. The light increased in excruciatingly small increments, and what he had initially perceived as cognizant movement became wisps of fog that coalesced into a solid wall in the distance. When he turned his head, he saw it was the same in all directions.

He became aware that he was in an awkward position. He looked down and saw that he was standing on the roof of a small building, with one foot planted on either side of the peak. The low susurrations of water drew his eyes downward, and he saw water licking at the eaves of the roof. Vertigo forced him to sit down, and he slowly lowered himself like a rodeo rider cautiously mounting a bull. He didn't know where he was or how he had gotten there, but he did know that he had come there to die.

He consciously suppressed all thoughts of what had led him to this decision, but he was confident it was the right thing to do. Although he was vaguely frightened at what was about to happen, he took solace in the fact that when it was all over, he would experience a simple, peaceful, pre-birth nonexistence.

He was prepared to die, but he suddenly decided that he had nothing to lose by giving God a chance. He whispered a prayer. "God, I'm sorry. I want to believe that Your Son died on the Cross for me. Please, help me."

He was about to continue when he heard a thud and felt a slight vibration. He looked down and saw a doughnut-shaped life preserver bobbing against the roof. He lifted a leg over the peak but stopped before sliding down. "No," he said aloud, "I want to die if I don't see a miracle." He threw his leg back over the peak and watched as the life preserver washed around the end of the roof and floated away into the fog.

He listened to the whispering of the water until the sound of a small engine broke the quietness. A little boat came gliding out of the fog, narrowly missing the end of the roof. When the two men in the boat noticed him, the one controlling the motor whipped the boat around. The engine slowed its downward progress but lacked the horsepower to overcome the current. Seeing what was happening, the other man grabbed a coil of rope from the bottom of the boat, held on to one end, and flung the coil. The uncoiling rope draped itself over the roof.

"Grab the rope!" the man yelled.

Having already decided to wait for a miracle, he watched the rope snake over the peak and down the side. The end of the rope plopped into the water just as the fog swallowed the boat.

He immediately heard a clatter and saw a helicopter hovering above him. A man leaned out of the open side door and tossed a rope ladder at him. When Jake ignored the ladder, the man began climbing down.

His attention was drawn away from the ladder when the building upon which he sat gave a violent shudder. Then, the roof flattened on the water and began inverting. He expected water and darkness to envelop him, but it didn't come. Instead, he found himself standing again, and the fog had become clouds, drifting lazily around his knees. This must be Heaven, he thought.

Tentatively, he asked, "God, are You here?"

*"**I have always been here**," came a powerful, soft voice filled with love and compassion.*

At first, Jake felt peace and love wash over him, but then, as the implications of God's existence dawned on him, he felt fear and confusion.

"But, God," he asked, "why didn't You save me?"

*"**My poor foolish son**," said the voice, "**I did save you**."*

His fear drained away, and the peace and love surrounding him was palpable.

*Before he could ask another question, the same strong, melodic voice declared, "**I am come again into the world**," followed by a clap of thunder.*

Jake bolted upright in bed. When he realized where he was and heard nothing unusual in the house, he dropped his head back onto the pillow, confused by the noise that had awakened him. Every nerve in his body tingled like a classic symptom of shellshock. He wondered if the mind could imagine a noise so loud that it could cause physical symptoms in the body. Whatever the tingling was, he hoped it would pass quickly because it was nearly 8:30, and he needed to retrieve his service revolver and take a quick shower before Nick got home.

CHAPTER 4

Stanley Gunther was fidgety, cradling the Uzi as he sat in the back seat of the Chevy Caprice. The Uzi was from Israeli military surplus, and he'd gotten it along with two others in a lucrative drug deal. The Chevy was light green and had been stolen just for this job. They were parked where they could watch the McCallum house but were hidden from view by the new greenery on the bushes and the three-board fence of the larger paddock attached to the barn.

McCallum was scheduled to report to a federal prison camp tomorrow, but Stanley intended to kill him today. What McCallum said during his sentencing hearing had so infuriated U.S. Attorney Daniel Sullivan and Stanley's brother, West Virginia State Police Sargeant Glen Stillwell, that they wanted him dead. McCallum had implicated them by name in open court as suspected of complicity in the drug business, and they were no longer satisfied with taking just his freedom and credibility.

"Idiot!" Stanley scolded the driver as he watched another light come on in the house. "You woke the whole damn house."

"Sorry," Wayne said, shrugging his shoulders submissively. "I stopped to confirm that McCallum's car was there the last two mornings, and nothing like that happened."

"I knew you were going too fast when you hit this gravel road," Stanley nervously complained. "You made enough noise to wake the dead."

The driver, Wayne Parsley, was twenty-nine, five-foot-nine, and slightly overweight. He kept his long brown hair tied back in a ponytail, and his cheeks and forehead were scarred from severe acne in his teen years.

After half an hour without any further reaction from the house, Stanley felt calmer. He was anxious for this drive-by shooting to succeed because he led his brother to believe that he'd hired a professional out of Cleveland to kill McCallum. However, Stanley had come up with this perfect plan. He did hire a professional from Cleveland, but he intended to use that guy for another job. He would do this job himself and use the professional to get rid of his second wife and her son.

Stanley had been with his first wife for five long years, and they had no children. Their relationship deteriorated to the point where she was ready to leave him. He didn't want her around anymore, but he couldn't let another man have her either. Most of all, he didn't want to live with the worry that one day, she might turn against him and reveal too much about his activities.

He had planned her death and had executed that plan to perfection, but a witness came forward, and Stanley was charged with murder. His associates from his nightclub convinced the witness to develop amnesia, and the murder charge against him was dropped for lack of evidence.

Stanley had started taking most of his meals in restaurants, and of all the pretty waitresses in all the fancy restaurants in Cleveland, he fell for the one who played hard to get. She resisted his charms and refused his advances until he finally offered to put a ring on her finger. Two and a half years after the death of his first wife, he married his current second wife, and she came with a five-year-old son.

After his second marriage, Stanley settled down. His constant legal battles became a thing of the past. For nearly two years, he didn't so much as even get a parking ticket. He was surprised when his half-brother, Glen, showed up at his bar. Glen offered him a lucrative position in the drug business in southern West Virginia. However, that position came with one non-negotiable provision: Stanley couldn't get into any sensational legal trouble, especially like what had happened with his first wife.

The day his older brother showed up in his nightclub was one of the happiest days in Stanley's life. Although they had different fathers, they grew up together with their mother, and Stanley had always resented his brother. Glen left Ohio to attend West Virginia University and then took a job with the West Virginia State Police, while Stanley barely finished high school and stayed in Cleveland to manage nightclubs until he could get his own.

Only one thing could have made Glen's visit to his nightclub any sweeter: Stanley wished their mother could have been alive to see it. If she said it once, she said it a hundred times: "Stanley, why can't you be more like Glen?" It was a fitting irony that Glen had become more like Stanley.

Stanley moved his family to a small Mingo County, West Virginia community two months after Glen's visit. He became the owner of the most popular nightclub in the area. In the first year, he expanded his business to own a second nightclub in neighboring Beecham County, West Virginia, just outside Logan. Both of the nightclubs were highly profitable, but the real money came from the drug business.

After more than four years of marriage, his stormy relationships with his current wife and her son were the only obstacles to an otherwise perfect set-up. Like his first wife, his second wife was on the verge of leaving him, and he couldn't say he'd be sad to see her go. Her son, Billy, was a problem from the start. He was a cute kid, and Stanley was initially determined to bond with him, but the first time he laid his hand on the boy's shoulder, the kid shied away. After that, the boy always stayed more than an arm's length away from him.

The drug business was great until the sheriff became a problem in Beecham County. He brought in the FBI and DEA, and their business started to suffer, experiencing significant drug losses. Something had to be done about it. Stanley went with Glen to meet with U. S. Attorney Daniel Sullivan, and they left the meeting happy, assured that a sting would be set up to oust the sheriff. The U.S. Attorney would use a memo from the Justice Department to direct the FBI and DEA to concentrate their efforts on political corruption investigations. They would use the Justice Department memo as cover to prosecute the sheriff, the chief deputy, and the deputy in charge of the drug investigations.

The prosecutions succeeded and should have ended the matter, but then McCallum made incriminating statements against U.S. Attorney Sullivan and Sargeant Stillwell in open court at his sentencing hearing. McCallum claimed to have written statements, voice recordings, videos, and other evidence against them – not yet enough for criminal charges, but enough to justify a more focused, thorough investigation.

Stanley's brother and the U.S. Attorney wanted McCallum shut up for good. When Glen insisted he use his contacts in Cleveland to hire a hitman, Stanley was nearly euphoric. It solved a problem he'd been contemplating for months: how could he bring a professional in to get rid of his wife and her son without risking his brother finding out? Glen's insistence on hiring a hitman would guarantee that his brother would enthusiastically ignore or quash any rumor of a hitman investigation.

Stanley sent Wayne to scout this area, and he discovered that McCallum rarely left the hollow where he stayed with his brother. Wayne reported that McCallum followed a morning routine like clockwork. While feeding the horses, McCallum would put two horses in the larger paddock and then lead one horse to a smaller paddock across the road. Shooting him beside the road would be as easy as shooting fish in a barrel.

Stanley had immediately set his plan in motion. He made a few phone calls to Cleveland, located his man, and briefly outlined his plan. Stanley would get his wife and her son to a restaurant, and then he'd find a reason to leave the table and go to the counter. The man would come in and, starting with the table where Stanley had been sitting, would open fire with his AR-15, then expand to other tables in that immediate area. He would flee, leaving behind many casualties. It was the kind of senseless violence that had become commonplace all over the country.

Stanley chuckled under his breath at how he'd played his wife like a fiddle. He ignored Wayne's sidelong glance from the driver's seat. His wife thought the sun rose and set on her son, and she would do anything to please him. Yesterday, Stanley turned on his charm and offered to take her and her son out to lunch this coming weekend.

The bitch refused, just as he expected. Saturday would be her son's birthday, and he knew she would have already made plans. He'd dangled false promises before her, lying about planning a surprise to please Billy. He said he wanted a better relationship with him and had made special arrangements for his birthday. Of course, there were no special arrangements, but she wouldn't live long enough to discover that lie. He refused to tell her what it was but assured her the boy would love it. He guiltily confessed he only wanted to take them to lunch so everything could be set up at the house. Just as he expected, she fell for that lie, too.

Today was Monday, and soon, the first phase of his plan would be accomplished: the deputy would be dead. He brought extra ammunition, and Wayne had questioned the necessity of so many magazines, but Wayne didn't know he intended to kill more than McCallum. Stanley also planned to kill two big dogs and a horse. And hopefully, if everything went smoothly, he would also kill the other two horses in the larger paddock.

He was more excited about killing the dogs and horses than the man. Killing people was business, but inflicting pain on animals and making them suffer – and the bigger the animal, the better – was fun. By Saturday night, he would be at home celebrating his new-found widower marital status while his wife, her son, and McCallum would all be at the morgue or in a grave.

CHAPTER 5

Jake waited in the kitchen until he heard his brother close his bedroom door. He heard Nick turn on the noisy window air conditioner that would enable him to sleep through the day. Its loud, white noise would muffle the noises outside his bedroom. Jake retrieved his service revolver from where he'd stashed it in his bedroom and stuffed it in his belt.

The dogs were jumping around, eager to go out, but Jake squatted, stroked their heads, and spoke to them like they would understand. "You guys can't go with me today," he said. "Be good, and don't make a racket, okay?"

Jake went through the sliding glass door onto the patio. The dogs sat in front of the door, watching him. As he was closing the door, he was distracted by a noise near the patio. He turned to see a large blackbird take flight out of the trees on the mountainside. After he watched the bird gain altitude, he stepped off the patio and headed toward the barn.

He stopped at the top of the hill and looked around. He hadn't noticed what a beautiful day it was. The temperature was perfect for an early spring morning, and the world seemed filled with activity. The birds, the insects, the ground squirrels, and all the other wildlife seemed to be bustling around, reveling in life. He breathed deeply of the fresh air, redolent with the sweet smell of spring flowers and blossoming trees. "It's a beautiful day to die," Jake whispered as he descended the hill.

When Jake reached the barn, he fed the horses and left them in their stalls. When his body was discovered, there would be a lot of activity. The horses would be safer in the barn, away from the emergency vehicles and onlookers.

Jake left the barn, crossed the graveled road, and hopped down the bank. He jumped across the little creek that was only two or three feet wide in many places. He passed through knee-high weeds, jumped up on a large boulder about waist-high, and sat down cross-legged.

Technically, he was no longer on his brother's property. The creek was the boundary line, and from where he sat looking down the hollow, the creek curved back toward the hillside. It left room for a small paddock on his brother's side of the creek, between the creek and the road. On his left, the property on which he sat turned almost immediately into a steep mountainside, and it belonged to Nick's nearer neighbor above him.

As Jake sat atop the boulder, he pulled the revolver from his belt and brought it to his lap. *Sarah*, he thought, but then pushed the thought away. He'd already done enough thinking. He started to bring the revolver to his mouth but stopped halfway and lowered it. He felt someone watching him, and at the same time, he felt a sudden change in air pressure, like he was deep underwater or high in an airplane. It was like he was holding large seashells to his ears, but instead of hearing a sound like the ocean, he heard a drawn-out whisper, "Saaaraaaaah."

The feeling of being watched, the change in air pressure, and the sound of whispering ended as suddenly as it had started. He put the gun barrel in his mouth but hesitated again when a sound made him think the whispering was coming back. After a few moments, he realized there was a difference and recognized what it was: the sound of tires moving slowly on gravel. A vehicle was coming down the hollow. He lowered the pistol. He didn't know if the car's occupants could see him yet, but he didn't want to make anybody witness his gross destruction.

Jake had seen many cars go up and down the hollow, and they usually proceeded slowly out of caution for the presence of horses, but this car was ridiculous. When it got closer, it slowed down so much that walking would have been faster. He turned his head and looked at the older model green Chevy. There was a male driver and one male passenger. His mind kept analyzing what his eyes had recorded even when he faced forward again.

The minute details of the car and its occupants continued to run through his mind. When he looked toward the car, the driver had acted squirrelly, immediately turning his head away. He appeared to be around thirty. His brown hair was swept back in a ponytail to reveal a thin, pock-marked face, and he wore headphones. The passenger was heavy-set, in his forties, well-groomed, and had short black hair. He was also wearing headphones. He was sitting in the back seat directly behind the driver; his window was down, and his stare was intense.

Warning bells blared in Jake's head. The seating arrangement was all wrong. It wouldn't have been so unusual if the car was in town. It could have been circling the block to pick up another passenger. But the seating was out of place here, up this hollow. Experience taught him that unusual circumstances should always put police officers on guard. He reexamined the headphones in his mind's eye and suddenly realized they weren't headphones at all; they were fancy ear protectors.

In a moment, the car would be directly across from him, and he jerked his head around again just in time to see the gun come level with the window. He twisted his torso to the left and kicked off with his right leg to propel himself behind the boulder. Even as he fell, he heard the chattering of the gun. It felt like he was moving in slow motion, suspended in mid-air for an eternity. When he finally hit the ground, he heard the last bullets ricochet off the top of the big rock and cut the weeds above him, within inches of where he lay.

Most people expect a bullet to bounce off a flat surface at nearly the same angle as it strikes, like the rails of a pool table. However, when a bullet hits a hard surface at an angle, it will rise only an inch or two and travel parallel to that surface. Jake learned this oddity about trajectories in theory at the Academy and witnessed it in practice during a murder investigation. He located the solid, deformed, killer shotgun slug exactly where the theory predicted the ricochet should have landed.

The instructors hadn't tried to explain the physics involved and admitted that it was counterintuitive and hard to believe without seeing it in action. In any event, Jake owed his life to this quirk of physics and the fact that the shooter had opened fire prematurely. If the incompetent killer had lowered his aim, much of the volley would have ricocheted off the top of the rock and shredded his body before he could drop below the rim.

When the Uzi fell silent, Jake started to rise, but he heard a *thump* on his side of the creek. He hesitated and held his weapon in a two-handed grip, expecting that someone had jumped across the creek to confirm he was dead. He jumped up when he heard the motor racing and the tires throwing gravel. He assumed a shooting stance, aimed at the car, and squeezed the trigger. He'd been trained at the Academy to fire twice, hesitate to assess the effect, and fire again if necessary.

However, a single *boom* was followed by an impotent *click*. He saw the rear windshield of the car implode, but with an empty gun, there was nothing more he could do. He remembered he had loaded the revolver with only one round. It was a Smith & Wesson .357 Magnum Revolver, and one hollow-point round would have literally taken the top of his head off. At the time, loading more than one round seemed ridiculous.

Jake lowered his arms in frustration as the car disappeared over the hill. His mind was in turmoil, torn by a plethora of emotions. Failure, anger, and helplessness were prominent, but other emotions competed for dominance. He put the gun to his head, pulled the trigger, and heard the dry snap of the hammer. A wild, frustrated laugh escaped his lips just as a bright light exploded inside his head, and he fell to the ground.

His eyes opened when he heard a deep-throated *Woof,* and he rose to see the dogs charging down the hill toward the barn. He expected to see his brother appear at the top of the hill, but that didn't happen. The dogs swerved around the end of the barn and came directly toward him. They were growling and snarling, their lips pulled back from their teeth.

For a moment, it appeared that they must not recognize him. He spoke their names in a quiet but commanding tone, "Rocky! Apollo!" He'd seen Apollo's eyes before, and they had never instilled fear in him, but now, those eyes reminded him of the eyes of the rottweilers in the old *Omen* movies. Although he'd imitated his brother's tone, the usually obedient dogs didn't break stride. It was clear they were in full attack mode.

Jake put his hands on the boulder and vaulted upward, even though he knew the top of the rock wasn't high enough to protect him from the dogs. They were big enough to easily leap onto the boulder, but it appeared to be the only position offering even a modicum of safety and defense potential.

The dogs crossed the creek, and Jake was surprised when they ignored him. Instead of attacking the boulder upon which he stood, the dogs attacked the weeds around the base of the rock. They each found a target, and their growls and snarls grew exponentially in the heat of battle. Looking at their snapping, biting, and slinging jaws, Jake saw that the dogs had attacked snakes. Oddly, it appeared that the dogs were the only vicious combatants. Even though the snakes were being chewed and slung about like wet rags, they seemed passive and resigned to being destroyed. The dogs finished their gruesome work and abandoned their quarry as though nothing unusual had happened.

Jake jumped down from the rock and, using a stick, pushed back the weeds to reveal the first snake. It was badly mangled, but he thought it looked like a timber rattler. A weak twitch of its rattle removed all doubt. It was mortally wounded, but it never ceased moving. When he was a kid, he'd heard that a snake wouldn't stop moving until the sun went down.

The northern copperhead and the rattlesnake were the only two poisonous snakes indigenous to West Virginia, and the more potent venom of rattlesnakes made them the deadlier of the two. However, fewer people were bitten by the rattlesnake because it usually gave a warning before it struck, notwithstanding that these two snakes had not. Contrary to their nature, these rattlesnakes had approached him, gave neither him nor the dogs any warning, and offered no resistance to being destroyed. The dogs most likely saved him from fatal bites when they caused him to leave the weeds and jump back up on the boulder.

Jake remembered the thump he'd heard while lying behind the boulder and finally spotted a black briefcase. He picked it up, jumped across the creek, and climbed the bank into the road. He glanced up at the house, but there was still no activity. The noisy air conditioner was doing its job. He had no idea how the dogs got out, but it was fortunate for him that they had. He called them to him and alternately cupped their heads, examining them for bite marks as he praised their actions. The rattlesnakes could have been nearly as deadly for the dogs as for him.

He laid the briefcase on the road and opened it. It contained nothing but a used baggie with a bit of white powder. A residue of white powder was all over the inside, and a tag attached to the handle identified it as a briefcase he'd last seen when signing it into the Evidence Room. It *had* contained much more of the white powder and other illicit drugs at that time. He realized that his fingerprints were already all over it.

"Oh, crap," he said out loud.

He quickly closed the briefcase as he looked down the road. He realized the armed attack must have been only one component of a larger plan. He was supposed to have been killed, and the briefcase was supposed to be found near his body. That meant cops would be showing up at any moment. His death was supposed to look like a drug deal gone bad.

"Come on, guys," he said to the dogs as he picked up the briefcase and ran toward the barn.

He couldn't let the briefcase be found. If it was, regardless of what else happened, he could be charged with stealing it from the evidence room, not to mention a drug charge for the missing quantity of powder and pills. He remembered a large brush pile behind the barn they had once considered using for a wiener roast. He stopped at the tack room, picked up a five-gallon can of gas, and found a lighter on a shelf.

He hurried around to the brush pile. He had no time for finesse. He quickly pulled several pieces of brush off the pile, opened the briefcase, and placed it in the middle of the pile. He grabbed the gas can and poured gas in and around both sides of the open briefcase. He replaced the pieces of brush and sprinkled more gas. He used the last of the gas to make a trail away from the pile, and when he lit the trail, he picked up the gas can and ran toward the barn. He stopped and turned around just in time to see the trail of flame touch the brush pile.

The pile of brush exploded with a *Whump*. The force of the exploding gas lifted the brush off the ground and sent a mushroom of fire high into the air. The pile of brush settled down into a roaring inferno.

Jake jumped and then laughed at his reaction. "That might have been just a tad too much gas," he said to the dogs and then noticed they were gone. He heard them barking and thought it must be their reaction to the igniting gas until he heard an approaching car over the roaring of the fire.

Jake rounded the corner of the barn to see a sheriff's department cruiser stopped on the road at the turn-in to the barn. Apparently, seeing Jake, the cruiser left the road and headed toward the barn. Jake returned the empty gas can to the tack room and walked toward the approaching car. When he met the cruiser, the driver's side window went down. The deputy didn't attempt to get out of the car because of the dogs.

"What's going on?" the deputy demanded without preamble.

"Marion," Jake said cheerfully. Then, mockingly added, "It's so good to see you, too."

The deputy scowled at the use of his middle name. "That's Deputy Mennis to you," he said. "And this isn't a social call."

Of the eighteen deputies in the department, this was the only one Jake actively disliked. Deputy T. M. Mennis had been in the department two years longer than him, but the sheriff had promoted Jake above him because the guy was an asshole. The new sheriff had wanted to fire him, but Jake had advised against it because of Civil Service. Either Mennis was stupid enough to let himself be used by the people who were trying to kill him, or the dumbass was knowingly involved.

The dogs continued to bounce around the cruiser, growling and barking. Jake pretended to quiet them.

"You need to lock those dogs up," Mennis said. "You don't mind if I look around, do you?"

"The dogs are on private property," Jake said, adding, "but I don't mind if you search the property." He watched the deputy's smirk of victory transform into a grimace of defeat when he added, "I'll just need to take a quick look at your search warrant."

"If you demand a search warrant," the deputy spat, "you must have something to hide."

You son-of-a-bitch, Jake thought. *You know exactly what I've got to hide. You're probably the one who took it out of the evidence room.* Jake had noticed Mennis scanning the ground in front of the barn, all the way to the road, obviously looking for the briefcase. He started to make an angry retort when he heard another car coming up the hollow. He turned his head to see a state police cruiser crest the hill.

Jake waited to see where the police cruiser would go. Apparently, the trooper noticed the sheriff's department cruiser and turned into the driveway to the barn. The dogs were still running around, so instead of stopping and getting out, the trooper pulled up so that his passenger side window was even with the driver's side window of the deputy's car. Jake had backed up against the sheriff's car so the trooper could get close. The trooper lowered his passenger side window.

"Jake," the trooper greeted him with an evident reluctance and an unmistakable coolness in his voice.

Jake knew Trooper C. W. Collins well. They had worked together several times, and he'd thought they were friends.

"Chad," Jake returned the greeting, ignoring the trooper's cold tone. "I'm glad you're here. I need a witness."

Jake turned his head toward the deputy and said, "Marion, I said you needed a search warrant to go any further," using his middle name again. After a few moments, he asked, "What are you going to do? And speak up so Trooper Collins can hear you."

The deputy stared straight ahead.

"We're waiting," Jake pressed.

Deputy Mennis didn't say anything. Finally, he dropped the car into reverse, backed up around the state police cruiser, and threw dirt into the air as he accelerated out of the driveway.

Jake laughed and said, "What a prick." Turning back to the open window, he said, "Sometimes, I like yanking his chain."

"You might want to be careful about that," the trooper warned, reminding Jake that he was no longer a comrade-in-arms.

"He's harmless," Jake said dismissively.

Jake didn't really believe that, but he was downplaying the threat the deputy posed, hoping to keep the situation light and the trooper from becoming too inquisitive. He knew the trooper didn't have much respect for the deputy either.

"I don't know what this was all about, and I don't want to know," the trooper said. "I just got a call to back up a county unit on a shots-fired call. The county unit's gone, so I have no reason to be here."

Jake offered his hand, but the trooper just turned his head.

"I got to go. Watch yourself," he said as he dropped the car into reverse.

"See you later," Jake said as he backed away from the cruiser.

When the trooper was gone, Jake turned back to the barn. Today hadn't gone as expected, and the experience profoundly changed him. *"The best-laid plans of mice and men,"* he grumbled but he no longer had the urge to kill himself. Something had happened inside his head when the light exploded, and he suspected it may have changed him in some significant way.

Something suddenly dug into the small of his back and made its presence felt. He discovered he'd forgotten about his service revolver. He sighed with relief that neither of the officers had noticed it, and he was glad he hadn't become aware of it sooner. He wasn't sure he could have kept it hidden from them without acting suspicious. He was in direct violation of a court order that prohibited him from possessing a firearm. Even though the tail of his shirt covered the gun, if the officers had gotten out of their cars, there was a high probability that the bulk under his shirt would have been noticed. Their tense conversation might have taken an ugly turn if that had happened.

His first order of business was to get rid of the gun. He'd started this crime spree by illegally possessing it, and now, in addition to that, he was guilty of attempted suicide, discharging a firearm, and destruction of evidence, not to mention deceiving his brother and lying to police officers. Bad behavior seemed to be self-propagating, one bad act necessitating another. He felt justified in everything he did today, but his conscience nonetheless bothered him. Even now, as long as he remained in possession of the gun, he felt like a criminal, as though he was in danger of sliding further into lawlessness.

Jake called the dogs and headed toward the house. He glanced back at the fire and continued up the hill, seeing that it posed no immediate danger. He found the sliding glass door partially open when he reached the patio. It was only about a foot wide but enough for the dogs to squeeze through. He must have left the door open a crack, and the dogs had widened it. That would explain how they got out, but it couldn't explain how they knew where the rattlesnakes were or why they had attacked the snakes with such single-minded aggressiveness.

He opened the door wider, and the dogs followed him in. He rechecked them to make sure they had no swelling. He was tempted to sit down and let the stress of the morning drain from him, but he had too much to do. He needed to clean the revolver, return it to the gun locker, and fix the damage he'd done to the locker. He'd known where the key was, but he'd broken into it to make it evident that nobody other than him was responsible for violating the court order. After he fixed the locker, he would need to move the horses from the barn to the paddocks. Finally, he needed to manage the burning brush pile until he was sure all traces of the briefcase were thoroughly destroyed.

As he cleaned the gun, he sorted through the morning's events. What his brother said last night seemed relevant and hopeful today. *Everything happens for a reason.*

The prophetic words in the dream the night before also seemed just as relevant. *Your life is about to become stranger than a Dean Koontz novel.*

CHAPTER 6

Stanley continued sitting behind the oversized, mahogany desk in the den after Glen was gone. He liked the masculine feel of the big desk that doubled as a repository for their drug inventory. He also liked the masculine feel of the room, but mostly, he liked the den for its privacy. Wayne, his helper, and Glen, his brother, were the only visitors allowed inside the room. It was strictly off-limits to his wife and her son.

Four days had passed since his failed attempt on McCallum. Unfortunately, McCallum had abandoned the routine that Wayne observed. He was late coming to the barn, and he didn't bring the dogs with him. He didn't even put the two horses in the paddock attached to the barn as he usually did. But worst of all, he didn't lead the third horse across the road to the smaller paddock. Wayne had assured him they would see the horses' heads when he moved them to the paddocks. But despite all that, he'd thought the gods must be smiling upon him when Wayne spotted McCallum sitting on a boulder beside the creek.

He'd had McCallum dead to rights and still couldn't imagine how he missed him. He'd been sure the "hit" had succeeded when he shoved the briefcase out the window. It was only when he heard the shot that imploded the rear windshield that he knew he'd failed. He'd dreaded facing his brother and had been prepared to take verbal abuse, but Glen had surprised him.

His brother had looked at the company books and accepted his explanation for the expenditure and failure of the hitman without question. Stanley had turned a total failure into a modest gain for himself. He told his brother he'd paid the hitman half up front and would pay the other half only after the job was done. He assured his brother the job would be completed, even if the hitman had to wait for McCallum to get out of prison.

What worried Stanley even more than his brother's reaction to the failed attempt was that McCallum saw him and Wayne. It hadn't crossed his mind to wear a disguise. He had fully expected that after they came face to face with him, McCallum would be dead. It would be nice if he never walked out of prison, but Stanley knew that if McCallum did, he would have to kill him, even if his brother no longer considered him a threat.

Stanley opened his wall safe and brought out his private books, where he kept track of the money he siphoned off the company profits. The company books his brother had seen contained nothing about the organization's members, but Stanley kept detailed records of his brother's associates, including the man at the top. He even made covert recordings and took incriminating pictures. It was his insurance policy.

Stanley was jubilant as he made notations of today's meeting in his ledger. He hadn't lied when he told Glen he paid the hitman half up front. That part hadn't been a lie, except that he'd paid for a different target. He'd made it clear to the hitman that his wife was the primary target, but there needed to be many collateral casualties to conceal that fact.

Delano Bouchard had already arrived in the area, and Wayne had met with him to work out the final details. Wayne reported that they checked out several fast-food restaurants and settled on the McDonald's at the crossroads in South Williamson. That McDonald's was in a relatively secluded area with several heavily traveled escape routes.

Wayne confirmed that he got another car for the job. He showed Del where he could hide his car and told him he'd pick him up from there and take him to McDonald's, where they would wait for Stanley and his family. Wayne would point out the target, let the hitman out, and stay nearby. After the hit, Bouchard would leave McDonald's on foot and run in the opposite direction from his car. Wayne would casually follow him, pick him up, and deliver him back to his hidden vehicle.

Per Stanley's orders, Wayne clarified to Del that while the wife was the target, if her son also died, it would be acceptable but not required. Stanley had been thinking about it and decided it might be fun to have the boy around. He fantasized about watching him suffer. He could make the kid's life a living hell without his mother around to protect him.

As soon as he finished with the books, Stanley poured himself a scotch on the rocks. He sometimes drank to excess, but he never touched drugs. After the fourth drink, he began to fantasize about the myriad ways he could torture the boy. The prospect of the pain and screams of terror he could draw from the kid became an aphrodisiac, lowering his self-restraint faster than the alcohol.

On other nights when he felt aroused, he would go out to find sexual release. With one phone call, he could easily arrange a rendezvous. It had been more than six months since he and his wife had slept together as husband and wife. His wife, Connie, found out about his involvement in the drug business and withheld sex as a means to modify his behavior, but instead of succumbing to her efforts, he'd found another source for sex. He was sure he could coax Connie into bed if he wanted, but tonight, his arousal was caused more by his desire to inflict pain and misery than by his sex drive. He was considering going to bed when a delicious idea suddenly occurred to him.

Stanley's excitement grew as he thought about how his actions tonight could set the tone for the boy's future, if he had one. He would have to be careful that he only hurt the boy in places where he would likely not show his mother, but his biggest problem was to find some reason to get Connie out of the house. It was after ten, and she had already put the boy to bed. After making a phone call, he found her in the kitchen.

"I'm sorry," he said, "but I've got to postpone the plans for tomorrow. I'll have to cancel the arrangements in the morning. I've got more work to do, and I just discovered an emergency at my Beecham County club. I have to run an errand tonight." With a shrug, he added, "I already gave Wayne the night off."

He saw her eyeing him suspiciously, but she didn't say a word. He'd used a sudden errand before to get out of the house. On those nights, he wouldn't return until the early morning hours. He knew she knew he'd spent those nights with another woman and counted on her thinking that that was what he was up to tonight. He hoped she would be willing to make it unnecessary for him to go out. He spun back around like a thought had just occurred to him.

"Would you be willing to run that errand for me?" he asked. "If you could, I could finish my work tonight and not have to cancel tomorrow's plans."

Stanley knew instantly that he had her. It worked like a charm. He had a package that needed to be delivered to Logan, but there was no rush. With that phone call, he'd arranged for the package to be received tonight. The package contained drugs, and although she would have nothing to do with his business, he was sure she would willingly accept this lie tonight for the boy's sake. She was so easy to manipulate when it came to her son.

"What's the errand?" she asked.

"It's not drugs or anything," he lied, "but it's something they need at the Beecham County nightclub."

He explained that it wouldn't take more than an hour and a half, and she wouldn't even have to leave the car. All she'd have to do was park in the Kentucky Fried Chicken parking lot. A guy would come to the car and ask for him. She could just push the trunk release and let the guy get the package.

He put the package in the trunk, and as soon as she got in the car and started down the driveway, Stanley hurried to his bedroom. He had at least an hour and intended to make the most of it. He quickly undressed and slipped a bathrobe on over his nakedness. He nearly ran in his haste to get to the boy.

"Wake up, Billy boy," he crooned, flipping the light on in the boy's bedroom. "Happy birthday," he said, shedding the bathrobe. "Look what a big surprise I've got for you."

Billy was asleep on his side facing the wall, so Stanley gripped his upper right arm and, none too gently, pulled the kid toward him, turning him onto his back. Stanley stood beside the bed, completely naked, stroking himself as Billy rubbed his eyes in the glare of the overhead light.

"Happy birthday, Billy boy," Stanley said again. "I decided to give you your present early. I'm sure you're going to love it."

When Billy didn't make a sound, and his only reaction was to turn back toward the wall, Stanley grabbed the sheet covering him, stripped it away, and tossed it to the floor. He pulled the boy onto his back again. He took the boy's pajama bottom in both hands at the waist and stripped it down his legs, taking his undershorts with it. He stripped the pajama top over his head, and Billy's limp arms offered no resistance.

"Say something!" Stanley commanded. "Scream!" He straddled the small, silent form on the bed.

Stanley was losing his excitement, being defeated by the boy's passivity. The boy's eyes were open, but they didn't seem focused on anything in this world.

Images of a doe flashed through Stanley's mind. He'd shot the deer at close range with a twelve-gauge shotgun. It was illegal to hunt deer with buckshot, but that didn't matter because it wasn't deer season, anyway. He got to the deer before it died, but it did nothing but stare up at him. It remained unresponsive no matter how much he kicked and prodded it. He finally killed the doe out of sheer frustration.

His excitement didn't come from sexual desire, so he needed to see or hear the pain. He knew he could exploit one anatomical difference between the boy and the doe. He'd learned from experience that the male of nearly every species had a spot so sensitive to applied force that even the most stoic male couldn't ignore the pain for long. It was also a spot a young boy was least likely to talk about or show his mother.

Stanley began applying pressure to the boy's testicles, slowly increasing the force in small increments. There was still no reaction. After a few minutes, he began to fear he might be causing an injury that would require a hospital visit. The little shit was defeating him, and he could no longer look into the boy's mocking eyes. He was becoming frustrated.

"I'll teach you," he snarled. "I didn't intend to do this, but you're giving me no choice. I'll show you pain."

Stanley shifted his weight to his left knee and rolled Billy onto his stomach. When he saw the profusion of scars on the boy's back, he let out a loud, raucous laugh.

"I see I'm not the only one who had to teach you a lesson," he said through cruel laughter. He kept laughing and gleefully rubbing his hand over the dehumanizing scars, letting the deformities feed the excitement in his crotch.

Stanley barely heard a screaming voice. At first, he thought it was coming from the kid, and it only fed his need to hear fearful suffering. He was locked into a world of sick desires, nearly oblivious to everything beyond his immediate pleasure. When he finally realized that a hand was pulling his hair, he backhanded the distraction, batting it away like a pesky fly.

The next thing Stanley knew, he felt a sting and heard the fleshy *thwack* as something hit the top of his shoulder blades.

Turning and seeing Connie, he shouted, "You stupid bitch, I'll kill you for that."

When he looked at her, she stepped backward. He put all his weight on his left arm and turned to dismount the bed, but she surprised him. Instead of backing farther away, she stepped forward, cocked the bat, and swung again. He saw the bat coming and ducked his head.

The bat landed on the crown of his skull with a *thunk*, like the sound of a ripe melon. If she'd had the power of a major leaguer, his skull would have been crushed like a baseball that sails out of the ballpark. But she just didn't have that kind of power. Stanley tumbled to the floor, but he wasn't even rendered unconscious. He was addled, but he instantly struggled to get up.

She surprised him again by her relentlessness. She stepped up and swung the bat, this time in a high overhead arc. He put up his arms and blocked the first and second blows, but as the blows continued to rain down on him, he could only wrap his arms around his head and absorb the pain. After a while, his arms fell away, and the blows fell on his unprotected head, gradually turning his world dark and silent.

CHAPTER 7

Entering the front door of the Prison Camp Administration Building in Manchester, Kentucky, Jake tried to remain upbeat and hopeful. Still, his first experience with a prison camp guard was so humbling and degrading that he could barely maintain even a pretense of positivity. The guard seemed to take a perverse pleasure in being insulting and physically abusive as he subjected Jake to the most humiliating cavity search imaginable. Jake was filled with grim hopelessness, convinced he couldn't endure this kind of degradation for fifteen months.

Yesterday, except for the ashes from the burned brush, Jake had restored everything to how it should be, and the noisy window air conditioner allowed Nick to sleep through it all. Jake had decided it would be safer for the family if he didn't tell them about the events of the morning. The briefcase was indistinguishable from the remains of the brush pile, and nobody asked why the pile of brush had been burned. Jake didn't volunteer an explanation for anything, but he showed Nick the still-quivering snakes in case the dogs later suffered any adverse effects.

The Prison Camp sat on the left in a subsidiary hollow, and a Medium Security Prison sat at the head of the main hollow. These were low hills instead of the high mountains, like in the part of West Virginia from which Jake came. Any infraction of the prison camp rules landed an inmate in that more traditional prison, and the length of their stay varied from days to indefinite, depending on the severity of their infraction. The nearness of iron bars and the Medium Security Prison's razor wire fence provided excellent incentives for following prison camp rules.

Directly behind the Administration Building was a large, square concrete pad with long concrete benches along each side, and it was commonly referred to as the quad. Sidewalks led from the quad to the other buildings. The first building housed the mess hall, and the next housed the library, gym, and other facilities. The last three buildings were two-story dormitories with left and right wings, like two buildings, joined at a slight angle. Those buildings housed the inmates, each floor an open bay. The open bays were divided into eight-by-ten-foot cubicles separated by five-foot-high, tiled cinder block walls.

The low hills formed a natural barrier around the compound, and the tree line was the unguarded boundary. There were no iron bars, and the prisoners were never locked in, not even at night. It would be no great challenge for a prisoner to escape, but that was a rare occurrence. The alternative to serving a sentence in this relatively low-pressure, non-violent prison camp was to be locked up in the nearby Medium Security Prison. There, the inmates were faced with iron bars and locked doors, armed guards, razor wire fences, and indiscriminate threats of violence.

As soon as they were finished in the admin building, the guard led Jake to a cubicle on the second floor of the last dorm. An inmate who would be his cube mate sat on the bottom bunk in the cube, and his actions did nothing to alleviate Jake's impression of hopelessness in the prison camp. As soon as they entered the cubicle, the inmate ignored them, got up, and slipped out without saying a word. Jake had gotten friendlier greetings from inmates he had arrested and put in the local jail back home. However, the inmate hadn't gone far because he returned as soon as the guard was gone.

"I'm Vincent White," the inmate said, offering his hand.

Contrary to his last name, the inmate was black. He was near Jake's height of six feet but a good fifty pounds heavier. He looked like an overweight Denzel Washington and appeared to be in his fifties or older.

"Jake McCallum," Jake said, shaking the extended hand. "Are we required to leave when a guard comes around?" he asked, needing to learn the rules of his new environment.

"No," Vincent said with a chuckle. "Most guards are cool, but Marshall Dillon's an exception. It's only prudent to leave when he comes around."

"The name tag on the guard's uniform said C.M. Wellingham," Jake said, confused.

"Marshall Dillon is a nickname given by the inmates," Vincent said, grinning at Jake's confusion. "His real name is Charles Marshall Wellingham, and most guards call him Marshall. The inmates call him Marshall Dillon because he's pretty much the antithesis of the upstanding TV character. He's ambitious and seems to believe that terrorizing the inmates and making their lives miserable is his path to success. He's condescending and abrasive, known for his penchant for degrading and humiliating inmates without cause. Best to avoid him when possible and not make eye contact with him when it isn't."

When he processed into the camp, Jake's possessions had been separated into two piles; one pile he could take into the camp with him and another that would be locked away. He was surprised when the guard put a Bible in the pile that he could keep, and he was even more surprised when he recognized it as one of Nick's most prized possessions. His brother had owned that Bible even when they were kids. Nick must have slipped it into his bag as a token of his concern for Jake's salvation.

After the first few days, Jake settled into a routine. The inmates enjoyed a degree of freedom in moving around the compound, but the prison camp was far from the Country Club that many critics claimed them to be. There was no golf course, swimming pool, or tennis court. The conditions in the inmate dormitories were not dissimilar to those in any Army barracks. In fact, except for avoiding the one guard, Jake found little difference between life in the prison camp and life in the Army. The most significant difference was that the camp intercom announced a count several times daily, and each inmate had to report to a designated area for a mandatory head count.

After reading two novels from the small prison library, Jake decided to spend time with the Bible instead of selecting a third. He approached the Bible without much enthusiasm. His primary motivation was to acknowledge his brother's gracious gesture, but just as importantly, it was another way to kill time.

Although he had read some of these verses before, he was surprised by the clarity they now revealed. What had once seemed as complicated as calculus was now as simple as two plus two. He didn't know the cause of the change but couldn't deny the effect.

It was a Scofield Reference Bible, and it linked each subject throughout the books of the Bible. His curiosity about different subjects took him from Genesis through Revelation. His realization of the main difference between the Old and New Testaments simplified the Bible and eliminated many claims that the individual books were self-contradictory.

He'd been in the prison camp for three and a half weeks, and as he walked around the compound, he considered what he'd been reading in the Bible over the past week. Other inmates were busy cutting the grass, trimming the bushes, and filling the camp with the sounds and fragrances of summer. Each inmate was assigned a job in the camp, but Jake hadn't yet received his assignment. He walked around the compound, letting his mind wander and his eyes rest from a morning of reading. He paused occasionally and closed his eyes to let the sun, the sounds, and the fragrances take him back to happier times.

Ordinarily, thinking about freedom and home was depressing, but Jake wasn't depressed now. He was in the grip of fascination with the new insights he found in the Bible. He felt like he was on the verge of an epiphany. He was about to discover something so humongous that it would change the world. He had to consciously suppress the anticipation like he did on Christmas Eve when he was a kid and couldn't sleep.

He was deep in thought, meandering around the compound, paying little attention to his surroundings, when he suddenly looked around as if awakening from a trance. He had entered the quad and could go no farther in that direction, so he executed an about-face and started back toward the dorms. Now, he walked at a more purposeful gait, intending to get back to the Bible. His thoughts were interrupted when he became aware that his cube mate had fallen into step beside him.

Vincent was coming from the camp library where he worked. They had taken only a few steps together in silence when Vincent said, "There's something you should know."

"Yeah," Jake said, "since when did the camp become co-ed?"

Jake was looking at a small group of inmates in front of the first dorm. One of the inmates had long hair, and from this distance, he looked and moved like a girl.

"Oh, that's just Frankie," Vincent said when he saw where Jake was looking. "He's been here for more than a week."

"By the looks of those guys swarming around him," Jake said, "I'd say that sooner or later, he's going to start some trouble. It wouldn't even surprise me if there weren't some self-appointed "Christians" (in air quotes) here who will see it as their duty to God to make his life miserable."

"Actually, the subject of Frankie came up in our last church service," Vincent said in response to the air quotes. "Our preacher, Eli Cavenaugh, talked about the sin of homosexuality," and without waiting for a reaction, he continued. "He said the followers of Jesus don't have to worry about other people's sins. He said Jesus directs us not to judge our neighbors. We can completely ignore Frankie."

Jake light-heartedly joked, "You mean the preacher said there shouldn't be any judges?"

Jake joked about judges because Vincent wasn't shy in talking about himself, and he had told Jake that he'd been a Circuit Court Judge in one of the northern counties in Georgia before coming here. Vincent had been here in the prison camp for more than three years, but his greatest regret wasn't that he was here. His greatest regret was the estrangement of his fourteen-year-old daughter more than twenty years ago. He often talked about her and admitted that her leaving was his fault. He'd been self-righteous, overbearing, and unyielding. He'd forced her to run away with the boy she loved, and he never saw her again.

"Not exactly," Vincent said without acknowledging Jake's quip. "The point was that if a Christian punished Frankie for the sin of homosexuality, it would condemn that Christian as surely as the sin itself condemns Frankie. Let he who is without sin cast the first stone. Only Jesus is qualified to punish sinners."

Jake was amazed. This had to be more evidence that something big was coming. Vincent echoed precisely what he'd been thinking minutes ago. It couldn't be just a coincidence that when he came to this prison camp, he'd been given a Christian cube mate. Jake was so engrossed in the conversation that he barely noticed when they entered their second-floor cubicle.

Vincent rummaged in his locker and retrieved his Bible. He pulled out a paper that had been folded lengthwise and inserted like a bookmark.

"The preacher handed this out last week," Vincent said, indicating the paper in his hand. "It's a letter to the Editor of the local newspaper. The Preacher said he'd felt compelled to write it as a tongue-in-cheek story. It concerns what we were talking about. As a matter of fact," Vincent added, "I've been meaning to ask you about church. I've noticed you read the Bible, but you don't attend any church services."

"I didn't know there were any," Jake said. "If anybody mentioned it, I guess I wasn't paying attention."

"We had the same preacher for a long time," Vincent said, "but he left a few months ago. We got a new preacher about the same time you got here." He glanced at his watch and said, "I've got to get back to the library. I thought it might be important for you to know about something immediately. I didn't chase you down to talk about Frankie and church."

"What's up?" Jake asked.

Vincent raised his head and stretched to his maximum height, looking around the bay. Like Jake, when he stretched, he was tall enough to easily see above the walls of all the cubicles. He stepped closer to Jake and lowered his voice to a confidential tone. His deep voice made it difficult for him to whisper.

"I have a friend who works in the admin building," Vincent said. "He told me about an inmate who processed in this morning. He said he overheard Marshall Dillon talking to the guy and heard your name several times. By the way they acted, even though he couldn't hear every word, he said he heard enough to believe they might be plotting something against you."

Vincent stretched and cautiously looked around the bay again. He wasn't being melodramatic; he was just being careful. Some inmates told the guards everything they heard, and it would be less advantageous to Jake if the guard knew he'd been forewarned.

"The inmate's name is Harley Humphrey," Vincent continued. "He's a big white dude and easy to spot." Pulling his index finger down his left cheek, he said, "He's got a long scar on the left side of his face."

Knowing that Vincent was more attuned to life in the prison camp than he, Jake asked, "What should I do about it?"

"Not much you *can* do," Vincent admitted, "except keep your eyes open. Avoid that inmate and that guard whenever you can, and don't let them catch you alone in secluded areas."

As he started toward the doorway, he handed Jake the letter he was still holding and said, "I got to go. I just thought I should warn you. They might not try anything for a long time, but then again, they could already have something in the works."

Jake yelled, "Thanks!" as Vincent headed out the bay door.

When Vincent was gone, Jake sat in the chair, laid the paper on the desk, opened it, and flattened out the crease. There were three pages, and he started reading. *Wow*, Jake thought after reading the first few paragraphs. He'd been amazed that he'd come here and gotten a Christian cubemate, and now, this letter could have been written about his own life, and it perfectly matched his thoughts about the Bible. It had been written by a preacher he'd never even met before.

After finishing the letter, Jake leaned back in the chair, stunned. He could no longer doubt that something huge was happening. The chance of two people having identical convictions about the Bible being drawn together from such disparate origins was tiny, but the chance of three – himself, Vincent, and Eli Cavenaugh – was astronomically small. It strained credulity to the breaking point. When the most obvious explanation occurred to him, he was awestruck by its implications.

God was real, and everything did indeed happen for a reason.

CHAPTER 8

Connie made it to the four-lane before the wrongness of what she was doing gripped her heart and caused her to turn around. When she entered the house, she noticed the door to the den was wide open, but Stanley wasn't there. She saw his books lying on the desk and the wide-open safe door. Something was wrong. He would never, even briefly, leave the door open and unguarded. She started to go in when she heard a sudden burst of wild laughter from upstairs.

"Billy!" she cried as she started toward the stairs.

She rushed up the stairs and into Billy's bedroom. She drew up short, frozen in shock by the horrifying spectacle of naked Stanley straddling her son on the bed. It was a nightmare, except she wasn't asleep. Billy's face was turned toward her, and his eyes were horrifying. His open, unblinking eyes, a common affectation of death, spurred her to action.

"What are you doing?" she screamed, pummeling Stanley's back with her fists. "Get away from my baby."

Her blows were having no effect. Her hands could find no purchase on his stocky, naked body, but she finally managed to get a handful of his short hair. She tried to pull him away from the bed, but he backhanded her, knocking her into the wall. As she fell, she slid sideways into the corner. She wasn't hurt, but she was frantic. Stanley was much bigger than her, and she didn't stand a chance against him.

She pulled herself up by holding onto something. When she stood up, she discovered she was holding a baseball bat. She approached the bed, cocked the bat, and swung for his head but hit the top of his shoulders instead. Her bad aim could have proven disastrous, but then, it actually worked in her favor. While Stanley was off balance, dismounting from the bed, she stepped up and swung again. Stanley tried to duck but moved his head directly into the path of the bat. It landed squarely on his skull but didn't knock him out, so she kept hammering him. When the adrenaline finally wore off, she sagged to the floor.

When she could move again, with her breath coming in sobbing gasps, she dragged herself to the edge of the bed and confirmed that Billy was indeed breathing. He lay on his stomach, exposed and unmoving, his left leg hanging where it had been carried with Stanley's falling body. His face was still turned toward her, and his expression hadn't changed. She pushed his leg onto the bed, wiped her face on the discarded bed sheet, and rested her head on her arm on the bed, too exhausted to move.

After a few minutes, her love and concern for Billy summoned an unknown reserve of strength. Using the bed to leverage herself off the floor, she pulled the discarded sheet with her and draped it over her son's naked body. She gently raised his sheet-wrapped form, turned him over, and slid under him to cradle his head. She caressed his face and brushed the hair away from his forehead, whispering soothingly into his ear.

"It's okay, baby, it's okay, baby. I love you." Eventually, she said, "Stanley's dead. He can't hurt you anymore."

After what felt like an eternity, Billy started reacting to her ministrations. She vigorously rubbed his arms, demanding he say something, trying to coax more interactions from him.

"Mom?" Billy finally said.

Her first thought was to get him to the hospital, but one glance at Stanley's blood-covered corpse informed her otherwise. She was seized by an eerie feeling more substantial than déjà vu. History had repeated itself in uncanny detail; a second drunken husband had viciously attacked her son. She'd caught both in the act and had beaten both to death with a club.

The first time was five years ago. She married Richard Sanchez because of threats from the child welfare department that if she got one more criminal charge, her baby would be taken away from her. Richard was a worthless gambler who dragged them from town to town, always chasing an elusive pot of gold at a blackjack table. When it happened, they'd been living at the edge of the desert on the outskirts of Needles, California.

She returned home from a long day of waitressing to find her drunk husband beating Billy, her four-year-old son. When she tried to intervene, Richard violently ejected her from the house and resumed beating Billy. He'd locked the door to keep her out, so she retrieved the tire iron from the trunk of their old Ford Pinto. By the time she'd pried the front door open, the house had gone silent, except for the whimpering of her son.

She'd found him on the floor, his shirtless back so uniformly covered with blood that it looked like he was wearing a red shirt. Richard was sprawled on the couch in a drunken stupor. Her body seemed to move of its own volition, crossing the room without any thought of moving her legs, and she'd swung the tire iron without conscious control of her arms. When she came to herself, she was holding the bloody tool, and he was dead.

She'd carried her son into the bathroom and washed the blood from his back. There were several deep gashes, and she knew she should take him to the hospital, but her husband was dead in the living room. Because of her criminal record, she feared she might go to jail and lose her son. She cleaned him up, smeared his back with an antibiotic cream, and covered it with a bandage. Billy slept throughout the ordeal, and she hadn't tried to arouse him because she feared he would suffer unbearable pain. She'd carried him to bed, placed him on his stomach, and knelt at his bedside to think and pray.

Sometime after midnight, she made a decision. Luckily, Richard hadn't been heavy-set like Stanley. She got a wheelbarrow from an outbuilding, stripped his dead body of everything, and loaded him into the wheelbarrow. She carted him out into the desert behind the house and dropped his body into an arroyo. Then she returned to the house and cleaned up all the blood. She loaded everything they owned into the Pinto and headed east. She stopped at several dumpsters to get rid of her husband's belongings. She doctored Billy while getting them away from California as quickly as possible. Billy had been courageous about it, never complaining. His back eventually healed, but the inadequate medical attention had left severe scars.

After covering Stanley, her current husband, with a blanket, she urged Billy to get up. They had to get away from here. Like the earlier flood of adrenaline, a presentiment of danger flooded her brain with an urgency to run. She could only pray that Billy's mind would heal more completely than his back.

Richard had no other family and no close friends who would report him missing. The big difference this time was that Stanley had connections that were as likely to get her killed as to land her in jail. Wayne was out in the gatehouse, and she had always been afraid of him.

Glen, Stanley's brother, was the most significant threat to their life and liberty. Staying and telling the truth was not an option. Stanley's brother would undoubtedly come after her in defense of his and Stanley's shared drug business, if not simply for the sake of family ties. Moreover, if Stanley's brother started investigating her, he might connect her to that other dead husband out in California. She didn't know if Richard's body had ever been found, but she couldn't take the chance. She couldn't go to prison and leave Billy all alone in the world.

"We have to hurry, baby," she said as she pulled his clothes out of drawers. She tossed underwear, socks, a shirt, and pants on the bed and said, "Put these on while I pack your suitcase."

While she was stuffing his clothes into the suitcase, she saw him getting out of bed and caught a glimpse of his scarred back. It wounded her heart that he turned around to face her while putting on his underwear. She feared that his obsession with concealing those scars might have the power to condemn him to a life of solitude. He was ever mindful of not letting anyone see them, not even her. She would never forgive herself for having put Billy in danger for a second time. She had to wipe tears from her eyes so she could see what she was doing.

"I swear to you, baby," she promised, "I'll never look at another man. From now on, it'll be just you and me." When she saw him stare at the blanket-covered lump on the floor, and even as her imagination told her it moved ever so slightly, she assured him, "Don't worry honey, he's dead."

She led Billy into her bedroom and quickly packed her own suitcase. Carrying both suitcases, she ushered Billy down the stairs in front of her. As they were passing the den, she remembered that the wall safe door had been standing open, and it occurred to her that she didn't have much money. Once, she had seen a lot of cash on his desk, and he might keep some of that money in the safe. They could get in the car and drive away, but with very little money, they wouldn't get very far. Taking the time to check the safe for money was worth the risk.

She steered Billy into the den, dropped the suitcases, and hurried to the safe. Her eyes lit up with hope when she saw the money. She found a leather satchel by the desk, emptied it, and raked the money into it. She was leaving when she noticed the open ledgers on the desk. She didn't know exactly what they were but knew they must be important. She put the ledgers on the money, making the satchel heavy.

"Can you carry a bag, honey?" she gently asked Billy. When he nodded, she handed him the lightest bag, which just happened to be his own.

They made it to the car, and she tossed all three bags into the back seat. She remembered Stanley's package in the trunk but left it there. When she abandoned the car, that package might give the police something to think about besides her and Billy. Wayne was coming out of the gatehouse as she sped down the driveway. He waved for her to stop, but she didn't even slow down.

She had no destination in mind, but she had some experience with running, so she turned north without thinking. Five years ago, when they'd been fleeing from the situation with Richard, she'd eventually headed north and wound up in Cleveland. She'd gone into a restaurant looking for a job and met Delmas Gilmeyer. He was in his mid-fifties and married to a sweet lady. Delmas gave her a job, and she and Billy had been happy there for nearly a year. The Gilmeyers didn't have children, and they'd tried to treat Billy like their own grandchild, but he rebuffed all of their attempts to show affection through physical contact because of the risk of them touching his back.

When Connie met Stanley, she hadn't fallen in love with him, but he had been persistent. When he offered marriage, she accepted only for Billy's sake. Billy was five years old then and deserved more than she could give him. Her sacrifice of submitting to a man she didn't even like was a small penance for having subjected Billy to Richard. She hadn't suspected then that she was moving Billy away from a safe albeit meager existence and delivering him into the arms of a monster.

It was nearly two a.m. when she drove into Charleston, West Virginia. She stopped at the first busy gas station she saw and parked in a quiet corner of the lot. At six a.m., after dozing fitfully in the car for a few hours, she got directions to the bus station. She knew she'd have to be more creative than the last time she ran. At that time, there was only a possibility that she was being hunted. This time, it was a certainty. The fact that Stanley's brother was a corrupt cop who could access and deploy official resources against them heightened their exposure.

At the bus station, she parked Stanley's car on the street, and they carried their luggage inside and stowed it in a locker. Then she hustled Billy back out to the car. She drove up the street until she found a suitable parking lot. She backed the car close to a concrete wall, locked it, tossed the key under it, and walked back to the bus station. The car would be found, but making its one license plate difficult to see might buy them a little time.

The first scheduled bus departure was for Cleveland, and she bought two tickets using Connie Jones, the fake name she'd used when she married Stanley. A half-hour later, they surrendered those tickets and got on the bus without their luggage. She turned her cell phone on and wedged it in the corner of the seat. She'd seen enough movies to know cell phones could be tracked. Minutes before the bus was scheduled to pull out, they got off when the driver's back was turned.

They didn't go back inside the bus station when they got off. Instead, they walked across the street to a restaurant and sat where they could watch the station. They lingered over breakfast until a different bus arrived, and several people got off. They returned to the bus station, and she found a pay phone. She checked the phone book for hotels and found two listings for Holiday Inn. She called a taxi, and they got their luggage from the locker and stood outside to wait, hoping to look like typical, just-arrived travelers. The taxi arrived within minutes.

"The Holiday Inn," she told the driver.

She didn't immediately give an address but waited to see if the driver would just take them to the nearest one. Their destination didn't matter because she only used it as a ruse. She was being more proactive in hiding their trail. She sat back and relaxed when the driver pulled away from the curb without questions.

When they arrived at the hotel, the driver took their luggage from the trunk and set it on the sidewalk. He offered to help them into the hotel, but she declined, quickly paying him to hurry him on his way. She immediately hung the heavy leather satchel on her shoulder by its strap. She didn't intend to check into the hotel, but she needed to go inside to use a phone. She carried her suitcase, and Billy brought his.

They went directly to the lounge area instead of the check-in counter. She set her bag down beside an overstuffed chair and told Billy to sit there while she looked for a pay phone. She intended to play it safe and, as much as possible, use only pay phones and public transportation. Pay phones had become more challenging to find now than they once were, but she finally located one in the alcove in front of the bathrooms.

She searched through the phone book and selected a different taxi service. She didn't want to take the chance of getting the same driver who brought them here. They took a taxi about 50 miles to Huntington, West Virginia, from one Holiday Inn to another. This time, she went directly to a house phone and called a local taxi to take them to the bus station. She bought two tickets on the first bus scheduled to leave town.

It was late evening when they arrived in Knoxville, Tennessee. There were racks of travel brochures and a bulletin board that displayed contact information for Lyft/Uber drivers. Connie found a pamphlet for *Dollywood* and decided that a crowded vacation resort should be safe. She called a Lyft driver to take them to Gatlinburg. With the driver's help, she found a place that rented rooms by the week.

In the first week, they stayed busy shopping and visiting all the attractions within walking distance of the hotel. She bought a new disposable cell phone, convinced that it couldn't be traced to her if she paid cash and didn't use her name. The following week, they took a shuttle to *Dollywood*. The vacation atmosphere appeared to be precisely what Billy needed. He seemed to improve right before her eyes, becoming more playful and happier by the day. She began to relax and enjoy the laughter and happiness around them, but then, the life-changing nightmares started.

It happened for the first time at the end of their third week in Gatlinburg. She was awakened at three o'clock in the morning by a scream. She jumped out of bed and rushed to Billy's side. He was crying and gasping for air, occasionally gathering enough breath to scream. She raised him and sat under him to cradle his head. When he finally opened his eyes, the blankness was the same as the night Stanley had pinned him on the bed.

She again caressed his cheeks and brushed the hair away from his brow, whispering love and encouragement into his ear. Finally, she was rewarded with life returning to his eyes.

"Mom?" he cried.

"I'm here, baby," she replied soothingly.

"Mom, it's Stanley," Billy nearly screamed. "He's coming after me."

"No, baby," she assured him. "Stanley's dead. He can't hurt you anymore."

"He's dead, but that only means you can't stop him."

His unfounded fear scared her, but she couldn't remember him crying before, not even after Richard had beaten him. He hadn't cried on that horrible night with Stanley. The crying was terrible now, but she could only pray that it signaled the beginning of a more complete healing.

Billy eventually went back to sleep, and he woke up at noon the next day, acting like he didn't remember having a chilling nightmare. She took him to McDonald's, and everything seemed to return to normal, but she felt uneasy. She was skeptical that it was over, that it was a one-time event.

CHAPTER 9

At the end of his fourth week in the prison camp, Jake received a copy of his appeal from his court-appointed attorney. It did nothing to improve his spirit or his low opinion of lawyers. After his conviction, he immediately requested the court dismiss his trial attorney. His request was accepted, and an attorney in Martinsburg, West Virginia, was appointed to handle his appeal. In their first phone conversation, the new attorney assured him he'd reviewed the file, and Jake's case had several good points for appeal.

Jake had cautioned the new attorney, Melvin Applegate, not to talk to the trial counsel, warning that he firmly believed the trial counsel had been complicit in getting him convicted. Yet, in the cover letter with Applegate's brief, the new attorney indicated that after consulting with the trial counsel, Jake's appeal was only "hanging by a thread."

Jake tossed the package into his locker, intending to forget about it. He hadn't expected much from the court-appointed lawyer, so he wasn't surprised. He wasn't a lawyer himself, but the appeal was so ambiguous that he didn't need a law degree to predict its outcome. He had no doubt the court would reject the appeal. Later, when Vincent came into the cubicle, he mentioned receiving a copy of his poorly argued appeal.

"It was so bad," Jake said, displeased with the attorney, "that I'd reject it myself if I were a judge."

The former Judge said, "You know you can do something about it, right?" Without waiting for a reply, he continued, "You can go to the library, look up relevant cases, and file your own appeal. Or, even easier, you can just attach an addendum to your attorney's brief. I can show you how if you like."

Vincent gave Jake a rudimentary course of instruction on using the law books in the library and offered to review any arguments he wanted to make.

Jake spent Friday and Saturday in the library. He found four specific issues, and Vincent assured him that they each held the potential to reverse his conviction if argued with proper case law. The more Jake learned about the issues, the more enthusiastic he became about his appeal.

On Sunday morning, Jake attended the church service for the first time. He wasn't the only new face. The preacher's popularity was growing, and one or more new inmates attended the service each Sunday. After an opening prayer, the preacher introduced himself and welcomed those attending for the first time. He briefly explained how he would conduct the service and how the inmates were expected to conduct themselves.

"Prison camp officials insist that I keep it somewhat formal," the preacher said. "My name's Eli Cavenaugh, and you can call me Mr. Cavenaugh, or you can just call me Preacher. Any honest discussion is not only permitted but encouraged. Disagreements are also allowed, but absolutely no violence. If you have something to say, please raise your hand. I've been told it's necessary to maintain order. Any questions?"

The room grew quiet, and Jake tentatively raised his hand. He'd never actively participated in a church service before, but he found a statement in the Bible that defied reason. He thought that maybe the preacher could explain it.

When the preacher pointed at him, Jake introduced himself and said, "I've been reading the Bible, and it seems reasonable and easy to understand, but I found something that doesn't make any sense to me."

"Sounds intriguing," the preacher said, resting his forearms on the podium, waiting for Jake to continue.

"I've always heard the Bible is one hundred percent true," Jake said, "but I found an obvious lie in it."

Jake opened his brother's well-used Bible and flipped through the first few pages of the introduction to the second page of scripture. He ran his finger down three-quarters of the page.

He read, "Relegate fossils to the primitive creation and no

conflict of science with the Genesis cosmogony remains." He kept his finger on the page to mark his place and, looking up, said, "I don't have a problem with that statement, but the next statement is the outright lie." He looked down and read, "Man is never found in a fossil state."

Jake expected to get hostile denials or vague take-it-on-faith justifications, but he was surprised when the preacher responded calmly and matter-of-factly.

Referring to the Bible in Jake's hand, the preacher asked without a trace of disapproval, "Who edited that book?"

Jake flipped back a few pages and answered, "Reverend C.I. Scofield."

The preacher held up his own Bible and said, "I've got that very same Bible here, but mine looks like it might be a little newer."

Jake watched as the preacher flipped through the first couple of pages and ran his finger down the page. He found and read the first sentence Jake had read, but then he stopped.

"Interesting," the preacher said as he came out from behind the podium to stand behind Jake.

Jake held his finger under the second sentence he'd just read. Looking over his shoulder, the preacher read aloud from Jake's Bible, then laid his Bible in front of Jake, marking the place with his finger.

"Read, please," he said.

Jake stopped after rereading the first sentence about no conflict between science and Genesis. "That's it," he said. "The lie isn't there."

The preacher picked up his Bible and returned to the podium with a spring in his step, obviously pleased by the discovery of the missing statement.

"I hadn't seen that before, but I'm not surprised. It proves to me that I'm not alone in questioning the original interpretation of the Bible," the preacher said. "Scofield's Bible was first published around 1909 and has been reprinted several times. When Jake's Bible was printed, that statement was most likely the accepted truth at the time, like the fact of a flat earth just a few centuries earlier. Obviously, somebody involved in the reprinting saw that statement in that edition, recognized time has proven it false, and wisely left it out of the newer editions.

"To more specifically answer your question, Jake," the preacher continued, "that statement is in the footnotes because it's interpretation, not scripture. The Bible promises the scriptures were given by divine inspiration, but it doesn't promise anybody was ever given the gift of divine interpretation."

They discussed many other things before Jake asked the question that had been uppermost in his mind since his dream about God saving him.

"Has God come into the world more than once?" Jake asked.

"I believe," the preacher said, "that after Adam and Eve were ejected from the garden, God established a pattern in which He would come back into the world at two-thousand-year intervals. When God comes into the world, He fills the earth with His awesome power, and some people can draw that power out and use it. Over time, that power dissipates and drains away, and that's why the strongest paranormal activity would also occur at these two-thousand-year intervals. The era of Melchisedec accounts for magicians who could duplicate many of Moses's miracles, and the era of Jesus accounts for the real witches the Bible says existed in the world two thousand years ago.

"The pattern began four thousand years ago with the man called Melchisedec. The Bible says that Melchisedec had no beginning or end. He was positionally greater than Abraham, and since Jesus was made High Priest after the order of Melchisedec, He was also positionally greater than Jesus, meaning that Melchisedec could be none other than God the Father incarnate. Melchisedec came into the world four thousand years ago unannounced and left the world. Then, two thousand years later, Jesus came into the world and was the prophesied God the Son incarnate."

After nearly an hour of discussion, during which he and the preacher were the principal participants, Jake asked the question that would define the rest of his life.

"So, it's been two thousand years since Jesus was in the world, and the power He brought with Him has dissipated and drained away. Are you saying it's time for Jesus to come into the world again?" Jake asked.

"No, not Jesus," the preacher corrected. "According to the Bible, other things must happen before Jesus returns. That's why I said a two-thousand-year pattern began four thousand years ago with Melchisedec. God is a Holy Trinity: three distinct individuals with three distinct personalities. Two of those Entities have already come into the world and gone. First, God the Father came in the earthly form of Melchisedec, and then, God the Son came into the world in the human form of Jesus. What must happen to complete that pattern?"

Jake had been greatly interested in the subject, and he was sure this was the epiphany he was expecting. He said, "If the Third Entity of God, the Holy Ghost, were born into flesh," he said, "it would do more than complete the pattern of the incarnation of the Holy Trinity. His presence on earth would also fill the earth with the awesome power that the Antichrist would need to draw upon for his personal supernatural power. And in addition to that," Jake concluded, "if the Holy Ghost were born into flesh, it would confirm what God told me in a dream."

The preacher grew excited, vigorously calling for silence when the inmates whispered loudly among themselves.

"Hold it down, please," the preacher said over the din. He looked at his watch. "We don't have much time, and I'd like to hear about this dream."

When the noise died, Jake said, "Have you heard the old joke about the minister who decided to test his faith while he stood on the roof of a building surrounded by floodwater?"

A few inmates said they had, but the majority had blank stares. The preacher seemed noncommittal. Clearly, his primary interest was to hear about the details of the dream from Jake before he had to close the service.

"Anyway," Jake continued, "in the joke, a minister is standing on the roof of a small building surrounded by flood water, and he decides to test his faith. He would refuse to do anything to save himself. He would put his fate completely in God's hands. He got three chances to save himself – a life preserver floated by, two occupants in a boat threw him a rope, and a helicopter lowered a rope ladder – but each time, he refused. He was determined to wait for God to save him. Finally, the roof of the building collapsed, and the minister stood before God. He asked God why He didn't save him; the punch line is in God's response. God said, 'My poor foolish son, I sent you a life preserver, a boat, and a helicopter. It was you who refused to accept any of them.'"

There was a respectable smattering of chuckles from the inmates who hadn't heard the joke before.

"My dream was like that," Jake continued, "but the difference between my dream and the joke was in God's response to my question of why didn't He save me. Instead of the punch line, God said, 'My poor foolish son, I did save you.' But that wasn't the end of my dream. Just before a clap of thunder woke me up, God said, 'I am come again into the world.'"

The inmates began talking among themselves again, even louder than before, but this time, they were silenced by the sound of the door being jerked open and the appearance of a guard. It was Marshall Dillon. He tapped his watch and said, "Now!" in a voice that would tolerate neither argument nor discussion. Obviously, he had no more respect for the inmates while they were in church than he did at any other time.

On Monday morning, Jake returned to preparing his addendum. First, there was the issue of No Victim/No Crime. Second, there was the Incidental Use of the U.S. Mail. Third, there was the Ineffective Assistance of Counsel. And finally, there was the issue of Selective Prosecution, in which Jake excoriated the U.S. attorney and the State Police Officer.

Jake spent the next two days in front of an old Underwood typewriter; his addendum was ten pages when he finished. He was required to send a copy to the U.S. Attorney, and he wished he could be a fly on the office wall when the U.S. Attorney got his copy. It felt good just getting those thoughts off his chest. He'd said some of those same things at his sentencing hearing, and the District Judge and the U.S. Attorney had done their worst. There was nothing more they could legally do to him.

Vincent was working in the library, so when he finished at the typewriter, Jake asked Vincent to look at his addendum. He waited while Vincent slowly read through the ten pages.

"Very good," Vincent said, returning the papers to Jake. "For what it's worth, I agree with everything you said." After a brief pause, Vincent added, "With that said, and meaning no offense, I do have one critique. You've included an inordinate amount of extraneous detail and contentious opinion in your addendum."

"No offense taken," Jake said, adding with a grin, "Also meaning no offense, but that sounds like a mouthy way of saying my arguments are too mouthy."

"Touché," Vincent said, returning the grin. "But seriously, what is it you want to accomplish with this? Do you want to win, or do you just want to use the appeal to express your outrage?"

Jake thought about it briefly and asked, "Can't I do both?"

"You can try," Vincent agreed, "but it doesn't take much for a Court to deny an appeal. Convoluted arguments and contentious opinions can sometimes be enough."

"What would you recommend?" Jake asked seriously.

"If you just want them to know how pissed off you are, then I'd go ahead and file this," Vincent said. "But, if winning's more important, I'd edit it and make it as cogent and concise as possible."

"Any chance you could help me with that?" Jake asked.

"Sure," Vincent said. "If you want to leave it with me for a few days, I'll see what I can do."

"Great," Jake happily agreed, handing him the papers and adding, "If you would mark it up and note any changes in the margins, I'll type it up again."

On Friday afternoon, Vincent returned Jake's addendum. It was only four pages and more neatly typed. All it lacked was Jake's signature.

Jake immediately took the material to the Administration Building, made copies, and mailed them to the Fourth Circuit Court of Appeals and the U.S. Attorney.

CHAPTER 10

It had been three weeks since he put his appeal in the mail, and word had quickly spread around the camp that Jake would soon be getting out of prison. The rumored certainty of his release grew with each passing day. It had been a short time since the filing, but according to the gossip, he had already won his appeal and was only waiting for the official notification.

Jake awoke on Saturday morning, savoring the familiar dream and needing a shower. He'd had the wet dream again. He was in Sarah's arms; the emotions were as vivid as their original union years ago. He described his dreams of God in the church services but never these dreams of Sarah. They weren't the kind of dreams you shared, especially in a church service.

Nearly every week, he had a new dream of God to discuss. It had become SOP to talk about his dreams and, sometimes, the preacher's dreams, too. Jake wouldn't talk about Sarah, but he had a dream earlier in the week that he could talk about. One of the other inmates had asked him, "Can God make a rock so big that God Himself can't move it?" Jake saw it as a philosophical question suggesting that an omnipotent being can't exist; either can't make the rock or can't move it. He'd been thinking about that question when he fell asleep.

In his dream, Jake was holding a rock, and he commanded the rock to grow. Then, he was flat on his back with the rock on top of him, crushing the life out of him as it grew. He woke up gasping for air, and the meaning seemed obvious. For God to make a rock so big that He can't move it, He would have to make it fill all of Creation, crushing even Himself out of existence. To prove His omnipotence, God would have to commit suicide.

After showering and dressing, Jake went to breakfast and then returned to his cube. He enjoyed Saturdays more than other days because it was usually quiet around the dorms. Saturdays were visiting days in the prison camp, so all the activities were centered around the admin building. However, even today, he might get a visit from another inmate. His cubicle had become the most popular in the camp. When other inmates had questions on legal matters, they came to see Vincent. When they wanted to talk about spiritual issues, they came to Jake.

Jake didn't receive a single visitor to his cube for his first five weeks in the camp, but he'd received more than a half dozen in the last few weeks. He didn't hang around the admin building on Saturdays because he'd told his family not to visit him there. So, instead of receiving visitors from the outside world, he could enjoy the quietness of the dorm until he got the occasional visitor from the "inside" world. Today, he spent the morning undisturbed on his bunk, reading and napping. After lunch, he returned to his cube and read the Bible at the desk.

Around two o'clock, an inmate stepped into his cube's doorway and asked, "Are you Jake McCallum?"

"Yeah," Jake said without looking up.

"I heard you can talk to God," the inmate said. "Can I talk to you?"

Jake was surprised when he looked up at his visitor. He got up, offered his chair, and sat on the end of Vincent's bunk. The inmate seemed anxious and timid, as though he feared a violent attack or expected to be angrily rebuked and ordered out.

"I'm Franklin Dorsey," the inmate said as he reluctantly sat down, "but everybody calls me Frankie."

"Well, Frankie," Jake said, "what did you want to talk about?"

Frankie visibly relaxed at the ease with which Jake used the familiar form of his name. Instead of fearing rejection, his hesitancy now seemed to come from trying to figure out how to say what he'd come here to talk about.

"Am I going to hell?" he finally blurted out.

"What do you think?" Jake asked.

Jake was amazed that even sitting face to face with this inmate, he still wasn't sure of his gender. He had clear, unblemished skin, big round eyes of an alluring shade of green, and lustrous brown hair that would be the envy of any girl. The only thing that betrayed the feminine quality of his appearance was his flat-chested, boyishly slender body.

"I don't know," Frankie said, "but I think my dad should." His face darkened with hatred as he added, "If I could, I'd kill him."

Frankie's hand lay on the desk. Jake patted it in commiseration, his every instinct telling him he was talking to a girl.

"You can talk about it if you want," Jake said.

Frankie described a textbook case of growing up gay. He had had an unhappy childhood, constantly feeling he never fit in. He'd felt more comfortable in the company of girls, and the boys often ostracized him. He'd done poorly in school and was a magnet for bullies. When he entered puberty, he never felt any sexual desire for girls and had been afraid to openly admit his attraction to boys. For the next couple of years, he'd tried to suppress his desires and deny those attractions, but he found that feeling nothing at all made him feel much worse than dealing with the truth. He'd felt suicidal during those early years.

His parents were deeply religious, but when he was around fourteen, his father stopped insisting he go to church with them. Frankie was sure he was an embarrassment to his father. Finally, when he was sixteen, his father caught him in a sexually explicit act in his room with another boy, and he turned and left the room without saying a word.

Frankie sent the other boy away and stayed in his room, vacillating between abject fear of what his father might do and guarded happiness that his secret was finally out in the open. Just before bedtime that night, his father returned and, in a preternatural calm, had begun explaining that homosexuality was sinful. For some reason that Frankie couldn't fathom, his father seemed to shoulder all the blame. Then, his father abruptly left the room again.

A half-hour later, his father returned. His calm, self-deprecating attitude was gone. The difference was Jekyll and Hyde. His father began angrily denouncing him and ordered him out of the house. The transformation between the previous and current visits had been so stark that Frankie couldn't be sure he hadn't fallen asleep and dreamed that first kind, compassionate dad.

"I put some clothes in a bag and left," Frankie said, concluding his story. "The last thing my father said to me was that I was going to Hell, and by the violent way he was acting, I think he meant that if I didn't leave immediately, he was going to send me there personally."

"What about your mother?" Jake asked. "Where was she that night?"

"I don't know," Frankie said. "I didn't ask, and she didn't say. A couple of months later, I called her after I'd found a man to live with. She met me at a restaurant, and we talked for hours." His voice choked with emotion. "She offered to leave him, but I convinced her not to. I was concerned that she couldn't make it on her own, and besides, I was happier where I was. I still see her, and I think she still loves me."

Having given punishment some thought, Jake had previously concluded that fathers were more concerned with right and wrong, whereas mothers were only concerned with love. He meant no disrespect to God, but he'd often thought the world would be much better if God were the Mother instead of the Father.

"Sounds like you made peace with yourself about your dad," Jake said, "so what makes you think he's worthy of hatred and death now?"

"My mom visited today. She just left," Frankie said. "She told me something she should have told me years ago." Frankie became secretive and lowered his voice. He looked around to ensure privacy. "She told me that I was born with both sexes. She told me that I could have been a girl. It was my father's decision, against the recommendation of the doctors, that I should be a boy. I was put through several operations and was given extensive hormone therapy while I was a baby."

Frankie hesitated, and when Jake didn't react, he angrily added, "Don't you see? If not for my father, I could have had a normal life as a girl instead of this hellish existence as a boy. I hate him."

Frankie began to cry in the silent way of girls, sobbing and emitting intermittent, high-frequency sounds.

Jake decided that loving was like the biblical burning bush, the flames of love giving away its essence while never diminishing the lover. Conversely, hating was purely self-destructive, the burning flames never touching the hated but entirely consuming the hater. Frankie was in danger of being consumed by hatred, and Jake patted his hand again in commiseration.

Frankie raised his head and wiped his eyes with his other hand. He didn't move the hand Jake had touched. After several swipes at his tears, Frankie stared directly into Jake's eyes.

Jake returned the stare for several seconds before he realized what was happening. The wetness of Frankie's eyes made them even more alluring and seductive. Jake had seen that look in girls' eyes before and knew what it meant.

"Stop that!" he said in a low but stern voice, deliberately snatching his hand off the desk.

Perhaps his voice had been harsher than he'd intended, or maybe Frankie just overreacted, but Frankie stood up so quickly and forcefully that he knocked the chair over.

"I'm sorry," he stammered while picking up the chair. "I didn't mean ..." he started but trailed off because he knew exactly what he'd meant, and he knew Jake knew. After an uncomfortable silence and finally getting the chair back in place, Frankie asked, "Are you a priest or something like that?"

Jake almost laughed because the question implied that he must have refused because he was forbidden to have sex. Apparently, Frankie wasn't accustomed to being rejected. He had probably never had an intimate conversation with another guy without that conversation leading to sex. Then again, Jake couldn't know what Frankie might have heard about him. "I heard you can talk to God," Frankie had said. Although he had an aversion to sex with other guys, he also felt no compulsion to compound his rejection of Frankie with unnecessary pain.

"Something like that," Jake said lightly. "But please, sit back down. There's something in the Bible I'd like to show you."

Jake opened his Bible and began leafing through the pages. He remembered reading a particular scripture because it had seemed so harsh. What male would willingly wound himself in the scrotum or cut off his own penis? When he found it, he read it aloud and then turned his Bible so Frankie could read it. It was Deuteronomy 23:1, which said that any male who was wounded in the stones or had their privy member cut off could not enter into the congregation of the Lord.

"You see," Jake said, "it's possible he had your salvation in mind when he wouldn't let them cut off your penis."

Jake couldn't know if Frankie's father considered this verse before deciding on Frankie's future. Still, given the Republicans' zealous proclivity for trying to force Christians to obey the Old Testament Mosaic law like the Pharisees of old demanded, it was certainly possible. He decided that for Frankie's sake, it was more compassionate to suggest his father could have been motivated by Frankie's own best interests.

Frankie stared at the verse for a long time before he said, "I was considering a sex change operation, but if my father was right, there's no hope for me."

"Not necessarily," Jake said. The Mosaic laws no longer apply if you accept Jesus' free grace. Jesus fulfilled the law; the only requirement now is to ask Him for forgiveness when you sin."

"Even me?" Frankie asked, amazed. "Jesus would forgive me?"

"Even you," Jake assured him. "If Jesus was present in the flesh and you asked for forgiveness, He'd forgive you and tell you to go and sin no more."

"But that's just it," Frankie said, "I don't think I can ... you know ... not sin anymore."

Jake knew the answer to this one. He turned to 1 Corinthians 6:9-11 and read the verses out loud.

"And such were some of you," Jake repeated after reading the verses. "These verses are about the unrighteous and include the effeminate. Do you think these people cleaned up their own lives before coming to God? Not likely. If they could clean themselves up, they would believe themselves to be good people and not in need of grace. It will be these self-proclaimed good people, being neither righteous nor grossly evil, neither hot nor cold, who will be spewed out of the mouth of Jesus for being lukewarm."

"But what if I am forgiven," Frankie said, "and then I ... you know... do it again?"

"When you accept Jesus as your Savior," Jake said, quoting the preacher almost word for word, "don't expect that you'll never commit another sin but be constant in prayer and continuously seek forgiveness. If you read the Old Testament – and the Old Testament is a teacher, not a guide to live by – you'll see that David was a man after God's own heart. The important distinction is that God had the foreknowledge to know that David would commit future sins, *even before* He chose him. The only reasonable explanation is that David prayed constantly and continuously sought forgiveness. Where sin abounds, God's grace doth much more abound."

Responding to Frankie's particular concern, Jake added, "In my opinion, whether you commit a thousand different sins or the same sin a thousand times, God is always faithful to forgive you. There is the risk that God will turn you over to a reprobate mind, as it says in Romans 1:28, but the greater risk is not in asking for forgiveness one time too many. The greater danger is in becoming inured to sin and not asking for forgiveness at all. Remember that sinning against the Holy Ghost is the only unforgivable sin in the Bible, but it's common sense that there is another, and that's the sin for which forgiveness was never asked."

Other than a cursory examination of the subject when he'd seen Frankie in front of one of the dorms, he hadn't given it much thought. Still, Jake felt satisfied that he'd answered Frankie's questions in a way consistent with the Bible. Homosexuality is a sin, but it's not unforgivable.

After Frankie left, Jake took a walk around the compound. Frankie's visit had taken longer than most. Walking down the sidewalk toward the admin building, he thought about his talk with Frankie. Whether he was helping the other inmates or not, he was at least increasing his own understanding of the Bible. Frankie's situation had a physical component, but what about other homosexuals? Frankie's hellish life – Frankie's own description of his life – was thrust upon him. But does the lack of a physical component make the confusion of sexual desire in others any less forgivable if forgiveness is sought?

Jake passed several other inmates on the sidewalk without acknowledging them, but he looked up when he passed a guard. It was common for the inmates to be courteous to the guards, but when Jake saw who it was, he looked away and kept walking. Eye contact was an invitation to conversation, and conversation with that guard was an invitation to disaster.

Visiting hours at the camp had ended, but the quad was crowded with inmates meandering around, still in a mood to socialize even after their visitor was long gone. It was already shadowy in this little valley between the hills, but it was a beautiful evening. The grass was freshly cut, and the hills were vibrant with multi-colored wildflowers against a backdrop of verdant growth. He drifted under the overhang of the admin building, imagining he was anywhere but in the prison camp. He was about to head back to the dorm when he saw Vincent approaching.

"Heard you had a visitor," Vincent greeted him.

Jake didn't have to wonder who Vincent was talking about. It wasn't unusual for him to have visitors, but only one inmate stood out from all the others. Rumors and gossip might take just days to spread in a small town, but here in the prison camp, it only took hours, if not minutes.

"Yes, I did," Jake readily conceded.

They strolled down the length of the admin building as they talked, only stopping when they reached the end. The building was red brick, but under the overhang, there was a row of plate-glass windows. The windowsills were three-and-a-half feet above the base of the building, and the window sections were about four feet wide and five feet high. Jake and Vincent stopped in front of the last window, and Jake leaned against the building with his arm resting on the windowsill while they talked.

"I was going into the gym when I saw you go by," Vincent explained. "Then, I saw Marshall Dillon acting kind of squirrelly, like he was following you."

Vincent started to say more, but he was interrupted by a burly inmate who boldly walked up and stopped before Jake. He was broad-shouldered, a couple of inches taller than Jake, and had a long scar on his left cheek.

"You're trying to steal my girlfriend," the inmate accused.

Even though it was unusual for a guy to speak openly about a homosexual relationship, even here in the prison camp, Jake knew to whom the inmate was referring.

He recognized the scarred inmate as being the one Vincent had warned him about. He moved only slightly, but the movement was enough for the arm on the windowsill to become cocked, ready for immediate action. He had always been adept at reading other people's intentions, and he knew immediately that this guy was primed for action.

"You're wrong. He's not my type," Jake said dismissively.

"What's that supposed to mean?" the inmate demanded, flexing his hands.

Jake knew the rules against fighting in the prison camp, but this guy would not respect a turn-the-other-cheek gesture. He would rather avoid this confrontation, but experience told him that this guy wouldn't relent, even if he were submissive. And if he submitted to this guy, others would assume they could force him into submission, and that could be a fate worse than death.

Jake prepared himself for the imminent attack. This guy was committed to assaulting him, so the best thing he could do was to let it happen while he could see it coming. He'd been right about Frankie causing trouble. However, Frankie wasn't the cause of this confrontation, only the excuse.

Jake said, "No offense to Frankie, but that means my minimum standard for a girlfriend is that she must have a vagina."

A crowd of inmates had gathered around them, and somebody snickered at Jake's remark, providing the attacker with a final stimulus for action.

"You son-of-a-bitch," the guy barked, drawing back his right hand clenched in a ham-sized fist.

Jake saw the swing coming, and he was prepared to block with his left and throw his right from the windowsill. However, the guy was so ponderously slow that, at the last instant, he decided to side-step the punch instead. He moved and reset himself on the guy's right, expecting the guy to check his swing and turn toward him for another swing.

From that point, the whole episode became surreal. The guy didn't check his swing. He followed through as though he hadn't seen Jake move, and he stepped forward with the swing and ran his arm through the window.

At the first crack of the glass, the crowd drew back, reacting like a single organism. The only person caught in a deadly shower of glass was the big guy who'd caused it. Shards of glass stuck in his head and shoulders, and when he pulled his arm back, the punctures were as numerous as quills on a porcupine. One large shard of glass was stuck in the middle of his forearm, and the copious amount of blood suggested an artery might be involved. He slumped against the building and started blubbering between screams for help.

It never ceased to amaze Jake. The toughest guys, the ones who love to inflict pain on others, cry the loudest and are the biggest babies when they are themselves hurt. The many years of police work had conditioned Jake to take charge in emergencies, and he was about to step forward when somebody caught his arm and held him in place.

He saw a guard breaking through the crowd on the other side and thought how fortunate it was that a guard had been so close when this happened. He started to step forward again, but when he saw who was holding his arm, he allowed himself to be pulled backward into the crowd. Acting on cues from Vincent, the other inmates closed ranks around Jake, and he was shouldered to the rear of the crowd.

The guard, Marshall Dillon, pushed through the crowd, demanding to know what happened. He glanced dismissively at the inmate crouched on the concrete and began eyeing the nearest spectators.

Vincent stepped forward and said, "This fool ran his fist through the window. Looks like he's bleeding to death."

The inmate had calmed down at the appearance of the guard, but upon hearing he might be bleeding to death, he started screaming again, demanding attention.

"Break it up!" the guard ordered, unable to ignore the injured inmate any longer. This area is off-limits!"

The crowd moved away, drifting toward the dorms. Jake and Vincent ambled along, letting the crowd disperse around them.

"What was that all about? Why did you pull me away?" Jake asked when they had a little privacy. "I was going to tell the guard what happened," Jake said.

"That's exactly what I thought," Vincent said, stopping in front of the gym. With a nod for Jake to follow, he added, "Let me show you something."

Jake followed Vincent as he walked around the front corner of the building and stopped near the rear corner.

"Like I was saying, I saw Marshall Dillon come this way acting squirrelly," Vincent said, "and when I peeked around the corner, I saw him standing right here. That inmate that attacked you was standing right where you're standing, listening to what the guard was telling him. That's what I was going to warn you about when that guy interrupted us. I suspected they might be up to something, but I had no idea it would happen so fast."

When comprehension showed on Jake's face, Vincent said, "That's right, it was a set-up. If you'd been involved in a fight or connected to the breaking of that window, you would have ended up across the street."

"Across the street" was the euphemism for the Medium Security Prison, which was around a curve, out of sight.

A violent death in a nonviolent prison camp would raise many questions, but if he'd been sent to the Medium Security Prison, his life would have been in serious jeopardy. Jake was sure this attempt came from the same people who tried to kill him the day before he came to the prison camp. While he was in prison, he wasn't a threat to anybody, but either the filing of his addendum or the rumors of his imminent release must have made him a target again.

Jake expressed his deep appreciation to Vincent for coming to warn him and for his intervention after the window was broken. Deciding that Vincent deserved to know the truth, they walked around the compound while Jake told his friend the whole story.

CHAPTER 11

Three peaceful weeks went by without incident, but Connie's uneasiness never disappeared. Then it happened again, and it was an identical rerun of the first time. Just after three o'clock, Billy woke up crying and screaming, fearful of things that could only be seen through his mind's eye. She was becoming increasingly anxious, concerned that Billy's health might be in jeopardy. The vacation atmosphere that had once been a balm had now turned depressing, rapidly becoming devoid of joy. She hated that Billy believed Stanley had the power to haunt his dreams, but she had no idea whether the dreams gave birth to that belief or whether that belief spawned the dreams.

The same night-time terror came again just two weeks later. After she got Billy calmed down, she gently withdrew from him and quietly crawled back into the other bed. She lay there staring at the ceiling, knowing he was finally asleep. She knew when he was faking, but she wouldn't tell him that. She was glad when he pretended to fall back to sleep because she knew that sooner rather than later, he would.

Billy never had nightmares like this before, not even after that dreadful man put deep cuts in his back. She had been afraid to take him to the hospital back then, too, and the cuts had turned into ugly scars. By the way he guarded them, she knew those scars had become the bane of his existence, and he was becoming antisocial, keeping away from anybody who might see or touch them. She had to do something to stop these nightmares before they could leave scars on his mind that affected his personality as detrimentally as the scars on his back affected his behavior.

At first, she'd consciously decided to avoid Cleveland because she was sure Stanley's brother, with help from Wayne, would look for them there. Now, she couldn't think of any other option. The Gilmeyers had been the only people who had ever helped them. Billy needed to be in a more structured environment of friends and family, but she was his only family, and Cleveland was the only place they had friends.

She knew it would be too dangerous for her to work in that same restaurant again, but she also knew the Gilmeyers owned other businesses, and maybe she could work at one of those. By now, Stanley's brother should have thoroughly searched Cleveland and determined they weren't there. She had already paid the rent here for another week, but that wasn't enough reason to stay. Besides, after two months here, simply packing and leaving without notice would probably be the safest. She couldn't wait for the nightmare to happen for a fourth time.

Eddie Blankenship was the Lyft driver who brought them there, and he had given her his business card and told her she could call him any time. He had reasonably predicted that, eventually, she would want to go somewhere else. She didn't know if anybody was hot on their trail, but she would play it safe and conceal their movements whenever possible. Since Eddie had proven safe, she would use him again. When she got up a few hours later, instead of using the phone in her room and possibly disturbing Billy, she stepped outside and used her new cell phone.

"Hello," a voice answered her call.

"Hello," she responded, "is this Eddie?"

"Yes, it is," he said.

"This is the lady with the boy you took to Gatlinburg a couple months ago," she said and continued, "You said I could call you when I was ready to go somewhere else. Do you remember that?" She didn't want to give a name because she couldn't remember what name she used the last time.

"I remember," he said. "It took us a while to find that place where you could rent by the week. Where and when do you want to go?"

"Tomorrow. Back to the bus station, I suppose," she said.

"You don't sound very definite," he said. "I'm not very busy, so I could take you anywhere you want to go."

"My son's not feeling well," she said. "We need to get to

Cleveland, and I wish we didn't have to ride a bus."

"I've got the time if you've got the money," he said cheerfully. "I can take you, but it would cost much more than a bus."

He explained that he'd been to Cleveland before, and from where she was, it would take approximately eleven hours. After some debate, most of which was just Eddie thinking out loud, he offered to take them to Cleveland for three hundred dollars plus expenses, which included gas, meals, and a hotel room for one night before his return trip.

Connie pretended she needed to see if she could get enough money and promised to call him back within the hour. Money wasn't really an issue, but she didn't want him to think she might be carrying a lot of cash. She had raked just over thirty-eight thousand dollars into the leather satchel when she took the money from Stanley's wall safe. She didn't mind paying a premium for the convenience of traveling by private vehicle, but she wanted a cover story to justify what might be seen as a ridiculously extravagant expenditure. She returned to the room and thought about it for a half-hour. When she had devised a reasonable story, she stepped outside and called him back.

"I talked to my husband," she said, blaming a fictitious husband for any possible extravagance. "When I told him about our son not feeling well, he insisted that our son not be subjected to another bus trip. He's wiring me some money, but he's concerned about the vague term 'expenses.' He suggested I offer you a flat fee of five hundred dollars."

Traveling with Eddie would be an extra layer of disguise. Her wig and glasses were better than nothing, but the presence of a man would provide a much more effective camouflage. Anyone looking for them would be looking for a woman traveling alone with her son. And although Eddie seemed harmless, she was painfully aware that she and Billy might appear to be defenseless targets. The involvement of a fictitious husband would also help ensure that Eddie didn't get any ideas.

"I can do that," Eddie said after a brief hesitation. "When do you want to leave?"

"I'll get the money later today or first thing in the morning," she said. "Could you be here around one o'clock tomorrow, right after lunch?"

"Sure," he said. "Are you still in the same place?"

"Yes," she said. "We'll be watching for you around one."

When she returned to the room, Billy was sitting in front of the TV. He was staring at the screen, but she couldn't imagine what might be happening behind his vacant stare. It was like the nightmares had disconnected him from the world. Since he'd had a nightmare last night, she felt confident they could make it to Cleveland before it happened again.

She immediately started packing their luggage. It was amazing how much extra junk they had accumulated in such a short time. It was good that she'd bought another suitcase. She disposed of the leather satchel and put Stanley's books in a box, wrapped it like a gift, and put it in the bottom of the new suitcase. She had no idea if those books were important, but she just couldn't bring herself to throw them away. She put some money in her pocketbook, then divided the rest into three stacks, hiding one stack in each of the three suitcases.

After she packed everything they wouldn't need immediately, she coaxed Billy away from the TV for lunch and a matinee. Afterward, they took a long walk, revisiting several local attractions. They capped the evening with dinner before taking an even longer walk. She wanted to work off as much excess energy as possible so they could better tolerate the long trip tomorrow. When they went to bed, she and Billy were good and tired, and she expected they would have a quiet night. However, around three o'clock in the morning, the horror was back. It was the first time the nightmare came two nights in a row.

Connie got out of bed the next morning, more anxious than ever to escape this place. The bad experiences were beginning to overshadow the fun they'd had there. She checked Billy to ensure he was still sleeping, went outside, and called Eddie again. She told him that she had received the money from her husband, and he could pick them up at his earliest convenience. Eddie lived relatively nearby, so he said he would be there in an hour and a half. She roused Billy, finished packing, and hurried next door to the restaurant for breakfast.

Eddie arrived promptly at ten. They quickly loaded their suitcases and were on the road within minutes. Eddie made several turns within the first ten or fifteen minutes, and then, for a long time, they moved in a relatively straight line. Since Eddie had said he'd driven to Cleveland before, Connie paid little attention to their routes. They stopped only for bathroom breaks and to pick up fast-food takeout, which they ate on the fly.

Connie rode in the front passenger seat. She told Eddie she wanted to give Billy room to stretch out, but her true motive was to create the appearance of a family unit. If she rode in the back seat with Billy, it would be evident to everyone that there was no family connection between the driver and his passengers. Billy was dozing, and she alternately napped and stared out the window at the passing scenery.

Hours later, she was staring out the window when she realized she was becoming tense. When they slowed and came around a curve, she recognized a Speedway gas station. She jerked upright in the seat, her body stiffening with shock. She knew this area well. They were just ten or fifteen miles from the house in West Virginia, where they'd lived with Stanley. She tried to conceal her shock while surreptitiously watching Eddie out of the corner of her eye. He wasn't doing anything suspicious, and she struggled to hide her apprehension.

"You okay?" Eddie asked, apparently picking up on her sudden anxiety.

It was several seconds before she could trust her voice not to betray her. "I'm fine," she finally said. "I was just surprised to realize I've been through this area before."

"Yeah," Eddie said. "If you've traveled from Gatlinburg to Cleveland before, this is probably how you came. As far as I know, it's the shortest, easiest route.

Eddie sounded so casual that it put her at ease, and she felt better after they passed the turnoff to the house. She tried to relax, but old and familiar feelings caused her heart to flutter. Less than an hour later, suppressed memories surfaced and brought her mind into sharp focus. The one and only man she'd ever loved had told her about the little community near Logan in which he'd grown up. When she moved into the area with Stanley, she'd refused to let herself think about it, and she had never before felt an irresistible urge to go there and locate his family.

Now, that community seemed to have the power of a black hole, and she felt the pull of its gravity. If she had been driving, she doubted that she could have resisted, but fortunately, the attraction seemed to diminish with each mile after they passed the turn-off. She had no reason to expect they would find any help in that community, and Cleveland was another five or six hours away. At least in Cleveland, there was some hope that they could settle down and resume a normal life.

They arrived in Cleveland before 9 p.m. Eddie wasn't very familiar with the city, but Connie guided him to a hotel with which she was familiar. They stayed there that first time they'd come to Cleveland, and the restaurant where she found a job and great friends was within easy walking distance. She'd started thinking about where to stay as soon as they entered the city and decided to use the same hotel. She and Billy had already been living in an apartment a few blocks on the other side of the restaurant when she met Stanley, so there was no way that Wayne would know to look for them at that hotel. At her direction, Eddie pulled the car under the portico.

"Billy's still asleep," she said to Eddie. "Would you mind waiting while I get a room?"

She liked the disguise of traveling like a family unit and decided to continue the ruse. She would create the impression that she needed lodging for a husband and her son. She went to the check-in desk and asked for a room for three, explaining that her husband and son were waiting in the car because her son wasn't feeling well. She registered as Mr. and Mrs. Edward Jones and faked a license plate number. She paid cash a week in advance and asked if there would be any problem leaving the car out front until they got everything to their room. She declined help from the hotel staff. When she returned to the car, she was pleased to see Billy awake and moving around.

"Could you help us get the bags up to the room?" she asked Eddie, and when he seemed reluctant, apparently expecting the hotel staff to do that, she added, "Last favor, I promise."

Eddie carried all three bags in one trip, Billy's smaller bag tucked up under his arm. When they went by the check-in counter, Connie put her arm around Billy's shoulder as though he required her attention. When they got to the room, she got money from her pocketbook while Eddie was putting the bags down. She counted out five hundred dollars and placed it in Eddie's hand. When he started to turn away, she held out another hundred-dollar bill.

"For your excellent service," she said. "We appreciate everything you've done for us. We'll call you if we ever need transportation around Knoxville again."

Eddie smiled, earnestly thanked her for the tip, and went away happy.

Getting Billy into pajamas took longer than usual. He had dozed intermittently for more than ten hours and seemed to be in a peculiar mood. In addition to the effects of the nightmares, she suspected he must be afflicted with some earth-bound cousin to jet lag. It was nearly midnight before she got into bed. She could only hope he would be better tomorrow.

It was nearly eight o'clock when she woke up, and the light coming through the drapes was bright. She looked at the other bed and was pleased to see Billy smiling at her.

"I'm hungry," he announced.

She slipped out of bed and embraced him, happier than she'd been in days. "Good morning," she said, feeling optimistic but unable to immediately ascribe a reason for it. She kissed his cheek and forehead, secretly checking his temperature. He felt normal. She continued, "I'm going to order breakfast from room service. Why don't you look at the menu over there? It's a special day. You can have anything you want."

While waiting for breakfast to arrive, they took turns washing up and getting dressed. Getting help from the Gilmeyers was their best shot at returning to a normal life, and she hoped that having Billy with her might help persuade them to render aid. As they ate, she tried to convey to Billy the importance of making a good impression on the Gilmeyers.

"We really need their help," she said. "I don't know where to go if they don't help us. They'd like nothing better than acting like your grandparents if you let them. So, please, please, please wear an extra-thick sweater and try to accept their hugs graciously."

She hadn't called to make an appointment because saying no over the phone was too easy. She thought it best if they showed up unannounced. She knew that Mr. Gilmeyer spent most of his weekdays in his office at the back of the restaurant.

When they entered the restaurant, a couple stood before the counter paying their bill. When the couple finished and moved away, the woman behind the counter saw them, gave a squeal of delight, and came out from behind the counter to hug them.

After the warm greeting, Hilda Gilmeyer seemed to suddenly remember something. She glanced nervously at the front door before hurriedly ushering them toward the back of the restaurant. She asked one of the waitresses if she would please watch the counter for a few minutes. That was what endeared her to so many people. Hilda was so kind and considerate to everybody, including her employees. Connie expected a similar greeting from Mr. Gilmeyer, but when they were rushed into his office, she was shocked by his reaction.

"What are you doing here?" he demanded when he looked up.

He jumped up and rushed around the desk, bypassing them to close and lock the office door. When he was satisfied that they were alone and safe, he turned and hugged them both.

"You shouldn't be here," he said. "Somebody has been here several times looking for you, and he could be watching or come back at any time."

"Who?" Connie asked, even though she suspected she knew. She wasn't surprised Wayne had come here, but she was surprised he'd let it be known that he was looking for her.

"He wouldn't give his name," Mr. Gilmeyer said, "but he was a big guy with a ponytail and a rough face."

Wayne had known she'd worked here, and she'd made it easy for them to trail her here from Charleston. She'd expected them to follow her, but she'd hoped they'd already come and gone, giving up on finding her here. With Stanley dead, Wayne would likely come here to recover Stanley's books if he were now working for Stanley's brother.

"I know who it was," she said. "It's a long story."

"I've got time for a long story," Mr. Gilmeyer said. Waving his arm to indicate the world beyond the door, he said, "It's safer here than it is out there. Indicating the two chairs in front of the desk, he added, "Please, sit down."

"I hate involving you in this," she said, "but I'm desperate, and there's nobody else I could turn to." They sat down, and she told him about Stanley and Stanley's brother.

Mr. Gilmeyer had met Stanley before she married him, and he didn't seem surprised that Stanley had turned out to be a bad person. In deference to Billy, she glossed over the cause, but she explained that she got into a fight with Stanley and killed him with a baseball bat.

"It was self-defense," she assured him, "but I knew I wouldn't get a fair deal from Stanley's brother, who just happens to be a dirty, drug-dealing cop. I was afraid they'd take Billy from me and send me to prison, so we ran."

He wasn't skeptical of her story and even seemed sympathetic to her and Billy's misfortune. "I'm very sorry about your troubles, and you were probably right to run," he said, "but I don't understand why you would come here. Surely, you didn't think they wouldn't find you here."

"No," she admitted, "but I know you have other restaurants around the city, and I hoped I might get a job at one of those."

Nodding his head, he said, "Yes, that might have worked, except they also know I have other businesses, and that man has also been to them. Even if you worked at one of those other places, it would only be a temporary solution because they'd recheck those places again sooner or later when they don't find you. You need a more permanent solution. It would also be best if you had a new identity and a new location. I'm sorry, but I don't know the kind of people who could get those things for you."

Connie started to get up, but Mr. Gilmeyer stopped her and motioned her back into the chair.

"I'm sorry," he said, "but I wasn't saying I wouldn't help you. I just didn't want to get your hopes up and then be unable to deliver. I don't know the kind of people you need, but I know people who know people. Maybe one of them knows somebody who can help you find what you need. If you like, I'll make some phone calls, but I warn you: the kind of paperwork you need will likely be very expensive."

Connie practically gushed with relief. "Please, anything you can do would be greatly appreciated." She patted her pocketbook and added, "And I do have some money."

She hesitated, torn between their best interests and concern for the Gilmeyers' safety. She couldn't stand the thought that she might bring danger to their doorstep.

"I must warn you and give you a chance to withdraw your offer to help," she finally said. "I know that man who came here looking for us. His name is Wayne, and he grew up around here. He travels in the same circles as those who can help us get what we need. He'll be all over it if he hears that a mother and son are shopping for new identities. He could be dangerous to you if he finds out you've helped us."

Mr. Gilmeyer thought about it briefly and said, "I'm glad you told me, but you don't have to worry. Like I said, I know people who know people. If this man starts pushing too hard, I can find people who can push back."

He took her current driver's license and asked several more specific questions. He wrote everything down, including her room number at the hotel. When he had the information he needed, he pushed a button on what appeared to be an intercom. He didn't say anything, but it must have been a signal because Mrs. Gilmeyer immediately returned to the office.

Connie thanked the Gilmeyers profusely and hugged both in turn. She nudged Billy.

"Yeah," Billy said, taking the hint, "thank you very much." He surprised his mother by not only accepting their hugs but even returning them.

After tearful goodbyes, Mr. Gilmeyer led them out of the restaurant's rear service entrance and told her the safest way back to the hotel.

"It would be best to stay off the street," he said. "I'll call you when I find out something. I won't send anybody to your room without calling first."

As soon as they were alone in the alley, Connie told Billy how proud she was of him. She realized he was more perceptive and capable than she'd thought. He was growing up so fast.

Two days later, Mr. Gilmeyer called. He had worked everything out but needed a bit more information, and then he gave her the essential details. She and Billy could keep their first names, but their last names would change. Their birth dates would change, and they would have new birth certificates. Her identification would even include a new driver's license and social security card.

"This is very credible paperwork," he assured her after finishing the details. "I was assured this paperwork is of the same quality as what is given to people in the Witness Protection Program. It will withstand the most intense scrutiny. Background information will be included, and the more you study that information, the safer you'll be."

There was a long pause before he said, "The only bad thing is, like I thought, it's very expensive. It will cost twenty-five thousand dollars."

Connie involuntarily gasped when she heard the price. She quickly did the math and figured it would take more than three-quarters of the money she had left, but in the end, the only math that really mattered was her plus Billy plus safety.

"I know that's a lot of money," he said, "and if you don't have that much, I can front you as much as you need, and you can pay me back whenever you can."

"That's very generous," she said, "but I've got that much. Tell them to go ahead with it."

"I already did," he said. They should have it ready by tomorrow afternoon, but let me ask you one more thing."

CHAPTER 12

Jake flipped through the Bible late Friday evening while lying on his bunk, looking for a topic to discuss at Sunday morning's church service. Six weeks had passed since he filed his addendum and a total of three months since he came to the prison camp. During that time, he became an avid reader of the Bible, participated in church services, and developed close friendships with Vincent and Preacher. His and the preacher's interpretations of the Bible were so compatible that their friendship seemed to have been foreordained.

The P.A. system interrupted Jake's search for a topic with an announcement. The message was short and abrupt: there would be no church service Sunday morning. There was no explanation or details. Like all communications to the inmates, the message was brief and issued in a cold, imperative tone. It was as though too much information might endanger camp security or any civility at all might undermine camp discipline.

Jake closed his Bible and set it aside. There was no need to prepare for a discussion that wouldn't happen. He retrieved a Steven King novel from his locker, intending to immerse himself in a world created by his second favorite author. He stretched out on his bunk again, but before he could become involved in the story, Vincent breezed into the cubicle.

"What's up with the church service?" Vincent asked.

"Don't know." Jake snapped.

Vincent ignored Jake's abruptness, got something out of his locker, and left the cubicle again.

Jake dismissed Vincent from his thoughts and went back to reading. He only read a couple of pages before he was interrupted again. Another inmate passing by stepped into the doorway and asked about the church service.

"I don't know," Jake said without taking his eyes off the page he was reading.

When the third inmate inquired about Sunday morning, without looking up, Jake snapped, "I don't know. I don't care."

"You don't have to be a prick about it," the inmate rejoined. "I just thought you might have heard something."

Jake realized he was peeved at the preacher but was acting like a jerk to everybody else. The preacher had denied him the courtesy of knowing why he wouldn't be here this Sunday, and he snapped at the others because each time they asked, it confirmed that he had a right to be peeved.

Friends, Jake thought, *who needs them*? After getting such a cold reaction from most of his casual friends and co-workers and losing even his best friends, he'd decided he didn't need anybody. There were lots of novels he hadn't read and lots of movies he hadn't seen. He'd previously decided he would be better off living vicariously through others in fictitious worlds, but here he was, reacting again to those same old feelings of being snubbed.

He didn't want to talk to anybody, so he laid the open book on his chest and closed his eyes. A short while later, he heard someone stop in his doorway, but he went away when Jake didn't acknowledge him. Before he knew it, all his pretense of sleep was gone. He awoke when the book slid off his chest, but the overhead lights had already been turned off in the bay, so he turned over and went back to sleep.

The next day, he awoke an hour earlier than usual. He got up, showered, and got dressed. He wanted to take a walk before the sidewalks became crowded with inmates expecting a visitor. Sleep hadn't improved his disposition. He felt aggrieved and had no desire to be sociable with anyone.

Like most Saturdays, he returned to his cubicle for a quiet day of reading, glad that most of the other inmates would be preoccupied with visitors. The morning went by uninterrupted, but after lunch, the P.A. system pulled him out of the fictional world he'd been visiting. Ordinarily, he could block out the loud announcements because they didn't concern him, but this time, the name called was his own.

At first, he moved leisurely, marking his place and putting away the book. He was sure he would find his name had been called by mistake when he got to the visitors' center. But, halfway through tying his shoes, he considered the alternative. If it weren't a mistake, his visitor would have to be a family member because they were the only ones on his visitors' list. He'd told them not to come, but the rules required him to put at least two visitors on the list anyway. Only an emergency could have brought them here. He hurried to the visitor center.

His first glimpse of his visitor should have calmed his fears, but it didn't. When he saw the preacher, his first thought was that something horrible must have happened. Devastating news was usually the kind of news that preachers were called upon to deliver. It could have been a bad accident, or worse, maybe whatever happened was his fault. The people who wanted him dead might have taken it out on his family.

"What happened?" Jake asked, shaking the preacher's proffered hand.

"Some kind of accident," he said. "I don't have all the details."

Jake swallowed hard, dreading the answer to his next question.

"Who?" Jake asked.

"It was my wife's father down in Houston, Texas." Seeing the confusion on Jake's face, he added, "I won't be here tomorrow because of a death in the family. Didn't they announce that?"

"They announced there would be no church service tomorrow, but that's all," Jake said, relieved but still puzzled. Any death was bad news, but this death didn't affect him because he didn't know the preacher's wife, much less her father.

"I don't mean to sound callous," he said, "and I'm sorry for your wife's loss, but what does that have to do with me?"

"Nothing," the preacher admitted, and realizing confusion still existed, added, "Let's start over."

As he shook the preacher's hand, Jake asked again with a wide grin, "What happened?"

"Don't start that again," the preacher said amiably. "Let's sit down."

When they were seated, the preacher explained. "We got the call early yesterday morning that my wife's father had been killed in an accident," he said. "I put her and the kids on a plane to

Houston. I planned on taking care of a few things before driving down this morning. I called and explained the situation because I wasn't planning to stop." He glanced at his watch and added, "Actually, I thought I'd be through Tennessee by now."

Jake found the explanation gratifying. The preacher hadn't snubbed him intentionally; the prison guards were responsible for the unintended slight.

"There's a strict visiting list here, and you're not on mine," Jake said. "How did you manage this visit?"

"I've got friends in high places," the preacher said, grinning as he raised his eyes toward the ceiling. "That, and my dad's a pillar of the community. I got him to make a few phone calls for me this morning."

"This is surprising," Jake said and asked, "What was so important that it caused you to stop here today?"

"A dream," the preacher said. "It was your dream about being on the rooftop during a flood."

"You became the minister on the rooftop testing your faith," Jake said, smiling at the joke.

"No," the preacher said. "It was your dream. It was like watching a movie, except I don't think any actor could ever imitate God's voice to the perfection of that dream. I saw you in your dream, just as you described it, and I heard God tell you He saved you." He hesitated momentarily and said, "Then the dream shifted, and I saw you sitting on a rock with a big silver gun in your hand. I saw a car coming down a gravel road, and I saw somebody in that car start shooting at you. There was another shift; the next thing I knew, I was part of the dream. I was standing at the door of a house above you on the hill. I opened a sliding door and let two big dogs out. They ran down the hill to you and seemed to attack something in the weeds. Does that make any sense?"

Jake was speechless. He hadn't told anybody about the rock, the car, the shooting, the snakes, or the dogs. Was it possible that it had been the preacher he'd sensed watching him, and could the preacher have let the dogs out? He'd heard that quantum theory suggested that effect could come before cause, but that stuff was way over his head. His first impulse was denial, but that didn't feel right. Obviously, the preacher had made considerable effort and sacrifice to come here and talk to him.

"Are you sure you want to know?" Jake said. "At the risk of sounding too dramatic, knowing too much about my past could be dangerous."

"Yes," the preacher assured him. Leaning forward, giving Jake his full attention, he clarified, "Tell me everything."

Jake briefly described his life up to the point of the federal prosecutions in his home county in West Virginia. Then, he began elaborating on the details more relevant to his state of mind. He admitted to his suicidal intent and that he was stopped the first time by a strange sound and a feeling of being watched. Then, he was interrupted after putting the gun in his mouth by two men in a car who tried to shoot him. Finally, he described how the dogs saved him from the rattlesnakes in the weeds.

The preacher could barely catch his breath. "Then it's true, God did save you," he said, his tone filled with awe.

"I don't know," Jake said, shrugging his shoulders. "Something happened to me on that creekbank. Light exploded in my head, and I woke up with a different attitude toward life."

"In the joke," the preacher said, smiling broadly, "the minister was given three chances to live, but he died. God told you He saved you, and you were given three chances to die, but you lived. Don't you see those amazing parallels between the dream and what happened to you?"

Jake thought about it briefly and conceded that the preacher had a point. He'd had three near-death experiences, all within the space of about ten minutes. He could claim a coincidence in the first two interruptions, but nothing short of quantum theory or a miracle could answer the question, *who let the dogs out?* He concluded his story with his arrival at the prison camp.

"And what about that?" the preacher said, jerking his thumb toward the rear corner of the building like a hitchhiker.

Jake knew instantly what he was talking about. Even after more than a month, the last window near the corner was still patched with plywood.

"It's been like that for a while, and I've been wondering why they haven't fixed it," Jake said.

"Me too," the preacher said, "so I did a little checking."

He casually looked around to ensure nobody was paying any attention to their conversation. The center had filled with inmates and visitors while they were talking, but everybody seemed absorbed in their own business.

The preacher said in a lowered voice, "I have it on good authority that it's a mystery. It's still under investigation, but it's the only window in the entire compound with real glass instead of shatter-proof plexiglass." Pausing for dramatic effect or to decide how to phrase it, the preacher almost whispered, "The original building blueprints show only six windows, and that's a seventh window. It's looking like they'll have to fix it without ever closing the official investigation." With an appraising look at Jake, he asked, "Do you know how it got broken?"

It was a reasonable question, but Jake suspected the preacher had already heard something about his involvement based on his tone and how he looked at him.

"I was there," Jake admitted.

After listening to the whole story, the preacher asked, "Did anything seem odd to you at the moment the inmate was swinging at you?"

"Sure," Jake said. "The guy moved like molasses in winter." After momentarily reflecting on it, he added, "The guy seemed not to have even seen me move."

"I heard you moved like greased lightning," the preacher said, confirming that he had indeed heard something. "One moment, you were in front of the window, and the next moment, you were standing to one side."

"It all seemed slow to me," Jake said with a shrug.

The preacher studied Jake intently and said, "It's been weighing heavily on my mind ever since that first day you talked about a dream in which God spoke to you, but I think you're why I was sent here to preach. It suggests an unbelievable revelation about God, but now I'm convinced it's true."

The preacher hesitated, obviously considering the best way to say what he needed to say.

"I've had dreams about you and the Holy Ghost," he finally said, fixing Jake with a direct stare. "I think He has already been, or very soon will be, born into flesh. Either you know Him now, or you will come to know Him. With everything that's happened, I think God's awesome power has already come into the world and is working through you. My dreams and what you've said here today have convinced me."

What the preacher said made sense and explained all the weird things happening in Jake's life. However, he'd listened carefully and thought he saw an obvious flaw.

"You said, 'or soon will be,'" Jake pointed out. "If the Holy Ghost hasn't yet come into the world to fill it with God's power, how could any of what's happened to me be attributed to Him coming into the world?"

"I said, or *very* soon will be," the preacher corrected him. "It's possible that the Holy Ghost has already been conceived by a virgin and not yet born, placing His age anywhere from zero to twelve years. I've seen no reason to believe He has already grown to adulthood and is walking among us." He eyed Jake and smiled as he suggested, "unless it's you."

Jake blinked in surprise and exclaimed in amazement, "Me? If I was God, do you think I would be in prison?"

"According to the Bible," the preacher said, "it wasn't unusual to find God's people in jail. Even Jesus allowed Himself to suffer imprisonment. But no, I don't believe you're the Holy Ghost incarnate. I just wanted to impress upon you how strongly I believe God is working through you."

Jake considered the possibility that he already knew the boy who could be the incarnation of the Holy Ghost. Of the few kids he knew under twelve, Walker's kids were the only ones with whom he was close. He thought of Walker Jr., and it brought a pleasant memory.

The last time he'd been playing with Junior, the boy had inadvertently addressed him as "daddy." Junior immediately recognized his error, giggled, and said, "Uhm … I mean Jake." Psychologists call that a Freudian slip, and Jake was proud that those kids evidently thought enough of him to accidentally conflate him with their father.

On the heels of that pleasant memory came an unpleasant thought. Was it possible that the kids had made similar slips to their father, accidentally calling Walker "Jake" before correcting themselves? Could that explain Walker's inexplicable accusation? Jake didn't think it could be the whole explanation, but he conceded that it could have been a contributing factor. The preacher's voice brought him back to the present.

"According to the pattern set by Jesus," the preacher said, "the boy won't come out of the womb with the ability to talk or with a present knowledge of who He really is. He'll likely be under twelve, and if he's old enough to talk, he might seem more mature than his number of years would suggest. He will probably know things without fully understanding how he knows, and he might also be associated with unexplained miracles. Most importantly, he will have been born of a virgin."

Jake considered Walker Jr. as a possible candidate for the Holy Ghost incarnate and instantly dismissed him. For the same reason, he also rejected Mark, Junior's younger brother. They both had an older sibling. Beautiful Sarah was the firstborn of the family. He wasn't close to any other young children, and he didn't know any young girl who was now pregnant.

"I'm pretty sure I don't already know any boy who could be the Holy Ghost incarnate," Jake said. "But why is it necessary that God can only come into the world as a child born of a virgin? The Bible says that Melchisedec had no father and no mother."

"With God, all things are possible," the preacher acknowledged, "but having one known example of how He *did* come into the world sets the standard. In Melchisedec's case, it simply means he had no *known* father or mother, or they weren't identified because they weren't germane to his life's story."

"Couldn't God have just formed a new body out of clay, or couldn't Jesus have taken possession of an already existing thirty-year-old body?" Jake asked.

"He could," the preacher agreed. "God could have created a brand new thirty-year-old body, but that body would have had no connection whatsoever with existing humanity. Also," he continued, "Jesus could have simply taken over the body of a living male, but to do that, He would, of necessity, be aborting the already existing soul of that body. The only reasonable way God can take the form of flesh without creating a new body, aborting a soul, or dispossessing an existing soul," he concluded, "is for the divine gamete to combine with the female gamete in a virgin to form the zygote before developing into an embryo."

The preacher slid a card halfway across the table, and Jake picked it up. It was a standard business card with the preacher's name, address, and phone number.

"Turn it over," the preacher said.

Jake did, and the preacher's home address and phone number were hand-written on the back.

"I'm serious," the preacher said emphatically. "I would welcome anybody to my place of work, but in a place like this, I must be discreet as to whom I would invite to my home. I have a wife and two young children."

"I understand," Jake said as he slipped the card into his shirt pocket under the watchful eyes of a guard. "I won't give out your address or phone number. As to the other matter," he added, "I don't know any boy who fits those qualifications, but if I should meet him, you'll be the first to know. I promise."

"One thing's for sure," the preacher said, "you won't meet him in here, and that's why I had to come here today. I can't shake the feeling that you'll be gone when I get back. I had to impress upon you the importance of knowing that a boy is out there, and you need to find him."

Jake believed every word the preacher said and returned to the dorm excited about his imminent release from prison. The following week was like a roller coaster ride, alternating between break-neck speed and a snail's pace. First thing Monday morning, Jake eagerly showered and dressed. The preacher predicted his release this week, and he wanted to be prepared in case it happened on the first business day.

But nine, ten, and eleven o'clock passed like time was the roller coaster on a quick downhill sweep. The minutes passed like seconds. He had assumed that notice of his release would arrive at the beginning of the workday, so around noon, it was as though the roller coaster of time had reached the bottom and began its long, sluggish climb back up the hill toward the next day. Tuesday, Wednesday, and Thursday passed in the same fashion.

By Thursday night, doubt had begun to chip away at his confidence in the preacher. There was only one business day left in the week, and if the preacher was wrong about his release, what else might he be wrong about?

On Friday morning, Jake awoke to a confusion of emotions. He'd slept later than usual, and the air in the dorm seemed stagnant but charged with anticipation, like the calm before the storm. He gathered his shower necessities into his spare laundry bag and went to the bathroom as usual.

The bathroom had eight shower stalls, each with its own door, and he chose to use the first one. After showering and drying off, he was pulling his jogging pants on when he heard furtive noises in the bathroom. It wouldn't be unusual to hear slamming stall doors or loud talk, but the apparent stealth was worrisome. When he cautiously pushed the door open, his wrist was grabbed, and he was unceremoniously jerked through.

Jake saw that an unknown inmate held his right wrist, and he was about to swing his laundry bag containing soap and other toiletries when another set of hands grabbed his left arm. He also didn't know this second inmate, and the two inmates forced him back against the closed shower door. The first inmate moved his grip to Jake's upper arm so a third inmate could take hold of his wrist. Jake knew this one.

"Let's see how fast you move this time, shithead," said the inmate who'd run his arm through the plate-glass window. "I'm going to do to you what you somehow did to me, but you'll be going to the morgue instead of the hospital."

The inmate turned Jake's wrist so that the palm was up, and the inside of his forearm was exposed. Jake saw a large butcher knife in his right hand. Undoubtedly, the knife would be retroactively reported missing from the Mess Hall. Above the hand that held the knife was a forearm so mottled with shades of pink as to give it the appearance of raw meat.

Their plan was obvious. They would slit his forearm, hold him until he bled out, and then place the knife in his dead hand. The official story would be that he had somehow stolen the knife from the Mess Hall and had committed suicide. It was a simple but elegant plan. Suicide involving prison inmates was neither uncommon nor unheard of, even in prison camps.

With the knife poised just inches above Jake's arm, the knife wielder grinned sadistically and said, "Any last words, asshole?"

Jake realized he wouldn't be "walking" out of the prison camp this week or ever. His death was inevitable. He closed his eyes in acquiescence and smiled at the irony of the preacher's prediction. He would indeed be gone by the time the preacher returned.

He waited for the sting of the blade. Although he'd closed his eyes, he could still perceive light through his eyelids, and he was surprised when the ambient redness suddenly changed into total darkness. He hadn't felt the sting of the blade, and he hadn't felt any weakness associated with blood loss. As far as he could tell, he hadn't lost consciousness.

The next instant following the darkness, every hand holding him let go simultaneously, repelled from his body as though he'd become a high-voltage conductor. He put a hand to his face to find out why his eyes wouldn't open and discovered they *were* open. The darkness he perceived wasn't private and internal. All the lights in the bathroom were off. There were no windows, and although several emergency lights were mounted on the walls, none had come on.

Jake stood still, and although he couldn't see anything, he heard the unmistakable sounds of a brawl. Apparently, the three inmates had moved away from him and were now fighting among themselves. He moved, guided by his hand to the wall, and turned two corners before reaching the door. He groped for the doorknob like a blind man, and when he found it, he twisted and pushed. The door opened outward a few inches, but then it rebounded like it had struck a doorstop.

A flash of light had entered through the door crack, and Jake didn't notice that the bathroom lights came back on in that very same instant. He still had the doorknob in his hand when somebody suddenly jerked the door open. It was Marshall Dillon, wearing a contemptuous smile, who confronted him. The smile melted away when he recognized Jake.

"I think somebody's fighting in there," Jake said, stepping around the shocked guard. He could feel the guard's eyes following him as he walked toward his cubicle.

Jake dressed as he listened to the commotion of the numerous guards and paramedics swarming in and out of the bathroom. All three of the inmates who had assaulted him were seriously injured. From the snatches of conversation he heard, one of them might even be dead. One of the guards told Jake not to leave his cubicle. The guard said he would be back in a few minutes, but it was more than an hour later when he returned.

Jake couldn't explain what had happened in the bathroom, even if he wanted to. He also knew that any admission to involvement in the altercation would likely land him in the nearby Medium

Security Prison. With that in mind, he kept his explanation brief and vague. When he came out of the shower, he'd heard fighting. He had exited the bathroom and found a guard blocking the door. He informed the guard that it sounded like somebody might be fighting in the bathroom.

He finished his brief account and waited for the many questions his broad statements would surely raise. He knew from experience that vague statements invariably hid details, and the devil was in the details. He was acutely aware that if he wasn't careful, he could be caught in a web of deceit like he'd caught so many others.

"Is this what you said?" the guard asked, turning the paper around so Jake could read it.

There were no additional questions. The guard was disinterested in what Jake said and had written it down in a perfunctory manner. Marshall Dillon had undoubtedly reported it differently.

"That's what I said," Jake confirmed after reading the brief statement.

"Sign it," the guard said, handing Jake the pen.

After retrieving his pen and Jake's statement, the guard said, "Wait here until you're called."

Jake returned to his relaxed, prone position on the bed and felt somewhat disappointed. He had implied that the first guard might have been serving as a lookout and blocking the bathroom door, but even that hadn't piqued any interest.

The dorm remained quiet, and he must have dozed off because the next thing he knew, he was summoned to the Administration Office. It was a quarter to one, and he was surprised that more than two hours had passed.

A few inmates were walking back toward the dorms, but the compound was mostly deserted. Vincent was standing at the front door of the Mess Hall about forty feet away from the main sidewalk. In response to Vincent's yelled question, Jake gave him a palms-up gesture with a shrug of his shoulders. He thought that if this didn't take too long, he might be back in time for lunch with Vincent. However, a minute later, lunch seemed highly unlikely. He passed Marshall Dillon, headed for the dorms, and he was carrying empty garbage bags.

Jake had seen a few inmates leave the camp, and their destination was somewhat predictable. If the inmate was routinely released, he gathered his belongings and was processed out, much like soldiers were released from military service. However, if the inmate was being shipped across the street or to another prison facility, he was called to the office and not allowed to return to the dorms. A guard was sent to collect his belongings. That must be what Marshall Dillon was doing with the garbage bags.

As they were passing, the guard stared at Jake with open hostility. Jake gave him a broad smile as he brazenly returned the stare. Marshall Dillon might have won, but Jake wasn't about to give him the satisfaction of seeing defeat on his face.

CHAPTER 13

When he reported to the administration office, Jake was directed to a chair and told to wait. A half-hour later, a guard opened a door and indicated that Jake should follow him. They entered a bare room containing only a table, and Jake was surprised that all his belongings were piled on it. They were sending all of his property with him, so evidently, they weren't intending to bring him back.

A second guard entered the room through a door opposite the one through which Jake and the first guard had entered, and he was carrying a stack of papers. The second guard said, "The court has ordered your release. You can read these later." He handed Jake the papers. "Change your clothes. Your brother is here to pick you up," and then abruptly left the room.

Jake stood there, staring at the door through which the guard had disappeared, too stunned to move. He finally remembered the papers in his hand and glanced through them, anxious to know the court's opinion. Skipping through to the court's finding, he was pleased that the court had reversed his conviction based on his first argument, but he was mildly disappointed that it rendered his other arguments moot and unaddressed.

"I'm in no hurry, but you can go home as soon as you change clothes," the guard still standing behind him reminded him. "I'll keep what belongs to the camp; you can take the rest."

Jake jumped at the first sound of the voice, having forgotten that the first guard was still in the room. As he changed clothes, Jake became more excited about going home, but he also wondered about the logistics of his release. Nick's house was more than a three-hour trip. If his brother was already here, he must have been notified more than three hours ago. That meant that while he was facing the knife and the three inmates in the bathroom, the prison officials already knew he'd been released.

It was apparent to Jake that Marshall Dillon had arranged the assault in the bathroom. Most likely, he was officially in the dorm to inform Jake that he was being released. At least, Jake was sure it would be the guard's story. Then, the severe injuries in the bathroom took precedence over everything.

When Jake was ready to go, he was led to a counter in another room where he was required to sign his release papers. The guard at the counter was the same one who brought the court documents to him, but Marshall Dillon was sitting behind him, glaring at Jake with undisguised contempt.

Jake looked up from the papers he was signing and made eye contact with Marshall Dillon. The guard's expression didn't change until Jake spoke.

"Mind if I ask you a personal question?" Jake asked.

Marshall Dillon straightened up and puffed out his chest. He was obviously happy that Jake must be foolish enough to give him one more opportunity to humiliate him.

"Not at all," Marshall Dillon said with a smirk.

"Is it really hard work being a prick all the time?" Jake asked, keeping his tone matter-of-factly and inquisitive, "Or do you find that it just comes naturally?"

The guard at the counter raised his hand to his mouth and coughed to cover a smile and a chuckle.

Marshall Dillon exploded out of the chair with an angry snort and charged the counter in a rage.

Having heard the quick movement behind him, the guard at the counter turned and held out his arms to keep the enraged guard from the counter.

"You can have him when I'm finished," the guard said to Marshall Dillon, making it clear that, for the moment, McCallum was his responsibility.

Jake didn't show any emotion or back away from the counter. His only reaction was a broad smile.

The guard managed to get Marshall Dillon back to the chair, and he returned to the counter. He quickly sorted the papers and gave Jake his copies.

"You'd better go," he said to Jake.

Marshall Dillon was still glaring at Jake, the contempt replaced by pure hatred.

After gathering his papers, Jake made eye contact with Marshall Dillon again. The guard at the counter turned and walked away to clarify that he was no longer involved.

"Now that we're both free men," Jake challenged without disguising his contempt, "if you'd like to continue this out in the parking lot, come on out. I'll wait for you."

Marshall Dillon bounded out of the chair again. This time, there was nobody to stop him. He raised his arms as though he intended to grab Jake, but when Jake didn't dodge or flinch, he seemed to realize he no longer had any authority over this man. He dropped his arms and stood there, fuming.

"Get out!" he shouted. "You son-of-a-bitch, get the hell out of my office."

It was no surprise to Jake that Marshall Dillon claimed ownership of the office. It was a common trait among the most egotistical of those endowed with authority. Jake had heard fellow police officers lay claim to "my road," "my town," and "my county." Once, he'd heard a particularly obnoxious officer inform a prisoner, "You're breathing my air."

Jake picked up his suitcase and, before starting toward the door, turned around and chuckled, "You know, that might be a record. I might be the first man thrown *out* of prison."

Marshall Dillon began to rant and curse, but Jake laughed loudly as he strolled out the door.

Nick had evidently been watching for him. He immediately pulled the car out of a parking space and stopped at the curb in front of Jake. Jimmy bounded out of the front passenger seat and greeted Jake with a hug, and Jake let him take the suitcase. Jimmy tossed the bag into the back seat and followed it in, leaving the front door open for Jake. Jake waited on the sidewalk for another minute. When it became evident that nobody was following him out, he climbed into the car.

Jake was disappointed that Marshall Dillon hadn't followed him, but it really wasn't a big surprise. Like a wife-beater who is a holy terror to his wife and kids, much of the guard's source of courage and strength came from the fact that he exercised some degree of authority and control over his victims. However, such bullies were usually cowards who would go to great lengths to avoid anyone who could and would fight back.

"Sorry about that," Jake said after he got in and buckled his seat belt. "I was having a little disagreement with one of the guards, so I invited him outside."

"Well, good to see that prison life hasn't changed your pleasant, nonconfrontational nature," Nick said and laughed. Then, before putting the car in gear, he said, "I'm tired. Any chance you feel like driving, Jake?"

It was nearly two o'clock on a Friday afternoon. Usually, Nick would have been getting out of bed about now, but he likely couldn't have even laid down today. When he got home this morning, he must have had to leave again almost immediately to be at the prison camp at this hour.

"Sure," Jake said. "I've missed doing normal stuff like driving."

Nick got out of the car and left the front door open. He opened the back door and displaced Jimmy from the back seat. They were quickly back on the road, and Nick spoke up from the back seat as he was getting comfortable, obviously intending to nap.

"By the way," he said, "Walker didn't come down the whole time you were in prison. There's no way he could've known you'd be getting out today, but he called last night. He was saying ... "

"If you don't mind," Jake interrupted, "I'd rather not talk about Walker." After a moment of silence, Jake apologized. "Sorry, but it's been a stressful week. I need a little downtime."

"Odd you should mention that," Nick said, perking up a little and leaning forward to talk. "We planned to go to Pittsburgh this weekend, and I've been wondering what to do about it. As soon as I got home this morning, I found out I could come pick you up. Jenny had already gone to work, so I called her on my way here. I told her I was coming to pick you up, but we put off talking about the trip until we got home."

Jenny's parents had moved to Pittsburgh soon after she and Nick married. They didn't visit them often because it was more than a five-hour trip. When they did visit, they took the dogs with them since Jenny's parents also had a dog in the house.

"Jenny's mother is having some kind of medical procedure Monday morning," Nick continued. "Jenny wanted to be with her.

She had to work today, so we planned to leave first thing in the morning. Both Jenny and I have already arranged to be off Monday and Tuesday. I got somebody to take over my duties at church this Sunday, and I arranged for a guy to feed the horses."

Nick paused for so long that Jake thought he might have dozed off, but he started talking again.

"Jenny should be home by the time we get there, and we'll figure it out then. We could cancel, or you could go with us, or if you're serious about wanting some downtime, you can have the house all to yourself for a few days."

"It's summer," Jimmy said, "and we haven't been fishing even once this year. If you come with us, Jake, we can probably find a good place up there to fish."

Jake laughed at Jimmy's innocuous spin on his absence. Jimmy made it sound like Jake had been busy or had voluntarily chosen to be away from home for the last few months, not like he'd been locked up in prison. Jake had always enjoyed being around Jimmy. He'd often fantasized about having children of his own, but the problem was that he'd have to find a wife first. He was becoming doubtful he would ever find a woman who could compete with his memories of Sarah.

Nick had never liked fishing, so Jake had taken Jimmy fishing many times, and he had become even more enthusiastic about it than Jake. It was tempting to go fishing, but Jake felt he'd been forced into the company of others for far too long, and a few days alone sounded great. He looked in the rear-view mirror and saw Nick napping against his suitcase, oblivious to the world, leaving Jimmy to carry on the conversation. Jimmy talked enthusiastically about local events and a horse he might be getting. When they were thirty minutes from home, Jimmy woke his dad so he could consult with his mother about dinner.

While eating take-out at the kitchen table, they caught up on the last few months, and Nick told Jake about the house at the head of the hollow that would soon be vacated. Nick explained that the old man who lived there had decided to move. The big house had finally become too much of a burden for him and his wife, and they were moving to a retirement community near their children in Ohio. Nick said he knew the old man well and could arrange for Jake to look at the house. Nick even suggested they might work out a deal with the old man if Jake liked it.

When Jenny mentioned she had talked to Donna today, Jake quickly let her know he didn't want to hear anything about Walker and Donna, and he abruptly changed the subject to their plans for the upcoming weekend. Jake was adamant about wanting to be alone. His feelings of the calm before the storm hadn't completely dissipated, and he needed some time to sort it out. He insisted that Nick and Jenny not change anything about their plans, not even their plans for the dogs and horses.

Jimmy volunteered to move his things back into the guest room, but Jake said it could wait until they returned. When Nick reminded him that the gun cabinet was still in the guest bedroom, Jake pointed out that he'd lost his right to possess a gun because of his felony conviction. Because the Court of Appeals reversed that conviction, he was no longer prohibited from possessing firearms. Later, when he read his court papers, Jake confirmed the validity of that assumption. Any court orders arising from his conviction were now null and void.

Although exhausted, Jake wouldn't go to bed while Nick, Jenny, and Jimmy were still making last-minute preparations for their trip. He said his goodbyes as they were going to bed because he didn't intend to get up before they left in the morning. When he lay down, instead of immediately falling asleep, a feeling of impending doom kept his eyes wide open. Finally, he got out of bed, retrieved his service revolver, loaded it, and laid it on the nightstand beside the bed. It was long after midnight before he finally drifted off.

Bright light was streaming through the bedroom window when he woke up. He laid still, savoring the silence of being alone. He looked at the clock and realized that everybody must be long gone. It was a little after ten o'clock. He felt rested and realized he'd slept all night without a dream for the first time in recent memory. He wasn't hurrying to get out of bed until he heard a loud *thunk* at the back of the house. Something must have delayed Nick's departure. He rolled out of bed and quickly got dressed.

Jake briskly pulled the bedroom door open and was about to step out into the short hallway when a man appeared in front of him, raised a gun to point directly at his chest, and pulled the trigger. Reacting to a preconceived expectation, Jake fell backward into the bedroom with the *boom* of the gun, only to realize that he hadn't felt the impact of a bullet. He rubbed his chest, and as impossible as it seemed, he pulled away a dry hand. He'd been shot in the chest at point-blank range, but there was no blood. He rolled over and discovered no pain either and, apparently, no wound. It was a miracle.

Jake looked toward the doorway and saw a man's shadow outside the bedroom door. His gun was lying on the nightstand at least ten feet away, and he had no other choice but to go for it. He pushed himself up, quickly took a couple of long strides to the nightstand, and grabbed his revolver. Even as he was snatching it up, he knew it had taken too long. The man was already behind him, inside the doorway, so instead of trying to turn and fire, he threw himself sideways at the bed. He landed on his back and rolled, letting his momentum carry him across the queen-size bed. He heard the *boom* of a second shot as he dropped off the opposite side of the bed.

Jake landed on the floor and, in one fluid motion, pulled himself to his knees, raising his gun into a two-handed shooting grip. With his left upper arm braced against the top edge of the bed, he squeezed off two rounds. He saw the man bounce off the door and drop to his knees with the impact of a bullet. But instead of falling to the floor, the man instantly got back on his feet, turned, and disappeared through the door.

Jake jumped up and went after him, pausing in the doorway to peek around the doorframe. When he saw that the man hadn't stopped in the short, unlit hallway, he headed for the next corner. After two steps, he heard the crunch of glass underfoot and instantly recognized the explanation for the "apparent" miracle. The man had approached his bedroom on the same side of the hallway as the door. Jake had forgotten about the wide, full-length mirror in the hallway. When he jerked his bedroom door open, the mirror must have made it appear like he'd suddenly opened a door directly in front of the guy. When the man fired, instead of killing Jake, he'd only shattered the mirror.

The noise of the crunching glass spoiled any attempt at stealth, so Jake sprinted into the living room and dropped into a shooter's crouch. Nobody was in the room, but from this vantage point, Jake could see through the dining room to the sliding glass door at the rear of the house. He glimpsed movement out on the patio. He ran to the door and found it pushed wide open. He stood in the open doorway in a shooter's stance, looking out at the patio and the mountainside only thirty or forty feet beyond. A foot lay on the edge of the raised patio, the attached ankle and leg trailing off to the man's body that lay face up on the ground.

Jake approached the foot, moving in stuttered steps with a two-handed grip on his weapon. A blood-covered left arm lay limp and useless against a man's body, and his right arm was stretched out at a ninety-degree angle to his torso. The gun lay several inches beyond an open hand that had apparently become too weak to hold it. Lastly, Jake looked at the man's face and was shocked when he recognized him. It was Marshall Dillon.

The guard's eyes were wide open, moving wildly as though searching for something in the cloudless sky. His breathing was sporadic and coming in noisy, rapid gasps, sounding like a woman in labor. As Jake watched, darkness came out of the guard's nostrils in a protracted exhalation. It gathered into a loosely defined dark mass about the size of a golf ball, seeming to throb with malevolence. It hung suspended over a chest that was no longer drawing breath.

As the darkness floated away, Jake stood transfixed, tracking the movement with his gun. At first, it drifted aimlessly, but then it gained speed as it traveled straight up the mountainside. Jake could barely track it through the thickened greenery, but he saw it hit a big black bird perched on a low tree limb. As though struck by a line-drive golf ball, the bird frantically fluttered its wings as it was knocked backward onto the hillside. The big bird thrashed noisily in the dead leaves for several seconds before it managed to regain the limb upon which it had been sitting.

Without making a sound, the big bird hunched forward and launched itself at Jake. Startled by the bird's unnatural attack, Jake dropped flat on the patio. He raised his gun, turning to track it as it passed overhead. He was about to shoot when it suddenly veered left, flapped its huge wings, and flew around the corner of the house. He saw it again when it emerged from the upper front side of the house, gaining altitude as it headed up the hollow. He watched it gain altitude, taking his eyes off it for only a moment to confirm that Marshall Dillon hadn't moved. When he returned his attention to the bird, he watched it as it circled high above the house and barn.

After completing a few circuits, the big bird began a dive that seemed to be aimed directly at him, and Jake brought his weapon up again. Then, the bird appeared to make a course correction, closed its wings, and turned the dive into a vertical drop. The bird hit a big flat rock, bounced once, and lay still. Jake watched until he was convinced there was no movement from either the bird or the dark mass that had entered it.

Jake sat down on the edge of the patio to consider his options. This wasn't like the last time. He couldn't put everything back in order and not tell anybody. This time, there was a dead body. This didn't appear to be part of a larger plan to incriminate or discredit him, but he did not doubt that if the wrong people got involved, every circumstance would be twisted in whatever way was most detrimental to him. But even as he pondered that, he realized he had no choice. He had no intention of illegally disposing of a dead body. All he could do was tell the truth and let the chips fall where they may.

Jake went inside to use the telephone. He'd carried a cell phone when he was working and even when he was home when he had an apartment that wasn't up a hollow. But up this hollow, like many other hollows in West Virginia, the cell phone service was so sporadic that it made carrying one pointless. It would likely be several decades before cell phone towers were plentiful enough on the mountaintops to make the signal reliable in the hollows.

Fifteen minutes later, an ambulance was the first to arrive. Jake knew one of the EMTs, so he explained the situation. They could check the victim to ensure for themselves that he was dead, but they couldn't move the body until the police arrived. This was a crime scene, and the shooting victim was also the perpetrator.

A few minutes later, a state police cruiser turned into the driveway and parked in the curve to allow room for the ambulance to depart when it was ready. Jake was heartened that the trooper was Chad Collins, an honest cop. After greeting Jake, he quickly took charge of the scene, taking notes and pictures and occasionally asking Jake questions.

"Is this his vehicle?" Trooper Collins asked. After seeing Jake's release papers, he was businesslike but no longer cold.

"No, that belongs to my brother," Jake said.

Jake had identified the body as Charles Marshall Wellingham, a guard from the prison camp. Jake recalled he'd been asleep and hadn't heard a vehicle, but the guy had to have had some manner of transportation. He must have parked nearby if he hadn't been dropped off.

Jake took Trooper Collins through the house and showed him the evidence of the shooting. He pointed out the two shots the guard had fired. But the most critical evidence he wanted documented was the two shots he'd fired. They proved he'd shot the intruder inside the house, and the intruder had run outside before he died. One bullet hole in the door was clean, but the position and blood splatter around the second bullet hole perfectly matched where the guard's chest would have been.

Trooper Collins took Jake's statement, and Jake was open and forthright in every detail, except he said nothing about the small dark mass that had come out of the guard. He couldn't prove he'd seen the mass, and any unsubstantiated details would only weaken his credibility. The Bible doesn't describe what the demons looked like when they came out of the two humans and went into the herd of swine, but Jake could think of no other reasonable explanation for the dark mass that went into the big bird.

Having come out of Marshall Dillon with his dying breath, the demons had nowhere to go, so they had gone into the big bird. When God set the Universe in motion, He established specific rules of order, like gravity, the motion of the planets, etc. We call those rules *natural laws* because they govern the natural world. It was only reasonable that God must have also established *unnatural laws* to govern the unnatural world. We don't know those rules because their very nature defies any meaningful study, but Jake was sure he'd just witnessed one.

He'd witnessed perhaps the most fundamental law governing the unnatural world. Apparently, demons can control animals for only a brief time before that animal destroys itself. Making a law that animals will choose destruction rather than accept possession must have been necessary to protect animals from demons. If animals could be possessed long-term, they could be enslaved by demons to be nothing more than mobile homes. It would allow demons to freely leave the unnatural world and interact with the natural world through those animals. Without such a rule, animals as we know them could not exist.

When Jesus cast the demons into the herd of swine soon after coming into the country of Gergesenes, the herd ran headlong into the sea to destroy itself. The big bird reacted similarly after its initial brief attack on him. It took flight and climbed to an altitude that ensured its destruction. The strange actions of the rattlesnakes also made sense in that context. The snakes lacked the physical ability to destroy themselves, but they could give themselves over to being destroyed.

As soon as the trooper was gone, Jake cleaned up the mess. However, this time, he was trying to eradicate only the mess, not the evidence that it had happened. He realized it was time to tell his family the truth. There was no longer any reasonable expectation that it was safer for them to not know. If any of them had been caught at home this morning, the guard's attack could have been catastrophic.

It was no surprise that Marshall Dillon had known precisely where to find him, but the direct, frontal attack was entirely unreasonable. The demon possession might account for some part of the guard's motivation, but Jake didn't know enough about demons or how long the guard had been possessed to tell if they were wholly responsible. He also didn't know any of the rules that govern demon possession of humans.

Wellingham had used a Smith & Wesson, Model 10, Snub Nose .38 Special. The fact that he had used a six-shooter in the assault wasn't weird, but the fact that he didn't have extra ammunition on him was inexplicable. The guard had staged an assault on a house with only the six rounds in his gun.

The mere fact that Marshall Dillon knew where to find him should have meant the guard also knew there was a possibility he could run into any of three other people and two large dogs. But the guard had noisily forced the sliding glass door open and boldly entered the house. Regardless of how quietly he'd approached or how slight the noise was when he entered the house, the guard should have anticipated that his presence could bring two big dogs running.

The bold attack was puzzling, but it made one thing perfectly clear. Jake needed to find his own place because it was dangerous for others to be around him. Nick had suggested that he look at the house at the head of the hollow and even offered to try to make a deal with the owner if Jake decided he wanted it. Isolating himself in that house could be the most practical and expedient answer to the danger he posed to others around him. It wouldn't hurt to look at the house. Maybe Nick could get the old man to defer payment or hold onto the property until he started drawing a paycheck again. To that end, the first thing he needed to do Monday morning was to arrange to meet with an attorney to begin proceedings to get his job back.

CHAPTER 14

On Monday, after a busy morning of making phone calls, Jake used his brother's car to go to Charleston to meet with an attorney. It was essentially a matter of opinion, but as far as Jake could deduce, Peal and Hoskins was the largest law firm in West Virginia.

His consultation with Sheldon Jamerson, a young associate with the firm, went very well. Jake intended to file lawsuits for everything possible. As Respondents, he named the State of West Virginia, a state police officer, the United States, two FBI agents, a DEA agent, the Federal District Court Judge, the U.S. Attorney, the trial attorney, the court-appointed appeals attorney, the Manchester Federal Prison Camp and the estate of the recently deceased, C.M. Wellingham.

Jamerson read his Fourth Circuit Court of Appeals decision and was eager to file his lawsuits. Jake also pressed the lawyer to prioritize his return to work. Although there was a reasonable expectation he would eventually be generously compensated for his confinement, there was still the matter of earning a living while the lawsuits made their slow journey through the cumbrous court system. It could be years before there was a final resolution. The Court of Appeals' decision did not address the issue of his job. That matter would require separate legal action, and only the Beecham County Deputy Sheriff's Civil Service Commission could order him reinstated.

Jamerson expressed his opinion that Jake's case represented big money and that he virtually guaranteed that Jake would soon return to work. Jake was adamant that he neither sought nor would accept an out-of-court settlement. He wanted all the issues exposed in open court so that he could then press for criminal prosecutions. Hopefully, the information brought to light in a trial would expose the corruption that would lead to the prosecution of someone higher up in business or government.

Just before noon Tuesday morning, Trooper Collins called. His tone was friendlier than it had been on Saturday. He wasn't required to make this call and was apparently doing so only as a courtesy to Jake.

"Just thought you'd want to know," he said after a friendly greeting. "I found Wellingham's car parked not far from the house Saturday. There was a 35mm camera with a telephoto lens in it. I had the film developed, and I just got the pictures back. Several pictures were taken of your brother's car farther down the hollow, leaving. You could easily count the people and dogs. I can't know what he had planned, but clearly, when he learned you were alone, his attack became a crime of opportunity."

They laughed and talked about old times for another ten minutes after Jake mentioned he expected to be back on the job soon. Before they hung up, Chad said he had closed the investigation. The pictures were no longer needed; he would mail copies to Jake if he wanted.

When Nick returned Tuesday afternoon, Jake sat down with the family and described what had transpired over the weekend. Nick received the information with his usual aplomb, so to ensure that everybody fully appreciated the ongoing danger, Jake told them about the attack the day before he reported to the prison camp. But, he decided it would not be useful to tell them about the two attacks in the prison camp. He just wanted to put them on alert, not make this a call to action. His greatest fear was that one of them might try to come between him and a would-be assailant. The dogs could have paid a terrible price for rushing to his aid if the rattlesnakes had acted more normally.

At Jake's request, Nick called the old man at the head of the hollow and arranged to see the house. When Nick got home from work the next morning, they went up to look at it. Jake liked the house the moment he stepped through the door. It had solid construction, and its ambiance was homey and peaceful. The old man explained that it was built when he was the pastor of a large church and that much of the construction had been done by the volunteer labor of the church congregation.

Jake had a few reservations about the house, but first and foremost was his lack of money. He did like that this property was at the head of the hollow, so it offered maximum privacy, but the big house and 365 acres of land were for sale for eighty thousand dollars. The problem was that Jake didn't even have eighty dollars to spare. His brother supplemented his remaining savings with food and shelter; Nick *even* provided the vehicle Jake used to travel back and forth to his lawyer.

The big house had six bedrooms and four baths: two bedrooms and two bathrooms on the first floor and four bedrooms and two bathrooms upstairs. It was ridiculously more than he needed. He explained to Nick that immediate solitude had been his primary motivation. If he had to wait until he returned to work – and the lawyer assured him it would be soon – to move in, he would be satisfied with an economical, one-bedroom apartment. It was even possible that he might get his old apartment back.

Additionally, cleaning and maintaining a house of that size would be a burden, and Jake reminded his brother that that was precisely why the old man was selling it in the first place. Even heating and cooling the unused areas of the house would be an unnecessary burden.

Nick, however, countered each of his objections. He knew the old man and was confident he could arrange an owner-financed deal. If a down payment was required, he could loan Jake money to cover that, including enough to tide him over until he returned to work. Regarding cleaning and maintaining the house, Jake could close off the entire second floor. The old man and his wife had kept the whole house open to accommodate the infrequent visits of their grandchildren.

"If you don't mess it up, you won't have to clean it up. And for the most part, if you don't tear it up, you won't have to fix it," Nick pointed out. "One of the best things about it," Nick continued, "is that the property has a gas well on it, just like mine. The natural gas is piped into the owner's house free of charge. It's a benefit that goes with the property when it's sold. If you buy it, that reduced cost alone makes the house nearly as affordable as renting and paying utilities for a decent-sized apartment."

However, it was Nick's final argument that convinced Jake to take it if a deal could be made. Nick explained that ever since he bought his property, he'd dreamed of owning all the property from his house up to the head of the hollow. He explained that he knew it was an impossible dream because buying the other two properties was beyond his and Jenny's resources, at least while they were still young enough to enjoy it. But now, if Jake bought one property, he could buy the other one, and together, they would own most of the hollow to do with as they pleased.

Jake wasn't in on the negotiations, but somehow, Nick arranged for him to move into the house four days later. The old man and his wife took only their personal belongings, so the house was wholly furnished. Some might think living alone in a big old house would be spooky, but not Jake. True, the house did have its creaks and groans, but he sensed that none of the sounds were malevolent. It was like living in a church, as though it had been sanctified and consecrated by the hands that built it.

For his second meeting with the attorney a week later, Jake had compiled all the information the lawyer requested. He provided all the details of the federal investigation in his county. He also brought audio and video tapes to corroborate his assertion of official misconduct and prosecutorial wrongdoing. He showed the attorney the evidence but refused to let it out of his possession until needed at trial, citing the chain of evidence rules. He had written long narratives about his trial lawyer, the court-appointed appeals attorney, and the attacks instigated by the dead guard while acting under the color of the federal government.

Jake had been home from prison for over three weeks, and he missed studying the Bible. Nick had unintentionally put a damper on that. When he offered to return his Bible, Nick refused to take it. At first, Nick had seemed excited that Jake was reading the Bible, but when Jake started explaining the book of Genesis the way the preacher at the prison camp had described it, Nick's enthusiasm waned until Jake finally stopped talking about it. He occasionally attended church, but those instances were becoming rare because he was quickly losing interest in that, too. The sermons preached at Nick's church were unenlightening at best and illogical and nonsensical at worst.

A week after his second meeting with the attorney, Jake was summoned to his office for a third visit. Jamerson refused to discuss why Jake needed to make the trip, claiming that it was something he couldn't talk about over the phone. When he arrived at the office, Jake was immediately led to a conference room and served coffee. He had taken only a few sips before Jamerson swept into the room. After a brief exchange of pleasantries, the lawyer opened the file, beaming with joy.

"This is a highly unusual case," the lawyer said, obviously excited about what he thought was great news. "I haven't yet filed anything with the court, but we've already received a very generous settlement offer."

The lawyer took a check from the file and slid it across to Jake, and Jake almost refused it without even looking at it. He would not have come if the words "settlement offer" had been used when Jamerson summoned him for this meeting. Curiosity got the better of him, and he picked up the check and looked at it. It was from an insurance company, and it was made out to him in the incredible amount of $150,000. When he looked at Jamerson, there was a broad smile on the lawyer's face.

"That's just an advance," Jamerson said. "The settlement offer is all-inclusive of the parties to be named in the lawsuits, and it's four million dollars." He pronounced the amount as though each word was a complete sentence. Four. Million. Dollars.

Jake took the papers without comment and began reading. He tried to maintain a poker face, but the offer boggled his mind. He had always lived from paycheck to paycheck and couldn't imagine what it would be like to be a millionaire. With that much money, he could retire in the lap of luxury. He could buy the property and never have to leave the hollow again. He could even buy that third property and present it to his brother as a gift.

"The advance is yours right now," Jamerson said. "If there's anything in the agreement you can't agree to, we can work it out, but if you'd like to sign it right now, you could have the full amount almost immediately."

Jake kept reading. At first, four million dollars sounded very generous, but the more he read, the more it felt like he was selling his soul. The amount was intended to compensate him for past grievances and buy his silence in the future. It required him to surrender all evidence within his possession or knowledge concerning all the respondents to be named in the lawsuits. It also required him to cease any investigations of the named individuals or their associates. Most strikingly, it required that he forfeit his job as a deputy sheriff and neither seek nor accept any job in law enforcement for ten years.

"I'll need some time to think about this," Jake said.

"You're the boss," Jamerson said amenably. "Take a day or two to look it over. Call me if you find a problem, and I'll try to hammer it out. If you don't see any issues, call me, and we'll set up a time for you to come in and sign it."

"Fine," Jake said, "but it might take more than a day or two. Have you filed for a hearing with the Civil Service Commission?"

"Not yet," Jamerson said, "but I have the papers ready. We have sixty days to ask for the hearing, and we still have a lot of time before that deadline. If you accept this agreement, returning to work will become a moot issue."

"But I haven't accepted this agreement," Jake reminded him, "and I'm not sure I will. I can't accept this either," he said, sliding the check back to Jamerson. "It would infer that I intend to accept the settlement, and it might give this law firm some expectation of a right to participate in my decision."

Jamerson seemed flustered and less amenable than he'd been just a moment before. "Mister McCallum, I'm obligated to do what I think is in your best interest. Resolving this case and giving you immediate access to the funds is possible. However, if the Court becomes involved, it's likely to take years."

"Mister Jamerson," Jake said, matching the lawyer's snooty formality and condescending tone, even though they had formerly been on a first-name basis. "Speed is not my primary concern. I made it clear from the start that I didn't want an out-of-court settlement. My decision to come to this law firm was purely arbitrary. I can, and if necessary, I will go to another law firm."

"Excuse me for a minute," Jamerson said, hastily standing and gathering the file. He added, "I'll be right back."

Jake occupied himself with continuing to read the agreement while Jamerson was gone.

When he returned, the lawyer apologized, "Sorry to keep you waiting. You're absolutely right. I've consulted with the senior partners, who authorized me to offer you this check." He handed Jake a check and a single-page document. "So that there's no misapprehension about the intent of the check," the lawyer said, "if you just sign that agreement, I'll make you a copy."

The document was concise and nearly free of legalese. The check had the law firm's name on it, and the document plainly stated that the $150,000 was a loan from the law firm. It was only repayable from the proceeds of the case, whether concluded by this firm or another, and whether by settlement or jury award. It further stated that the loan in no way, shape, or form obligated Jake to this law firm or to accept any settlement offer.

Jake could think of no logical reason to reject it. He could certainly use it. He could repay his brother, make a significant payment on the house, and have enough left over to last him several months. He should be back at work long before the money ran out. Jake left the lawyer's office with the check and a promise to call him with his decision.

Late Tuesday evening, the day after returning from the lawyer's office, Jake sat on his front porch reading his Bible, flipping from one book to another, studying eternal punishment and the nature of Hell. He was surprised that Hell wasn't a final destination. Hell itself was scheduled to be emptied out and destroyed in the Lake of Fire. When the phone started ringing, he retreated into the house, surprised that it was almost dark.

"It's your nickel," he said affably, expecting it to be his brother.

"Hey, how you doin'?" the flat voice on the phone said.

It had been months since he'd heard that phrase in that voice, but he instantly knew who it was. "Fine," Jake said, and after a brief pause, he added, "Who is this?"

Walker had wounded him deeply, and he didn't intend to let it go that easily. He owed him a huge apology, and Jake would settle for nothing less.

Walker identified himself, seemingly unaware of Jake's cold greeting.

"I've been waiting for you to call," Walker said, "but I couldn't wait any longer."

"Why would you be waiting for *me* to call *you*?" Jake asked. "*I* didn't kick *you* while you were down. *I* didn't accuse *you* of doing the worst possible thing one friend can do to another."

After a long, uncomfortable pause, Walker said, "A guy gave me something that was very convincing. But that's not what I'm calling about now."

The emotion in Walker's voice perturbed Jake. It was making him increasingly hard to understand.

"Didn't Nick tell you about Sarah being in the hospital?" Walker asked. "I called him a couple of weeks ago and told him to tell you to call me. Sarah's been asking for you. She asked for you right up to when she went into a coma."

His words and weird timbre chilled Jake to his core. "What's wrong," Jake asked, fear smothering his wounded pride. He remembered that both Nick and Jenny had tried to say something about Walker, but he cut them off, making it clear he had no desire to hear about Walker and Donna.

"She's dying," Walker said, his flat voice brutal in its harsh pronouncement.

"What're you talking about?" Jake asked, unable to imagine any reality in which that could be possible.

"She started having headaches about two months ago," Walker said, his voice softening but still strange. "She went downhill fast. She went into a coma about a week ago, and now, they don't expect her to make it through the night. That's why I couldn't wait any longer for you to call."

"Can't they operate?" Jake asked. "Is it a question of money?"

"No," Walker said. "In fact, they're going to operate. I've given the doctors permission, and they'll do it at seven in the morning, but there's no hope she'll live through it."

"What do you mean, no hope?" Jake said. "If there's no hope, why would you let them operate?"

"I'm not supposed to talk about it," Walker said. "I just had a weird urge to call you. I got your number from Nick."

Jake couldn't believe what he was hearing. Walker was making even less sense than the last time he'd talked to him. It felt like the world lurched backward, and an old, familiar anger and disgust began rising in him.

"Where's Donna?" Jake demanded.

"Jake, she's got a brain tumor," Walker said, continuing as though Jake hadn't said anything. "But it's no ordinary tumor. It's one hundred percent fatal, and it only affects girls from four to six years old. Other girls have already died from it, and many more are in the earlier stages."

"Brain tumors?" Jake questioned. "I haven't heard anything about a tumor epidemic."

"That's why I'm not supposed to talk about it. We were asked to cooperate by keeping quiet to prevent a panic."

"Who wants you to keep it quiet?" Jake asked.

"The doctors," Walker said. "There's a team of doctors here from the CDC in Atlanta."

Walker abruptly excused himself, and Jake was left with his own thoughts. The CDC was the government. It was the government that had sent him to prison, and the government had been complicit in the attempts on his life. He wanted to scream, why are you trusting Sarah's life to the government, but what Walker said when he returned on the phone was so devastatingly horrible that Jake couldn't think straight.

"The doctors haven't been able to learn anything about those tumors from the autopsies," Walker said. "They think if they look at it while the patient is still living, they might save some of those other little girls."

"You're letting them perform an autopsy on her before she even dies?" Jake blurted out, stupefied. When Walker didn't immediately reply, it suddenly occurred to him what was wrong with Walker's voice. "Are you drinking?" Jake accused.

"Yes, I am," Walker admitted, obviously glad to unburden himself with the confession. "It's the only thing that's helped me sleep for the past few weeks." After a brief pause, Walker said, "She's going to die, and nothing can stop that. If her death can help save other lives ..." he trailed off. He was quiet for another moment, then said, "You know if she could make the decision herself, she'd want it that way, Jake."

The trouble was Jake did know. She was the most generous, the most kind-hearted, the ... He consciously pushed those thoughts away. *There was no time for that.*

"Do you know for sure there are other lives involved?" Jake asked, his distrust of the government still worrying him.

Walker's speech was becoming more slurred now that he wasn't making any effort to hide his drinking.

"I've seen the files," Walker said. "They're all little girls and more than one hundred have already died. It's the other thousands still living that might be helped. Right now, none of the doctors know how the girls got the tumors or how to get rid of them. The tumors disappear immediately with death."

That information did nothing to alleviate Jake's concern about the government. In fact, the specificity of the age and gender of those attacked strongly implied an intelligent design. Intelligent design suggested a designer and made the existence of a government experiment a real possibility.

"Can I see her?" Jake asked. "Do I need a special permit?"

"There's no problem getting in," Walker said. "As far as anybody except the doctors know, it's a regular tumor."

"Where's Donna?" Jake asked again.

There was another long pause, and he thought Walker was going to ignore the question again, but when Walker spoke, his slurred speech was so choked with alcohol-soaked emotion that Jake could barely understand him.

"She won't leave the hospital, Jake," Walker said, his words punctuated with sobs. "It's been nearly two weeks since she's been home. She refuses to accept the truth. I'm afraid when it happens, when Sarah dies, it's going to destroy her, too. If you see her, please, please don't offer her any false hope." He stopped to catch a noisy breath and added, "Tell her we need her. Tell her she needs to come home to her family."

CHAPTER 15

Jake got off the phone as fast as he could after learning that the boys were not in the house with Walker. They had been with Walker's mother for the past two weeks. Again and again, Walker insisted Jake not give Donna any false hope, but whatever he was drinking was taking full effect, and Jake was becoming disgusted listening to him. It seemed Walker's main concern was Donna. It was as though he had already accepted the death of Sarah. By the end of the conversation, Sarah was forgotten, and Walker was nearly blubbering over Donna.

Jake had only half listened to the last several minutes of the conversation, distracted by worries of government involvement. The government wouldn't be experimenting to find a defense against five-year-old girls, but they could be experimenting with methods to target narrowly defined groups. An experiment could have gotten away from them. Was it possible his connection to Sarah made her a candidate for such an experiment? He loved that little girl, and the possibility he could be responsible for her death almost made him wish he were with Walker, sharing his bottle of mind-numbing, liquid comfort.

Twenty minutes after he hung up the phone, Jake was driving to the hospital in Logan. Besides making a substantial payment on the house, he had used part of the check from the lawyer's office to buy a one-year-old Jeep, a small CJ5, four-speed on the floor, and a canvas top. He had been concentrating on the cause of the brain tumor to delay thinking about the more painful issue, but now that he was on the road, he couldn't avoid what lay at the end of this short journey. According to Walker, she would be dead in less than ten hours, if not from the tumor itself, then from the doctors who claimed it was necessary to observe the tumor before it vanished with her death.

He had driven only a few miles before he had to pull off the road. It was like trying to drive through a rainstorm. Tears of regret were streaming from his eyes and clouding his vision because he had let his foolish pride stand in the way of having contact with Sarah. Clearly, Walker would have let him visit her in the hospital if he'd just called as soon as he got out of prison. Now, he would never be able to talk to her again.

When he could see again, he got back on the road. As he drove, his regret turned to anger. He recently deduced that God wasn't so monstrous as to create sentient beings just to doom the majority of those beings to suffer for eternity. It was an illogical supposition that those beings brought it upon themselves and forced God to punish them. Eternal torment was much too cruel a penalty for such a short, unasked-for, no-choice existence. Annihilation of the consciousness would be a much more merciful fate.

However, now he faced a situation in which God did appear monstrous. Sarah was a warm ray of sunshine in a harsh, cold world, and she didn't deserve to die. He thumped the heels of his hands on the steering wheel and railed against God. "A monster is as a monster does!" he yelled, hurling the accusation toward the heavens like a demented Forrest Gump.

By the time he pulled into a parking space at the hospital, Jake was physically weak and emotionally drained. He rested his head on the steering wheel and waited for his strength to return. Reason and logic reasserted themselves, and he reconsidered his outburst against God and repented. He gathered his strength and mentally prepared himself for the ordeal to come.

By the time he rode the elevator up to the third floor and approached Sarah's room, his feelings of anger, resentment, and hopelessness were replaced by trepidation. The main thing he now felt was fear at the prospect of the frightful sight of a comatose little girl. To a lesser extent, he was concerned about meeting Donna. He was about to see her again for the first time since that disastrous visit from Walker over four months ago. He had no idea what kind of reception to expect. He pushed the door open and went in, determined that he would spend as much time with Sarah as Donna would allow.

As he entered the hospital room, Jake saw Donna sitting in an easy chair with her legs folded under her, reading a book. Except for the meager light filtering through the window from the parking lot, a floor lamp behind her chair provided the only illumination. Donna lowered the book and looked up as he entered. When she recognized him, she leaped out of the chair and wrapped her arms around his neck.

"It's so good to see you," she said. "It's been too long."

"Yes, it has," Jake said, returning the hug, pleasantly surprised by her warm greeting.

After a long embrace, Donna stepped back and said, "Ever since we heard you were back, Walker's been putting off calling you. I think he was waiting for you to call him."

"I should have," Jake conceded. "I'm so sorry, but I didn't know about Sarah until less than an hour ago."

He didn't try to explain why he had refused to listen to their messages or how much Walker's accusation had hurt him. He had no idea how much she knew about it.

He purposely averted his eyes from Sarah's bed. Now that he was this close, the urgency in seeing her was replaced by dread. Hearing about her condition had been bad, but seeing her was bound to be so much worse.

"Whatever happened between you two," Donna said, "please work it out. He needs you, Jake. He's been drinking lately, and I'm afraid he might crawl into a bottle and never come out."

Apparently, Donna wasn't aware that Walker had severely restricted his access to her and the kids. It was encouraging that both had asked for help, each for the other.

"Everything's going to be all right," Jake tried to assure her.

When she began to sob softly, he was reminded of Walker's admonitions against offering her any false hope, but he quickly dismissed them. He had no intention of offering her any hope for the living flesh. The only hope he wanted to remind her of was the certain hope of the resurrection.

Through intermittent sobs, Donna said, "She seems to be slipping deeper and deeper into the coma, Jake. She hasn't said a word in the past two days, but before that, she kept calling your name and asking for help. She seemed convinced that you could help her."

Jake was angry and insulted that Walker had waited until he was drinking before calling him, but now, he could almost commiserate with him. It had to be a terrible thing for a father to hear. It would be heartbreaking to listen to your child begging for help you couldn't provide. How much more painful must it be to listen to that child calling out for help from another man? In that realization, he recognized the source of Donna's hope and the cause for Walker's warnings.

"You don't really believe I could help her, do you?" Jake asked. "What could I possibly do?" He was trying to be realistic, not dash any hope she might have. Her faith made her receptive to God; that was the only real hope he meant to remind her of.

"I guess not," she said as she wiped the tears from her eyes. "I guess if I really believed it, I would have called you myself."

Jake could delay no longer. He moved to Sarah's bedside. It was a good thing there was a chair beside her bed because the moment he saw her, all his strength drained out of his legs. He would have wound up on the floor if he hadn't caught the chair and managed to sit down.

Although she was covered by a crisp, white sheet with only her head and hands exposed, he could tell by the outline of her body that she had grown taller since he last saw her, and the perception of greater height only seemed to punctuate her gauntness. The skin on her thin face was taut and mottled with gray. Her eyes seemed sunken, and her once golden hair, although neatly combed and fanned out around her head, was limp and lackluster. It was a mocking reminder of its former glory. Her lips were thin, and her mouth seemed drawn wider than it should be, slightly turned down at the corners.

Her hand on the other side of the bed was wrapped with tape to secure an I.V. needle, but her hand closer to Jake lay exposed and inviting, as though Donna might have recently held it and had not put it back under the sheet. After recovering his equilibrium, Jake leaned forward and took Sarah's hand, but he quickly let go and jerked away as though she was repulsive.

He surreptitiously glanced at Donna, but she continued staring out the window. He was glad he didn't have to explain his reaction. It felt like an electrical shock. There was a sharp impact, followed by the sensation of bugs or tiny worms, highly energized and moving in crazed, frenetic motions.

A whisper of sound caused him to look at Sarah's face, but nothing about her expression had changed. He was doubting that the noise had even come from her when Donna suddenly appeared at his side.

"What was that?" Donna asked, obviously excited by the slightest possibility of any change in Sarah's condition.

Jake was amazed that Donna had even heard the sound from her position at the window. He'd been right beside Sarah, and the sound had been so indistinct and fleeting that he doubted he had even heard it. Donna had been standing at the window, lost in another world, but apparently so attuned to her child that even the most minute sound could draw her attention.

"I don't know," Jake replied truthfully. He watched as Donna thoroughly inspected Sarah for any change. She had just straightened up from her examination when there was another sound.

"Help me."

Those two words had been so faint that they were barely audible, but they had both heard them. Donna's hand flew to her mouth with a gasp.

"She knows you're here, Jake. Somehow," Donna whispered in awe through her fingers. "she knows you're here."

Jake didn't know if Sarah had reacted to his touch, but he'd already decided what he would do. His reaction to touching her the first time had been involuntary, startled by the unexpected sensation. This time, however, he would be prepared and wouldn't break contact no matter what happened.

When he covered her hand with his own, the sensation was the same as the first time. There was a sharp impact followed by the frantic motions of what felt like tiny worms, and the longer he held her hand, the more it felt like those worms were trying to break through his skin. An idea suddenly formed in his mind. Since this sensation felt like electricity, another similarity might exist. Maybe whatever this was could flow from one body to another. He bowed his head and closed his eyes.

"Dear God in Heaven," he whispered, "please let this be why I'm still living. Please let me take this little girl's place. Please, God, please, make her sickness my sickness; let her tumor be my tumor; make her pain my pain, and let her demons be my demons. In Jesus's name, amen."

Jake became aware of a vague light in the total darkness. He knew he was still in the hospital room and still holding Sarah's hand, but he also knew he was somewhere else. He was standing alone, surrounded by impenetrable darkness, except for a dimly lit, oval-shaped object directly in front of him. It was only slightly longer than tall and dimpled like a golf ball. It was grossly spongy and repulsive, but he immediately heard Sarah's voice again as soon as he touched it.

"I'm in here, Jake. Help me." The voice seemed to be coming from inside the repulsive object.

Jake made a fist and punched the object several times, and after poking and prodding, he discovered he couldn't rip it apart and destroy it, but he could penetrate it. Finally, he ducked his head, and using his fists like a jackhammer, he started forcing his way through, like a boxer driving his opponent across the ring. It felt like it was composed of hands trying to grab him, but he was as slippery as a greased pig at a state fair. He inched forward, keeping every muscle in his body vibrating with effort so the hands couldn't get a firm grip.

As he moved forward, he could feel the wall of the object closing behind him, but at the same time, the diffused light he was approaching was becoming brighter and taking on definition. He knew the end of the struggle must be near, but he felt himself becoming sluggish. A seed of doubt began to leach away his remaining energy in a way that physical exertion did not. Constant handling of the pig at the state fair wore away the grease until it could eventually be caught, and it seemed that something like that was happening to him.

"Help me, Jake."

It was Sarah's beautiful voice, and it sounded so close. It provided the extra lubricant Jake needed. He exploded through the last inches of the wall and came face to face with Sarah.

The little girl leaped into his arms. He enfolded her, covering her cherubic face with kisses. She looked like she did several months ago when he last saw her, not like she looked lying in the hospital bed. She seemed to be composed of light, but the warmth and texture of her skin were that of flesh and blood. She draped her tiny arms over his shoulder and nuzzled his neck like she'd done so many times. Jake extended one arm to look at his hand, and he, too, seemed composed of the same light.

"I love you," Jake said, hugging her tightly.

"I know," she whispered. "Make them go away."

She sounded like she was winding down, as though she knew she could lower her defenses once locked in his embrace.

Jake felt a hand on his shoulder, shaking him. He opened his eyes and looked up at Donna. She was crying, shaking him with one hand and holding her other hand over her mouth. When she saw that she had his attention, she took her hand away from her mouth and pointed at Sarah's face.

A little color had returned, and the enigmatic frown was gone, replaced by an equally enigmatic smile. It was amazing that such a slight shift of facial muscles could have such an overall effect on her appearance. Now, instead of detracting from her beauty, her gauntness only served to emphasize it.

"Shhh, shhh, shhh," Jake soothed Sarah. "It's okay, honey. Nobody's going to bother you."

"She's beautiful," Jake said to Donna, his reaction the same as it had been the first time he saw her five years ago.

He was cognizant of the fact that he was in two places at the same time. He was in a hospital room talking to Donna, while at the same time, he was inside the tumor inside Sarah's brain, holding Sarah in his arms and talking to her. Six months ago, he would never have let this situation progress to this point. He would have broken contact and distanced himself from Sarah, not out of fear but out of unbelief.

Everything happens for a reason.

With her head on his shoulder and her arms around his neck, Sarah continued to mumble, but she'd surrendered to exhaustion, and Jake couldn't pick out any individual words. He held her with one arm and kept the other hand moving over her neck and back to assure her of his presence constantly.

Donna had moved away from his side and kneeled before the easy chair. Jake could hear her whispers but not her words. When she got up, she returned to his side.

Jake's left hand had become numb. The steady stream of bugs, tiny worms, or whatever it was that left Sarah's hand and entered his hand had now reached his wrist. It felt like battalions of ants on the march, advancing into his hand so excruciatingly slowly that it seemed they must be marching in place several steps for each step forward.

"I was praying for my baby," Donna said, standing beside Jake again. As though she had heard his prayer, she added, "But I also prayed that no harm would come to you."

"It's all in God's hands," Jake said.

He was about to speak more, but a nurse bustled into the room. She was carrying a large plastic bag, the clear liquid inside puffing it out to a cylindrical shape. She went about her business quickly and efficiently, superficially apologizing for the interruption. She completed her task and bustled back out of the room.

Thinking ahead to the morning, as soon as the nurse was gone, Jake asked Donna, "Would you do me a favor?"

Donna was still standing by the bed, wringing her hands and staring at Sarah.

"What?" she said, reluctant to take her eyes off Sarah.

"Please," Jake implored, "We need your help."

His sincere, pleading tone finally convinced her to give him her undivided attention.

"She's going to be all right," Jake said, "but she might need your help in the morning."

Jake was sure he was right. Donna relaxed her worried expression, obviously enthused by the prospect that her baby would be alive and need her in the morning.

"It's quite possible," Jake continued, "that neither Sarah nor I will have enough energy to object to whatever the doctors want to do in the morning. Besides, you're the only one to whom the doctors and nurses are legally required to listen."

"What do you want me to do?" she asked, obviously eager to fully embrace any glimmer of hope.

"Don't let them touch her in the morning," Jake said, indicating Sarah. "Barricade the door, if necessary. No more medication and definitely no operation."

Nodding her head, she said emphatically, "I will."

"You need to rest," Jake said. "You can't stop them in the morning if you're asleep." Indicating the easy chair, he said, "Try to get comfortable. Get some sleep if you can."

With a backward glance at Sarah, she went to the easy chair. As she settled in, she looked at Jake and said, "She's going to be all right?" Her tone made it as much of a statement as a question.

"She's absolutely going to be all right," Jake promised.

Like Sarah, she surrendered to exhaustion, resting all her hope and trust on him. When Donna closed her eyes, Jake returned his attention to Sarah.

Several minutes later, he glanced at Donna and saw a big smile on her face. He couldn't tell whether she was awake and thinking or asleep and dreaming. Either way, he could see that she appeared pleased.

Jake was happy for her until his thoughts turned to Walker. He had explicitly warned Jake numerous times against giving Donna any hope that Sarah wouldn't die, but he'd done so much more than that. He'd caused her to believe in the *certainty* of Sarah's recovery. *May God forgive me if I'm wrong because Walker never will.*

After that thought crossed his mind, Jake was astonished that it had occurred to him. It was an expression of doubt for which there existed no evidence or justification. Apparently, as the Israelites proved while wandering in the desert, doubt is no further from the human heart than the next breath of air.

CHAPTER 16

The door opened, and the overhead lights came on. Jake was sitting in the chair, leaning on the bed with his head resting on his arm. In response to the noise and light, he jerked upright, and a bolt of pain shot through his head. He was aware that he was in the hospital room, but he nearly panicked when he realized his other self was no longer holding Sarah. His left hand was still in contact with her hand, so he closed his eyes and tried to visualize the tumor. Nothing happened except for more awareness of a low-grade, general pain in his head.

He glanced at his watch, saw that it was almost five a.m., and realized that he must have fallen asleep. He moved his left hand and found that it was no longer numb. He could feel Sarah's warm hand and sighed with relief when he realized he could feel the "ants crawling up his arm" sensation just above his wrist. He was no longer inside the tumor because the tumor was inside him. It was gone from her brain, and she was no longer in a coma. She was sleeping peacefully.

The sensation extended from his wrist to his head. The part just above his wrist was the tail end of the beast. Its malignant head was already metastasizing in his brain, setting off a war with his immune system. Right now, the "worms" felt generalized all over his brain, but he expected that soon, his immune system would corral them and force them to condense, becoming a tumor once more. When it had fully reassembled itself, he would become as incapacitated as Sarah had been.

"... surgery," a voice standing beside Jake said.

"Huh?" Jake said, not hearing what the nurse said but only then becoming aware she was talking to him.

"I'm sorry, honey," the nurse said. "You must leave the room. It's time to prepare her for surgery."

Taking Jake's inattention for a mental problem, the nurse talked slowly like she was speaking to a child or a mentally challenged person.

Jake glanced at Donna, but she was still sleeping, undisturbed by the nurse's entrance. "I'm sorry," Jake said, "but apparently, you didn't get the word. The surgery has been canceled." When the nurse didn't move, he added, "Please be so kind as to turn the light off on your way out."

When the nurse still didn't budge, he nodded toward the door and gestured with his right hand, making an unmistakable request that she leave.

"We'll see about that," she said, giving him a distrustful look as she turned on her heels. She went out the door in a huff without touching the light switch.

Jake turned back to Sarah and examined her more closely. He stroked her head with his right hand and tried to detect even the slightest reaction. Nothing. He withdrew his left hand, held it away from her, and brought it back to touch her hand again. Still nothing. He studied her slow, steady breathing, watching the rhythmic rise and fall of her small chest. Her color had fully returned, and her face had a healthy glow.

He considered trying to wake her up but decided against it, concluding that she must need the sleep. She could use the rest; besides that, she was a very perceptive little girl. He had no idea what she intended when she asked for his help, but he wouldn't take any chances. If she woke up now and realized what had happened, she might try to reverse the process to save him. She might somehow take the tumor back from him faster than he'd managed to take it from her.

He thought about getting up but remembered the sharp pain. He knew he should leave, but he couldn't go until he was sure Sarah was safe. The doctors might examine her and decide surgery was no longer necessary. Still, on the other hand, armed with Walker's authorization, they might try to rush her into the operating room. He gently brushed a kiss across her hand and slid his chair back, away from the bed.

He had no way of knowing at what point he might become

incapacitated by the tumor. To be safe, he decided not to stand up until he was ready to leave, and he was determined to leave the hospital without assistance. He would honor his commitment to take Sarah's place. He would not seek or accept medical attention. He would leave quietly with the tumor and take it home to suffer its effects in private.

"Donna, wake up," Jake said. Without raising his voice, he repeated, "Donna, wake up."

Her eyelids fluttered, and she stirred but didn't open her eyes.

"Donna?" he said again, and her eyes popped open.

"Jake," she said dreamily. "I was having such a wonderful dream." Suddenly remembering where she was, her eyes focused, and she nearly screamed, "Sarah!"

"She's okay," Jake assured her, and as Donna moved toward Sarah's bedside, he confidently added, "She's just asleep. She's going to be all right." He was about to explain that Sarah's tumor was gone now, but he was rudely interrupted by the door being flung open.

"That's him!" the nurse bellowed, pointing at Jake. She was leading a small group of men.

Two men stepped up beside the nurse, and two others stood just inside the doorway, one holding the door open. One of the men beside the nurse wore a dark brown suit, had short brown hair graying at the temples, and was probably in his mid to late fifties. *He might be a doctor*, Jake thought, *or he might be a government bureaucrat*. Jake suspected the latter. The other man beside him, closer to Jake, appeared slightly younger and wore hospital scrubs. He was obviously a doctor.

The two muscular men standing in the doorway were dressed in white from head to toe. They were obviously orderlies but seemed out of place in a regular, local hospital. They looked like they would be more at home at a mental institution, restraining wild, unruly patients.

Addressing Jake, the doctor said firmly, "Sir, we have authorization to begin surgery on this patient immediately. You'll have to leave."

"No," Jake said, "the surgery has been canceled." Indicating Donna, he said, "She's the child's mother, and she's canceling the surgery."

Donna was focused on Sarah, paying no attention whatsoever to the new arrivals.

The man in the suit didn't bother introducing himself or showing credentials as proof of his legitimate authority here. He just took the doctor's arm and pulled him backward until they had switched places.

"I'll handle this, Ed," the Suit said. To Jake, he said, "We don't have time to play games. You can walk out on your own, or you'll be removed." Glancing meaningfully at the orderlies, he added, "By whatever force necessary."

Jake took an instant dislike for the man. He exhibited hateful, aggressive traits Jake associated with Republican officials, acting more like overlords than public servants. This was a critical moment. More likely than not, if he tried to spring from his chair to oppose them, he would land on his face and be carried from the room, unable to offer any meaningful resistance. They apparently had no intention of letting Donna cancel the surgery, so that left him with very few choices. He could acquiesce, but that really wasn't a viable option since the surgery would mean certain death for Sarah. They were in no mood to compromise, leaving him only one course of action. His only hope was to make them believe he was capable of extreme violence.

"I'm willing to die trying to stay here," Jake bluffed, pausing to confidently slide his hand under the tail of his shirt at the small of his back where he usually carried a gun. "The question is, are you willing to die trying to remove me?"

That threat had worked for John Wayne, but John Wayne had been sitting horseback, visibly armed to the teeth. Jake hoped his movement had been authentic, dramatic, and convincing enough to cause the men to believe he was armed. Otherwise, this might be the shortest standoff in history.

The Suit turned to the orderlies and was about to wave them forward, but the doctor grabbed his arm.

"Gentlemen, gentlemen, let's remember where we are." The doctor sounded conciliatory, adding, "There's a more civil way to handle this." To Jake, he said, "What's your name, sir?"

After Jake gave his name, the doctor waved the orderlies off and got the reluctant Suit turned around. Before going out the door, the Suit turned to glare at Jake.

Jake deflated like a balloon as soon as the door closed. Maintaining a threatening posture had taken a lot out of him. He glanced at Donna and saw her full attention was still focused on Sarah. She seemed happy, blissfully locked in her own world, unaware of the confrontation that had just transpired a few feet from where she stood. Jake sagged in the chair and closed his eyes, expecting a few minutes of rest would allow him to recoup the energy he had expended.

Like most hospital room doors, the door to this room was oversized in width to permit easy passage of beds and equipment. Jake's head was down, and his eyes were closed, but when the door was thrust open, he jerked his head up, alerted by the sound and sudden difference in air pressure the large door produced. As another bolt of pain shot through his temple, he chastised himself for having relaxed too quickly and letting them catch him off guard. However, what he expected to happen didn't. Instead of pouncing on him to subdue and remove him from the room, one individual stepped directly in front of him, and the others stopped in the doorway.

"I couldn't believe it," Walker said. He was angrier and more threatening to Jake than he'd ever been in his life. "I couldn't believe it when they called and told me what you were doing. I warned you about giving Donna false hope, but I never dreamed you would go this far."

Walker was beside himself with anger. He ranted and railed at Jake more harshly in public than Jake had railed against God in private. Jake suspected Walker's hangover might be a contributing factor to his surliness.

Jake couldn't understand how Walker could have gotten here so quickly until he looked at his watch. He had assumed that only seconds had elapsed between the closing of the door and its reopening, but nearly an hour had passed. His energy level hadn't improved, and he finally understood that both his declining energy level and the missing block of time were symptomatic of the tumor that was attacking his brain.

"Get up!" Walker demanded, clenching and unclenching his fists. "Get up so I can knock you back down."

The Suit was holding the door open, smiling smugly at Jake.

"Donna?" was all Jake managed, but he hoped his tone would

remind her of what he'd asked her to do this morning.

Donna appeared to be engrossed with Sarah, oblivious of her surroundings, just as she had been since waking up this morning. However, her actions proved otherwise. She wheeled around to face Walker.

"Stop it!" she exclaimed. "Leave Jake alone. Either help me or get out!"

Jake was more shocked than Walker by the vehemence in her voice. Clearly, she was aware that Sarah's life hung in the balance of what was transpiring in this room. He suspected she hadn't been as oblivious to the earlier confrontation as she had seemed.

"They need ... It's time for ... Walker stammered, the fire of his anger gone.

"Nobody's touching my baby," Donna declared to the room. "She needs me." In a softer voice, she said to Walker, "She needs you, too."

Walker dropped his head, sufficiently chastised. He slowly turned to leave the room, but he wasn't finished with Jake. "I'll be out in the hall waiting for you," he promised threateningly.

Walker left the room, and the other men went with him.

Jake turned to Donna when the door closed and said, "You did great." He smiled reassuringly. "I'm sure Walker will be all right when Sarah wakes up."

Jake arose from the chair, slowly and cautiously, like a decrepit old man. He was dizzy, his head ached, and for a moment, he thought he might black out.

Donna stepped forward and took his arm to steady him. "Jake?" she said. "Jake, what's wrong?"

"I have to go," Jake said.

"No, you don't," Donna said. "Don't listen to Walker. You can stay here as long as you like."

The tumor was stealing his equilibrium, but for the moment, he could defeat it with concentration. Jake mustered all his energy, hugged her quickly, and started for the door. The tail end of the sensation in his left arm was up to his elbow now, and he had no way of knowing how long he might remain ambulatory. At any moment, the debilitating effect of the tumor might become too strong to overcome.

Donna started to follow him, but he gently admonished her,

reminding her that Sarah was still in danger.

"Don't leave her until she wakes up," he said, immediately leaving the room before she could argue.

The door closed behind him, and he stopped when he saw Walker striding toward him. He closed his eyes for just a second to summon more strength. The next thing he knew, he was sitting on the floor, his back against the wall, and Walker was kneeling in front of him.

"Jake?" Walker was saying, "Are you all right?"

"I'm okay," Jake mumbled, not opening his eyes.

Walker shook him again and repeated, "Jake?"

"I'm okay," Jake said, opening his eyes and appearing to be a little more alert.

He was aware that Walker's animosity toward him had abruptly morphed into concern, and he was pleased. It was the mark of family. Family members could fight with each other and commit atrocities against each other, but even during an altercation, an outside intruder could have a unifying effect. It was what made domestic violence calls so dangerous for police officers. In this instance, the outside intruder was the unseen brain tumor.

"Where's your gun?" Walker asked.

"I don't have one with me," Jake said, aware that Walker probably looked for it while helping him sit down.

"When the doctor called me, he wanted to know if you might be carrying a gun," Walker said. "I told him you probably were."

"Thanks," Jake said. His mind was muddled. Walker hadn't intentionally helped him, but the only thing preying on his mind was the need to leave. "I have to go," he said.

Walker didn't back away to allow him to stand up, and he didn't offer him a helping hand.

"Why did you do that?" Walker asked in a complaining tone. "I told you what this would do to Donna. Now, she might never recover." His anger started to return as he demanded again, "Why did you do that?"

Jake was relieved when Donna came to his rescue.

"Walker!" Donna screamed from inside the hospital room, her voice slightly muffled by the door but still loud and clear.

Jake heard joy and excitement in Donna's voice and could only surmise Sarah had awakened.

Obviously expecting to hear the very worst, Walker suddenly became a broken man.

"Oh God, oh God," he said, "it's happened just like the doctors said it would."

Walker extended his hand to help Jake get up. When he was on his feet, Walker turned and started toward the door, then stopped and turned back to Jake.

"Well, come on," he said, "come and see what you've done." With a catch in his throat, he added, "You can watch my wife fall to pieces while she's holding my dead little girl."

Jake had pushed his back against the wall while Walker pulled him up. He was aware of Walker moving away, but he had no intention of following him. His mind was fixated on one task: he must get home. He stood against the wall, struggling with the pain in his head and the dense fog that was beginning to coalesce in his mind. It took every ounce of his concentration to start moving again.

CHAPTER 17

A s soon as Walker turned away, Jake took his first step in his arduous journey, every move requiring concentration. His motions were too jerky to appear normal. He was aware that he was moving like a drunk, but simple inebriation would have been far less debilitating. As he was moving, what had seemed like fog coalescing in his mind began transforming into what felt like a thick swarm of angry bees.

Jake struggled into his Jeep in the parking lot. He immediately started it, dropped it into gear, and drove away. He knew rest was no longer an ally. Energy expended couldn't be regained, and any period of immobility threatened to lengthen itself into permanence. If he closed his eyes to rest, he would risk passing out and being hauled back into the hospital, where he would become nothing more than a medical curiosity. The doctors could surely do no more for him than they'd done for Sarah.

After leaving the hospital, he was fortunate to catch all the green lights since it reduced the number of times he had to change gears. He liked driving a standard, but coordinating the clutch, shifter, and gas pedal right now nearly became his undoing. Shifting gears required effort, and effort required an expenditure of energy that was in increasingly short supply. After passing the Mall, the traffic became lighter, and keeping his eyes open soon replaced changing gears as his most significant challenge.

Before long, he started coming up behind other vehicles and slamming on his brakes, only to realize the other cars were hallucinations. Phantoms. The dashed lines in the middle of the road that separated the two northbound lanes took on a hypnotizing effect. By the time he finally reached his exit, he was nearly in a trance. He turned left off Corridor G onto a two-lane road, and although the narrow road required more effort to navigate, he was thankful for the change of pace. It was curvy and just wide enough to allow two-way traffic, but at least there were no mesmerizing center markings.

He drove the first mile with no problem, but then he rounded a curve onto a straight stretch, and a protracted blink caused him to jerk the wheel. The next thing he knew, he was in the ditch on the left side of the road. He dropped the Jeep into low gear and tried to power out, but the rear wheel in the muddy ditch just spun without effect. He engaged the four-wheel-drive and got the same result. He was crestfallen to realize that the front wheel hubs were locked out, and he would have to get out of the Jeep and manually twist the hub lock on each wheel.

The ditch was nearly two feet deep, separating the road from the steep mountainside. Both front and back wheels on the driver's side were in the ditch, but the wheels on the passenger side were still on the edge of the pavement. The bank dropped precipitously on the other side of the road before sloping gently to a field several hundred feet wide. If the Jeep had gone off the road on that side, it most likely would have flipped over. On the other side of the big field, a creek bed lined with trees separated the flat land from the opposing mountainside.

Jake pushed the door handle down, and the lightweight door fell open, stopping when it hit the steep mountainside. He eased out of the vehicle and managed to close the door. He extended his arms for balance as he took the few steps to get to the front wheel, alternately touching the Jeep and the mountainside. He held onto the fender to support his weight as he lowered himself into a sitting position on the hillside, letting his legs straddle the wheel. A flash of déjà vu connected the straddling of the wheel to straddling the peak on the rooftop, and it took a minute for his clouded mind to separate dream from reality.

As he twisted that hub lock into position, he realized that doing the other side was going to be much more difficult. He used the fender to pull himself to his feet and the bumper and grill to get around the front end. His movements were so deliberate, and his dependence on the Jeep so great, that anybody watching might have thought him blind and using the contact for guidance.

Finally, he stood beside the passenger side wheel, trying to decide the best way to get to the wheel hub. Lowering himself to a full sitting position was out of the question. The fender on this side was cocked much higher than the side in the ditch. He decided that squatting would likely be less disorienting than bending over or dropping to his knees. Gripping the fender with both hands, he cautiously lowered himself into a squat. He knew his time was short because the feeling had returned to his left arm. The crawling sensation had progressed into his shoulder.

He twisted the hub lock into position and was ready to get up when the buzzing in his head changed to stereophonic. It took him several seconds to realize that part of the buzzing was external. It was the tires-on-pavement whirr of an approaching car, and it was coming from the direction he'd been traveling. He was squatting on the pavement on the wrong side of the road, directly in the path of the oncoming traffic. Intending to stand up against his vehicle and let the car go around him, he pulled himself up too quickly. Blinding pain filled his head, and he lost his grip on the fender. He staggered backward, desperately trying to keep his feet under him, fearing that if he went down, he would never get up again under his own power.

He was nearing the edge of the pavement before the searing pain in his head moderated enough for him to regain control of his legs. When he stopped, he instantly recognized that he was still standing on the asphalt. He took one more step backward to get off the pavement, deciding to wait and let the car pass between himself and his vehicle. When he realized he could no longer hear the approaching car, he looked in that direction and was momentarily gratified that it had stopped.

The car was still about eighty feet away, and Jake thought the driver must have seen trouble ahead and stopped to gauge the situation. Traffic on this narrow road was predominately local, and it wasn't unusual for drivers to make courteous concessions to their neighbors.

After a full minute, when the car didn't make a move to go on its way or offer help, Jake started across the road. His gait was slow, and his steps uncertain. He was moving like a novice on skates, trying to walk before rolling. When the engine revved up loudly and the tires screeched, he didn't need to look at the car to know what those sounds meant.

His instinct for self-preservation told him to run and get off the road, but his intellect overruled the instinct. Sudden movements would only invite disaster, and he took only a couple more steps before he accepted the cold, hard truth: he wasn't going to make it. He stopped near the center of the road and turned to face what would surely be the instrument of his destruction. He had expected to die from the tumor that was invading his brain, but really, what difference did it make? Perhaps this was God's way of mercifully sparing him hours of agony that might precede death by the tumor. He whispered thanks to God for Sarah's life.

When the car was close enough for him to see the occupants, the scene suddenly turned surreal, like the incident at the prison camp when the inmate's swing had become unnaturally slow. Even though he could see the front wheels pointing toward him, the whole car seemed to be shifting sideways, away from a collision course with him. The commotion in the car appeared as though the occupants were wrestling over the steering wheel, and it soon became clear to Jake that neither was in control. The vehicle was moving in a direction independent of the front wheels. It was exempt from natural law, traveling in a straight line even though the front wheels were turned to the extreme right.

It became apparent that the slow car would miss him, and Jake watched as the passenger returned to his seat. Now, with both facing forward, Jake recognized them as the same two who had tried to kill him the day before he went to prison. Jake watched as they passed him harmlessly, only inches away. The driver's hands were on the steering wheel, still trying to make the car turn right, while the passenger raised an Uzi to the open window.

After it passed, the force holding the car in a straight line suddenly let go, returning it to the jurisdiction of natural law. The external force of the extreme position of the front wheels finally acted upon the object in motion. The car tried to make the sharp turn, but the front tires gripped the pavement, causing the driver's side to dip. The rear passenger side raised and came around until the car was crosswise of the road. The forward momentum caused the car to roll. It flipped bottom over top for several revolutions before leaving the pavement and rolling over the bank. It was like watching a movie while standing on the movie set.

Jake stood motionless, staring at where the car had vanished, waiting for the inevitable fireball. After several seconds passed, he realized this wasn't a movie set. This was real life, and dazzling pyrotechnics were the exception rather than the rule. He had investigated a few cars that had rolled over mountains, and none had ever exploded. But, when he thought about it, waiting for a fireball might have been as much wishful thinking as it was expectation. A big explosion would have ensured that those two would never come after him again.

He turned away from the scene and refocused on his primary objective. He managed to pull himself around the front of the Jeep and work his way to the door. He cautiously climbed in, started it, and put it in low gear. The Jeep crawled out of the ditch easily with all four wheels engaged. He shifted the lever back into two-wheel drive and continued on his way.

He put the incident behind him and applied all his concentration to driving. He couldn't afford any further delay. The crawling sensation had left his shoulder and was now in his neck at the base of his skull. He was concerned that he might lose consciousness at any moment. Darkness pressed around the edges of his vision, making him feel like he was driving through a tunnel.

Jake finally pulled in front of his house and killed the engine. It would feel so good just to lay his head on the steering wheel and rest, but he wouldn't let himself do that. The end was in sight, but if he failed to get inside the house, all his efforts since leaving the hospital room would have been in vain. If he were discovered unconscious outside his home, out of an abundance of caution, anybody who found him would call an ambulance.

He pulled himself out of the Jeep and used it for support for as long as he could. He held the keys in his right hand, pushed himself away from the Jeep with his left, and started toward the porch steps. The steps were only six feet away, but his awkward gait turned into a lunge before he could reach them. Only four steps led up to the porch, but he fell hard onto the board flooring when he missed the first step.

The pain in his hands might have been excruciating, except that his whole body had gone numb. He sprawled forward, the keys slipping out of his hand and skidding across the porch. He counted his blessings that they had gone toward the door. Otherwise, the mere act of retrieving them might have defeated him. Still on his hands and knees, he crawled across the porch.

When he picked up his keys, he attempted to stand, but his energy was nearly depleted. He settled for rising to his knees. He finally unlocked the door and, holding onto the doorknob, shuffled forward on his knees as he pushed the door open. He paused, still holding onto the doorknob for support, trying to focus his mind. He had to remove the keys because their presence would likely invite anyone noticing them to come in to inquire if leaving them there had been an oversight.

After much fumbling, he got the key out of the lock. He crawled and shuffled his knees around to make room for the door to close. He put all the force he could muster into slamming the door, and the equal and opposite reaction to the applied force sent him sprawling backward.

He considered staying there on the floor, but grim determination made him roll over and bring his arms and knees under him again. The buzzing in his head blocked out all external stimuli, and the narrowing tunnel he was navigating was nearly closed. He knew his time was up.

He dragged himself down the hall and through the open door to the edge of his bed. He grabbed the edge of the dangling sheet and took it with him as he pulled himself onto the bed. As he rolled toward the wall, he dragged the sheet over him. He was still wearing his clothes and shoes, but he hoped the sheet would hide that fact for as long as necessary. Before he finally surrendered to the darkness, his final thought would have made him smile if he'd had enough energy. Like his heroes in the old Westerns, he would die with his boots on.

*****

Stanley blamed Jake for his woes, taking it as a personal affront that Jake refused to die. Jake had even jinxed his plan to get rid of his wife and her kid. Connie had tried to kill him, and if Wayne hadn't found him when he did, she would have succeeded. His memories of that night were disjointed and confused. He had opened his eyes when he heard Connie talking, but the darkness remained unrelieved, and the next time he opened his eyes was when he woke up in the hospital. Ever since McCallum got out of prison, he and Wayne had been watching and waiting, looking for an opportunity to kill him.

Stanley managed to keep his domestic situation and the missing books hidden from his brother, but that couldn't last forever. Sooner or later, Glen would demand to see the books. Fortunately, Connie and Billy had no other family and very few friends to miss them. Marge Zimmerman, a nosy neighbor, was the only one likely to start rumors about his wife's disappearance, but he'd already secured her as an unwitting confidant.

Stanley *wanted* to kill McCallum because McCallum had become his Moby Dick. He *needed* to kill McCallum to get in his brother's good graces, but he *had* to kill McCallum because he could identify him and Wayne.

They had resumed the stakeout this morning, parking near the mouth of McCallum's hollow a half-hour before dawn. They had seen little traffic, and Wayne suggested a bathroom break and a cup of coffee. They were headed to the convenience store out by the four-lane when they saw the vehicle in the ditch. Stanley hadn't known McCallum owned a Jeep, but as soon as he saw the figure squatting beside it, he recognized him. He commanded Wayne to stop, and while keeping his eyes on McCallum, he fumbled the Uzi out from under the seat.

By the time he got the weapon into his lap, Stanley had become more interested in Jake than in the Uzi. It looked like McCallum must have been out drinking all night. He'd watched him stagger backward across the road but stop at the penultimate moment. Now, Jake was standing on the berm of the road, looking in their direction, obviously offering them the right of way. *The spirits of fate were finally smiling on him again,* he thought as he waited for McCallum to start moving.

"Go! Hit'im hard!" Stanley yelled, even as Jake was taking his first step.

Wayne wasted no time. He'd immediately understood Stanley's intent. He revved the motor, dropped the car into gear, and held the gas pedal to the floor.

They covered more than half the distance to McCallum when it started going wrong. Stanley had watched Jake stop near the center of the road and turn toward them. The car had been lined up perfectly to catch McCallum with the center of the hood, but then he started drifting off-center. He hadn't taken his eyes off him, so Stanley knew McCallum wasn't moving. He grabbed the steering wheel and tried to correct its course, but when it wouldn't turn any farther to the right, he returned to his seat. He grabbed the Uzi, but the car was doing nearly sixty and accelerating when they pulled alongside Jake. He didn't even have time to stick the gun barrel out the window.

As soon as they passed McCallum, Stanley felt a violent jerk of the car, and then it felt like he was inside a clothes dryer. He woke up, sprawled on top of Wayne. When he rose to look around, he saw that Wayne's head was turned at an impossible angle, his neck obviously broken.

Even though it was unregistered and couldn't be traced to him, Stanley still needed to find the Uzi. That particular model wasn't easy to come by, and although he owned three, he didn't want to lose even one of them. He finally found it lodged between Wayne's back and the seatback. He crawled over and around the steering wheel and exited the car through the hole where the windshield used to be. Setting a fire was the last thing he did before leaving the scene.

CHAPTER 18

"Jake? Wake up, Jake. Jake?"

Jake heard his brother calling as though from a great distance, and he opened his eyes.

"What're you doing here?" Jake croaked in a dry, raspy voice.

"Trying to wake you up," Nick said with obvious relief.

Reality came flooding back to Jake. He had crawled into bed in his own house, expecting to never wake up in this world, but he'd obviously been wrong.

"What time is it?" he asked.

"A little past two," Nick said. "Are you all right?"

"Sure," Jake responded. "Why are you up so early?"

It must have been past eight when Jake got home this morning, so he'd slept under six hours. It felt much longer.

"I always get up early on Fridays," Nick reminded him.

"But today's Wednesday," Jake countered.

"Man, you must've really been out of it," Nick said. "I called Wednesday night but never got an answer. Walker came up yesterday evening, and when he couldn't get you to the door, he came and got me. Your Jeep was here, so we came inside. We shook you and yelled, but you never stirred. You seemed to be just sleeping deeply, so we left. I came up as soon as I got up today, and you looked like you hadn't moved a muscle. I've been shaking you and yelling for five minutes. I was just about ready to call an ambulance."

Jake threw the sheet aside and sat up on the edge of the bed. It had been three days, which explained his extreme hunger, parched throat, and desperate need to use the bathroom. He was still fully clothed, boots and all.

Nick gave his clothes and boots a questioning look but didn't say anything.

"How's Sarah?" Jake asked as he slowly stood up.

His mind felt clear, and he couldn't detect a single trace of the debilitating tumor. His slow movements were born more from caution than necessity.

"Walker said Sarah's supposed to get out of the hospital today with a clean bill of health," Nick said. "I'll make some coffee while you're in there," he added as Jake crossed the room toward the bathroom.

By the time Jake entered the kitchen, Nick was already sitting at the table with a cup of coffee. Another full cup was on the table, waiting for him.

"Thanks," Jake said as he sat down. "Man, I'm so hungry, I could eat a horse."

"Bacon, eggs, and potatoes would probably taste better," Nick said. "I just talked to Jenny. She didn't work today and was fixing breakfast when I left. She's got it ready and will be bringing us a plate." Looking more closely at Jake, he asked again, "Are you sure you're okay?"

"I will be when I get some food," Jake assured him.

"What happened?" Nick asked.

Jake started with the phone call from Walker and apologized for not having let Nick give him Walker's message. Nick listened attentively without saying anything until Jake described how he'd been sure the entire tumor had left Sarah's brain.

"According to Walker, the tumors in all the other little girls disappeared shortly after Sarah's," Nick said.

Jake thought he detected a slight note of incredulity, as though Nick thought his presence at Sarah's bedside might have been purely incidental to all of the tumors disappearing. Hearing Jenny coming with the food, he wrapped up his story without questioning Nick's remark.

"Anyway," he finished the story, "when I knew Sarah was okay, I came home and went to bed."

When the food was on the table, Jake ate ravenously and waited at the table for Nick and Jenny to finish. He briefly recounted his story for Jenny's benefit. He remembered the incident with the other vehicle when he finished with the same broad statement about coming home and going to bed.

"By the way," he said, "was there a car wreck out on Big Branch Road Wednesday morning?"

"As a matter of fact, there was," Nick said. "It was a bad one. The driver was killed. Did you see it?"

"A car passed me, and it looked like it might have been out of control," Jake said offhandedly.

"It rolled over the bank," Nick confirmed. "Somebody saw the smoke and called the Fire Department. The car was stolen, and the driver was burned. They just identified him this morning. They said his name was Wayne Parsley."

The car had exploded after all, Jake thought. The driver's name didn't mean anything to him, so he asked, "What about the passenger?"

"Passenger?" Nick asked. He looked at Jenny, and she shook her head. "We didn't hear anything about a passenger."

"Oh," Jake said, "I thought there was a passenger. I was sleepy, and I guess I wasn't seeing very well by then."

He didn't want to worry them unnecessarily, and he had already told them about two attempts on his life, so he didn't tell them about this latest attempt. He realized that since the passenger had escaped the car and wasn't found at the scene, he had most likely set the fire to cover his tracks.

After eating, Nick announced that he and Jenny were going to the store. Jake asked them to pick up a few things for him. When they were gone, he showered and stretched out on the couch. He wasn't sleepy, but he still felt a little tired. He was thinking about the relationship between the driver and the passenger.

The passenger was likely in charge and had walked away from the wreck. Although it wasn't Jake's fault, the passenger might still hold him responsible for the driver's death. Jake might have escalated the hostilities just by surviving the attack. If another attack came – and the passenger's survival made that a reasonable probability – the assailants might not wait to catch him alone the next time. He might have inadvertently heightened the danger for anybody around or connected to him.

He picked up the phone and called Nick, thinking they might have stopped at the house before going to the store. They should already be on high alert, but he should remind Nick to be extra cautious because the danger might have increased. When there was no answer, he tried Nick's cell phone, but apparently, he didn't have it with him.

At a quarter till six, Jake's phone rang. He'd expected Nick and Jenny to be gone all evening. "That was fast," he said when he picked up the phone.

"Is this Jake McCallum?" the voice on the phone said.

"Yes, it is," Jake said pleasantly, recognizing the lawyer's voice.

"I've been trying to reach you for two days," Jamerson said petulantly, priggishly adding, "You need to get an answering machine."

Jake took immediate offense to his tone. "Is that your expert legal advice?" he asked sarcastically.

The lawyer ignored the question. "I want you in my office first thing Monday morning," he commanded.

"What's up?" Jake asked more evenly.

He objected to the lawyer's attitude, but because he'd just been thinking about it, he was curious to know if the recent death of one of his assailants had anything to do with the proposed meeting.

"We'll talk about it Monday morning," the lawyer said.

Jake wondered if the loan he'd accepted gave the lawyer the impression that he could boss him around.

"We'll talk about it now," Jake said firmly. "Let's not forget who works for whom."

"I said ..." the lawyer started.

Jake didn't wait for him to finish. He hung up the phone Five minutes later, it started ringing again. He let it ring six times.

"Hello," Jake said lightly, as though he wasn't expecting a call.

"We seem to have gotten cut off," the lawyer said, obviously flustered.

Jake didn't hide his anger. "We weren't cut off," he said. "I hung up. I figured if you can't provide more timely answers to my questions, I'll find a lawyer who can."

After a brief pause, the lawyer said, "My apologies. I've been really busy, and it's just that I wanted to share this good news with you in person."

"What's the news?" Jake asked bluntly, his tone clearly furious and demanding an answer.

"We have a new offer," the lawyer gushed. "Ten. Million. Dollars." This time, he pronounced the amount like a game show host, telling the lucky contestant how much he'd won.

"I'll think about it," Jake said without much enthusiasm. "Anything else?"

"It's your decision, of course," the lawyer said, almost pleading, "but I must recommend you accept this offer."

As the lawyer prattled on about the benefits of accepting the offer, Jake thought about the danger his presence might now bring to those around him. He considered telling the lawyer about the latest attempt on his life and the death of one of the two assailants, but he decided against it. Unlike the attack by the prison guard, there was no physical evidence that connected the car wreck to the driver's attempt to run him down.

The thought flickered through Jake's mind that accepting this offer might neutralize the threat to those around him. Money wasn't that important, but he'd learned that not having any could be a major inconvenience. The fact that this more than doubled the original offer wasn't a deciding factor, and he wasn't aware he'd decided until he heard himself say it.

"I'll accept the offer under one condition," Jake said, speaking over the lawyer's rambling rhetoric.

"Excuse me?" the lawyer said.

"I'll accept the offer under one condition," Jake repeated.

"I'm listening," the lawyer said, his tone a mixture of hope and cautious joy.

"I want a card that permits me to carry a concealed weapon anywhere," Jake said. I plan to travel as soon as this agreement is signed."

Jake had surprised himself again. That was another decision he made without knowing he'd made it, but he immediately knew it was true. He would travel around the country and let the dust settle on this case, presenting only himself as a target. Besides, traveling would also serve another purpose. Although he would rather become a recluse, content with passing the remainder of his years with old movies, music, and books, he remembered how much the preacher had stressed that there was a boy he needed to find. None of the young boys with whom he now had contact – neither family nor friends – was the Holy Ghost incarnate. If he stayed secluded in this hollow, he would negate any possibility that the preacher's prophecy might be fulfilled.

"That's it?" the lawyer said with amazement. "All you want is a gun permit?"

"Basically," Jake confirmed.

"That's not a problem," Jamerson said. I'm not currently aware of anything like a national gun permit, but if there is such a thing, I can personally guarantee one within a couple of months."

"No," Jake said, "you weren't listening. It's a condition of my acceptance. Unless, of course, you're okay with waiting a couple of months to conclude this agreement."

"Let's be reasonable," the lawyer begged, reverting to a wheedling tone. "I'm sure you're aware that gun permits routinely go through the County Sheriff's Office, and they require time for processing."

"I'm aware of that," Jake said, "but that's not what I want. I'm talking about the Law Enforcement Officers Safety Act, a federal law that gives active and retired police officers the right to carry a concealed handgun. The only requirement is a photographic ID card from a local, state, or federal government agency. I expect you to prevail upon the U.S. Attorney to get me one. He can use my driver's license photo."

"I'll see what I can do," the lawyer said, "but I can't make any promises."

"Then, I'll make this simple for you," Jake said. "This is a deal-breaker. No card to carry a gun, no settlement. I'll go to trial, with or without you."

"Please, Jake," the lawyer cajoled. "Let's be reasonable."

"Getting the ID card should be a piece of cake for U.S. Attorney Sullivan since he owns the Beecham County Sheriff," Jake said, "and while you're at it, you can deliver a message to Sullivan. Tell him I said he can send more gunmen at their own peril."

"What does that mean?" the lawyer asked, perplexed now.

"You don't need to understand it," Jake said. "Sullivan will know what I mean."

Jake said nothing more about the ambiguous warning. His demand for the "gun permit" and the message to the U.S. Attorney were intended as shots across their bow to let them know he wasn't intimidated.

"I'll be in your office at nine o'clock Wednesday morning," he continued, returning to the matter at hand. "If you fail to get the ID card by Tuesday evening, let me know, and we won't have to waste each other's time on Wednesday."

He gave a curt goodbye, hung up the phone, and went to the kitchen. It hadn't been long since he'd eaten, but he felt hungry again. He sat at the kitchen table with a jar of peanut butter, a pack of saltine crackers, and a Coke. He thought about his conversation with the lawyer and wondered what the Bible said about becoming wealthy. The preacher at the prison camp had been adamant that God was using him, and he wondered if wealth would affect his usefulness.

When he finished his snack, he took his Bible out on the porch to look it up. More than an hour later, after he determined that the evil lay in the love of money, not the money itself, he started to go back inside when he heard a vehicle coming. It was about time for Nick and Jenny, so he waited. When the vehicle came around the curve, he could see it wasn't his brother's car, but he waited anyway. It was Walker.

Walker parked in the driveway and pulled two shopping bags out of his car.

"I stopped down at Nick's," he said. "Jenny sent these."

"Thanks," Jake said, meeting him at the top of the steps and taking the bags. "A few things go in the refrigerator. Pull up a chair. I'll be right back."

When Jake returned to the porch, he resumed his relaxed posture with his feet up on the banister. Walker copied his posture, and they sat silently for several minutes, unsure how to move past their earlier confrontations. The accusation made months ago and the threats of violence made just days ago at the hospital seemed to be insurmountable barriers.

"This is something I should have done long ago," Jake finally said, breaking the silence. He retrieved the Bible from the banister where he'd laid it and handed it to Walker. When Walker took the proffered Bible, Jake put the palm of his left hand on it and raised his right hand. "I solemnly swear," he began, "I have never had carnal knowledge or any improper contact of any kind with your wife. I love your wife and kids, but that's mostly because they're yours." He took the Bible, leaned back in the chair again, and returned his feet to rest on the banister.

Walker was silent and red-faced for several minutes. Then he smiled. "You shouldn't swear," he said.

"You shouldn't make me have to," Jake rejoined, grinning to take the sting out of the rebuke.

"I'm sorry," Walker said. "I'm really, really sorry … for everything."

It was the straightforward apology Jake had wanted, but it wasn't as satisfying as he'd imagined. He felt just as embarrassed for having received it as his friend did for having made it, so he quickly changed the subject.

"How's Sarah?" he asked.

After a brief pause, Walker said, "Our little girl is doing great."

There was no emphasis on any word, but Jake couldn't help but notice the word "our." It was clear Walker was reinstating his honorary possessive claim toward his children.

"Did Nick call and tell you I was coming?" Walker asked.

"No," Jake said, not immediately grasping the point of the question. "I was expecting Nick back from the store. I just happened to be sitting here."

"I mean that," Walker said, indicating the forgotten book in Jake's lap.

"Oh, the Bible," Jake said, realizing that he hadn't really talked to Walker for nearly five months. Walker must have assumed the Bible was there solely to swear on it. Jake added, "I was reading it before I saw you coming."

"Since when do you read the Bible?" Walker asked.

Walker and Donna had been Christians from their youth, and although he'd accompanied them to church several times, he'd never carried a Bible or shown any real interest in it.

"I recently had some spare time to read," Jake said with a grin. After a brief pause, he added more seriously, "I met a preacher at the prison camp who had a way of explaining the Bible that made perfect sense to me."

Jake had been excited about showing his family and friends the reason and logic in the Bible. That reason and logic should make it easier for anybody to believe it. However, when he'd talked to Nick, the reason and logic had seemed to fall on deaf ears. He could only assume it was his fault. He must not have laid a proper foundation. Now, he had another opportunity, and he intended to be more diligent with the basic facts.

Jake described how Chapter 1 of the book of Genesis began and ended the original six days of Creation. He explained how Adam and Eve were created in Chapter 2 as additions to the original Creation. He described how they had been kicked out of the Garden into a world populated with flora, fauna, and Gentiles. After explaining that cavemen were the Gentiles created on the sixth day – before God planted the Garden of Eden – he paused to gauge Walker's interest. He saw little encouragement. When he began reconciling the Bible with science, he expected it to stir some excitement in Walker, but it didn't.

He had to admit that Walker was no more swayed by reason and logic than Nick. He considered how the preacher might handle this when he remembered doubting Thomas and realized he was trying to convince the wrong people. Nick and Walker were already Christians, and they had already "not seen, and yet have believed." The "Doubting Thomas" in this situation was himself. Seeing the reason and logic in the Bible was necessary for him, but for them, it was just unnecessary, uninspiring rhetoric. Because of their prior, whole-hearted acceptance of the traditional view, Walker and Nick were less likely to be persuaded by a logic-based interpretation of the Bible than many nonbelievers. He changed the subject again.

"I might be leaving in a few days," Jake said, "and if I go, I don't know how long I'll be gone. I'm going to ask Nick to have some work done on the house while I'm gone and, knowing how much you like grills, I thought if you have time, maybe you do something with that one out back."

"Sure," Walker said, obviously eager to get beyond the past few months. "What've you got in mind?"

"Just fix it like you would if it was your own," Jake said. "Go wild. Nick can get any materials you need."

"Where are you going?" Walker asked.

"You might say I'm going to try to find God," Jake said.

"Didn't know He was lost," Walker said mischievously.

"He isn't," Jake agreed with a grin and added more seriously, "It would be more accurate to say that I hope to put myself in a position where God can find me."

Jake explained the preacher's prophecy that an incarnation of the Holy Ghost – a boy conceived by a virgin like Jesus – has come into the world. He explained how 2 Thessalonians 2:7 says there will come a time when the Holy Ghost must leave this world to allow the Antichrist to rise to power, but the Holy Ghost must also stay in the world to save people.

"The preacher said the only way that verse could be true was if there were two Entities of the Holy Ghost, like when Jesus came into the world: one ethereal and the other flesh and blood. The preacher thinks the Holy Ghost has already filled the earth with the awesome power of God. When the Antichrist begins his rise to power, the ethereal Entity will stay, but the flesh and blood Entity of the Holy Ghost will leave," Jake said.

Continuing his explanation, he told Walker about God's two-thousand-year pattern and the residual power God would leave on the earth. He explained how some people could draw out that power and use it for magic, as would the Antichrist. He spoke of the expectation that the Holy Ghost's current age would be anywhere from zero to twelve, allowing for the possibility of a pregnant young girl.

Jake wasn't surprised that Walker maintained a jocular manner throughout, as though he suspected Jake might be setting up a joke. Jake concluded by saying that the preacher insisted that he, Jake, might already know the boy who was the Holy Ghost incarnate, or if not, he would soon meet him, thus the need for the trip.

"Junior and Mark have to be ruled out," Jake said, "because neither of them was the firstborn."

Walker reacted more seriously to that declaration. There was no punch line and the momentousness of what Jake had been saying finally wiped the grin from Walker's face and the mischief from his eyes.

"To even consider that one of my kids might be God in the flesh, like Jesus, is mind-boggling," Walker said.

CHAPTER 19

Since the lawyer didn't call to cancel the appointment, Jake was in his waiting room at 9:00 a.m., Wednesday morning. The longer he waited, the more convinced he became that the lawyer had failed and was giving him the runaround. Unless Jameson had a valid, reasonable explanation, he was ready to leave and look for another law firm. Twenty-five minutes after his appointment, he was escorted into an elegant conference room most likely reserved for VIP meetings. Jameson was present, but now he appeared to be only a junior member of a team of lawyers led by a much older gentleman.

The older lawyer was Clarence Hoskins, one of the law firm's founding partners. Within two and a half hours of his arrival, Jake became a millionaire. He was surprised when the ID card he demanded was better than expected. Instead of a Photo ID from the Beecham County Sheriff's Department, it was an ID card from the U.S. Marshall's Service, and a federal judge cosigned it. It was good in all fifty States.

Jake hadn't been in any hurry, but he rushed them through once they started. He claimed he was eager to travel and planned an extended trip with Las Vegas as his first destination. Truthfully, he wasn't keen to go anywhere, but it seemed like a believable desire for someone who had just come into unexpected wealth. His real motivation for enthusiastically advertising a destination was to draw any possible assailants away from family and friends while he searched for a particular boy.

Although the senior partner advised him that his law firm could handle all the transactions with the settlement funds, Jake was concerned that these lawyers had become too comfortable working with his enemies. During a break with the lawyers, he visited an accounting firm in the same building and quickly engaged the services of an accountant. The accountant accompanied him back to the meeting with the lawyers, and after that meeting concluded, Jake followed the accountant back to his office.

Amazingly, attorney fees were also included in the settlement. After the firm took out the loan, Jake was left with 9.85 million dollars. He gave the accounting firm broad discretion in investing 9 million dollars but arranged for immediate access to the other eight hundred fifty thousand dollars through his local bank.

He also arranged for Nick to have access to the account. When he got home, he explained his travel plans to Nick and told him he needed to go to the accounting firm as soon as possible and sign some papers. Nick would have access to the funds for repairs to Jake's house and could buy the third property for himself, giving the two of them the ownership his brother had wanted.

The next day, after wrapping up a few banking details, he made several phone calls in preparation for his trip, and the only call that caused him any concern was the conversation with Sarah.

"I don't know how long I'll be gone, honey," he said. "I'm just going to take a short vacation." He assured her several times that he wouldn't be away nearly as long as the last time he'd gone on a trip. He hadn't tried to explain prison.

"You'll see Sarah soon," she'd said.

"I'll see you just as soon as I can, sweetheart," he assured her.

What she'd said sent a chill through him. Her inflection was all wrong, and her choice of words was out of character. She'd always been very precocious, but she'd never referred to herself in the third person. He questioned Walker when he came back on the phone, but Walker assured him he'd seen nothing concerning her health to worry about.

Shortly after sunrise the next morning, Jake threw his fishing gear and two suitcases into the Jeep and was on his way. When he stopped in Charleston for breakfast, he realized the Jeep was inadequate for this trip. He'd been looking forward to cruising with the top off, but he became aware of the security problem the canvas top created. Anytime he left the Jeep unattended, he would risk his property. The clothes weren't so important, but he had money and guns in the suitcases he didn't want to lose.

After breakfast, he drove around Charleston until he found a car rental service. He chose a nondescript Ford that appeared to be the kind of car that could go through any neighborhood, rich or poor, without drawing much attention. He had the rental service put his Jeep in storage until he returned.

He had no specific destination in mind, but since he'd pretended to be going to Las Vegas, he got on Interstate 64 and headed west. After passing through Lexington, Kentucky, he felt a vague sense of unease and thought about a different destination. He could reverse direction, but he didn't want to go back the same way he came. He stopped for the night at a hotel to think about it.

The next morning, he chose a different route. He continued west until he reached Interstate 57 South. He felt better as soon as he changed direction. After an hour or so, he switched to Interstate 24 East. When he got to Nashville, he turned onto I-40 toward Knoxville, and the uneasiness morphed into anticipation as though he was being drawn toward a destination.

Seeing billboards advertising the Great Smoky Mountains, Jake realized that a vacation resort would be a great place to meet kids. He had been on the road for two days, and for all the good it was doing him, he might as well still be secluded in his own house. He hadn't even spoken to a child since he'd been on the road. Like he'd told Walker, the best he could do was to put himself into a position where the boy, the Holy Ghost incarnate, of whom the preacher had spoken might find him.

He arrived in Gatlinburg late in the evening and found a hotel room. He had a good feeling about the place. Watching kids having fun was entertaining for a few days, but he was ready to move on by the third day. He didn't know what he was looking for, but this wasn't where he would find it.

When he left the resort area, he didn't bother to look at a map. He just began meandering, taking any road that was posted as eastbound. About the time he decided he must be in the middle of nowhere, he found himself back at another entrance ramp to Interstate 40. He got on the Interstate and continued east, and it wasn't long before he crossed into North Carolina. When he came to Interstate 77, he decided he should head south. If he went north, in six or seven hours, he would be back in Charleston, West Virginia, having gone in a huge circle and accomplished nothing, so he headed South. However, a half hour later, he noticed that he had somehow ended up on I-77 North.

When he saw a sign for Mt. Airy, North Carolina, he decided to exit the Interstate. He had once heard Andy Griffith was from Mt. Airy, supposedly the inspiration for the town of Mayberry in *The Andy Griffith Show*. According to that show, fishing was a recurring theme, and he thought he might find a place to use his fishing gear there. A hotel stood near the Interstate, so he decided to spend the night and get a fresh start in the morning.

Early the next morning, he got on U.S. 52 South, expecting his destination to be Mt. Airy, but he passed through the town without any inclination to stop. An hour or so later, he entered the city of Wharton, North Carolina. He found the local river, and when he saw a spot that looked well-used because several forked sticks were already in the ground, he thought he'd try it. He parked, got his gear out, and threw his hook out to the middle of the river. The current washed the line into the deeper water under the trees. He didn't have to wait long before he hooked a big catfish. He reeled it in, took it off the hook, and let it go.

He had seen enough. He liked the area, and it looked like the fishing would be good. Most of all, it just felt right. He gathered his gear and headed back to the car. He'd find a place to buy a fishing license for this State and then find a hotel. He was stowing his gear in the trunk when a voice behind him made him straighten up and turn around.

"Give me your money." the voice commanded.

Jake turned around to see a guy about eight feet away. He was wearing a ski mask, a long-sleeved shirt, and gloves. He was pointing a chrome-plated revolver at him. It looked like an old .22 caliber Saturday Night Special, and Jake thought it was more likely to blow up than to fire an accurate shot. The image of the barrel of his .357 Magnum as he'd brought it to his mouth suddenly flashed through his mind, and the juxtaposition of the two barrel sizes struck him as hilarious. He began laughing.

"I'm serious," the guy said, nervously waving the gun to draw Jake's attention to it. "I want your money."

"No, I don't think so," Jake said as his laughter trailed off.

He trusted his ability to read people, and the vibe he got from this guy wasn't threatening.

The guy was close to Jake's height, but he appeared to be skinny. Other than that, Jake couldn't tell much else about him except that, by the sound of his voice, he was young.

"I'll shoot," the guy threatened.

The gun wavered again, not to draw attention to itself this time, but from apparent nervousness. The guy moved slightly to his left, and his feet got tangled in a dead tree limb.

While the guy was momentarily distracted, Jake stepped forward, grabbed the gun with his left hand, and knocked the guy's grip off the weapon with his right. His skinny opponent stumbled backward and fell.

The young man's body language telegraphed submission. A huge sigh of relief whispered across his lips as though he'd been relieved of a burden. He didn't try to get up.

Jake deftly tossed the would-be robber's revolver into his trunk with his left hand as his right hand went under his shirt at the small of his back and pulled his .380. As he brought the gun to bear, he didn't flip the safety off, but he cocked the hammer. It was a deafening sound, not because it was loud but because when most guns were cocked, it usually meant that it was only a twitch of the finger away from explosively discharging a deadly wad of lead. However, the .380 was equipped with a rolling block safety that held the hammer off the firing pin by a movable metal block. That safety feature made the cocked hammer more menacing, but at the same time, it also made the gun safer.

"Please, mister," the guy said. "My gun wouldn't even shoot."

"Take off the ski mask," Jake ordered.

When the mask came off, he turned out to be a handsome black kid.

"How old are you?" Jake asked.

"Seventeen," the kid said.

Like the guy he'd faced back in the prison camp, Jake was confident in his ability to read this guy's intentions. Some guys are prone to violence by nature; others could be driven to violence by circumstances, but some are practically incapable of violence. This kid was a card-carrying member of that third group.

Jake lowered the hammer of his .380, tucked it in his belt, and turned his back to fish the kid's gun out of the trunk. It wasn't loaded, and when he pulled the hammer back to look at the firing pin, there wasn't one.

"How many people have you robbed with this thing?" Jake asked, as much amused by the harmless youngster as by the useless gun. The kid probably thought the anonymity created by the shirt, gloves, and ski mask made him look formidable.

"You were my first," came the reply. "I needed money, and it seemed like a good idea at the time."

"Well, it wasn't," Jake said as he cocked his arm back and threw the useless gun through the trees. He heard a satisfying "plunk" as it landed in deep water.

"Find a job," Jake said as he turned away.

During his lifetime, Jake encountered many people who wanted money from him. Some unabashedly begged for it, and others held up signs promising to work for food. Sometimes he'd felt inclined to give, and sometimes he hadn't. He turned around to see the kid walking away dejectedly.

"Wait a minute," Jake called after him.

The kid turned and waited as Jake approached him.

"Why do you need money so badly that you would try to rob people for it?" Jake asked.

The kid fidgeted, either embarrassed by his need or resentful of this stranger's inquisition. Apparently, his need was so great that it allowed him to disregard those emotions.

"My mom needs medicine, and me and my brothers and sister need food," he admitted. "My mom's sick, and we have nothing to eat. On top of that, my sister's pregnant, and she's only fifteen."

Find a job, he'd said. It had rung hollow in his own ears. He'd expected it to relieve him of any further responsibility, but it hadn't. It was a self-righteous gesture, like offering to pray for a genuinely hungry person instead of sharing food that would fill their stomach.

When the younger kids were mentioned, Jake was reminded of his primary reason for being here. The younger brothers weren't relevant to that purpose, but the pregnant sister was, particularly if the father was unknown.

"Does your sister know who the father is?" he blurted out without thinking it through.

"F*** you," the kid said disgustedly as he turned and walked away.

"Wait a minute," Jake said, instantly recognizing his unintended slur. "I'm sorry. I didn't mean that the way it sounded."

The kid wouldn't stop. He apparently heard Jake coming up behind him because he took off running.

Jake wouldn't let it end like this. When the kid took off, Jake turned on the speed and tackled him before he'd gone thirty feet.

The kid struggled to get away, but there was no fight in him. When Jake got him pinned down, he sat on his chest.

"Listen to me," he said. "I'm sorry, but I didn't mean what you thought I meant. I have a good reason for asking about the father. I just phrased it wrong. Now, I'm going to let you up. I want to help you, but you can take off if you don't want my help."

Jake rolled off the kid, stood up, and backed away. When the kid was up, Jake turned his back to him to prove he could take off if he wanted. Apparently, the kid's need was significant enough for him to take a chance on a stranger.

"Come on, I'll take you home," Jake said without looking back.

When the young man started toward the passenger side, Jake stopped and took something out of a suitcase before closing the trunk. When he got in the car, he introduced himself and learned the kid's name was Chalmer Thomas.

He made several turns and drove about a mile. He was appalled when he stopped the car in front of the house to which he'd been directed. Calling it a house was being too generous. It was nothing more than a run-down shack.

Two young boys played on a large pile of dirt in the front yard, building roads and bridges for their little toy cars. Jake followed Chalmer into the shack. It was poorly furnished but clean. A young pregnant girl sat on a worn couch, flipping through an old Sears catalog.

"Look at this, Chal?" The girl held up the magazine so Chalmer could see the picture she'd been looking at. "I want this for my little girl." She shrank back when she saw Jake.

"Congratulations," Jake said, "so, you're going to have a girl?"

"Yes," the girl said, eyeing Jake with suspicion.

Jake was surprised he had so quickly gotten the answer to a question he didn't know how to ask. This girl would have a baby, but it wouldn't be a boy. Now, he just had to decide how much money to give Chalmer, and he could be on his way.

"Chalmer, is that you?" a weak female voice called from another room.

"Yeah, Momma, it's me," Chalmer called back.

"Come here," the voice in the other room commanded.

Chalmer went into the other room, and as though the kid was exerting some magnetic force on him, Jake felt himself being pulled along in his wake. A woman lay in bed, and she was talking to Chalmer when Jake stepped out from behind him. She cringed and pulled the sheet to her chin.

"Who's that?" she demanded of Chalmer.

"I'm sorry for the intrusion, Ma'am," Jake said, embarrassed that he'd entered the privacy of the woman's bedroom. "I'll wait in the other room."

As he turned to leave, Jake saw the old newspaper articles decorating the walls. The picture accompanying one extensive article caught his eye. He saw a familiar face in it and moved closer to read the caption underneath. He wondered if these people knew the man in the picture.

"Who's this?" he asked without turning around.

"That's my grandfather," Chalmer said proudly.

Jake was speechless for a moment. What were the odds? He tried to recall what Vincent had said about an estranged daughter. He had talked about her a lot, but obviously, he wouldn't know anything about grandchildren.

"If this is your dad," Jake said, addressing the woman in the bed, "that would mean you must be Odessa. He hasn't seen you since you were fourteen."

Shock overtook the woman's face, and she looked wide-eyed at her son.

"What've you been saying about me?" she demanded.

Chalmer was more shocked than her because he knew he hadn't said anything to Jake about his mother.

Jake quickly explained that he knew Vincent White, and Vincent had told him about a daughter he'd regretfully never seen again after she ran away from home. Jake asked her for permission to pray with her, and when she welcomed the offer, he knelt by her bed and took her hand.

"Dear God," he whispered after a short prayer, "let me help this woman. Let her sickness be my sickness, let her pain be my pain, and let her demons be my demons. Amen."

Jake waited another minute before he let go of her hand, but he already knew it hadn't worked. There hadn't been any shock or sensation of worms flowing from her hand into his. He didn't mention what he'd hoped would happen. They talked a while longer, and she admitted she loved her dad and collected everything she found about him in the news. She'd wanted to contact him but feared he must hate her.

"I have to go," Jake finally said, "but I know your dad loves you and would want to hear from you. I'll give Chalmer his address. I also think he would want you to have this."

Jake took the wad of one-hundred-dollar bills out of his pocket and handed it to Odessa. It was part of a stash he carried for emergencies, and this situation certainly qualified as an emergency. It was five thousand dollars, and there was another wad just like it hidden in the other suitcase. He said goodbye and asked Chalmer to walk to the car with him.

Jake found a pen and paper in the glove box and wrote down Chalmer's contact information. On another piece of paper, he wrote down his own information. He included his house phone as well as his cell phone number. The cell phone wouldn't do much good when he was home, but it was useful while he was still on the road. He got Vincent's contact information from his billfold and wrote it under his. Then, he popped the trunk and got the wad of money from the other suitcase.

"I owe your grandfather a huge debt, and I'm paying it forward. There's just one more thing I think he'd want me to tell you." Without the slightest suggestion of anger or animosity, he said, "If you ever try to rob anybody else, I *will* come back, I *will* find you, and I *will* kick your ass." Softening the well-meaning threat, he handed Chalmer the cash and said, "I want you to have this." When he handed him the paper, he added, "If you ever get desperate enough to rob again, call me instead."

When he left Chalmer, he drove back into town, looking for a bank. He could get cash from an ATM, but he wanted to use a bank for a money transfer instead because of the ATM's daily withdrawal limit. It was a few minutes after twelve, but if he hurried, there should be enough time to complete the transaction before the bank closed for the day.

It was a good-sized town, and it took only a few minutes to locate a bank. He went into the First National Bank of Wharton and asked to talk to somebody about a money transfer. He was shown into a waiting area and treated to a cup of coffee, but nobody was in any hurry to help him. When twenty minutes passed without progress, he doubted he could accomplish anything today. A few minutes later, he was encouraged when he was ushered into a small office.

He gave his information to an older lady and waited while she contacted his bank. She had always been courteous, but after she talked to his bank, her attitude became more respectful and helpful. She couldn't do enough for him. An hour later, he left the bank with his stash replenished and a new bank account. That account was now owned by Odessa Thomas and Chalmer Thomas and held another fifty thousand dollars. Their need was desperate, and the bank would contact them and inform them that a new account had been set up in their names.

He strolled down the street, breathing deeply of the fresh air, relishing a renewed feeling of purpose. It was providence that he'd found Vincent's estranged family, and he was happy to have found a way to make a payment on a debt. As he crossed the street toward his car, he suddenly felt an irresistible urge to talk to Sarah. He took out his cell phone and automatically checked for a dial tone. Back home, as often as not, he wouldn't have one. Instead of getting in his car, he stepped to the back of the sidewalk and stood with his back against a brick wall. He was conditioned by the spotty reception back home to expect that if he moved too much, he was likely to lose the signal.

He punched Walker's number into the phone, and as he was waiting for the connection, he saw a young boy walking down the street toward him. The kid was alone, and his head was down. There was something about the way the boy moved that held his attention. As the boy passed within a few feet of him, Jake turned to watch him, vaguely aware that the phone was ringing on the other end. Apparently, feeling Jake's eyes on him, the boy stopped, turned around, and raised his head to meet Jake's gaze. Jake felt goosebumps on his arms. There was something hauntingly familiar about the boy. He remembered the phone in his hand when he heard the answering machine pick up.

"It's me. I'll call back later," he said distractedly into the phone without taking his eyes off the boy.

The phone almost slipped from his hand as he disconnected, and he glanced down. When he looked up again, the boy was gone. He scanned the area and saw him crossing the street. The kid ran down the block and disappeared around the corner. Jake continued holding the phone as he stared at the vacant corner, trying to understand what he'd just seen and felt.

The boy's movements had first attracted his attention, but when the kid stopped and looked at him, Jake glimpsed something in his face that set off a cascade of emotions. While he was sure he didn't know the boy, he felt a wave of love and uncanny attraction. *The Holy Ghost in the flesh,* he suddenly thought. It was an exciting thought, and as far as he could tell, it was the only reasonable explanation.

CHAPTER 20

Jake watched farther down the street, hoping the boy would reappear. He planned to stay in this area but now, he was reluctant to even leave this street. When he stepped away from the brick wall, he saw that he'd been leaning against an apartment building, and his car was parked directly in front of its door. A sign affixed to the inside of the glass door advertised a completely furnished apartment for rent.

He still held the phone in his hand, so he punched in the number on the sign. If he got this apartment, he would be within walking distance of the river, but more importantly, he *had* to see the boy again, and this street was his only connection.

He got the apartment, and in this case, "completely furnished" meant the bedding, kitchen utensils, and most other necessities were included. He might want to stay only a night or two, but he couldn't have gotten the apartment on that basis. He overcame the requirement for references with a generous cleaning deposit and a month's rent in advance.

Although the apartment was entirely furnished, Jake needed a few personal items, including food and drinks, to stock the pantry and refrigerator. He went to the Walmart he'd passed when he took Chalmer home and found everything he needed, including a fishing license. He bought enough food, snacks, and drinks to allow him to spend several days in the apartment without going out if he chose to do so. After he put away his purchases, he scouted the streets, looking for the most direct route to the river.

During the next six days, after a leisurely breakfast, he spent the mornings on the riverbank. He returned to the apartment for a late lunch and then spent most afternoons loitering on the street, watching for the boy or sometimes just roaming the streets. He saw several boys, but none ever inspired more than a glance. It wasn't until the seventh day that he finally made contact; as it happened, it was extremely hard contact.

The seventh day started just like the previous six, offering no hint that the past was about to collide with the present to produce a future beyond his wildest dreams. He was taking his usual route to the river when he turned a corner and stepped directly into the path of a running boy. The rods and tackle box flew from his hands, and he tried to catch the boy to keep him from falling, but the kid eluded his every effort to grab him. When their feet became tangled, they both fell to the concrete.

Even as they landed together on the sidewalk, the boy twisted and wiggled away from him. Just as the boy sprang to his feet and ran, Jake recognized him as the boy he'd been trying to find. As he got up, Jake saw the reason for the kid's headlong flight. He was being chased by five other boys who whooped and hollered like baying dogs excited by the chase. Had he not collided with Jake, the first boy might have already lost his pursuers, but now, it would take several blocks to regain the lead he'd lost.

Jake stood to watch the chase. The first boy was faster than his pursuers and would eventually outrun them, but then he made a costly blunder. The kid crossed the street and turned into a dead-end alley. Unlike most other alleys, a high, solid wood fence blocked that alley. Jake had discovered it while looking for the shortest route to the river. The kid was trapped. Jake closed the tackle box and picked up the rods. He started to follow the boys when a glint of silver and yellow caught his eye. It was a knife that had fallen out of his tackle box. He fished it out of a crack in the sidewalk and put it back in the box.

He hesitated as he approached the mouth of the alley and heard the boys' commotion. He could charge up the alley and break it up, but all the boys would likely disperse and run away, including the one he wanted to meet. He could do nothing and wait for it to be over and take the boy home or to the hospital, depending on the severity of any injuries. That would guarantee him more time with the boy, but he couldn't stand by and let the kid take a beating just to satisfy his desire to talk to him. As he set the rods and tackle box down, a more appealing third option occurred to him. He took the yellow-handled knife back out of the tackle box.

The knife was just a cheap trinket he'd bought in Mexico during a weekend trip while he was in the Army stationed at Ft. Hood, Texas. He'd been twenty years old at the time, but he'd been suitably impressed by the shiny yellow handles, the silver ends, and the switchblade action. When he got over his fascination with the knife and had no other use for it, he relegated it to the tackle box. He was sure it would impress these boys, who appeared to be around ten years old.

With the knife in hand, Jake moved swiftly up the alley. The clamor of the altercation masked the sound of his approach. He stopped within a few feet of the melee, completely unnoticed. The kid with his back to the wooden fence was the only one who faced him, but he was too busy covering his body to look beyond his attackers. Fortunately, the boys were too tightly packed around their victim to be able to inflict any real damage.

"Hey, you!" Jake shouted in a loud, angry voice. All the boys jumped at his booming voice, startled by the anger and surprised by his nearness. They all turned to face him.

Taking advantage of an opening in front of the boy, Jake stepped forward to confront him. He pointedly ignored the others. "Does this belong to you?" he angrily accused the boy.

He extended his hand with the knife, palm up so that all eyes were directed toward the knife. It was slender and sleek, with bright yellow handles capped with a silver nub on each end. He gently undulated the muscles in his hand so that the knife moved as though it was alive with malicious intent. He deftly pressed the release button with his thumb, and a tapered silver blade flicked out and locked into place. Then, gripping it with the tips of his fingers, he dropped his hand to his side and closed the blade against his upper thigh. As though drawing a gun, he thrust the knife forward and pressed the button to demonstrate how easily and quickly it could be brought into action.

He closed it again and looked at the kid. He had intended to maintain his anger at the boy until the others were gone, but his heart melted when he saw the kid's face, and he couldn't sustain even a pretense of anger. The familiarity was still there, but now the face was darkened with a mixture of fear, hurt, and confusion. Blood from his nose was smeared across his face by the back of his hand, but the kid wasn't crying.

"You must have dropped this when you knocked me down back there," he said, making it a simple statement instead of an angry accusation. "You shouldn't be carrying something so dangerous." He stepped closer and gave the kid a conspiratorial wink the other boys couldn't see. He said, "I was going to call the cops, but now I see why you would carry it."

He glanced at the other boys with disgust, took the kid's right hand, and placed the switchblade in it to correctly position the button for action.

"That should make it a fair fight," he said, taking a few steps backward.

The kid extended his arm threateningly and pressed the release button. As Jake expected, one of the boys mumbled something about home and walked away. His two closest confederates called after him and turned to follow. All three instantly broke into a run. Having been deserted by more than half their number, the other two quickly followed suit.

Jake chuckled as he stepped forward and held out his hand for the knife. "Bullies are like that," Jake offered in the way of advice, "stand up to them, and they'll leave you alone."

The boy imitated Jake's actions in closing the knife on his thigh before handing it over. Jake was pleased and impressed that he'd accomplished the feat without cutting himself. Jake slid the knife into his pocket and held out his hand again.

"I'm Jake," he said.

After a brief hesitation, the boy wiped his hand on his pants and shook hands. "I'm Billy," he said. "Thanks for helping me."

"I'm going fishing," Jake said. "You're welcome to come along if you like."

"I can't," Billy said. "I have to go home."

Although Jake had said he was going fishing, he didn't move. Billy's appearance, mannerisms, and even his voice resonated with some mysterious quality that piqued his interest. He wanted to know more about him but didn't know how to ask him if he was God. Billy also implied that he was leaving, and Jake didn't know what was holding him in place. The silence hung between them, quickly becoming awkward.

"I go fishing about this time every day," Jake finally offered.

"I've got an apartment a couple streets over where I saw you the other day. If you ever want to go fishing, I'll be around."

Jake turned and started walking down the alley. He stopped at the mouth of the alley to pick up his rods and tackle box, and then he started down the street.

"Hey, mister," Billy called after him.

Jake turned around and saw Billy standing in the mouth of the alley.

"You can call me Jake," Jake said.

"Can I have my knife back, Jake?" Billy asked with an impish grin.

Jake laughed. The kid was gutsy and had a sense of humor.

"I guess I did say it was yours," he said. Looking seriously at the boy, he asked, "How old are you?"

"I'm … eight," Billy said falteringly. "But I'm not a stupid little kid," he added defensively.

Jake pulled the knife out of his pocket and looked at it. "I'm not sure your father would approve," he said.

"I don't have a father," Billy said, "but if I did, I think he would be okay with it."

Ordinarily, Jake wouldn't even consider giving a switchblade knife to an eight-year-old boy he didn't know, but these were exceptional circumstances. The kid had just answered the question that cut to the heart of his search for the Holy Ghost incarnate. He wanted to know more, but too many questions too fast might drive the boy away. Instead, he decided that giving the kid the knife might provide a connection for getting the information through the natural course of friendship.

"Tell you what," Jake said. "I'll give you this knife under one condition. I don't want you pulling it on anybody. It would be as serious as pulling a gun. You have to promise me you won't carry it around. You'll take it straight home and put it in a safe place."

"I will," Billy said breathlessly. "I promise."

Jake held out the knife, and Billy closed the distance between them and took it out of his hand slowly and gently, like a dog taking a morsel from fingers that it was careful not to nip. Billy cradled the knife in both hands and looked at it in awe as though it were a treasure of tremendous value.

"Thanks," he said as he carefully slid it into his pocket.

Jake was amused as he watched the boy handle the cheap trinket with such reverence. He expected that when the knife was safely tucked away, they would talk more, but when the knife was secure, Billy wheeled around and took off like a shot.

*****

Billy rubbed his eyes in the glare of the overhead light and saw Stanley standing beside his bed, naked. He began to moan and whimper, feeling the effects of the pain in his groin even before the cause was administered. He turned away, but he was roughly pulled back onto his back.

"Happy birthday, Billy boy," Stanley crooned. "I've decided to give you your present early."

The voice and appearance mutated and took on more ominous and hideous qualities, but Billy knew it was still Stanley. He wanted to get up and run but couldn't move a muscle. The bed became like a spider's web, holding him tight while the evil thing approached. He continued to whimper as he felt the sheet being stripped away from his body. He lay motionless as Stanley stripped away his underwear and pajama bottoms, forcing his arms over his head with the pajama top. He felt Stanley straddling his legs as he climbed onto the bed.

The Stanley thing had become Stanley again, and he began applying pressure to Billy's testicles. He maliciously smiled down at Billy while slowly increasing the pressure and encouraging him to scream.

Billy began to feel the pain that radiated from his testicles to his belly button, but he couldn't react.

Through a haze of tears, Billy saw Stanley stand on his knees and tower over him. Somehow, he knew what Stanley would do next, and his eyes filled with fresh tears.

"Billy, there's nothing wrong with being scared. It's what you do despite being scared that's important."

Billy turned his head toward the voice and saw another man beside the bed. He had no fear of this man and was sure this man held no ill will toward him.

"He's a bully," the man said. "Stand up to bullies, and they'll leave you alone. You have the knife."

The tears dried in Billy's eyes as he recognized Jake and remembered the knife. Before Stanley could grip his arm to turn him over, Billy slid his right hand under his pillow and felt the hard plastic and cool metal. He grabbed the knife with his fingertips like Jake had shown him, jerked his arm forward, and extended his fist toward Stanley's face.

Stanley was shifting his weight from his right knee to his left knee when he stopped mid-stride to look at Billy's proffered hand. Billy pressed the release button with his thumb and was instantly gratified by Stanley's look of shock and fear when the shiny silver blade flicked out. Stanley's eyes widened as he pulled his head back to get his face farther from the blade.

"Get off me!" Billy demanded through clenched teeth.

Billy dug his right heel into the bed, and with every ounce of his strength, he kicked upward with his left leg, aiming for the bulbous flesh between Stanley's legs. When his leg met resistance, Billy turned with the kick, intending to knock Stanley off the bed. However, he must have misjudged his strength because he felt his momentum pulling him off the bed, too.

He woke up when he hit the floor. He was tangled in the bed sheet, but he could instantly recall the dream. This time, it had been different. He hadn't been awakened by the shame of the phantom pain in his testicles and the scars on his back. This time, he'd fought back, and he'd won.

He heard his mother calling his name, followed by the sound of her footsteps. She was coming. He couldn't wait to tell her how he'd beaten Stanley and that he didn't have to fear him anymore. He wanted to tell her about Jake and how strange it felt when Jake took his hand to place the knife in it.

Suddenly, the thought of the knife paralyzed him. She would disapprove of him having the knife. He'd brought it home and put it where she couldn't find it. After he'd gone to bed and she left the room, he retrieved the knife, hiding it under his pillow. He didn't know if she would take it, but he couldn't take that chance. The knife was his only defense against Stanley.

The knife was in his hand when he'd fallen out of bed, but it wasn't there now. He must have dropped it. He frantically swept his hands around the floor but couldn't find it. Even when the overhead light came on, he continued to search, squinting his eyes against the sudden brilliance.

His mother rushed in, knelt beside him, and scooped him into her arms. She cradled him and tried to soothe him, much like she'd done on that faraway night when the real Stanley attacked him and caused him real pain.

Billy gave up on the search, relaxed in her arms, and closed his eyes. His only defense against her prying questions was to pretend he was falling back to sleep. He could only hope she wouldn't find the knife. He was sure that without it, Stanley would come after him again. After several minutes, he allowed his mother to help him back into bed.

She picked up the crumpled sheet and shook it out. He rose up and watched the floor, but the knife didn't fall out. After she spread the sheet over him, she went to the door and switched the light off, but much to his disappointment, she didn't leave the room. She returned, sat down on the edge of the bed, and resumed caressing his cheeks and forehead.

He had been slipping out of his bedroom window for the past two weeks while she was at work. He went out the window the first time just to prove to himself that he could. The roof of the building next door wasn't far away. He left his window open while he searched for a way off the roof. He found a many-limbed tree at the back of the building, and after that, he left his window raised about an inch and went a little farther each day. He had a vague sense that he was searching for something, but he had no idea what it might be.

How could he tell his mother about Jake when he didn't understand it himself? He'd stayed away from the street where he first saw him. He'd been spooked by his stare and his interest in him. However, even though he'd tried to avoid him, he ran straight into his arms. At first, he thought Jake must be working with the boys chasing him, but then he'd helped him. He couldn't tell his mother anything about Jake because he wanted to learn more about the man. If she knew he was exploring the streets alone, she would never give him the opportunity and freedom to go out and find him again.

He felt himself being seduced into sleep by her comforting ministrations. He couldn't allow that. He had banished Stanley from his dreams, but if he didn't find the knife, Stanley would come back. He couldn't explain it to his mother. She would consider the knife too dangerous. At best, she'd lock it away and promise to return it when he reached a more suitable age. At worst, she would dispose of it.

He turned away from her gentle touch, turning his back to her, hoping she would think he was asleep and leave the room. Then, he could find the knife and put it back under his pillow.

After turning away from her, he slid his right hand under the pillow to where the knife would lay once he found it. He thrilled at the touch of hard plastic and cool metal. It was already there, under his pillow, magically returned by itself. He wrapped his fingers around it and then surrendered to sleep, convinced Stanley could never touch him again. The knife was his defense, his weapon, his talisman.

*****

Connie felt exhausted and finally returned to the musty couch in the living room. The small apartment had only one bedroom, and Billy had taken the couch at first, but after a few uneasy nights, she insisted they trade. What happened tonight seemed to justify that decision. She dozed in a fitful sleep, one ear tuned to the bedroom. She fully expected another outburst at any moment, and it didn't improve the quality of her sleep that the bedroom remained quiet She could see the front door from the sofa, and she took some consolation in the fact that at least he couldn't leave the apartment without her knowledge.

Life was beginning to beat her down. Every time she started to feel like they had risen above their troubles and that life would be good, she was knocked down again. She had thought they might have finally found peace here since they had arrived in complete anonymity, and she had been warmly welcomed into the job that Delmas Gilmeyer had arranged.

In Cleveland, Mr. Gilmeyer had said that he had a friend in a small town in North Carolina, and he'd asked if she'd like him to call and see if his friend could give her a job.

She had thanked him profusely. He had made deciding what to do next so much easier. "I can't thank you enough," she said.

They'd settled here in North Carolina over two months ago, and the nightmares had become a constant dread in their lives. The frequency of the nightmares varied, but tonight, there was a new, more dangerous dimension. Previously, his outbursts had been limited to crying and screaming that woke her up. The addition of this physical quality scared her. Even more foreboding, the screaming and crying were gone, and it had only been the *thump* on the floor that had awakened her.

Even though she'd done everything for Billy, she'd also had a selfish motive; she needed him. Billy's father was dead, and twice, she had entered into marriage to provide him with a father and a normal family life, but both ended in utter disaster. The first man in California had put ugly scars in Billy's flesh, which might have the power to make him a hermit. The second man put nightmarish scars in his mind that might have the power to take his life. Both times, fearing she might lose Billy, she had run.

She was forced to reconsider her priorities. She might have to let Billy go. For the last two weeks, she'd been feeling like she was losing him. Billy was withdrawing into an inner world beyond her reach. He had become less communicative and more secretive. *Now*, she sadly thought, *maybe he needs professional help more than he needs me.*

The new identities were expensive, but the documentation was excellent. The background information on her new name, Connie S. Horton, was so meticulous that she was confident that her identity would never be questioned. Billy worried that the new identification made people think he was a stupid little kid, but his background information contained school records showing that he would be entering the third grade.

She had found this apartment within walking distance of her job. It was a one-bedroom walk-up on the second floor, but it was cheap enough to allow her paycheck to comfortably cover their monthly living expenses. Except for Billy's nightmares, life got back to normal again. But, two weeks ago, Billy's nightmares took on a new intensity and increased in frequency. She'd been awakened by his screams three times during the past two weeks, not counting tonight. This latest episode served to underscore the fact that she had to get help for him.

When she went to work, she left him in front of the TV, but she could tell he was distracted and disinterested in the program that had previously held his attention. He'd become uncharacteristically silent during the last two weeks, but last night's terror was the final straw. She'd checked her health insurance as soon as she started to work and found that it didn't cover the kind of professional help Billy needed. If she'd just stayed in West Virginia and faced Stanley's brother, at least the State of West Virginia might have provided the professional help Billy required to help him cope with his traumatic experience.

While walking to work, she decided to hold their new identities in reserve and take Billy back to West Virginia. Her heart broke at the thought of losing him, but she realized that her own selfishness posed a greater danger to his health than the authorities. She would face whatever she had to face, but her highest priority must be to get treatment for him.

When she arrived at work, she had a few minutes before her shift started. She dug the cell phone out of her purse and found a quiet corner. She called Marge Zimmerman back in West Virginia. They were only casual friends, but Marge was a gossip, and Connie needed to know what to expect when she returned home. Marge was the person most likely to tell her. If she were wanted for murder for killing Stanley, she would undoubtedly reveal that news. She expected an unfriendly greeting from Marge, so she was totally unprepared for the friendly reception she got and the shock that followed.

After warmly greeting her, Marge said, "Stanley asked about you just the other day. He told me about the argument." Obviously pleased to have been made a party to such juicy gossip, she said, "Did you come back home, dear?"

Connie was speechless. Over five months had passed since she thought she'd killed Stanley, but Marge had talked to him just a few days ago. *Stanley wasn't dead.*

She didn't realize she was making sounds of distress until Marge asked, "Are you okay, honey? Are you in trouble?"

"I'm fine," she said when she found her voice. "No, there's no trouble," she added, covering her shock as best she could and then waiting for Marge to spill everything she knew.

"Did you know Stanley was in a terrible car accident right after you left?" Marge asked.

"I heard he had some serious injuries," Connie said evasively.

Marge told her everything Stanley had said. At first, she thought Marge sounded as though she'd rehearsed what she was saying, but then she realized this was likely not the first time Marge had repeated Stanley's lies. Everybody in the neighborhood must have heard the story by now.

Stanley had concocted lies that accounted for his injuries and also explained her and Billy's absence. According to Stanley, there had been a stupid argument, and he left the house mad and got into a bad car accident. Then, two days later, he awakened in the hospital to learn that his wife and son had left him. Stanley called every week or so to see if Marge had heard from her.

After telling what she knew, Marge started asking prying questions. What was the argument about? Was she ready to accept Stanley's apology? Where was she? When would she be coming home?

It was contrary to Stanley's character to talk to Marge and enlist her aid. He loathed the woman and constantly berated Connie for associating with her. Stanley had invented a plausible scenario in which he came off as the victim. Then, knowing that Marge was possibly the only person who might provide clues to her whereabouts, he pretended to take Marge into his confidence. Connie belatedly realized that Stanley was using Marge, and she had sprung the trap he'd set for her.

Connie deflected Marge's questions and hurriedly got off the phone. Her head was buzzing. The initial shock of Stanley's recovery weighed heavily on her mind, but other equally shocking realizations soon eclipsed it. She did not doubt that Stanley meant to find her and Billy, kill them, and use Marge as an alibi. That revelation chilled her to the bone. The prospect of prison was the lesser of two evils now.

She stood for a long time with her forehead pressed against the wall, trying to control the tremors and involuntary shudders. The fear was mingled with anger at herself for having fallen victim to Stanley's design again. He had foreseen that she might contact Marge, and by her own responses to Marge, she had unwittingly validated every lie Stanley told.

She forgot to turn the phone off because she had too much to think about. She had taken those ledgers from Stanley's desk because she was sure he was dead. Now, she recognized that it had been a foolhardy thing to do. A careful study of those records was sure to reveal Stanley's drug dealing activities and her possession of them, not to mention the money from the safe, virtually guaranteed he would come after her.

What should she tell Billy? For several months, she'd been trying to convince him Stanley was dead and they were safe. She told him he could start school here, and none of his new classmates would ever know anything about Stanley. Those assurances had done nothing to dispel Billy's nightmares, and as bad as they were now, how much more devastating might those nightmares become if he learned Stanley wasn't dead and was actively hunting them with murderous intent?

On the other hand, if she told Billy the truth, the knowledge of Stanley's living threat might rob him of the ability to haunt Billy's dreams. Fear of the living might be easier to deal with than fear of the dead, but she wasn't qualified to tinker with Billy's mind and make such a consequential, potentially destructive decision.

CHAPTER 21

J ake was going through his morning on autopilot. He couldn't stop thinking about the kid as he was washing up and having breakfast. He was sure he must be the boy the preacher talked about. There was something disturbingly familiar about him, but it was elusive. The familiarity inspired instant love and longing, but a vague sense of communing with the dead came unbidden to his confused heart.

He wondered if that perception of the dead could somehow be related to the boy's identity. If this boy was the incarnation of the Holy Ghost, might Jake not be intuitively discerning some measure of an Ageless Presence in him? But that wasn't reasonable. If anything, he ought to be sensing infinity and immortality, not the finite state of the dead.

Moving slowly, he picked up his tackle box and rods. He lacked enthusiasm for sitting alone on the riverbank, but he had no other choice. He wanted contact with the kid but had neither an address nor a last name. He could only keep to his routine, making himself available for the kid to come to him.

He went down the stairs and out of the building carrying his rods and tackle box. As soon as he was on the sidewalk, he felt he was being watched. He started down the street and pretended to notice his shoe was untied. He stopped, leaned the rods against the nearest parked car, and set the tackle box on the hood. He lifted one foot to the car's fender and pretended to work on the shoelace while covertly scanning the street. He wasn't concerned about a complaint from the owner of the car because he'd deliberately waited until he could use his own.

The only suspicious activity he noted was inactivity. A solitary figure was standing still, watching him from across the street. After retying his shoe, he faked a yawn so that he could look directly at the motionless form. It was Billy.

Jake raised his hand in greeting, and the boy returned the gesture, but he didn't otherwise move. Jake waved his arm again, but this time in a "come here" motion. After a brief hesitation, the boy crossed the street. He approached Jake but stopped in the street, keeping the car's hood between them.

"Hello, Billy," Jake said, the pleasure of seeing him again evident in his voice.

Billy nodded his head in greeting, but he didn't speak. He looked at Jake appraisingly as though sight alone might tell him everything he needed to know about this man.

"Well, Billy, you want to go fishing?" Jake suggested companionably, picking up the tackle box and rods.

Billy still said nothing.

Jake might have thought the boy was mute if he hadn't heard him speak on a previous occasion. Seemingly unconcerned about Billy's silence, Jake hoped he could break the ice by mentioning the one thing they had in common.

"Do you have your knife with you?" Jake asked.

"I don't carry it with me," Billy immediately responded, patting his empty pockets as proof.

"Good," Jake said with a genuine smile, "I'm glad to see you're a man of your word." Holding out the rods as an invitation, he said, "You can carry these."

"I don't know how to fish," Billy said as he moved around the car.

"No problem," Jake said. "I can teach you everything you need to know in about five minutes. The hardest part is making up a good story about the big one that got away."

*****

Billy was passing the same spot for a third time when he stopped to watch somebody coming out the door of an apartment building. He immediately recognized Jake. He didn't want Jake to see him, but there was no time to hide. Not wanting to draw attention to himself, he froze, not knowing that standing still while others were moving around him was precisely what made him stand out. Billy sighed with relief when Jake started down the street, but then Jake stopped to tie a shoe. When he yawned and stretched, Jake looked straight at him.

Billy was petrified for a moment, but when Jake smiled and waved, he could do nothing but return the wave. When Jake gestured for him to come over, he crossed the street, surprised by his own willful compliance, which was more of a reflex action than a conscious decision. He stopped beside the car and studied Jake, hoping to confirm that there was not the slightest hint of evil intent in the man.

Then, the most amazing thing happened. Jake asked him about the knife and called him "a man of his word," obviously pleased with him. It was the first time he'd seen that kind of delighted, honest acceptance of his existence in any eyes other than his mother's. The men his mother brought around, including the two she'd married, had pretended to like him, but he hadn't been fooled for a minute. He'd recognized their evil intent toward him long before their actions proved it to his mother. He could discern no such evil intent in Jake.

He hadn't planned on making contact with Jake when he left his apartment. Last night, he fell back to sleep soon after he touched the knife and knew he was safe from Stanley. This morning, he awakened from his most peaceful sleep in a long time. He took the knife from under his pillow and hid it behind the bottom dresser drawer. He couldn't let his mother find it. Not only might she take it, but she would surely demand to know where he'd gotten it. That would be the end of his secret daytime excursions.

He believed the knife held magic power because he needed to believe it. He was vaguely aware that losing the knife on the floor might have been part of his dream, but he preferred to believe the knife had magically rematerialized itself under his pillow. That belief reinforced his conviction that he no longer had to fear Stanley. And, if the knife was magic, what about the man who had given it to him? What about Jake?

Jake had appeared in his dream to help him again, and Billy didn't know if the knife had brought him or if Jake possessed his own magic. Billy refused to consider the possibility that the entire episode had been wholly manufactured by his own mind. He was very curious and eager to learn more about Jake, and as soon as he hid the knife, he began formulating a plan.

The first part of the plan was easy. All he had to do was remain silent. He had no faith in his ability to lie to his mother, so his best course of action was silence. If he began telling her anything about the man or the knife, one question would lead to another. She would uncover his every deceit, and he would lose her trust and his freedom to roam.

The second part of his plan was a little more demanding. After his mother went to work, he slipped out the bedroom window and went searching for the man. He hadn't planned on being seen. He would only locate the man and watch him from a distance until he knew more about him. He would concentrate his search on the street where he saw him that first time. Jake said he had an apartment on that street.

*****

On their way to the river, Jake regaled Billy with a story about fighting a big fish for a half-hour before getting it near the bank. He described in detail how he'd carefully played the fish, finishing his story with a declaration that the fish got away, but it weighed two pounds and six and a half ounces. Billy didn't know enough about fishing to ask the proper question that led to the punch line, so Jake asked it for him.

"Want to know how I knew exactly how much it weighed, even though it got away?" Jake asked. When Billy nodded, Jake said, "It had scales on its tail."

The joke deserved a grin, or at most, maybe a chuckle, but Jake was pleasantly surprised to hear Billy laugh out loud. It appeared to Jake that Billy was as happy as he was that they were together. They walked in companionable silence for a while, but when they crossed the road to the riverbank, Jake noticed Billy had become noticeably subdued and apprehensive.

While standing at the river's edge, using the worms he'd dug the day before along the riverbank, Jake showed Billy how to thread a worm on a hook and cast a line. He could feel the boy's anxiety and saw Billy visibly relax when they got their lines in the water, placed their rods in the forked sticks, and moved back from the water's edge to sit down.

Jake wanted to know more about this kid, but he was concerned that he might push him away if he appeared overly inquisitive. He decided to take it slowly and limit himself to innocuous inquiries. However, they had very little time to talk about anything before the excitement started. Almost simultaneously, Billy's rod bent down, and a big fish broke the surface of the water.

"You've got a big one!" Jake said excitedly. "Grab your rod!"

Billy went for one rod, and Jake went for the other. Jake quickly reeled his line in to keep it from getting tangled with Billy's. Out of the corner of his eye, he saw Billy pull his rod back behind his head, nearly bending it double. It was the natural reaction of a novice. Luckily, the drag was set high enough to allow more line to play out, so it didn't snap.

Jake tossed his rod on the bank and stood beside Billy. He resisted the urge to grab the rod from the boy's hands. Because of the way the fish was breaking the surface, Jake could tell it was bigger than anything he'd been catching.

"Play him," Jake advised. "The harder it fights, the faster it'll wear itself out, and you can reel it in."

The fish was getting closer to the bank because of the river's current and its own efforts. Jake advised Billy to walk along the river's edge while reeling in the line.

"Slow," Jake cautioned. "Watch your step."

The excitement was contagious and must have made Billy a bit reckless. After only a few yards, he stepped too close to the edge, and the bank began crumbling beneath him. His balance became precarious, and he fumbled the rod. In his attempt to catch the rod, he fell face-forward into the river.

"Aaiee!" Billy shrieked before contact with the water took his breath away.

Jake was a few steps behind Billy, and he laughed uproariously, entertained by what he thought must be a purposely exaggerated reaction to falling into the water. The current near the bank was practically nonexistent, and the water wasn't deep. Jake continued to laugh, waiting for Billy to stand up so he could tease him about the poorly executed dive, but Billy didn't stand up. He'd hit the water in a prone position, and instead of getting his arms and legs under him to stand up, he flailed at the water as though his torso was in the grip of a beast.

It took Jake only seconds to recognize the danger. You could drown in mere inches of water if you didn't lift your face out of it. He jumped flat-footed into the river, landing only a few feet from Billy, and was at Billy's side in two steps. His progress was hampered more by the silt on the riverbed than by the knee-deep water. He grabbed Billy under his shoulders and lifted him out of the water. He wrapped his arms around the boy's chest and pulled him tightly against his own chest. The kid was crying, sputtering, and coughing. His arms continued to claw at the air, and his feet kicked spasmodically, still fighting the water.

"Billy!" Jake said firmly. "Stop it, Billy." When he finally convinced him to stop struggling, he said more soothingly, "You're all right, pal. I've got you."

Billy began to calm down, continuously wiping hair and water from his face with both hands.

"I'm going to set you down now," Jake said, "and we're going to walk out of the water. It's not deep."

When he tried to put him down, Billy panicked and grabbed frantically at his arm.

"It's okay, buddy," Jake said. "I won't let go."

When they reached the bank, Jake released Billy, but the kid looked so dejected that he put a hand on the boy's shoulder. He was surprised when Billy shrugged away from his touch. Billy was wearing a long-sleeve flannel shirt like he'd been wearing on the other occasions he'd seen him. He'd wondered why the kid wore the heavy garment in such a temperate climate. He hadn't noticed anything odd while they were in the water, but during the brief touch of his shoulder, he'd felt a lumpiness as though his undershirt was bunched up or some foreign debris was trapped under the flannel shirt.

Jake sat down on the bank, and after a few minutes, Billy sat down, too, but he seemed to deliberately choose a spot far away. Jake had no idea what that was all about. He could only guess that maybe the boy had a phobia that made him sensitive to unnecessary physical contact.

Billy sat with his head hanging between his raised knees, his arms wrapped around his ankles.

"I'm sorry," Billy finally said without raising his head.

About what? Jake thought but didn't ask. He was waiting to see if Billy would explain his distance, but apparently, that wasn't what was on the kid's mind.

"I'm sorry about losing your fishing rod," Billy said.

"Don't worry about it. I can get another one," Jake said.

"I'm sorry about getting you wet," Billy said.

"I'll dry," Jake said in the same gentle, dismissive tone.

"I'm sorry for everything," Billy insisted, raising just his eyes to peek at Jake.

This time, Jake concluded that Billy must be apologizing for being so standoffish. His heart went out to the kid. He wanted to put his arm around his shoulder and tell him everything was all right, but he realized that preventing just such an impulse as that might be precisely why the boy had chosen to sit so far away. He attempted to lighten the mood.

"I guess congratulations are in order," Jake said. You're now a fisherman with a bona fide story about the big one that got away." When Billy didn't react, he added, "It's a shame, though."

Billy's head came up, and he stared at Jake.

"You didn't get it close enough to see its scales," Jake clarified, "so you can't say exactly how much it weighed."

Billy's darkly clouded face broke into an uncertain smile. His posture relaxed, and he looked appreciatively at Jake.

"I think that's enough fishing for today," Jake said, standing up and brushing sand off his pants. His shirt was damp, his pants were soaked, and his shoes were squishy. "Let's go home."

Billy didn't object. He was wet and covered with mud and sand from head to toe. He got up to follow Jake. He picked up the other rod on the bank while Jake repacked the tackle box.

Both were wet and dirty, and Jake hated to part like this, but he knew the danger of taking such a young child into his apartment. However, he felt strongly about this boy, and seeking God born into the world again was a noble cause. Indeed, rumors started by any neighbors or even possible allegations of pedophilia were an acceptable risk.

"How about we go back to my apartment, clean up, and then I drive you home?" Jake suggested.

Billy seemed to seriously consider it for a long time before he said, "I can walk home."

"I know you can," Jake agreed, "but I wouldn't feel right about it. Yesterday, I sent you home with a knife, and if I send you home muddy and half-drowned today, somebody might think I'm a bad influence on you. Besides," he added in a more serious tone, "you might need some help explaining the muddy clothes."

"Mom's going to kill me," Billy agreed, clearly having already given his mother's reaction some thought.

"Plan B," Jake suggested. "You clean up, and we rinse and dry your clothes before you walk home."

After a long hesitation, although Billy was obviously reluctant, he finally agreed.

They walked back to the apartment side by side, and Jake was happy for Billy's company. He shifted the tackle box to whichever hand was closest to the boy to avoid inadvertently touching him. Sarah and her little brothers had known hugs and kisses from birth, and they not only accepted such close contact but often demanded it. This kid was different. Even when he was within arm's reach, his standoffish, lone-wolf demeanor sent out an I-don't-want-to-be-touched vibe.

The first order of business when they were in the apartment was to remove their shoes. Jake took them to the kitchen sink, rinsed the mud and sand off them under running water, and set each pair in a loose cradle of aluminum foil. He put them in the oven, turning the heat low.

"How would you like your shoes cooked, sir?" Jake asked as though he was a waiter in a restaurant.

"Well done," Billy said with a grin.

"Excellent choice, sir. If you will follow me," Jake said as he effortlessly transitioned from waiter to butler.

"Your bath, sir," he said as he hung a fresh towel. "I'll find you something to wear while your clothes dry."

He went out of the bathroom, closing the door behind him. He went into his bedroom and looked through his small assortment of clothes. He knew he had nothing to fit Billy, but he found a pair of black jogging pants with a drawstring at the waist and elastic at the ankles. They would be ridiculously baggy on him, but it was the best he could do.

He returned to the bathroom, tapped on the door, and pushed it open. He was surprised to find Billy standing in front of the sink, still fully clothed, instead of in the shower.

"You can wear this," Jake said, tossing the pants on the counter.

Billy critically examined the garment and said, "I'll need a shirt, too. Something with long sleeves."

Jake hadn't expected the kid to be so particular about clothes, but he was willing to please. He returned to his bedroom and got one of his own flannel shirts. It would be much too big, but the kid could use it like a bathrobe. Back in the bathroom, he tossed the shirt on top of the pants, bowed curtly with one arm at his waist, and said, "Will there be anything else, sir?"

Billy didn't answer, smile, or move except for an involuntary shudder. He looked like he was facing the electric chair instead of a harmless shower. *Boys don't like baths*, Jake reminded himself, but seeing the boy shiver again, he decided the source of his shaking might be more than just a dislike of baths. He needed to get out of those cold, wet clothes.

"Get a hot shower before you catch pneumonia," Jake ordered. His tone was gentle, but he dropped the subservient pretense. "You can pile your wet clothes on the floor, and after you shower, I'll throw them in the washer for a rinse."

Jake backed out of the bathroom and pulled the door closed. He returned to the kitchen and sat at the table on one of the wooden chairs. After a few uncomfortable minutes, he decided he didn't want to put on clean clothes until he showered, but even dry, dirty clothes would be more comfortable than what he was wearing. He went into his bedroom to change and heard the shower running as he passed the bathroom. He would wait until Billy was gone before taking his own shower.

As he passed the bathroom again, he heard nothing but silence within. He thought he might as well get Billy's clothes and put them in the washer. He tapped on the door, hesitated for a second, and pushed the door open. Billy was standing in the bathtub with his back to the door, vigorously toweling his head. The shower curtain was pushed back, and Jake got a full view of Billy's bare back. An involuntary, audible gasp escaped his lips.

Billy had been drying his hair and must not have heard the tap on the door, but he definitely heard the gasp. His head jerked around toward Jake.

"Aaiee!" Billy cried. As he turned, he grabbed the curtain,

pulling it to cover his back. He ended up facing Jake with the curtain behind him, and as soon as he recognized his error, he quickly pulled the curtain in front of him.

Jake picked up the pile of wet clothes and backed out of the bathroom, pulling the door closed with him. Jake backed across the narrow hallway until he bumped into the washer. He heard Billy crying as he turned and dropped the clothes on the washer. *That poor kid*, he thought.

"I want my clothes," Billy yelled.

The words were drawn out and barely intelligible because he hadn't stopped crying, and he was nearly choking on the sobs.

"Put the dry clothes on," Jake said without moving.

"No!" Billy shouted. "I want my clothes! I have to go home."

"Put the dry clothes on," Jake insisted.

He didn't know what to do, but he had to do something. The kid was inconsolable. Jake opened the bathroom door, went in, and sat down on the closed lid of the commode.

Billy took a step backward – as far as the confines of the bathtub would allow. He had completely wrapped himself in the shower curtain. After a few minutes, his crying turned into sobs and defensive anger.

"I want my clothes," he demanded again.

"We need to talk," Jake said calmly and reasonably.

"No! Give me my clothes," Billy said more defiantly, "I have to go home!"

Jake couldn't stop his mind from reviewing the images recorded through his eyes. He had witnessed scars from child abuse before, but none had ever affected him so profoundly as what he saw on Billy's back.

Some unknown instrument of torture had left a profusion of raised, interlacing welts all over Billy's back and upper arms, from the bottom of his buttocks to the top of his shoulders. Jake could tell the scars weren't fresh, but they appeared luminous, as though angered by the successive submersions, first in cold water and then hot.

Billy had tried to hide his back, but he'd turned too late. Under other circumstances, Billy's blunder in his attempt to cover his back would have been comical, but there was nothing humorous in this situation. What was most apparent to Jake was that Billy was more ashamed of the scars on his back than of the nudity of his front. In that flash of insight, he understood why Billy wore flannel shirts and why he didn't want to be touched near his back and shoulders. When he'd put his hand on Billy's shoulder, he'd felt the lumpiness of Billy's skin, not foreign debris.

No clear plan of action presented itself to Jake. So far, his only course of action was inaction. He knew he couldn't return Billy's clothes. If Billy left under these circumstances, Jake was sure he'd never see him again. And yet, Billy was in no mood to talk. Calm, rational persuasion wasn't an option. This situation called for more drastic measures.

Clink, clank. Two plastic hooks supporting the shower curtain snapped under the constant pressure Billy exerted on them. Jake took that for a sign. He leaped up, grabbed the far end of the curtain, and yanked it down and forward. Clink, clank, clank, clank. The plastic hooks snapped in rapid succession from back to front, like ripping open a shirt with snap buttons. When the curtain was free of the rod, he stepped forward and wrapped the end around Billy. Holding him with one arm, Jake used his other arm to sweep his legs out from under him, like he'd done to Walker's kids many times. Billy was bigger, but it still worked, and he fell into Jake's arms. He pulled Billy out of the bathtub.

Jake sat on the floor and tightly cradled Billy in his arms, rocking back and forth as he recited Psalm 23. After finishing with "I will dwell in the house of the Lord forever," he added, "Father, if it be thy will, please let me take this thorn from this boy's flesh. Please God, let his scars be my scars, let the pain these scars cause him be my pain, and let his demons be my demons. In the name of your Holy Son, Amen."

By the time he finished, Billy had become silent and unmoving, as though he'd been rocked to sleep. Jake had been holding his left palm flat against Billy's back, but a thin layer of plastic curtain separated flesh from flesh. He wondered if skin-to-skin contact might be crucial because he had felt nothing through the thin layer of plastic curtain. After his failure with Vincent's daughter, he doubted it would work, but Billy deserved his best effort. Maybe his being a child like Sarah would make the difference. He stopped rocking and lifted his left hand to Billy's neck. He placed the palm of his hand on the exposed skin at the back of his neck and slid it down beneath the curtain.

"Uuhhnn," Billy groaned but offered no resistance.

Jake rubbed Billy's back until he found the most concentrated area of scars. The skin felt as rough as alligator hide and had the consistency of vulcanized rubber. It was as unpleasant to the touch as it had been appalling to the eyes.

"Our Father which art in Heaven, hallowed be thy name," he recited, resuming the rocking as he began saying the Lord's prayer. After he finished with "deliver us from evil," he repeated his appeal for God to let him take Billy's scars.

When nothing happened again, Jake withdrew his hand and sat unmoving and completely silent. He relaxed his tight grip on Billy, but Billy made no move to free himself.

"I'm sorry," Jake finally said, "but it's not working."

After a brief silence, Billy asked, "What's not working?"

Jake told him the whole story about what happened to Sarah. He described her birth, her kind, innocent soul, and his great love for her. He told Billy about her brain tumor and how it had nearly killed her, but God had allowed him to draw that tumor from her brain into his. He explained the possible need for skin-to-skin contact to let the affliction pass between them.

"I took the tumor from her brain, and I had hoped to take the scars from your back, but it didn't work." Apologizing again for his failure, he said, "You still have the scars, but they're not a problem between us. I've seen them and touched them, and you don't have to hide them from me anymore."

Jake got up and set Billy on his feet. "I'll get your clothes," he said. "If you still want to leave, you can, but I hope you'll stay so I can rinse and dry your clothes. Nothing has changed between us."

When Billy didn't move or say anything, Jake had no choice but to get his clothes. He left the bathroom and picked up Billy's clothes off the washer. He hesitated, saying another short prayer to give Billy an extra minute to change his mind. When he returned to the bathroom, he was pleasantly surprised to see Billy pulling on the jogging pants.

"I'll just toss these in the washer," he said, indicating Billy's clothes. "If you're in a hurry, I can just run them through a rinse cycle, but if you've got time, I can do the regular wash and spin."

"We didn't spend much time fishing, so I've got time," Billy said, grinning sheepishly because it had been his fault that the fishing trip was cut short.

Everything happens for a reason.

Standing at the washer after putting Billy's clothes in, Jake thanked God for His tender mercies. *God truly works in mysterious ways,* he thought again. This incident had held the potential for disaster, but God had used it to bring him closer to Billy than years of casual friendship could have done.

CHAPTER 22

Connie was mentally and physically exhausted when she entered the apartment's front door. It had been a long, hard day. She brought dinner home from the restaurant because she was too tired to cook. Running from the law was stressful, but it was a much more frightening experience to be running from a murderous madman.

She'd hoped physical activity would give her tortured mind a rest, but it hadn't. She'd tried to avoid thinking about the life-changing questions, but they seemed to ambush her at odd moments. How long did she dare work here? Was it safer to stay in one place or keep moving? How could she hold any job to support them if they were constantly on the move? Would it help Billy to know that Stanley wasn't dead? Different permutations of those questions and others plagued her all day.

She had been settled in this job for over two months and was just beginning to feel safe. She had dared to dream about Billy starting the new school term, even imagining they might have found a normal life here. Then, two weeks ago, when Billy's nightmares worsened, dreams of a normal life started fading. Today, when she found out Stanley was alive and hunting them, her dreams of normalcy disappeared altogether. Her whole world became filled with foreboding and portents of danger.

When she was inside the apartment with the door locked behind her, she was so weary of the myriad questions that she wished she could just lie down and sleep. Sleep seemed so enticing because she had been getting so little lately. But its primary attraction was that it offered an escape from reality, and an escape from all the questions was what she yearned for at the moment.

She was mildly relieved to see Billy sitting in front of the TV. She worried about him spending too much time with the "boob tube" as his only companion, but today, that worry seemed trite and inconsequential. They were safe and together, and that was all that really mattered to her right now. Billy surprised her when he bounded from the floor to greet her with a hug. He was exuberant and full of life – a drastic change from the sullen mood he'd been in when she left this morning.

Curious, she asked, "Why are you so happy?"

Smiling for the first time today, she was pleased and energized by Billy's change in mood and spontaneous show of affection. Her dreams of normalcy were gone, but as long as she had Billy, she still had hope.

"No reason," Billy said, "I'm just glad to see you."

Even though she couldn't interpret his emotions as readily as she once could, Connie knew her son was in a strange mood. He was becoming secretive, but she didn't have the energy to call him on it today. Instead, she decided to harbor a secret of her own. She would pretend that her day had been routine as usual, unspoiled by the earth-shattering news about Stanley. Billy wasn't troubled by the danger Stanley posed in his nightmares for the moment, and the overwhelming news of the real-life threat the not-dead Stanley posed could wait.

Despite her secret about Stanley and Billy's strange mood, the evening passed more happily than they had known for a long time. She noticed he had little appetite, but the meal was enjoyable. Afterward, they played a board game and finished the evening by making popcorn and watching TV together. It wasn't until bedtime came that the threat reasserted itself.

If the previous night was any indication, tonight held a potential for physical injury in addition to the usual terror. He could fall out of bed and break something. She needed to stay awake and listen so that she could interrupt the nightmare before it could progress into the more dangerous physical stage.

*****

Billy had beaten his mother home, and he was glad to see her when she came through the door. He was feeling guilty about the wonderful day he'd spent with Jake, as though what he was feeling double-crossed her, and he owed her a hug. He desperately wanted to tell her about his new friend. He wanted her to know about Jake and the knife and the dream in which they helped him banish Stanley. He wanted to tell her about falling into the river and talk about what happened in Jake's apartment. Being held by Jake had seemed natural and peaceful, stirring emotions that were new and beyond his understanding.

However, Billy couldn't talk about these things with his mother because he intended to return to Jake's apartment the following day after she went to work. If she knew about it, she would surely forbid it. She had repeatedly told him that she would never allow another man to come into their lives. He was afraid she might decide to pack up and leave without even meeting Jake, choosing to avoid the man rather than risk another Richard or Stanley fiasco. How could he make her understand that Jake was nothing like those two men?

While they'd been sitting on the riverbank, Billy worried about his wet, muddy clothes. He might be able to crawl through the window and remove his filthy clothes without making too much of a mess, but it would be impossible to keep his mother from noticing the clothes in the laundry. She would start asking questions and wouldn't stop until he told her everything. He'd be lucky if he were allowed out of her sight again before he was twenty-one. So, when Jake announced plan B, Billy accepted with only minor trepidation.

The main source of his apprehension was that if Jake knew his secrets, he might stop liking him. He worried about keeping the scars on his back hidden and didn't want Jake to see him climbing through his bedroom window. He felt drawn to Jake and didn't get the slightest bad vibe from him. He didn't know why Jake had singled him out, but he liked the attention and didn't want his secrets to bring that to an end.

He'd panicked when he saw Jake staring at him from the bathroom doorway. But it wasn't his physical safety that concerned him. He feared what Jake must be thinking. When Stanley saw his back, he laughed and taunted him scornfully. He could only imagine how much more painful those taunts would be coming from Jake. He had demanded his clothes out of self-defense, wanting nothing more than to get out of there before Jake could mock him and throw him out.

However, Jake proved he was different. The only time he'd willingly gone anywhere alone with Stanley was last year when he tagged along on a hunting trip, and it had been such a disaster that he'd tried to block it from his mind. Stanley had been cruel, taking pleasure in the pain he could inflict on any living creature, but he didn't see any evidence of that in Jake. After getting over the shock of being pulled from the bathtub, being cradled in Jake's arms felt strangely comforting.

When Jake let him go, he said nothing had changed between them, but everything had changed for Billy. Jake had changed his whole world, adding a dimension to his life he'd never known existed. He had imagined that no man would ever care about him, but Jake did, and Jake was as magical as the knife. The story about the little girl proved that.

Jake was like Superman. He was everything Billy wanted to be when he grew up. Jake intrigued him, but what impacted him most was that Jake obviously and sincerely *liked* him. The prayers and the story about the little girl were awesome. Jake couldn't take away the scars, but more importantly, he didn't mock and wasn't repelled by them.

Billy tried to act the way his mother would expect. He wasn't hungry so soon after eating pizza at Jake's, but he ate as much as he could. He knew she was withholding something, but he couldn't risk questioning her for fear that she would question him. He ate popcorn and watched TV while thinking about seeing Jake again. He went to bed looking forward to tomorrow but couldn't go to sleep because he couldn't stop reliving today.

*****

As soon as Billy was gone, the apartment seemed empty and lifeless, like a deserted stadium after a championship game. Sitting alone on the couch, Jake began thinking about what he and Billy might do tomorrow. Going fishing and returning to watch TV was appealing, but he wondered if Billy could ever fully enjoy fishing. The kid was terrified of the water, and that terror was what was dangerous, not the water.

Billy had come out of the bathroom and curled up on the couch, wearing Jake's oversized sweatpants and shirt, like a baby wrapped in swaddling clothes. That image reminded Jake why he had actively sought to befriend this kid. He needed to find out everything he could, and to do that, he required Billy's trust. Fortunately, the accidental discovery of the scars on the boy's back went a long way in that regard.

"I won't ask you a lot of questions or pry into your business," Jake said as soon as Billy was settled on the couch, "but if you need anything, all you have to do is ask."

They sat on the couch and talked until a pizza arrived. They had many likes in common, including their favorite drink and what was on their pizza. They'd watched TV while eating a meat lovers' pizza and drinking Cokes. Billy fell asleep in the middle of his third slice and had drifted sideways, coming to rest in the crook of Jake's arm. Jake had let him sleep until he became concerned about the shoes in the oven.

When Jake moved, Billy had awakened and was immediately concerned about the time. He was worried about getting home late. He had gone out the door within minutes, dressed in dry clothes and oven-warmed shoes. He thanked Jake for the pizza and asked if he could return the following day.

Jake had been mildly disappointed that Billy still refused to let him drive him home, but he could hardly blame the boy under the circumstances. What kind of monstrous mother must he have to have administered such malicious beatings? And the scars were surely evidence of medical neglect. Even if she were faultless in that regard, how could she allow such a young kid to roam the streets alone?

After thinking about Billy's fear of water, he decided on an activity for tomorrow that would be as much fun for him as it would benefit Billy. Still, much would depend on finding the right accessories. He left the apartment in a rush, happy to be going on a mission. He had to find the right swimsuit. Ordinary swimming trunks wouldn't do because Billy would never agree to go shirtless. He needed to find a swimsuit that would cover him from elbows to knees.

He found what he was looking for in the clothing department of Walmart, but when he questioned a saleslady about alterations, she sent him in a whole different direction. She suggested he look at biking outfits. They had just received a large shipment and came in the knee and arm lengths he desired. Jake found the shorts and jerseys, but all the salespeople in Sporting Goods were less than helpful men. He returned to the saleslady and asked her for assistance. She was accommodating, and after he approximated Billy's height and weight, she made an experienced guess at the sizes he would need.

Next, he looked for a public swimming pool. The river was a choice of last resort. It would be more fun in a cleaner, safer environment with other people engaged in the same recreation. He could get a room in a hotel with a swimming pool, but he really wanted a public facility where he and Billy could share relative privacy within a crowd.

He finally located a public pool within fifteen minutes of his apartment. It was already closed for the day, but the sign informed him it would reopen at ten o'clock the next morning. He returned to his apartment, satisfied with his accomplishments and looking forward to tomorrow.

Jake thought about Billy's scars and how modern technology made most unsightly scars a thing of the past. Plastic surgery and skin grafts could now erase most disfigurements. In Billy's case, the extensive work that would be necessary might ordinarily be cost-prohibitive, but Jake's life wasn't ordinary.

Your life is about to become as strange as a Dean Koontz novel.

Besides a few major purchases and everyday living expenses, he had millions of dollars and didn't know what he was supposed to do with it. Before he tried to go to sleep, he made a promise to himself. Whether or not Billy was God's third and final incarnation in the flesh, he would allocate whatever funds were necessary to erase those scars from his back. It pleased him that he'd found such a worthy cause.

Everything happens for a reason.

*****

Stanley couldn't sleep. He lay awake in the hotel room just off Interstate 77 at the Mt. Airy, North Carolina exit. His sleeplessness was caused by thoughts of what the morning would bring. His mind was churning with one fantasy after another. He was going to kill his wife and her son, but that would be the reality, not the fantasy. What fueled his excitement and inflamed his libidinous thoughts was the myriad ways by which their deaths could be accomplished. The more pain, the better. He planned on having as much fun as time and circumstances allowed.

Time was the most restricting factor. If not for the necessity of returning before a protracted absence could become an issue, he could create his own circumstances. But, as it was, his nearest neighbor and recent confidant, Marge Zimmerman, might become suspicious if he was gone on a trip at the time his wife was killed. He needed to minimize her suspicion. He needed to return home and phone Marge on his landline, worriedly asking for any new information about his recalcitrant wife. He needed to secure the old biddy as an ally before the discovery of the bodies could turn her into a gossip-spreading enemy.

Marge was a nosey busybody, and he detested having anything to do with her, but she could start vicious gossip about him that might get back to his brother, and he couldn't risk that. He had called Marge several times over the past few months, and each time he'd talked to her, she had become less helpful and more inquisitive. He was second-guessing the wisdom of enlisting her aid and drawing her attention to his business when it had unexpectedly paid off this morning.

Marge had called, excited by her news. She had just gotten off the phone with his wife. He had allowed Marge to go on and on about every detail of his wife's call, but he'd stopped listening long before she'd run out of words. Interestingly, his wife had said nothing about the incident that put him in the hospital and her on the run with her son. More importantly, she had said nothing about his business. His contrived story about the argument and his horrible car wreck remained intact.

Although he'd pretended to need to hear about his wife, he lost interest as soon as he learned the exact time of the phone call. After he finally managed to graciously extricate himself from the conversation, he hung up and made several more phone calls. By early afternoon, through his brother's connections with the phone company, he had learned the call came from a cell phone that wasn't immediately turned off. They determined the phone had been stationary for several hours in a restaurant in North Carolina. He knew the instant he got that information that he'd found her. She had been working in a restaurant in Cleveland when he found her the first time.

A week after Wayne's death, Stanley hired two men he'd previously employed in Cleveland. They were brothers, and he didn't hire them because it took two men to replace Wayne. He hired the two of them because they came as a package deal. They were both equally competent killers, but Carl, the younger of the two, was slow-witted and largely dependent upon his older brother, George.

Stanley had two problems – Jake McCallum and his wife. He had been told to lay off McCallum after he'd been bought off, but he had no intention of doing that. McCallum had gone on a trip but would be back sooner or later. Until then, finding his wife was his top priority.

He was so confident she would be employed at that restaurant that he hadn't waited for confirmation. That would have involved a risk of alerting her, and since Marge had told her that she'd been talking to him, any little suspicion might cause her to rabbit. He didn't want to get down there just to find she was gone again. It had been nearly four o'clock before they got on the road, and it had taken almost six hours to reach the hotel.

He was formulating his plans on the way, and when they stopped for dinner, he called the restaurant to find out what time it opened in the morning. He had a few hours to kill, so he stopped at the hotel for a bit of rest. He wanted to arrive at the restaurant at least an hour before it opened. He planned to grab her before she entered the restaurant and force her to return to wherever she and the boy were staying.

First, he would retrieve his books and whatever money was left from his safe, and then, after a couple of hours of fun, he would leave them dead. He would hurry home before their bodies were discovered and create an alibi with Marge. If circumstances permitted, he would leave them alive – but just barely – and return home with Carl, leaving George to let them suffer until they were dead before flying home.

After nearly an hour of daydreaming about what he would do to his wife and her son, Stanley decided that the most entertaining scenario was to make his wife watch while he finished what he'd started with her son. Finally, he forced himself to stop thinking, clear his mind, and sleep. George and Carl were in the next room, and he was sure they were already sleeping like babies. He sometimes envied stupid people. All of their gratifications were in the here and now, rarely wasting time dwelling on the past, and too simple-minded to worry about making plans for the future.

CHAPTER 23

Connie awoke to the sound of the alarm clock. She was surprised that she'd slept soundly throughout the night. The last thing she remembered was lying awake, ears attuned to the bedroom. No sound from the bedroom had awakened her, but suddenly, she had a vague sense of danger and impending doom. She rushed to the bedroom door and threw it open.

Fearing the worst, she stared at Billy's still form under the sheet and, for a horrifying moment, imagined he wasn't breathing. Rushing to his bedside, she placed a hand on his forehead, and euphoria flooded through her when she felt the heat of life on his face. A loud exhalation startled her, but she was giddy with relief when she realized it had come from her. She hadn't realized she'd been holding her breath.

"Mom?" Billy said, sitting up, rubbing his eyes in the blinding glare of the overhead light. "What's wrong?"

"Nothing, honey," she said, embracing him lovingly. "Are you okay? How did you sleep?"

After Billy assured her he'd slept well and felt good, she went to the kitchen to fix breakfast. She didn't understand it. She had also slept well and felt good, so why wasn't she happy? Fear and foreboding clung to her like an offensive odor as she tried to shake off the malevolent premonition.

They ate silently, him quiet and her preoccupied with thoughts of Stanley. There was no way he could find them, she decided. Their new identification would keep them safe. She'd called Marge from an unregistered cell phone, and there was no way Marge could get her location from her Caller ID. But Connie still couldn't shake the feeling that something was wrong. Reason argued safety, but her intuition screamed danger.

When she was ready to leave for work, Billy was sitting in front of the TV as usual, but he had already gotten dressed for the day. Sometimes, he would still be in his pajamas when she came home in the evening. She thought it was an encouraging sign that he was fully dressed. Because of her sense of impending danger, she didn't want to leave him alone, but she also didn't want to lose her job. She planned to ask for a few days off, and if she could begin that time off immediately, she would be back in about thirty minutes. She'd decided what she would do but didn't have time to discuss it with Billy. There would be plenty of time for that when she returned.

She left the apartment with cautious optimism, feeling better after having made some decisions. She would get a few days off, and during that time, she would write a letter to Stanley in which she would promise to forget about him if he forgot about her and Billy. She would include a separate letter to acknowledge she had no intention of ever coming home. He could take that to a lawyer and get a no-fault divorce. She would pack those letters in a bundle with his books, but she wouldn't mention the money since she'd already spent most of it. She would mail the package to Stanley, and she could only hope he would stop looking for them and leave them alone.

She was fully absorbed in her thoughts as she approached the restaurant door. She was trying to figure out how far she should travel by bus before mailing the package and how many days she would need to take off from work. She hadn't noticed the man standing on the sidewalk in front of the restaurant. He had been casually leaning against the building, but as she was about to pass in front of him, he stepped forward to block her path. She still wasn't fully aware of his intentions until she tried to sidestep him, and he moved to block her again.

When she realized she was in danger, she turned to run, but the man grabbed her arm. A big black car screeched to the curb, and the back door was flung open. The man shoved her through the door and followed in after her. Another man was already in the back seat, and he helped drag her in. She nearly fainted when she recognized the second man.

The driver pulled away from the curb. After a few minutes, he turned a corner and pulled to the curb again, apparently waiting for instructions.

"Where's the kid?" Stanley demanded. "Where're my money and books?" He slapped her hard across the face with the palm of his hand without waiting for an answer.

She howled in pain and crouched in the corner of the rear-facing seat behind the driver of the Stretch Limo, trying to get as far away from Stanley as possible.

The man who had followed her into the car took her pocketbook and began rummaging through it. Within a few minutes, he found her keys and an old paystub with her address.

Stanley didn't take his eyes off her. He watched her cry, thoroughly enjoying her pain.

The man brusquely tossed the purse back at her. He read the address aloud.

"Find it!" Stanley commanded.

Connie started sobbing more quietly into her hands. He pulled her toward him, drew back, and slapped her again to renew the pain. Although he mainly connected with the backs of her hands, her head snapped back with the force of the blow, and the pain started her howling again.

The address was only a few blocks from the restaurant, but they circled several blocks before finding the right street. When they stopped, the driver jumped out, hurried to the apartment building, and held the door open.

Stanley didn't immediately make her get out of the car. He held her in place as he quietly scolded her, warning her of the dire consequences to her son if she attracted attention.

Aside from the occasional passing car, this street was relatively deserted. As Stanley held her by the wrist and continuously shushed her, he pulled her out of the car while the other man followed closely behind, forcing her to keep moving. Stanley wrapped one arm around her shoulders, hurried her through the door, and hustled her up the stairs.

Connie became quiet and cooperative when she saw the driver go into her apartment. She needed to hurry after him. She had been stupid and careless for having been found so quickly and trapped so easily. Evidently, he'd found a way to trace her phone call, but the only thing she could think of right now was to get to Billy before these burly men could hurt him.

As soon as they were inside the apartment with the door closed, the driver, Carl, she would later learn, returned from a cursory search of the premises.

"Nobody here," he reported.

When Stanley looked at her, her perplexity showed on her face. She had expected Billy to be here.

"Search every inch," Stanley commanded, throwing her onto the couch.

She began sobbing again when she landed, silently scolding herself for failing to think quickly enough to invent some other place Billy might have gone. He must have found a hiding place in the small apartment, and she had just ensured that they would search until they found him.

"Nobody here," the driver reported again when he returned to the living room.

"It looks like he was here," the other man said as he came out of the bedroom, "but he's gone now. The bedroom window is raised a little, and the rooftop of the next building is pretty close. He must've gone out that way."

Connie was temporarily relieved by the news. Somehow, Billy must have seen them coming and gone out the window. She was thrilled he'd had the presence of mind to escape. She was happy he wasn't here, but simultaneously, she feared what might happen to him all alone on the street.

*****

Jake came out of the bathroom and stopped when he thought he heard an unusual noise in the hallway. He quietly retrieved his service revolver from the bedroom and went to the front door. He eased the door open, inspecting the hallway while keeping the weapon concealed behind the doorframe.

"Billy?" Jake said when he saw the boy sitting on the stairs. "Why didn't you knock?"

"I didn't want to wake you," Billy said as he got up and started toward the door. "I know it's still kind of early."

"I wasn't asleep," Jake said, "but even if I were, I wouldn't have minded if you woke me. Come on in."

Jake left the door open as he returned the gun to his bedroom. When he returned to the living room, the door was closed, and Billy sat on the couch. Jake tossed him the TV remote and said, "I'm going to get some coffee. You want something to drink?"

"Coke," Billy said, turning on the TV.

When Jake returned with his coffee and Billy's coke, he sat down beside Billy and watched TV. When his coffee was gone, he stood up and got a wad of keys out of his pocket.

"I was planning on going to McDonald's for breakfast," he said. "You hungry?"

"No," Billy said. "I already had breakfast."

"Then I'll just pick up something at the drive-through window and bring it back here," Jake said. "You can go with me or stay here and watch TV."

"Doesn't matter to me," Billy said nonchalantly.

"Then come along," Jake said. "I like your company."

Billy bounded off the couch, obviously happy to be going. They were back in the apartment within twenty minutes. Billy hadn't wanted anything, but Jake got two breakfasts, anyway. Billy looked malnourished, and he was concerned the boy might not be getting enough to eat.

After they finished breakfast – and Jake was pleased to see that Billy had eaten nearly half of his – they cleaned up their garbage and returned to the living room. In companionable silence, they watched one of Jake's favorite old TV shows, *Little House on the Prairie*. When it went off, it was ten o'clock, but Jake hadn't yet broached the subject of swimming with Billy because he was sure Billy wouldn't be thrilled with the idea.

"What shall we do today?" Jake asked, taking an indirect approach.

Billy seemed to consider the question seriously before suggesting, "We could go fishing."

Jake nodded in agreement and said, "We could, except you and the river don't play well together." Grinning, he added, "We might end up swimming again." Then, in a tone that suggested he thought it was a great idea, he asked, "Why don't we skip the fishing and just go swimming?"

"I don't know," Billy said hesitantly.

Jake placed a hand on Billy's shoulder and felt gratified when the boy didn't shrug away.

"Do you trust me, Billy?" he asked, looking him straight in the eyes.

Billy nodded his head without the slightest hesitation.

"I won't hurt you," Jake promised, "and as much as it is within my power, I won't let you get hurt. Do you believe me?"

"Yes," Billy said happily.

"Will you let me teach you to swim?" Jake asked.

"Yes," Billy eagerly responded.

"Good," Jake said, "I'll be right back." He went into the bedroom and got the swimwear he'd gotten for Billy. "Go in the bathroom and try these on," he said, handing the biking shorts and long-tailed jersey to Billy.

Billy turned them over and over in his hands. He didn't get up or say anything.

"The pool's opening about now," Jake said. "As soon as you're ready, we'll go."

"Pool?" Billy questioned. "I thought you meant the river. I don't want to go where other people will see me."

"Feel the material," Jake said. "It's thick. Even when it's wet, you won't be able to see through it."

He rubbed the fabric between his thumb and forefinger to demonstrate.

Billy still didn't move or say anything.

"I know you're ashamed of those scars," Jake said, "so I picked this material with that in mind. When I meet your mother, I want to talk to her about plastic surgery."

"Mom said surgery would cost too much," Billy said.

Jake wasn't surprised it had at least been considered. He had seen how extensive the scarring was and could understand that the number of surgeries required would be very expensive. "You let me worry about that," he said. "It won't be a problem. The only thing I'll need is your mom's permission."

Billy's eyes became glassy, and he jumped up and ran to the bathroom, taking the shorts and jersey with him. Jake could only wait and see what the boy would do.

"Everything all right in there?" Jake yelled toward the bathroom after several minutes of silence. He was about to get up and check on Billy when he heard the bathroom door open. Billy came timidly into the living room.

"Turn around," Jake said, twirling his index finger in the air. After Billy made a quick rotation, Jake said, "That looks great, and it's nearly a perfect fit."

The shirt sleeves extended to his elbows, and the shorts extended to his knees.

"I look like a geek," Billy said.

"That was the style back in the 1920s," Jake said. "It looks good on you."

Jake had anticipated that objection and found a few pictures in magazines to show Billy. This swimwear did resemble those pictures from a bygone era when it was unfashionable to show more flesh than necessary.

"You can just wear it, and I'll put extra towels in my bag. You won't have to change again until we get back."

"They'll laugh," Billy protested. "Everybody will laugh at me."

"Who cares if they laugh?" Jake said dismissively. "I'm not laughing."

"Yeah, but you're different," Billy said.

"It'll be all right," Jake promised, moved by the compliment. "You'll never see any of those people again. Besides," he added as he turned toward the bedroom to get his bag, "you won't be the only one there dressed like that."

Billy relented without further objection. When they entered the parking lot at the pool, the day's festivities were already in full swing. Although the lot was crowded, Jake lucked into a spot just being vacated near the entrance. High-pitched squeals of youthful laughter punctuated the rambunctious racket coming from the people in the pool area.

Since Billy didn't need to change, Jake took him into the pool area and showed him where to wait. He told him he could sit on the edge and put his feet in the water if he liked, but he couldn't go in until Jake returned.

"Five minutes," Jake said as he headed toward the dressing rooms, knowing he would have to hurry because he could feel Billy's discomfort. The kid had already drawn several stares.

After changing, Jake stepped through the door and looked toward where he'd left Billy, but he couldn't locate him until he turned to close the door. Billy was standing against the wall. Jake took the towels off his shoulder and extended both arms straight out from his sides.

"Ta-dah," Jake said. Except for the difference in size, Jake was wearing a swimsuit identical to Billy's.

Billy laughed, and Jake was pleased by his look of relief and approval. He playfully tossed one of the towels in his face and said, "Come on, let's get wet."

Jake shook out his towel and slung it over the chain-link fence surrounding the pool area's concrete apron. Billy followed Jake's lead, jumping several times before he managed to get his towel hanging beside Jake's on the high fence.

Jake went to the nearest steps that led down into the water and demonstrated the safe, proper way of entering. They were at the shallow end, and the water wasn't quite up to Jake's waist. He backed away a few steps and beckoned Billy to join him.

"Trust me," he encouraged when Billy hesitated.

Billy eased himself down the steps, entering the water. When Billy's feet touched the bottom, Jake placed a steadying hand on his shoulder. Just as Jake had expected, nobody was paying any attention to them. After a few initial stares and whispered comments, everybody returned their attention to the water and their own activities.

Jake had never taught anybody to swim, but when he realized Billy trusted him more than he feared the water, he knew Billy had already conquered the most significant obstacle to swimming. Jake started with the most essential, fundamental rule: hold your breath when your face is in the water. Billy was an apt pupil, and soon he was swimming underwater. Next, he was dog paddling, and eventually, he began swimming on top of the water. He even seemed to be enjoying himself. They'd been at it for over two hours before Jake called for a break.

When they climbed out of the water and started toward their towels, Jake positioned himself so that Billy would be walking near the edge of the pool. After only a few steps, Jake pointed toward the other side of the pool and said, "What's that?" When Billy turned his head to look, Jake pushed him, sending him toppling into the water.

"Aaiiee," Billy said as he fell, but this time, it wasn't loud and more a cry of surprise than a shriek of terror.

Jake stepped forward and leaped over where Billy had landed, executing an about-face in mid-air before touching the water. He kept his feet under him as he landed, standing just behind Billy. He watched as Billy floundered for a few seconds and then stood up, wiping water and hair from his eyes while searching the poolside for Jake.

Jake stepped up behind him and put his arms around Billy.

"Congratulations," he said, "you passed. You're ready for the deeper water."

A lifeguard's whistle sounded, and a youthful voice came over a megaphone. "No jumping off the sides!"

Jake acknowledged the warning with a wave.

"Quit jumping off the side," he said playfully to Billy. "You're going to get us in trouble."

They laughed happily as they climbed back out of the water. This time, they retrieved their towels and sat on a bench, each obviously enjoying the perfect day.

After ten minutes, Jake asked, "Are you about ready to go back in?" as though Billy had been the one who called for the break. Jake was painfully aware he wasn't a kid anymore and couldn't maintain constant motion like Billy.

They went to the deeper water, and Jake patiently showed Billy how to tread water, stop, and then start again. Billy caught on fast, swimming like a duck born to water. After a while, Jake called for another break and suggested they get something to drink. They climbed out and started toward the snack bar.

Billy pointed to the other side of the pool and said, "Look!"

This time, Jake was the one near the edge of the pool. He instantly recognized Billy's ploy. He was accustomed to making snap decisions, and options flashed through his mind even as he turned his head and anticipated Billy's push. He knew he could resist the push, and neither would go in the water. He could turn an awkward fall into a smooth dive, use Billy's momentum against him and throw him into the water, or allow the push and drag Billy in. He chose none of those options.

Instead, in the spirit of fun, Jake allowed himself to be pushed, and he made a sound of surprise as he windmilled his arms, trying to regain his balance. He hit the water with a loud splash, and while underwater, he heard a "sploosh" near him and knew Billy had followed him in. He surfaced, turned in the direction of the sound, and waited.

Billy's head broke the surface, and his face was turned toward Jake. As Billy brushed water and hair from his face with both hands, Jake caught a glimpse of another countenance commingled with Billy's features. It was so quick that it might have been imagined, but it triggered a wave of love. One thing became crystal clear: he'd found who he'd been seeking. This was the boy the preacher had implored him to find.

Billy laughed, obviously delighted with thinking he'd turned the tables on Jake, who feigned indignation as he splashed water at Billy. Their horseplay was interrupted by another blast of the lifeguard's whistle.

"You two, out of the water for one hour," the lifeguard ordered over the megaphone from his lofty perch. "One more infraction," he added with as much authority as his youthful voice allowed, "and you'll be banned for the day."

As they climbed out of the water, Jake still pretended to be seriously annoyed with Billy.

"See what you did? You got us in trouble," he accused, laughing as he playfully grabbed Billy in a headlock.

Billy laughed as he tried to free himself, obviously enjoying the roughhousing.

When Jake noticed they were directly under the watchful stare of an already aggrieved lifeguard, he whispered conspiratorially into Billy's ear, "Cool it, the lifeguard's watching." He released Billy, careful to not cause him to fall.

"I'm hungry," Billy announced.

"Well, thanks to you," Jake said with a chuckle, "we have some time to kill. I could go for a hot dog."

They laughed as they walked away from the water's edge. Jake pulled Billy close again and casually draped his arm around his shoulders.

When they reached the snack bar, they took their place at the end of a long line. As they moved a few steps toward the window, Jake realized he would need to pay for whatever they got. He left Billy standing in line while he went to get money from his clothes. When he returned, Billy was near the front of the line, so he gave him the money and told him what he wanted. He perched on the end of the nearest unoccupied picnic table where he could keep an eye on Billy.

A big man came to the snack bar, stopped to survey the crowd, and apparently decided he was entitled to go to the front of the line. He moved directly to the concession window, pushing others aside whenever necessary. The crowd grumbled and complained, but nobody tried to stop him. The man was slightly over six feet and probably weighed over 250 pounds. His belly hung over his skimpy trunks, and the grossness of the overall effect made Jake wish the 1920s style of swimwear was mandatory.

Jake didn't like the guy pushing everybody around, but he was determined to mind his own business. He didn't move from his perch until he saw the man roughly shove Billy out of his way. Jake was off the table like a shot and at Billy's side. He poked his finger into the back of the brute's shoulder. When the big man turned around, Jake angrily objected to his actions.

"That's my kid you're shoving around."

CHAPTER 24

Connie worked herself into a nervous wreck, scared out of her wits one minute and grasping at a glimmer of hope the next. Stanley took one of his men out to search for Billy twice, and they came back empty-handed both times. She was happy when they returned without him the first time, but she felt disappointed the second. She was glad he wasn't there, but she was also worried *because* he wasn't there. She didn't know what might be happening to him.

As far as she knew, Billy had never set foot outside the apartment alone during their whole time living there. He couldn't know the immediate neighborhood, much less what lay beyond. Was it possible that two catastrophes could have struck at the same time? Could someone have come in the window and forced him out? Since they were on the second floor, she'd never paid any attention at all to that window.

Stanley hadn't physically assaulted her since it appeared they weren't going to find Billy. She believed Stanley was concerned that Billy might bring the police there. She'd spent hours trying to decide on her best strategy if the police did show up. By early evening, she was happy Billy still hadn't shown up, but she was despondent that the Police hadn't either.

*****

Jake struggled to control his anger. Seeing bullies in action always pissed him off, but in this case, it wasn't his distaste for bullies that had propelled him off the table. He'd brought Billy here, and that alone made him responsible for him, but the fact that he promised Billy he would neither hurt him nor let him get hurt added another layer to that responsibility. But he didn't recognize the primary source of his anger until he'd heard himself declare how he felt about the kid. He'd said, "That's my kid," and instantly realized he loved the boy.

The big man turned and frowned, laughing derisively as he looked Jake and Billy up and down.

"If I've ever seen a couple of pansies," he said, "it's you two." Taking a step toward Jake, he placed his right hand on Jake's chest and said, "Maybe you'd rather I pushed you."

Jake had hoped for anonymity in the middle of a large crowd, but at the same time, he realized how they were dressed was bound to make them stand out from the crowd to some degree. The lifeguard's whistle had sounded many times, and he'd issued many warnings to other people, but their unique swimwear was likely why he'd easily identified them as two-time offenders. However, he hadn't expected their swimwear to make them look like easy targets to an overgrown bully.

With practiced ease, Jake placed his left hand on top of the big man's hand and gripped it. He pulled it away from his chest, simultaneously twisting the hand toward the man while bending it down on his wrist. At the same time, he took a half-step into the big guy and cupped his elbow in his right hand, completing what the police academy instructor had called a "gooseneck" hold. Its effectiveness depended entirely on a judicious application of force to the hand bent down on the wrist.

Several times, the man balled his meaty left hand and attempted to swing, but Jake increased the pressure each time until the hand dropped back to his side. Too little or too much pressure would have allowed him to complete his swing. However, the right amount of pressure partially paralyzed the other muscles, giving them a minimal range of movement.

After several minutes, Jake spoke to the man quietly through clenched teeth, not attempting to conceal his anger or disguise his contempt.

"You will apologize," Jake threateningly whispered, "or I'm going to rip this arm off and beat you with it."

The man grunted as a new shock of pain coursed through his right arm. After a few more minutes, his hostility, aggressiveness, and macho pride suddenly deserted him.

"Okay, okay," he said, "I'm sorry."

"Not to me," Jake said, "to the boy and the other people you shoved."

"I'm sorry," he said, looking at Billy. Turning his head toward the crowd, he repeated louder, "I'm sorry."

Jake released the hold and took a couple of steps backward.

"You broke it," the man complained, straightening his right arm and gingerly cradling it in his left.

"It's not broken," Jake assured him. "It'll be fine in ten or fifteen minutes." He waited for the man to declare his intentions, but after a few minutes of nothing but complaining from him, Jake said, "If you want to continue this discussion outside of the pool area, I would be happy to oblige. I can wait until you get feeling back in that arm."

The big man didn't look up. Still cradling his right arm, he ducked his head and walked away.

"Go ahead and get the food," Jake said to Billy. "I'll be back in a few minutes."

Jake followed the man close enough that he had to know he was there. He knew that as much as bullies liked to inflict pain and cause embarrassment to others, they lived in mortal fear of that same thing happening to them. He expected the threat from this man to be over, but he wanted to make sure. He followed him into the building, and after the man claimed his clothes and went into a dressing room, Jake returned to the snack bar.

By the time he returned, Billy was paying for their food, and he helped carry it to a table. After Jake said the blessing, they started eating their identical snacks without talking. After several minutes, Jake became concerned about Billy's silence. He was aware that Billy was sneaking peeks at him while he was eating. He tried to engage him in conversation several times, but Billy seemed preoccupied. Jake knew some people couldn't easily process violence, and he was concerned about what the altercation at the snack bar might have done to Billy.

Their penalty out of the water was nearly expired, but it was getting late. He hadn't intended to keep Billy at the pool so long, but now he was reluctant to leave. They had been having such a wonderful day, and he didn't want the confrontation with the bully to be the context in which Billy remembered this outing.

"You want to go back in the water?" Jake asked to gauge Billy's mood.

"Sure," Billy said immediately and enthusiastically.

As they headed toward the water, Billy became as energetic and playful as he had been before the incident at the snack bar. Jake was glad to see that the violence hadn't been so overwhelming as to end their fun.

"Let's try the diving board," Jake suggested.

"I can't dive," Billy thought it necessary to remind Jake.

"Can't never did do nothing," Jake quipped. "Just follow me and do what I do."

He got in line for the low diving board, and Billy willingly and happily stuck close to him. As they moved up the line, Jake explained what they would do.

"You're not supposed to jump off the sides of the pool or the sides of the diving board," Jake explained, "but you can go off the end of the board any way you want. This first time, we'll walk out and just step off the end of the board. Watch me and do what I do, okay?"

Billy nodded. When it was Jake's turn, he walked to the end of the board, turned sideways, and side-stepped off. He came up facing the near side of the pool and, with a few easy strokes, made it to the side. He put one hand up on the ledge and turned to see Billy standing on the end of the board.

"Come on," Jake called encouragingly. "I'll be here to help if you have any trouble."

Billy had stopped, but after Jake's encouragement, he turned sideways and side-stepped off the board without hesitation, just as Jake had done. He made it to Jake's side without the slightest difficulty. Jake pulled himself onto the side of the pool and extended a hand to Billy.

When they were both sitting on the side of the pool, Jake said, "You did great. You want to do it again?"

"Yeah," Billy said eagerly, "that's fun."

Jake was having a great time, too. He'd always loved this about being with Jimmy and Walker's kids. He could experience the world anew through their eyes. Right now he felt like the world held great potential for fun and adventure, like the freedom of running wildly through the mountains. He was experiencing companionship, contagious laughter, and the perfect combination of sun and water.

When he noticed the time on the clock mounted on the building, he snagged Billy's arm as he hurried toward the diving board for the umpteenth time.

"It's getting late," Jake said, pointing at the clock. "We'd better be going soon."

Billy glanced at the clock and said, "Okay, just one more time."

Upon leaving, when Jake came out of the dressing area, Billy stood by the door, scowling at two little girls walking away.

"Those girls," Billy said, "keep laughing at me."

"They're just flirting with you," Jake said. "They think you're cute." When Billy continued to scowl, Jake added, "I think you're cute, too. Come on, let's go."

When they'd been in the car for several minutes, Jake noticed Billy reverting to silence again. "You have fun today?" he asked.

"Sure," Billy said offhandedly and returned to silence.

It felt like the same silence as when they were eating, but this time, Jake was sure it had nothing to do with the violence.

"Anything wrong?" he asked.

"No, I had a great time," Billy said, and in almost the same breath, he blurted out, "Are you married, Jake?"

"Nope," Jake said. When Billy didn't say more, Jake added, "Some people might say I never made the same mistake once."

"Do you want to get married?" Billy asked, the words rushing out of his mouth as he looked hopefully at Jake.

Jake gave him a severe, appraising look. "You are cute," he said, "but you're a little short for me."

Billy laughed. "I mean my mom," he snickered.

"I suppose I'd have to meet her first," Jake said pointedly.

"Oh, you'll like her," Billy promised. He added more seriously, "She cooks really good, and she hardly ever snores."

Jake laughed happily at that naïve, unsolicited testimonial. He loved how young minds worked. They'd had a great day together; now, it became an amusing ride home.

At Billy's suggestion, they went back to Jake's apartment so he could change clothes. Then, the plan was for Jake to take him home and meet his mother. However, after he changed clothes,

Billy abruptly altered that plan.

"Are you sure I can't take you home?" Jake asked again as Billy was about to go out the door.

"Mom will already be mad when I get home," Billy said. "I'd better tell her you're coming first."

*****

Billy wanted Jake to take him home and meet his mother, but while changing his clothes in Jake's apartment, he imagined what it would be like when they met. Not being in Jake's presence to bolster his picture-perfect image of Jake and his mother together, his fantasy collided with reality. His mother would be mad at him for going out the window. At first, he'd imagined Jake would help calm her anger, but what if she did accuse Jake of being a bad influence? What if her anger made her say things that caused him to hate her?

He decided that surprising her with Jake might not be such a good idea. It might be better if she was prepared. She should cook a big meal and get all dressed up. He wasn't sure why those things mattered, but he'd gotten the idea from TV and movies that they did. He decided it would be best to face his mother's wrath alone. He told Jake he would talk to her and find out when Jake could come to dinner.

Billy left Jake's place in high spirits. He was nearly halfway home when his high spirits began to fade. He couldn't account for the change, but his bad feelings were becoming stronger the closer he got to his apartment. The world seemed to lose color, and the air became stagnant. His pace slowed as his emotions became more engaged with his thoughts.

He was so happy just minutes ago, but now, he was dreading the encounter with his mother. That must be what was causing the bad feelings, he decided. She wouldn't be as receptive as he first imagined, and she might be so mad that she wouldn't even listen. It was probably good that he changed his mind and decided not to bring Jake. He would see how she reacted when he told her about climbing out the window before he mentioned Jake.

When he entered Jake's apartment this morning and turned the TV on, an old movie was playing, but he hadn't cared. He felt more relaxed and comfortable there than he'd felt in his own apartment, and it didn't matter what was on the TV. There was an inexplicable feeling of safety and companionship with Jake that he'd never felt before.

When Jake brought up swimming, he wanted to refuse because he was afraid of the water, but he didn't want to disappoint Jake. When they entered the pool area, he stood by the chain-link fence and watched Jake disappear through the door to change clothes. He wanted to go to the main pool and sit on the edge like Jake suggested, but his feet wouldn't move in that direction. People walked by and seemed to become more aggressive with their words and stares now that he was alone. Two girls about his age walked by, and when he looked at them, they turned to each other, giggled, and hurried away.

He deeply regretted that he'd come and wanted to leave, but he couldn't go without Jake. He walked over near the door Jake had gone through and leaned against the wall, staring at the pool. His fear of the water had become secondary to his loathing of the people scurrying around like ants at a picnic. When Jake came out, he would demand that Jake take him home immediately. He was disappointed that Jake had lied to him. He didn't see a single person here dressed as geeky as he was.

However, when Jake came out wearing his new swimsuit, Billy's anger, tension, and disappointment instantly evaporated. He laughed with genuine relief and happiness, surprised and delighted by Jake's bold display of his larger but identical swimsuit. His trust in Jake soared to new heights.

When Jake followed the man away from the snack bar, a teenager behind Billy said, "Hey kid, your dad's really cool," and a few others in line agreed with that assessment. Billy hadn't considered for a second that he should correct the impression that Jake was his father. He'd felt so proud that Jake had befriended him and thought, *wouldn't it be great if Jake was my dad*? He'd been thinking about that the whole time they were eating, trying to figure out a casual way to bring it up and suggest that Jake marry his mother.

He suddenly realized he was on his own block when he saw what he believed was the front of his apartment building. It was more a guess than recognition because he didn't usually come this way. He always used another street and went to the alley behind the building next door. He was using this more direct route because his mother would already be home from work.

He was on the opposite side of the street from the apartment building, and as he got nearer, a man walked out of the building and stopped on the sidewalk, turning to face the door through which he'd come. Billy felt no alarm because he assumed the man must have come out of one of the other apartments in the building. However, when he saw a woman following the man, he stopped dead in his tracks. It wasn't a *woman*; it was *his mother*.

The emotion that halted his feet and gripped his heart now was anger, not alarm. How could his mother do this to him? She had promised to never again bring a man into their lives, and Billy didn't want any man in their lives unless that man was Jake. He was on the verge of running to her and telling her she'd lied to him when another man came out and joined them. The presence of a second man changed the whole complexion of the scene, and he concealed himself behind a parked car.

His mother didn't seem happy. Could those men be the police? Had she called them because he was late coming home? Then, an even worse possibility occurred to him. Had they found out she'd killed Stanley and had somehow tracked her down? Was she being arrested? However, as he watched, a third man exited the building. That man didn't change just the complexion of the scene. He changed the very nature of reality.

Every bit of energy drained from Billy. He was paralyzed. He couldn't move, couldn't breathe, and couldn't even bat an eye. His brain felt frozen, but one cold phrase circulated through his mind like an icy draft. *It's Stanley. It's Stanley.*

After what seemed like an eternity, the paralysis gave way to involuntary shudders, and tears filled his eyes. The anger in his heart was replaced by abject fear. His mind refused to focus. It was as if the cold phrases had bunched into an ice jam. His body parts seemed to want independence from each other, and his mind lacked sufficient conscious will to provide cohesion. He felt like he might come apart and fly off in every direction.

Stanley began to move away from the door, but Billy's eyes had become so clouded with tears that all detail was lost. Did Stanley look this way? Was he coming over here? Finally, the fear that had paralyzed him now seized his body and compelled the only defensive action possible. He dropped to his knees and buried his face in his hands.

Stanley had come back from the dead. *Surely, such power as that must come with some all-knowing ability.* He and his mother had put a lot of distance between him and themselves, yet Stanley found them. He knew hiding behind a car couldn't protect him, but he could do nothing except shake and tremble as he waited for the cold touch of Stanley's dead hand. He was freezing all over, but a wave of warmth suddenly rushed down the insides of his legs and pooled around his knees.

CHAPTER 25

As soon as Billy was gone, Jake showered, dressed in fresh clothes, and stretched out on the couch. He had enjoyed the day and wanted to relax while he thought about Billy, the ride home, and a very interesting question Billy had asked. *Do you want to get married?*

There had been a time when he would have answered that question with a definite yes. But, after several failed relationships over the years, he had come to one inescapable conclusion: relationships can't be sustained without love. He lost the only love of his life years ago, and no other girl had ever come close. Every time he thought he was over Sarah, something happened to make him think of her, and his love for her was rekindled to the exclusion of all others. He had accepted that normal family life was not in his future, and he had embraced Walker's kids to fill that void in his life.

However, Billy's question reawakened the possibility of a family and caused him to fantasize about a future in which he had both a wife and a son. Billy had naively offered his mother's hand in marriage, and Jake couldn't deny that the idea appealed to him. Perhaps an arranged marriage was his best hope for happiness. Even if he couldn't fall in love with Billy's mother, it was possible that a shared love for her son might sustain a workable, lasting marriage.

A loud banging invaded his thoughts, and he was annoyed by the interruption. When he pulled the door open, he was surprised and confused by Billy's appearance. Billy looked like he'd just climbed out of the water and hadn't dried off yet. His hair was wet and plastered to his head, and water beads shimmered on his face.

Again, Jake saw a fleeting vision of another countenance in his face. Before he could say anything, Billy rushed through the door and wrapped his arms around his waist.

"He got her, Jake," Billy cried, "Stanley got her!"

Jake pulled Billy into the room, closed the door, and wrapped his arms around the boy's shuddering shoulders. He felt the scars on his back, but neither reacted to them.

"Who got who?" Jake asked, still confused.

He realized that the source of Billy's wetness was sweat and tears, and a heavy scent of urine was wafting up with the boy's body heat.

"Stanley," Billy said between sobs. "Stanley got my mom, and he's going to kill her."

That information didn't help. Jake put paper towels in a wooden chair and sat him at the kitchen table. He quickly got an icy Coke from the refrigerator and waited while Billy took a long pull on it before asking more questions.

"Who's Stanley?" Jake asked.

"He's ..." Billy hesitated as he struggled to find the words to explain Stanley. "He's my mom's husband," he said. He had calmed down a little, but now, fear and urgency crept back into his voice as he declared, "He was dead, but he came back. He'll kill Mom. We have to help her."

A year ago, Jake would have quickly dismissed a claim of coming back from the dead, but not now. His experiences with supernatural events made his mind more open to the possibilities. If Billy was who he thought he might be, a person being brought back from the dead wasn't unprecedented.

Billy asked for help, and Jake responded just as promised. According to Billy, the situation called for immediate action. Responding to Billy's urgent plea, Jake went to his bedroom, got his service revolver, and concealed it in his belt under the tail of his shirt. Billy said there were three men; if they were as bad as he said, it was only prudent to be armed. They walked quickly to the apartment, and Billy led Jake to his bedroom window.

After climbing through the window, Billy looked around before informing Jake that his and his mother's clothes were gone. He explained that although his mother slept on the couch in the living room, they shared the closet and drawer space. Aside from a loose bundle of bedding, the bedroom was completely bare of personal effects. The mismatched dresser and chest flanked the bare bed like denuded trees, their lack of surface clutter a telltale sign that the bedroom was unoccupied.

It took only a few minutes to discover that the rest of the small apartment was the same – utterly devoid of any personal effects. Except for a note with some money on the kitchen table, there was nothing in the apartment to suggest that Billy and his mother had ever lived there. The note said, "PLEASE COME HOME – USE CABS AND BUSES." It was printed in large block letters and so vague that it proved nothing.

Jake took the money from under the note and threw it on the floor like garbage. He didn't want it, and Billy wouldn't need it. They were about to leave the apartment the same way they had entered when Billy remembered something.

"Wait," Billy said, going to the heavy dresser.

He knelt and pulled out the bottom right-hand drawer. It was empty, but he was interested in something behind it. He maneuvered his hand around the back of the drawer as only a child's arm could do, and in an instant, he pulled out the shiny, yellow-handled knife Jake had given him. A huge smile lit his face as he held it out for Jake to see, and then he carefully slid it into his pocket.

A sharp rap on the front door startled them. Jake hustled Billy out the window and quickly followed him. They crept out of the alley and stationed themselves so they could see the front door of the building. A few minutes later, an old, slope-shouldered man with bushy gray hair emerged.

"Know him?" Jake asked Billy.

"I think he owns the restaurant where my mom works," Billy said. "He came here once before."

Jake saw no reason to involve the old man in something potentially dangerous. The old man went to a blue sports car parked at the curb, got in, and drove away. Jake and Billy walked back to Jake's apartment unhindered.

"Start from the beginning," Jake said as they sat at the kitchen table again. He insisted, "Tell me everything you know about this Stanley and why he would kidnap your mother. The more I know about the situation, the better the possibility I can help."

Billy told Jake about his mother marrying Stanley Gunther and coming from Cleveland to live in a big house in West Virginia. Recalling details involving his mother had a calming effect, and just as the urine was drying on his pants, the sweat was cooling him as it dried on his face.

Questions and comments occurred to Jake, but he waited. It was a tremendous coincidence that Billy had lived within an hour and a half's drive of him back in West Virginia.

Billy shifted uncomfortably and averted his eyes from Jake as he told him about Stanley coming into his bedroom on that fateful night. He haltingly described how Stanley stripped him of his pajamas and laughed as he rubbed the scars on his back. Red heat reclaimed his face as he stumbled through a vocabulary inadequate to express his pain and shame. He used childlike phrases like "my things" to describe where Stanley had squeezed him and caused pain in his groin.

When Billy came to the point where his mother entered the bedroom during Stanley's attack, Jake interrupted him with a question.

"This Stanley," Jake said, "is he the one who put those scars on your back?"

"No," Billy said, "That was my father a long time ago." After hesitating, he blurted out. "I think Mom killed him, too."

"Go on," Jake said, feeling a profound sorrow for Billy's short, turbulent life. "What happened when your mother came into the bedroom?"

Although Billy had been in a daze that night, he had been aware of what his mother had done. Jake became increasingly impressed with her, even though the fact that she was currently married confounded his fantasy of an instant family. When he described seeing Stanley again in front of his apartment, Billy admitted that he'd been so scared that he'd peed on himself. He hung his head in shame as he mumbled a question.

"Jake," Billy said, "Do you hate me for … you know … with Stanley?"

Jake was shocked by the question. He leaned over and wrapped his arms around Billy's shoulders. He hugged him tightly, ignoring the unpleasant odors that came from the boy's urine-stained, sweat-soaked body and clothes.

"I don't hate you, pal," Jake said, and after a brief pause, added, "I love you, and I thought you knew that."

"But I did it," Billy insisted, his chin resting on Jake's shoulder. "I let Stan …"

"No!" Jake cut him off, refusing to let him finish that thought. "You listen to me, pal," he said, cupping his face in both hands to force eye-to-eye contact. "You didn't do anything wrong. What this man Stanley did to you was not your fault. You could no more have stopped him than you could have stopped … the man who put those scars on your back."

He'd hesitated before saying "the man" because the paternal ascription of "your father" just wouldn't roll off his tongue. It was partly because the term might have implied some impurity in Billy because of family association, but mostly, it was because Billy could be wrong. Jake couldn't discount the unexplained familiarity in his face, the lingering conviction that he was meant to find this boy, and the instant love he'd inspired.

"I love you," Jake said again. He lowered his hands to Billy's shoulders and added, "I love you, and I don't blame you for being scared, either. Heck, if I thought a real zombie was coming after me, I'd probably pee my pants, too."

"Really?" Billy asked.

"Really," Jake affirmed, handing Billy a stack of napkins off the counter. "There's nothing wrong with being scared. It's what you do despite being scared that's important."

Billy paused in the middle of wiping his face to stare at Jake with a quizzical look on his face.

"What?" Jake asked.

"Nothing," Billy said, "it's just that I think I remember you telling me that in a dream."

"Then it must be true," Jake said, smiling.

That hyperbolic reasoning didn't exactly support his conclusion, but it might help Billy if he believed it was so.

"Are you ready to do whatever it takes despite being scared?" Jake asked.

"I'll do whatever you say," Billy said with conviction, a determined look on his face. "I promise."

Jake had seen nothing in the apartment to contradict what Billy had told him. The fact that Billy's mother had given him the only bedroom in the apartment and had taken the couch for herself bespoke volumes for her care of the boy. She had placed herself between her son and the door to the outside world, notwithstanding that she had been clueless that her son was visiting himself upon the outside world through the bedroom window. Jake thanked God that Billy had gone out that window and spent the day with him. Otherwise, he would have disappeared from the face of the planet without a trace, along with his mother.

"We have to go after her," Billy insisted as soon as he finished his story. "He's going to kill her."

"Act in haste, repent in leisure," Jake said, sure that the maxim was especially true in this situation. "We don't have to rush to West Virginia because he won't do anything to your mother until he finds you. You're a loose end. The note and the money make that obvious."

"We have to go after her," Billy repeated. "If you won't go with me, I'll go by myself."

He got up and started for the door. He'd taken nothing from what Jake said except that Jake was refusing to leave immediately to go chasing after his mother.

"Wait," Jake said, starting toward his bedroom. He turned and said, "I'd rather you don't leave, but if you must go, let me get you some money for cabs and buses. I don't want you to have to go back to that apartment."

"I thought you would help me," Billy said, standing by the door, choking back sobs, trying not to cry.

"I will," Jake said, "but you promised to do what I say. Are you a man of your word or not?" Jake didn't want the kid to go, but he couldn't let him dictate their actions, either.

Billy rushed to Jake and threw his arms around his waist again. He freely and loudly released his pent-up grief. He knew he had to have Jake's help. He had the magic knife, but the knife wouldn't be enough against a dead man. His only hope against Stanley's magic was Jake's magic.

"It'll be all right," Jake promised as he hugged the kid tightly. "We'll leave first thing in the morning." Catching another whiff of the odors radiating from the boy, he added, "We both need a night's rest, and you need a shower."

Jake managed to rehang the shower curtain, and while Billy was in the shower, he found the same clothes Billy had worn yesterday and traded them for the boy's soiled garments. He was pleased that Billy totally disregarded his comings and goings from the bathroom this time.

Jake threw Billy's clothes in the washer, adding everything of his that was dirty. He packed most of his other things in anticipation of permanently vacating the apartment. He would be taking Billy back to West Virginia and couldn't think of a single reason why he should return here.

After Billy showered, they sat on the couch together as before. Jake wanted Billy to tell him every detail he could remember about the house in West Virginia. The first shock that Billy hadn't mentioned before was that Stanley was a drug dealer, and the second shock was that Stanley had a brother who was not only his business partner but also a cop.

Billy didn't know if the brother was local, state, or federal, and Jake wasn't sure it made any difference. Corruption in his own county involved all levels of government, and the fact that Billy had lived in an adjacent county made it highly probable that there was a connection. If he wasn't careful, he could be pulled right back into conflict with his old enemies.

Sitting on the couch listening to Billy, Jake decided on a plan of action that should be high impact but low risk. Rather than forcing a confrontation, he and Billy would find the house and watch it from afar. When the opportunity presented itself, they would grab Billy's mother and spirit her away. He would provide Billy and his mother with enough money to permanently disappear.

But, even as he conceived the plan, looking at Billy, he realized a part of him hoped the plan would fail. Providing them with money was the least of his concerns. He had thoroughly enjoyed the fantasy of marrying Billy's mother and living happily ever after, but her husband's existence made that an impossible dream. What success would mean was that he'd lose Billy.

*****

Stanley paced the floor all day, his plans in a constant state of flux. He thought it would be a fun day when he captured his wife so easily and found the apartment so quickly. However, the expectation of fun quickly vanished when the kid wasn't in the apartment and couldn't be found. He'd attempted to appease his wife in case the local police showed up, but the necessity of that precaution only angered him more.

His anticipation of fun quickly gave way to drudgery, and by mid-afternoon, he was so aggravated that he was sorely tempted to kill the bitch and take his chances. However, he knew Billy was a bright kid, and the chances were too great that he might still lead the police right to his doorstep, and he couldn't afford another dead wife scandal. By late evening, he devised a new plan. If he couldn't find the kid, he'd take his wife back to West Virginia. A room in the basement could easily be turned into a prison cell. He could hold her there until the possibility of the kid involving the police was no longer a threat.

Stanley wanted to arrive home in the middle of the night, so after a couple more hours, he couldn't wait any longer. Before leaving, he left a note and money for the boy.

It was after midnight when they pulled into his driveway. As he expected, nobody was stirring, not even nosey Marge Zimmerman. He would call her tomorrow and act concerned that she hadn't heard anything more from his wife.

Earlier, when they stopped at a Quick Mart for gas and sandwiches, she'd used that opportunity to attempt to escape He had taken her to the bathroom around the side of the building and had waited outside. When she'd come out, she had instantly broken into a full run toward a deserted shopping center behind the store. Luckily, George had finished gassing up the car and intercepted her. When Stanley got in the back seat with her, he had flown into a rage. He would have beaten her to death right there if George hadn't warned him of a police car patrolling the area just then. Stanley put Carl in the back seat with her because he couldn't trust himself to be within arm's reach of her.

When the car stopped in his driveway, Stanley jumped out and told Carl, "Keep her in the car until I talk to George." He instructed George, "Lock her in her bedroom for tonight. Tomorrow, find somebody to turn that basement room into a bedroom. Have Carl take whatever she needs down there from her bedroom. Have steel or something put over the window and door so nobody will have to constantly stand guard."

He hated her and looked forward to killing her, but he didn't trust himself not to kill her too soon if he had to be around her. He wanted to ensure she was secure to prevent having to go down there himself to deal with her. If he didn't hear from the kid in a few days, he would send George back down to North Carolina to look for the boy. The less he had to depend on Carl to keep her secure in George's absence, the better.

*****

Jake was up before daylight the next morning. While waiting for Billy to get up, he put on a pot of coffee and moved the clothes from the washer to the dryer. He was sitting at the table when Billy came in, moving slowly in the baggy clothes.

"Did I wake you?" Jake asked.

He smiled when Billy just shrugged. In that instant, he glimpsed himself in the boy's reaction.

"What time is it?" Billy asked.

"Time for you to get a watch," Jake said, and when Billy didn't crack a smile, he added, "It's a few minutes past seven." Jake got up and busied himself with the toaster. "How about toast, jelly, and orange juice?" he asked. When there was no response, he answered himself with his best impression of Billy. "Sure, Jake, I like toast, jelly, and orange juice."

He turned and looked at Billy, encouraged by a tenuous smile. Jake lingered over the light breakfast and coffee until he heard the dryer stop.

"You can change clothes while I finish packing," Jake said. He gathered the rest of his things, threw them in the suitcases, and was ready shortly after Billy was dressed. He didn't bother cleaning the apartment. He'd paid a large cleaning deposit and wasn't planning to wait around to ask for it back.

The next order of business was to stop somewhere along the way and buy a few changes of clothes for Billy. It was impossible to know how long it would take to spirit his mother away, and even when that job was accomplished, Billy couldn't very well go into the house and pack his clothes. Jake didn't look forward to the ordeal of shopping.

As he pulled away from the curb, a brilliant idea occurred to him. There was a helpful saleslady at the local Walmart. She had guessed a nearly perfect fit for Billy based on a description alone. With the boy standing right in front of her, it should be a breeze for her to select suitable sizes. He hoped she would be willing to provide a little personal service.

Jake made a slight detour, and luckily, the saleslady was working an early shift. He explained what he wanted, and when she agreed, he found a nearby bench to wait while she and Billy did the actual shopping. When she brought the first few selections to him, he clarified that Billy had complete authorization to choose at least four changes of clothing and more if he wanted it.

"If he wants it and it fits," he said, "you don't need to bring it to me for approval."

Billy and the saleslady were all over the clothing department, picking out a few things here and a few things there. After a while, Jake had to get up and stretch his legs. He meandered up an aisle, and when he heard the saleslady talking in the next aisle over, he paused to listen.

"You know," the saleslady said, "most parents aren't so easy to deal with. You're lucky your father trusts your judgment."

Jake held his breath. Depending on what Billy said, the saleslady might become less cooperative, or if Billy said too much, she might even slip into the back to call the police. He sighed with relief and pleasure when he heard Billy's response.

"I know," was all Billy said, simply but sincerely.

Billy hadn't made a Freudian slip like Walker's kids. At least in the eyes of the saleslady, Billy had willingly and purposely granted Jake the status of father. He returned to the bench to wait, *like a good father should*, he thought.

As they were leaving the mall, Jake noticed a Dick's Sporting Goods store at the other end. He made a slight detour and stopped there. They needed binoculars so they could watch the house from a safe distance, and the better the binoculars, the more distance they could put between themselves and the house. The store had a large stock, and Jake selected a pair the clerk assured him was the best on the market. He bought two pairs, figuring that Billy would be better able to identify people and objects if he also had a constant view of the house.

Finally, they were on the road, and Jake estimated they should arrive in West Virginia at around seven. That would give them more than an hour to locate the house and find a vantage point from which to watch before it got dark. Ideally, they would spot her quickly, drive up to the house, pick her up, and be several states away before anybody realized she was gone. However, he wasn't optimistic about finding ideal circumstances, and he was prepared to wait and improvise as necessary.

After having made only a few brief stops along the way, it was just a little past six-thirty when they rolled into the neighborhood. Billy was uncertain of his ability to locate the house, but within minutes of turning off the four-lane into the community, they came to a "Y" intersection he remembered. Billy was confident about where the house was from there.

Jake saw the house through the open double wrought-iron gates in the high cinder block wall as they drove by. The driveway went past a small brick house and continued for about twenty yards before it circled in front of a much larger brick house.

It took Jake more than an hour to locate a suitable vantage point from which to watch the front of the house. It would have been easier to watch the rear of the house from the tree-covered mountainside, but that vantage point was unlikely to yield any helpful information. Instead, he chose the rooftop of a deserted building at least eighty yards away. The excellent binoculars made surveillance from that distance possible. They were settling into their watching positions as twilight came.

The rooftop was radiating heat, but it was tolerable. Jake hurriedly studied the house and surroundings before it got dark. He noted the two cars parked in the widened part of the circular drive and paid particular attention to the trees and bushes between the wall and the house. As twilight came, a dusk-to-dawn light came on in the grassy center of the driveway, and a streetlight came on just outside the gates.

There was no movement from the houses or grounds for the first couple of hours of their observation. Both the little house near the open gate and the bigger house above it remained dark, as though they were uninhabited. The scene was so dull that Billy fell asleep, his head resting on his forearm on the parapet.

Jake had his glasses down when a sudden flash of light at the front of the house caught his eye. He raised his glasses, but by the time he focused on the house, the light had just as suddenly disappeared. It must have been the front door because someone was walking toward the cars. Whoever it was stayed at the periphery of the light, and the only thing Jake could tell for sure was that it was a man, not Billy's mother.

He didn't arouse Billy because the guy got into a car. Both cars were black Lincoln Continentals, and the man used the one that wasn't a Stretch Limo. He watched the car drive out of the gate and through the community. There was no other movement for nearly an hour. When the same car pulled back into the driveway, it stopped near the gate, so he aroused Billy.

"Watch this car down near the gate," Jake said quietly. "A man just got out of it. See if you know him."

Billy was instantly alert. He picked up his field glasses and pointed them toward the gate. The man from the car was closing the gates, and he was clearly visible because he was nearer the streetlight than he'd been to the dusk-to-dawn light earlier. After closing and locking the gates, he returned to the car.

"Know him?" Jake asked without lowering his glasses.

"No," Billy said, "but I've seen him before. When they took Mom, he was one of the two men with Stanley."

At least, Jake thought, that's confirmation we're in the right place, watching the right house. He watched as the man parked the car back in its original position and entered the house. There was a bright flash of light when he opened the front door, and when he closed the door, there was nothing but darkness. The house remained utterly dark, as though a black hole had swallowed the man and the light.

Billy had no explanation for the darkness. He remembered looking out of the windows when he lived in the house, and he could even remember being out after dark and seeing light inside. Obviously, the windows had been covered. The darkness remained unrelieved until dawn.

They sat on the rooftop all night, sometimes dozing, and their effort produced nothing in the way of helpful information. They were both hungry and needed freshening up, so they got in the car, drove through Williamson, West Virginia, and crossed the bridge into South Williamson, Kentucky. There were several fast-food restaurants there, but they didn't stop. Mostly, the concern was for

Billy, but either of them might be recognized in these environs. They went nearly twenty miles into Kentucky before stopping at a restaurant.

The gates were open when they were back in position, and the same car was gone again. Jake silently scolded himself for having been gone so long. Billy's mother might have been in that car. They might have missed an easy opportunity to steal her away. Now, they had no other choice but to wait and watch.

Jake's mind was put at ease half an hour later when he saw that their absence this morning had made no difference at all. The car returned, and the sole occupant was the same man who had used the car the night before. However, realizing they had missed nothing by being gone was of little comfort, considering the larger truth it foretold. It was likely Billy's mother's movements were restricted, and she wouldn't be coming out to them. He would have to go in and get her.

They watched the house all day without seeing anything of interest. Aside from two more errands run by the same man as before, there was no activity around the house. Then, as if the day had conspired to hoard all its action for one quick burst, a couple of hours before dark, three things occurred in rapid succession: an old nemesis arrived at the house, a violent thunderstorm threatened to fry them or knock them off the roof, and Jake spotted another watcher on a nearby rooftop.

CHAPTER 26

Jake was eating peanut butter nabs and drinking a Coke when a state police cruiser entered the community. It turned in at the gate, continued up the drive past the little house, and stopped in front of the big house.

"It's Stanley's brother!" Billy exclaimed in a hushed but eager tone. In the car on their way here, he'd told Jake that the first time he'd met Stanley's brother, he'd taken an instant dislike of him and never thought of him as an uncle.

By the time he got his binoculars focused, the man was already walking toward the front door. Jake needed to know the identity of this other dirty cop, this brother to Stanley. He didn't know any cop by the name of Gunther but might recognize him if he saw him. The state trooper stood facing the door but turned and looked back toward his car. Jake was shocked when he recognized the man. This wasn't another dirty cop. *This was the same dirty cop from his County.* It was Sgt. G. R. Stillwell.

Jake had no sooner recognized his old nemesis than a streak of lightning danced across the sky. The accompanying thunder shook the building, and a sudden gust of wind threatened to knock them off the rooftop. The sky had been overcast all day, and the clouds had darkened so stealthily that the thunderstorm had arrived without warning. In the few seconds that Jake was distracted by the sudden storm, the door opened and closed. Except for the police car now parked in front of it, the house had returned to its dull, uninteresting self.

The lightning was dangerous, and Jake was about to drop his binoculars and hustle Billy off the rooftop when he happened to spot a man on another rooftop closer to Stanley's house. The man held binoculars to his face. He appeared to be watching the same house as them! Jake could tell little about him except that he wore a tailored dark suit and had dark hair. His hands and the field glasses obscured his face. Just as Jake lowered his binoculars to get a better idea of the location of that other rooftop, scattered fat drops of water became a pelting rain.

He urged Billy to run for the car. When he refocused his binoculars for one last look at the other man, he was gone. Jake identified the rooftop on which the man stood as an occupied apartment building that he had considered using himself. It would have served well for a quick look but was too risky to use as a long-term observation post. The tenants were likely to become suspicious of a constant presence.

Who was the man? Was he a casual Peeping Tom, or did he have a vested interest in the house? Was he friend or foe to the occupants of the house? Had the storm driven him from the rooftop, or had he withdrawn because he'd spotted them? Jake was still considering all the possibilities when he rejoined Billy, who had stopped and waited for him. They were both soaked to the skin when they got in the car.

After ten minutes, the downpour showed no sign of letting up, and Jake became increasingly anxious. They were sitting in the car behind the building, and for all practical purposes, he was rendered deaf and blind. That other watcher and a battalion of bad guys could surround them without him seeing or hearing anything. The possibility that this location might be compromised, the fact that he was effectively rendered deaf and blind, and the fact that he now knew these were violent, dangerous people combined to give Jake ample motivation to vacate the area.

He started the car, and after a few slow, cautious maneuvers, he drove away as fast as the weather allowed. He made several random turns to see if they were being followed. The blinding rain worked as much for them as against them, hiding their withdrawal even as it hindered their speed.

"Do you know Stanley's brother's name?" Jake asked Billy while looking at the rear-view mirror and negotiating turns.

"Sure," Billy said. "It's Glen."

"Do you know his last name?" Jake asked, still paying less attention to where he was going than where he'd been.

Billy rolled his eyes toward the top of the windshield and squinted as though trying to read a name written there.

"I don't know for sure," Billy said with a shrug. "I guess I always thought it was Gunther."

He must be a half-brother, then, Jake thought.

After a few more turns, Jake realized they were back at the junction of U.S. 119. Nobody was following them, but he decided they should leave the community anyway. He needed time to think. The man on the other rooftop and the brother/cop put new wrinkles in the situation. He had accepted that some level of violence might be necessary, but if the unknown man had identified him, violence would be inevitable. Since this involved the same people who had tried to kill him, if they knew he was involved with Billy, they might well marshal an army against him or, at a minimum, use Billy's mother as bait for a trap.

He turned north on U.S. 119. He had considered going south into Kentucky to find a hotel, but when he thought about the distance it would take to make him feel safe, he realized he could just as quickly go to his own house. Being gone for a few weeks made it unlikely that his hollow was under surveillance. Besides, he talked to Nick yesterday, and Nick told him he'd made some security additions to the hollow.

"What about Mom?" Billy questioned.

"We're going to spend the night somewhere else," Jake said. "We'll come back tomorrow."

After leaving the storm behind and stopping to eat, they started up Jake's hollow at twilight. He saw no changes until he was less than thirty yards from his brother's house. A gate supported by big square brick pillars blocked further progress. In addition to the gate, an eight-foot-high chain-link fence was attached to the backside of each brick pillar and disappeared up the mountainside through the trees.

"Do drug dealers live here too?" Billy asked.

He had been quiet for so long that Jake thought he must be asleep. "No, nice people live here," Jake said, laughing at the absurdity of his strait-laced brother being a drug dealer. But from Billy's perspective, there probably wasn't much difference between this fence and the wall they'd been watching. "Some people just like their privacy," he added.

Jake got out of the car and walked toward the gate. Flood lights mounted on high poles just inside the gate came on as he approached. The lights weren't blinding because it wasn't yet fully dark, and he could see the video cameras mounted on the poles above the lights. The gate wasn't locked, so he pushed it open and drove through. He stopped, and as he closed the gate, he noticed the cameras were tracking his movements. He waved meaningfully at whoever might be watching. The lights went off as soon as he drove away from the gate.

"That's my brother's house," Jake said, pointing to the house on the knoll on the left when they crested the little hill.

He wished he could have gotten home without alerting Nick to his arrival. The less his brother was involved, the less legal liability he would incur. He hadn't yet decided what action to take, but there was a possibility that no matter what he did to free Billy's mother, he could be reigniting a war between himself and the drug dealers. At a minimum, he might be jeopardizing the settlement that had made buying much of this property possible.

Before rounding the curve that would put the house out of sight, Jake saw headlights coming out of his brother's driveway through the rear-view mirror. He had intended his wave at the cameras to be a "disregard my presence" wave, but evidently, his brother hadn't understood. Jake parked in front of his house and waited. The house was dark, and its two-story frame loomed massive in the meager light from the darkening sky.

"Wait here," he said to Billy as he exited the car. His brother had pulled in behind them, and he wanted to greet Nick and send him back down the hollow before he could see too much or ask too many questions. However, Nick was out of his car before Jake could stop him.

"I know, I know," Nick said with a wave that approximated the wave Jake had made at the cameras. "I got that. You're not here, and I haven't seen you in weeks, but you might need these next time you're here." He tossed a small wad of keys to Jake and added, "I had all the locks changed, and there are also keys for my house and the gate."

Jake hefted the wad of keys as though to guess its weight before tossing it back. He stepped aside and indicated that Nick should precede him. With an elaborate sweep of his right arm, he said,

"After you. Age before beauty."

"Intellect before idiot," Nick rejoined as he went around Jake.

They went up the steps, laughing. Nick deftly selected the proper key, unlocked the door, and returned the keys to Jake. He searched the inside wall with his hand and flipped two switches. The outside light came on quickly, followed by the overhead light in the living room. Then, Nick hurried to a keypad beside the switches and entered four numbers.

"I need to show you the security system," Nick said. "I know you said you didn't need a den, but it seemed like the best place for the security hardware. They finished most of the renovations and should finish the rest in a few days. All six bedrooms and four baths will be completely furnished and functional."

"Just a second," Jake said and stepped to the edge of the porch. He motioned for Billy to come in. He put his arm around Billy's shoulders as they entered the living room.

"This is my good friend, Billy," Jake said. And to Billy, he said, "This is my older-but-none-the-wiser brother, Nick."

Nick shook Billy's hand. "It's a pleasure *not to* meet you," Nick said with a wink. In response to Billy's puzzled look, he added, "I'm not supposed to know you're here, so I didn't meet you." Placing a hand at the corner of his mouth as though confiding a secret, he jerked his thumb to indicate Jake and loudly whispered, "Watch this guy. He's a thoroughly dangerous man."

Billy grinned.

Nick proudly showed them some of the repairs and changes. Then, while Jake and Billy got their suitcases out of the car, he returned to his house to get a few perishables lacking in the kitchen. Jake tried to dissuade him from going to the trouble since they would only be spending one night, but Nick insisted. When he returned with bread, eggs, milk, and a few other items, he brought Rocky and Apollo with him.

Billy was ecstatic with the dogs. He squealed with delight as he and the dogs romped around the living room before exploring the big house together.

"Do you sit in front of the security monitors watching the cameras at the gate?" Jake asked Nick, impressed that his brother had so quickly become aware of their arrival.

"Don't have to," Nick said, proud of the work he'd done to

improve the security of the hollow. "There are sensors and cameras placed strategically all around the property. You tripped an alarm before you got to the gate. It's all computerized and has the latest shape recognition software. It can tell the difference between two-legged and four-legged creatures. You don't have to worry about anybody sneaking up on you. You have the same security monitors as I do in your den, and I'll show you how to use them when you've got more time."

When Nick said goodbye, he assured Billy he was welcome to visit the dogs any time and suggested they might have time to ride the horses the next time he came.

After Nick was gone, Jake and Billy had a light snack before getting ready for bed. Both were exhausted. Jake gave Billy the bedroom next to his, leaving the door open and the light on in the bathroom down the hall.

"I'll be in the next room," Jake said as he tucked Billy into bed. "If you need me, just yell or bang on the wall. Make yourself at home. My house is your house." Jake turned to leave, but Billy stopped him before he got out the door.

"Jake?" Billy said. When Jake turned around, Billy said, "When we get my mom, can we come back here and stay with you?"

"There's nothing I'd like better, pal," Jake said. "Now get some sleep, and you can sleep as late as you want in the morning. We're likely to have another long day tomorrow."

Jake knew he needed to get some sleep, too, but devising a plan to free Billy's mother still occupied his mind. First, there was Billy's safety to consider. He couldn't very well concentrate all his efforts on freeing his mother if he were distracted by the need to protect the boy.

Second, was Billy's mother still alive? Billy said Stanley would kill her, but knowing that Billy was a loose end made that unlikely. However, now that he knew how murderous these people could be, he had to reconsider that possibility.

Third, if she were being held captive, how could he free her? Gunmen were a ubiquitous element in the illegal drug trade, and he would have to assume there would be at least three gunmen in that residence.

Finally, he had to be realistic. He had already tried to bring this criminal enterprise to justice, and he'd gone to prison for his efforts. He'd accepted that the corruption was too powerful for him to bring down, so he needed to resolve the whole situation without exposing his involvement. He couldn't think of a solution to any of those problems, so he closed his eyes and concentrated on looking for shapes in the darkness behind his eyelids until he fell asleep.

When Jake awoke the next morning, he took a long, hot shower in the adjoining bathroom. He'd told Billy to sleep as late as he wanted, so he took his time. When he started toward the kitchen to make coffee, he heard the shower running in the hall bathroom. Apparently, Billy was up. He started the coffee and put bacon on to fry. Nothing made a house smell homier in the morning than coffee brewing and bacon frying. He was stirring eggs in a bowl when Billy walked in.

"Good morning," he greeted Billy. Jake was cheerful after a good night's rest. "Sleep all right?"

"Fine," Billy said with a grin. "I dreamed me and Mom lived here with you, and I had dogs and horses."

"Dreams do sometimes come true," Jake said happily. "Pull up a chair. Bacon, eggs, and toast will be ready in a jiffy." After pouring the eggs into the frying pan, he turned around and said, "By the way, I like your new clothes."

Billy was wearing the clothes he'd picked out himself. Like Jake, he was dressed in loose-fitting blue jeans, a white T-shirt, and a button-up shirt that he left unbuttoned and untucked.

"Thanks," Billy said, obviously pleased.

Jake scraped the scrambled eggs from the frying pan, dividing them between two plates. He sat down and prepared his food when everything was on the table. He sprinkled a liberal amount of salt and pepper on his eggs and spread a thin glaze of jelly on two slices of toast. He saw Billy doing the same thing. Before they started eating, Jake covered Billy's hand with his own and bowed his head. After he said the blessing over the food, he added, "And Lord, if it's Your will, show us the way to find Billy's mother and free her. Amen."

"Amen," Billy added, his eyes becoming glassy.

While they ate, Jake laid out the difficulties ahead. They would face at least three gunmen, and they weren't even certain that his mother was in the house. The only thing he didn't tell Billy was how dangerous he knew these people to be.

In response to Jake's dire pronouncements of the dangers and uncertainties, Billy said, "I've been thinking. What if I call the house and ask to speak to my mom?"

Jake set his coffee cup down, got up, and stepped around the table until he was behind Billy. He wrapped his arms around the boy and planted a noisy kiss on his cheek. Most of the noise was generated between his lips, and it sounded like a kiss Bugs Bunny might give Elmer Fudd.

"That's for being so smart," Jake said. "You just figured out how you can get the most critical information we need." He sat back down, laughing at the surprised look on Billy's face.

Billy broke into happy laughter, too.

While eating, they discussed the phone call, and Jake realized his phone couldn't be used. Most home phones were equipped with Caller ID; if they made the call from there, his involvement would be immediately exposed. Moreover, Stanley might be able to trace all phone calls coming into his house through his associates. Since Billy was expected to be somewhere down South, Jake decided the call should come from that area.

Since he hadn't unpacked, Jake returned his same suitcases to the car, with replacements for the dirty clothes he'd taken off. Billy returned his two suitcases along with his dirty clothes since they didn't know when they might return here. They were repacked and on the road before eleven.

When they got out to Corridor G, instead of heading back toward Kentucky, Jake turned north toward Charleston. It would be closer and faster to go through Marmet, West Virginia, to get to the south-bound Interstate rather than going through Kentucky. Coming back to Stanley's house, it would be closer coming through Pikeville, Kentucky.

Going south on I-77, they crossed the Virginia state line in less than three hours after leaving Jake's house.

"Does Stanley's house have a security system?" Jake asked. "Alarms," he clarified, "do you know if there are any alarms in Stanley's house?"

Billy considered it and said, "Yeah, I think so. Once, when I slipped out of the house late one night, Wayne caught me. He said I set off an alarm."

"Who's Wayne?" Jake asked. Was he also with Stanley?

The alarm was bad news, but the possibility of the presence of another armed man was even worse.

"He's another guy that works for Stanley," Billy said, "but he wasn't with them when they got Mom."

The name "Wayne" rang a bell in Jake's memory, but he couldn't recall the context in which he'd heard it.

It appeared to Jake as though Stanley had stopped masquerading as a family man and was turning the property into a drug dealing compound. Now, he had to assume that he would face four gunmen when he entered the house. That made it even more important to confirm that Billy's mother was in there. This could turn into a very messy business.

Jake decided not to go any further south when they reached Wytheville, Virginia. From there, they could get on Interstate 81 and head south until they could turn north toward Pikeville, Kentucky. It would be the same route they had followed when they came up from North Carolina the first time.

Jake drove around until he found the Greyhound bus terminal, which was closed. It was a small bus stop open only when buses were scheduled in or out, but there was a truck stop within easy walking distance. It would be a reasonable destination for anybody waiting for the next bus.

"You're all alone," Jake said to Billy when they stood before one of the few pay phones. "I'll be standing right here beside you, listening in, but I want you to make him believe you're all alone." Holding up one finger for special emphasis, he continued, "The one most important thing is that you talk to your mother. You want to come home, but you won't unless he lets you talk to her. Can you handle that?"

"I'll try," Billy said, sounding much less confident now than when he'd first proposed the phone call.

"You'll do fine," Jake said, putting more confidence in his voice than he felt. If Billy messed up and gave it away that somebody was with him and helping him, the very difficult job might become impossible. The element of surprise was their best weapon and their greatest hope for success.

"It's very important that you act like a little kid who wants his mommy," Jake said. "Don't talk about anything else." Holding up one finger again, he said, "No matter what he says, keep insisting on talking to your mother."

Billy punched in the number, and when the operator told him how much to deposit, he told Jake. Jake dropped in the coins, and the phone started ringing on the other end.

"This is Billy," Billy said. "I want to talk to my mom."

Jake cringed. Billy didn't sound at all like a little kid. He sounded smooth and practiced. If not for the fact that he asked for his mom, he could have been a young, competent businessman taking care of business. Jake crowded his head against the phone so he could hear the response.

"Just a minute," the male voice on the other end said. The phone clunked like it had been dropped on a hard surface.

Billy was smiling broadly, obviously proud of what he'd accomplished. His mom would be coming on the phone any second. When the phone rattled on the other end, Billy excitedly said, "Mom?"

"Hello, Billy boy," came a new voice from the other end.

Jake knew it was a male voice, but he couldn't have identified it even if he'd heard it before because his ear was too far from the receiver. He heard the words, but they sounded tinny, like the sound of headphones before they're placed tightly over the ears. However, it was obvious that Billy recognized the voice. The smile froze on his lips, and then it melted away entirely, leaving his face slack and expressionless. Tremors racked his small body, and beads of sweat appeared on his upper lip.

"My name's just Billy," Billy said.

Jake was sure Billy had intended to sound tough and harsh, but the fear in his voice was pitiable. However, Jake was glad to hear it in this instance.

"Where are you?" Stanley asked. "Your mother and I have been worried sick about you."

Jake draped one arm around Billy's shoulders and gave them a light squeeze for encouragement. He thrust one finger in front of Billy's face. It worked.

"Is my mom there? I want to talk to my mom," Billy said, sounding more in control and impassive.

"She can't come to the phone right now," Stanley said. "Tell me where you are, and I'll come get you."

Jake flashed one finger in front of Billy's face again.

"I want to talk to my mom!" Billy insisted.

"Well, you can't talk to her," Stanley said dismissively. "Just come on home, and you can talk to her when you get here."

"No," Billy said steadfastly. "I won't come home until I talk to my mom." He was nearly in tears.

"Call back in half an hour, and she might be here," Stanley finally said.

Jake pressed the disconnect lever and held it down.

*****

Stanley continued holding the useless receiver, surprised that the line had gone dead. He had expected the boy to beg and whine more. He hated the boy more than his mother and loved tantalizing him with hope. When the recording started, "If you wish to make a call ..." he finally hung up.

It would be perfect timing if he could get the boy here quickly. His brother had just visited and wouldn't return for at least three days. Glen and all his associates were leaving tomorrow on a three-day junket to Atlantic City. The boss had summoned them. That was the only way his brother referred to him, but unknown to Glen, Stanley had proof of the boss's identity.

Glen had talked excitedly about being invited to the high-level conference, but Stanley had been worried the whole time his brother was in the den. The door to the basement was in there, and if Connie had started screaming, Stanley would have had a lot of explaining to do.

Fortunately, no sounds had come through the closed basement door. The woman had rarely raised her voice once she was settled in the basement and most of her needs were met. She was getting regular meals, and she could have anything she wanted from her bedroom. She was securely locked away, and Stanley preferred not to see her again until he could indulge his darkest desires.

Another thing that had worried Stanley during Glen's visit was the possibility that he might be expected to go with them. Sure, it might be fun and beneficial, but Stanley needed to solve a few personal problems before enjoying a pleasure trip.

He looked at the Caller ID and saw that the call had registered as a pay phone. He immediately picked up the phone and checked with his contact at the phone company. He expected the boy to still be in North Carolina, most likely staying in the deserted apartment. He wished he'd sent George back to watch that apartment until he learned the call hadn't come from North Carolina. It had come from a pay phone inside the Pilot Travel Center in Wytheville, Virginia. His contacts at the phone company informed him that the truck stop was across from a small Greyhound bus terminal. The kid was already halfway home; he just needed to entice him to come the rest of the way.

Stanley leaned back in the chair, his hands folded under his chin, thinking. He had the bait to coax the boy home, but other than letting the kid talk to his mother, there was no way to dangle that bait. He could refuse to let the boy talk to her and insist that he could only speak to her if he came home, but that would likely lead to a long delay. It could take the kid several days to work up the nerve to come and see for himself. Stanley didn't want any more delays. His brother would be out of town, and he wanted to resolve this before he got back.

Stanley thought of the cordless phone. There was a cordless phone in the living room. He could bring the base in here and hook it up beside his desk phone. When the kid called back, he could send George to the basement with the cordless. He could listen to them, and when he was sure the kid had taken the bait, he could simply unplug the base.

Stanley made the preparations and waited. The half-hour passed, but the phone remained silent. Each minute beyond the appointed time made him less optimistic that the kid would call back. *He must be hanging around the truck stop,* Stanley thought. Maybe something was keeping him from the phone. A truck stop could be a dangerous place for a little kid, and Stanley couldn't suppress a grin at all the frightening possibilities.

Finally, twelve minutes past the half-hour, the phone rang. Stanley quickly picked it up. When he heard Billy speak, he motioned George to take the phone to the boy's mother.

"Billy, boy," Stanley said, tauntingly. "Your mother will be on the phone in just a moment. She doesn't have much time," and there was a long, menacing pause before he added, "So you'd better talk fast." Silence filled the interval.

"Hello," Billy's mother said hesitantly.

Stanley was glad he'd made this arrangement. Just hearing her voice made him wish his fingers were around her neck. He put his hand on the plug as he listened, preparing to disconnect the base to set the hook when the bait was taken.

"Mom?" came the excited voice from the other end of the line.

"Billy?" his mother said with a gasp. "Billy, is that you?"

"Mom, are you all right?"

Connie shouted hysterically, "Run! Billy, run! Don't come ..."

Stanley held the plug from the base in one hand and the desk phone receiver in the other. "Sorry," he facetiously crooned into the receiver, "but she seems to have been disconnected." Before he could say anything more, he heard a click on the other end. "Billy? Billy?" he said into the dead phone.

He had been disconnected. He had expected the kid to grovel and be more cooperative. *Maybe he pulled the plug too quickly.* He would rather have sent George to Virginia to pick him up, but after he thought about it, he was confident it would work out anyway. The kid knew his mother was here, and despite her warning, he was sure the kid would come.

CHAPTER 27

Stretching the metal cord taut, Billy backed away as far as he could from Jake's outstretched hand. He sobbed, unwilling to relinquish his only connection to his mother. Jake was keeping his finger on the disconnect lever as he continued holding his hand out for the receiver.

"I want to talk to Mom," Billy said pleadingly. His eyes were glazed, and when he blinked, a teardrop squeezed out of the corner of his eye and drifted down the side of his face.

"Stop it!" Jake commanded quietly but forcefully. Billy didn't immediately respond. Jake repeated the command and, still holding out his hand for the receiver, added, "Now!"

Billy reluctantly complied.

Jake put the receiver back on the hook. He hadn't heard their tones clearly, but he understood that Billy's mother had tried to warn him away, and the man Billy called Stanley had made a taunt, not an apology.

He grasped Billy by the shoulders and said, "Listen to me, partner," in a low, sympathetic voice. They hadn't attracted undue attention yet, and he wanted to keep it that way. "The man wasn't going to let you talk to her anymore. He's got her, and now he wants you." He pulled Billy to him, hugged him tightly, and added, "He wants you, but I'll fight the devil to keep you."

Billy wrapped his arms around Jake's waist and held on just as tightly.

"Come on," Jake whispered when he noticed they were beginning to attract a few stares. "We found out what we needed to know." Then, he reminded Billy, "We've got a job to do."

Jake started making plans even as they hurried back to Stanley's

254

house in West Virginia. He wanted to study the wide area between the wall and the house as much as possible before it got dark. If he couldn't get in the house without setting off an alarm, he needed to know the best places to hide to catch them off guard when they responded. He was fully armed. His service revolver was under his seat, the .380 under his belt at the small of his back, and a little .25 automatic in his front pocket.

In about three-and-a-half hours, they were back on the roof of the deserted building. Jake carefully scanned the rooftop on which he'd seen the other man. Then, he swept the binoculars back and forth over the grounds in front of the house, memorizing each place of concealment. There was a large shrub near the front door and other large shrubs farther from the house. He needed to get to the one at the front door before anybody responded to the alarm. From there, he could move inside quickly before noise from the first responder could bring a second.

The same car made a few trips out, but other than that, the evening passed uneventfully. It was after ten p.m., and Jake still hadn't figured out the most pressing problem. He had to decide what to do with Billy. He wanted to include Billy in the decision-making, but they needed to discuss it in a safer environment. They got in the car, crossed the river into South Williamson, Kentucky, and pulled into the Walmart parking lot.

It had been on his mind since they left the truck stop. While on their way up from Virginia, he almost decided to hide Billy in a hotel room until he could come back for him, but each time he got near a hotel, he'd felt misgivings and hadn't stopped. While on the roof, thinking about the dangerous search and confrontations with the four gunmen, he realized the source of his misgivings. There were too many variables and opportunities for failure. Billy would be left stranded and all alone in the world if something went wrong and he couldn't return for him.

There was another option he liked better, but it had a significant drawback, too. If Billy agreed, he would have just enough time to run him back to his house in Beecham County. That way, if neither he nor his mother could return for him, Billy could go to his brother's house for help.

Involving his brother was the major drawback to that option. Thus far, he had involved his brother very little. However, if it became necessary for his brother to provide for Billy, Stanley might discover it, and Nick would become irrevocably at risk. If Stanley learned of Billy's whereabouts, he wouldn't stop the hostilities until he had his hands on the boy.

Jake was torn between the two options. The hotel room might be adequate, but his house would be safer. The problem was that he might fail Billy with the first option, but he could fail both Billy and Nick with the second.

Jake pulled into a cluster of vehicles in the middle of the parking lot. He parked the car, switched off the lights and motor, and turned to Billy.

"I don't think there will be a better time to do this than tonight," he said. "I'm not going to lie to you. It'll be dangerous, and there's no guarantee of success."

He broadly outlined his plan to Billy, and he pulled no punches. He pointed out how many gunmen he might encounter and concluded his plan with a dire risk assessment of that unknown man on the other rooftop.

"That guy's a wild card in a deck full of jokers," Jake said, and not sure if Billy understood, he clarified, "If that guy's connected to that house, and if he sees me go over the wall, we've lost before we get started."

He waited for Billy's reaction to all the gloom and doom. The kid sat slumped in the seat, head down, staring at his hands in his lap. He had a pained expression on his face. He started to say something but then closed his mouth.

"I couldn't decide where to leave you," Jake said, finally getting to the point. "I thought about a hotel room, but if something happens and I can't get back to you, you'd be stranded and all alone. The best option, I think, is where we stayed last night so you could go to my brother's house if necessary. Do you have any problem with going to my house?"

Billy didn't move, didn't answer.

"What do you think?" Jake prompted.

"I thought I was your partner," Billy finally said, moving nothing but his lips.

"You are my partner," Jake said. "That's why I wanted your opinion." Jake was glad to see the boy perk up a little, but what Billy said next filled him with endearing wonderment. This eight-year-old kid continued to amaze him from the moment he'd seen him taking a beating from a gang of little heathens.

"If something bad happens to you and Mom," Billy said, and turning to look directly into Jake's eyes, added, "I want it to happen to me, too."

At that moment, Jake realized the real cause of Billy's sullen posture. It hadn't been hopelessness and fear. He was upset and felt hurt and betrayed because he'd been excluded from the plan of action. It was a third option that Jake had declined to consider because Billy had peed himself at the sight of this man named Stanley. He had even trembled at the mere sound of the man's voice on the phone.

"Stanley's in that house," Jake said bluntly. Hoping to dissuade Billy, he added, "Going in there might mean coming face to face with him."

"I don't care," Billy retorted defiantly. "I'll face him."

Jake wanted to discourage the boy from wanting to participate in the assault, but at the same time, he was calculating the difference the boy's presence could make. They expected Billy to show up, and trying to catch him could occupy their full attention. It would make it much easier for him to get behind them. Billy's participation in the raid would improve their chances of success by orders of magnitude if he was up to the challenge.

Jake noticed Billy's hands moving, and when he looked down, he saw the yellow-handled knife. He hadn't seen him take it out of his pocket, but it was now in his hands, and he was fingering it like a rosary.

"I'll kill him if I have to," Billy said.

Jake was pleased that the boy's tone sounded hardened by resolve rather than retribution. He smiled adoringly at the kid and wondered if that woman inside the house realized what a special son she had. He didn't want to expose Billy to danger, but he couldn't argue with his "all for one and one for all" musketeer sentiment of a shared fate.

Jake had tentatively set three a.m. for the optimum hour for the raid. Not knowing the men's schedules inside the house made the timing of the action completely arbitrary. He chose that hour because even if the men in the house weren't asleep, the rest of the neighborhood ought to be. They still had more than three hours in which to adjust his original plan to include Billy, and he saw no reason to change that time.

Billy listened raptly as Jake explained his role in the assault. Upon hearing how he was to set off the alarm to pull somebody out of the house, Billy suddenly remembered a detail from his previous encounter with the alarm.

"When I set off the alarm that time, Wayne didn't come out of the house," Billy said. "He came from the gatehouse."

It sounded minor, but Jake was glad he hadn't proceeded with his original plan. While they'd been watching the house, there had been no activity around the gatehouse, and he had assumed it was deserted. He might have set the alarm off and been watching the front door when the response came from behind him. It was still possible that the gatehouse was abandoned, but now, it couldn't be entirely ignored.

They had seen only one man coming and going from the house, leaving three other men's whereabouts in question. Perhaps one of the men stayed in the gatehouse to monitor the security system, or maybe the system would no longer be in use if all four armed men stayed in the big house.

Fortunately, Billy's participation in the new plan would correct any problem the alarm might have caused in the original plan. With Billy's assistance, setting off an alarm was no longer integral to the plan. Billy could knock on the door of the gatehouse first. If there was no response, he could go to the front door of the big house and do the same thing.

"You'd have to stand far enough away from the doors so that you couldn't be quickly jerked inside," Jake cautioned, explaining the new gambit. "Then, you'll have to run past where I'll be waiting. There's a big bush beside both front doors."

"But we'd still have to find Mom," Billy said, adding, "and the guy who comes out might be too mean to help us."

"Right," Jake said. He waited patiently, giving Billy every opportunity to back out. Confrontations were harder for some people than for others, and they were especially difficult for some kids. But again, Billy was full of surprises.

"What if I let him catch me," Billy suggested. "He would take me to Mom, and you could follow us."

"That would be dangerous," Jake said, "extremely dangerous.

Stanley would have you as much as he has your mother."

"But you'd come and get us," Billy said.

There wasn't a trace of doubt in his voice. Jake thought about the faith of a child. It was no wonder Jesus found children so endearing. It was a much more daring role than he would ever have suggested Billy take, but he had to admit it held the best chance of avoiding violence. He could free Billy and his mother, and they could be long gone before their escape was discovered. All for one and one for all, he reminded himself.

After more than an hour of strategizing, there was little left to say about the plan. The bulk of that time had been spent with Jake coaching Billy on how to act and react, what to do if this should happen, and what to do if that should happen. When he could think of nothing new to add, he left Billy in the car and went inside to get a roll of duct tape. He might only need it if somebody was in the gatehouse, but he might also need to bind the one who takes Billy to his mother. Getting the tape had been his reason for choosing that parking lot.

As he was getting back into the car, Jake felt a stabbing pain in his upper thigh. He stopped to rub the area and discovered the little automatic had turned sideways. He shifted it to a more comfortable position before getting in the car. He considered leaving it in the car since he usually only carried it as a backup for the .380. However, since he was now carrying the .380 as a backup for his service revolver, the little .25 had become superfluous. If things went sour and he was taken prisoner or killed, they would thoroughly search him. In any case, having a third weapon would do him no good.

A scary thought materialized in his mind as he considered leaving it behind. *What if Billy was taken to Stanley instead of his mother?* There should be a contingency plan just in case it does go bad. It might prove completely unnecessary, but the more he thought about it, the more it seemed the little weapon must have come to his attention for a reason. He sat in silence for a few minutes before getting back out. When he got back in, he laid the little gun between himself and Billy.

"This is Plan B," Jake said, indicating the .25 automatic.

Billy had said nothing since Jake's return from the store. He took the bag when it was tossed to him, and he had busied himself with opening the roll of tape and getting it ready for use. When he saw the little gun, he put the tape aside and waited for Jake to tell him about Plan B.

After explaining how the .25 worked and having Billy work the slide to inject a round into the chamber so many times that it was becoming boringly repetitive, Jake started the car and put it in gear. He drove to the end of the lot and turned behind the building. There was just one more detail, and it required privacy. The .25 had to be hidden where it was least likely to be found. He wished he had a few days to prepare Billy better, but every instinct argued against delay. *He who hesitates is lost.* Fifteen minutes later, they were on their way to the house.

Jake parked on the street two blocks from the house and left the key in the ignition. If they were successful, Billy would lead his mother back to the car while Jake ensured nobody followed. He had given Billy his brother's phone number and told him about the emergency money in his suitcases.

"Fifteen minutes," Jake reminded Billy. "Don't wait any longer than that, and that's an order. I expect you to follow my orders. If I'm not here by then, it'll be because I'm leading men away from you, and you might have to insist that your mother drive away. Call my brother and tell him you're coming to my house. I'll come there as soon as I can," he concluded.

He gave Billy the option of saying a prayer before they got out of the car. Jake had been praying silently ever since he accepted Billy's offer to participate. He was pleased when Billy took his hand and bowed his head.

"God," Billy said, "please help us save Mom." He looked up at Jake expectantly and asked, "Was that all right?"

"That was perfect," Jake said.

They casually strolled up the street, trying to look as innocuous as possible for two people out for a stroll at three o'clock in the morning. As they passed the Zimmermans' house, Jake draped his arm around Billy's shoulders, making it harder for her to recognize him. Billy had warned him that he'd heard that Mrs. Zimmerman was the nearest neighbor and the most apt to be peeking out a window at any hour, day or night.

A short stretch of semi-darkness prevailed between the last streetlight of the neighborhood and the one in front of the gate.

When they neared the midpoint between the two lights, Jake quietly said, "Now!"

The wall was only two steps from the sidewalk. Jake cupped his hands to accept Billy's foot and quickly boosted him to the top of the wall. As Billy dropped to the other side, Jake levered himself up and over. One moment, they were on the sidewalk, and the next moment, they were gone.

As they had planned, they made a beeline for the gatehouse door. Jake concealed himself behind the nearest bush while Billy hurried straight to the door. Billy rapped softly on the door and waited. His knock wasn't loud enough to rouse anybody from bed, but if they were alerted by an alarm, the rap should be loud enough to bring them to the door. When there was no response to a second and third knock, Jake was confident the gatehouse was as deserted as it appeared. When he was in place behind the bush near the front door of the big house, he gave Billy a nod. The boy went directly to the door and rattled the doorknob. It was locked. There was a doorbell, but he ignored it and thumped quietly on the door with the heel of his hand. Jake wanted him to draw only the nearest occupant, not the whole household.

"Mom?" Billy called out just above a loud whisper. After a long interval with no response, he looked toward Jake, and Jake nodded. Billy went through the routine again. He shook the knob, thumped on the door, and called out. After a shorter interval, the light beside the door came on. Billy was backing away as the door opened, and as Jake had told him, he called out again, "Mom?" Then, "I want my mom," he continued to insist as he backed up a couple more steps. "Tell her to come out here."

The man who responded to the knock took several steps out the door and stopped. The brighter light he stepped into exposed the Uzi he carried, increasing the threat his ape-like silhouette had created in the doorway.

The man looked at Billy, looked left and right, and scanned the area to the wall. Apparently, satisfied that the boy was alone, he started toward him.

"Come here, kid," he said as he reached for Billy.

Billy backpedaled a couple more steps to draw the man further from the door, and he turned to run when the man reached for him again. When the big hand clamped onto his shirt collar, he struggled to get free, flailing his arms and twisting his body while spouting a steady stream of protests.

"Leave me alone! Let me go! I want my mom!" Billy protested. After several more repetitions, the protests became unintelligible screams and screeches.

The man was facing away from the house, and Jake used the distraction to slip through the open door. Billy had played his part to perfection. He held the man's attention so completely that a platoon of soldiers could have slipped into the house.

Jake quickly scanned the house's interior to ensure none of the other men were nearby. He was in a reception area with a high ceiling. A wide staircase was straight ahead in the distance, and he could see it led up to a second-floor balcony. Off to the left were two closed doors, and off to the right was an open archway that led to other parts of the house. The interior was dimly lit by a chandelier that was obviously controlled by a lowered rheostat. Nobody was in sight, so after he mentally noted the location of the next nearest place of concealment, he turned his attention back to the man and the boy.

He peeked around the doorframe and saw Billy still struggling and screaming. He worried the kid might no longer be putting on an act. It also occurred to him that he hadn't thought to tell Billy how long he should keep up the act.

As Jake watched, the man let go of the Uzi, and it swung from a cord that looped over his shoulder. The man grabbed the back of Billy's shirt with both hands, used his foot to sweep Billy's feet from under him, and slammed him chest-first to the concrete.

Billy hit the walkway hard with a loud "umph." Jake was incensed by the man's brutal actions. He stepped out in the doorway and raised his heavy service revolver to shoulder height, the muzzle pointed skyward. The man rolled Billy onto his back, still presenting his own back to Jake, and Jake fully intended to bring the heavy revolver down on his head. They would have to find Billy's mother on their own. He was just two steps from the man when Billy's voice stopped him.

"I'm okay," Billy said, as though to himself.

"You won't be when the boss gets his hands on you," the man snarled with a chuckle.

Jake started backing up, keeping his eyes on the man. If the guy turned around, he would have no choice but to complete the attack. When Billy crossed his legs and locked his ankles, Jake smiled. He'd told him to do that if anybody started searching him.

Jake made it back to the doorway and was about to turn around to hide when the man's voice stopped him.

"What's this?" the man looming over Billy said, his tone a mixture of amazement and amusement.

For an instant, Jake regretted not having taken the man out when he'd been so close. He prepared himself for an all-out charge, but before he could move, the man held his hand out to the side, and after a barely audible "snick," a slender silver blade appeared. Jake relaxed and moved back inside the door. He had forgotten about Billy's knife and was relieved the knife was the only thing the man found.

"Is this a present for your old man?" the man asked, closing the knife and putting it in his pocket. "I'll give it to him for you," and added with another chuckle, "but maybe not the same way you wanted to give it to him."

"I want my mom. Take me to my mom," Billy demanded, kicking a glancing blow to the man's shin as they stood up.

"Listen, you little shit," the man said with a quiet vehemence, "you do that again, you won't be seeing nothing but stars."

Jake had moved through the archway and was squatted behind an easy chair, waiting to see which direction the man would go. *Cool it, kid*, he thought when he heard the man's threat. He couldn't see them but repositioned his body, prepared to dash at them if necessary.

Billy seemed to move more willingly when they came into view, but it might have been because he had no other choice. The man was lifting him by the back of the collar so that only the balls of his feet touched the floor. Jake expected them to go toward the stairs or come through the archway, but the man stopped at the first door on the left and pushed it open.

"I'm not allowed in the den," Billy said helpfully.

As soon as they entered the door, Jake sprang up and sprinted silently across the carpeted floor. He pressed himself against the wall beside the door. He heard Billy speak again and knew, by the sound of his voice, that they were still moving away from him. He smiled at Billy's clever improvisation. He hadn't thought of having him announce where they were going.

"Is my mom down there in the basement?" Billy asked loudly.

"Shut up!" the man spat.

Jake waited a few seconds before looking into the room. It was spacious and handsomely furnished. The huge wooden desk looked heavy and well-made, and the other furnishings were of the same high quality. *Apparently*, he thought, *crime does pay*.

He quickly moved to the other open doorway in the room and saw the stairs. He was poised to start down them when he heard a door slam. There was a clanking noise, like metal against metal. He backed away from the stairs and crouched behind the far end of the desk.

The man came up the stairs and went directly out of the den, passing within ten feet of Jake. As soon as the man was gone, Jake went through the door and swiftly descended the stairs. He was thankful the door was open and the light was left on in the basement, but he knew he would have to hurry because it might also mean an intended quick return.

The stairs ended on a concrete floor, and off to the right, the light was swallowed by darkness. He got the impression of a large, open space. On his left, a cinderblock wall separated one section of the basement from the rest. A single, bare light bulb dangled from the ceiling in front of the door. It must be the door he'd heard close from the top of the stairs.

He had expected at least a padlock, but he was delighted to see that the door was built to swing outward and secured only by a metal crossbar resting in metal brackets set on each side. It was simple but effective, obviously constructed to keep someone locked in, not out. The wooden door itself was dotted with rows of large bolts with nuts.

This is perfect, he thought, lifting the crossbar free of the brackets and setting it aside. When Billy and his mother were out, he would close the door and replace the crossbar, leaving behind no clues to their escape. He smiled at the thought that he was creating a locked-door mystery. The prisoners would appear to have vanished from inside a locked room.

After setting the crossbar aside and easing the door open, he immediately saw the purpose of the bolts. They secured a quarter-inch sheet of metal to the inside of the door, making it impossible to punch holes in the wooden door. After a backward glance at the stairs, he stepped through the open door, intending to quickly usher Billy and his mother out of the room. He opened his mouth to speak, but the vision standing in the center of the room stilled his tongue and took his breath away.

He furiously struggled to comprehend, but his mind couldn't understand what his eyes told him. Sarah, a haunting vision of loveliness, stood there in the basement. It's Sarah, but it can't be, his mind argued. It's Sarah, but this must be a dream. It's Sarah, but she died in California. It's Sarah, maybe I'm dead. He vaguely heard somebody calling his name, but it seemed to be coming from a great distance.

Reality shimmered like a mirage, and he was suddenly sitting on a rock below his brother's house with a gun in his hand. The air pressure changed, and he heard a drawn-out whisper, "Saaaraaaah." Then, his whole world suddenly went away. It was like someone had reached into his brain, flipped a switch, and turned his mind off.

CHAPTER 28

Billy panicked when the man grabbed him by the collar, but the jolt when he hit the concrete took his breath away, cleared his mind, and helped him regain his senses. He went more willingly down the basement stairs, proud that he'd done his job of getting Jake inside the house. When they got to the door in the basement, the man fumbled the bar, and Billy saw an opportunity to break free, but he didn't. He was eager for the door to be opened so he could see his mother.

The man opened the door and announced, "You got company." He pulled Billy forward and propelled him into the room like he was tossing out a bag of garbage. He immediately backed out, closed the door, and replaced the bar.

As soon as his mother saw him, she came running. When the man threw him into the room, Billy tried to keep his feet under him, but he didn't see the single step-down on the floor, and he stumbled and fell into her arms. She hugged him tightly and nearly smothered him with kisses.

"Mom … Mom …" Billy repeatedly tried to get her attention, but she was overjoyed at seeing him.

She stopped kissing him only long enough to pull him into a tighter embrace, and then she pushed herself back and held him at arm's length to look at him.

"You shouldn't have come here," she gently scolded. "I told you not to come. Oh God, you shouldn't have come."

"Mom, I have to tell you something," Billy said urgently.

She pulled him into another tight embrace before she pushed him away again and ran her hands all over him like a blind person "seeing" him with her hands. "Have you gained weight?" she asked, cupping his chin and squeezing his cheeks. "Where did you get those clothes?" She scanned him from head to toe. "They fit well, but I didn't buy them."

"Mom!" Billy said exasperatedly, "We don't have much time. My friend is coming, and we have to be ready to …"

She shushed him in mid-sentence, pulled him to her, and embraced him protectively. She was looking over his head toward the noise at the door. When it was pulled wide open, she forced him behind her back with one arm, surprising him with her strength. He tried to look around her, but her arm was like a steel vise. Then suddenly, her whole body went rigid. He poked his head around to see the man standing in the doorway.

"Jake!" Billy cried excitedly, and then he looked up at his mom. "Mom, this is Jake," he said. "This is who I was trying to tell you about. Mom?"

When she didn't respond, he moved her arm to her side and came around her. She was staring at Jake, but her face looked weird. He took her arm and shook it, but it felt unnaturally stiff, as though it possessed limited flexibility. He had no idea what was wrong with her. He ran to Jake.

"Jake, what's wrong with her?" he asked. When Jake didn't respond, he took him by the arm, but he was in the same eerie condition as his mother. Billy ran back and forth between them, unable to rouse either from their zombie-like state.

Finally, he got a slight reaction from his mother when he waved his hand directly in front of her eyes. He stopped waving and held his hand motionless, blocking her view of Jake. She blinked, but before she could completely snap out of it, Billy heard a "whap" behind him. He turned around in time to see Jake falling into the room. The man who had brought him into the house stepped into the room, and Stanley came behind him.

*****

Connie sat on the bed. She couldn't sleep. She was worrying about the phone call she had gotten from Billy. When the overhead light came on, she stood up, nervous and scared at the prospect of receiving a visitor. Nothing good could bring visitors to her cell at this late hour.

Carl's appearance in the doorway frightened her for a second, but as soon as she saw Billy, she ran toward him. Carl seemed to throw Billy at her, and fortunately, she managed to catch him before he hit the floor. She hugged him tightly and couldn't stop kissing his cheeks.

She was anxious to know if he was hurt. She ran her hands all over his head, shoulders, and arms, checking for injuries. Then, she cupped his chin.

"Have you gained weight?" she asked.

There was something different about him, she thought. His cheeks might be a little fuller, but the difference in him seemed less tangible than weight and yet just as substantial. When she looked into his eyes, she saw it: confidence. He hadn't come to her cowering and whimpering like a whipped puppy. He exuded more self-confidence than she'd ever known he possessed.

Finally, she noticed the clothes. With her hands on his shoulders, she pushed herself a half-step backward to look at him. The clothes fit well, as though they belonged to him, but she hadn't bought them. Billy's demeanor and the way he was dressed stirred long-dormant memories.

"Where did you get those clothes?" she asked. "They fit well, but I didn't buy them."

She heard the bar being lifted from the door again. She silenced him, pulling him into her and wrapping her arms tightly around him. When the door opened, she forced him behind her back. At that moment, she felt less like a weak, petite woman and more like a mother bear protecting her cub.

A dead man stepped into the room. It was Jake McCallum. Her mind searched for an explanation until suddenly, all conscious thought deserted her.

*****

Stanley was surprised when Carl woke him. Carl had caught the kid and locked him in with his mother. Stanley could have waited until morning, but this was dim-witted Carl, and he wanted confirmation that both his wife and her son were secure. He was surprised that capturing the boy, like his mother, was quicker and easier than he'd expected.

He was even more surprised when he reached the basement and found the door wide open, and a man stood in the doorway. Stanley didn't even have time to fully internalize the enormity of the situation before Carl stepped forward and slapped the man over the back of the head. He used a lead-filled, police-issue sap Stanley had obtained from his brother.

"Well, well, what do we have here?" Stanley said happily. It looks like my little honey caught two flies."

Carl quickly collected the revolver from the man's belt and then more thoroughly searched the body. He immediately found the roll of duct tape and the .380. After he finished his search, he rolled the body farther into the room.

As the man rolled over, he crossed the step-down and landed on his back. His head bounced once on the floor, and his eyes fluttered open and became fixed on Stanley.

"You …" he said, but he went silent as his eyes closed again.

Stanley stared down at Jake McCallum for several seconds in mute incomprehension. This was McCallum. What was he doing here? He'd dropped out of sight a few weeks ago, and never in his wildest dreams had Stanley considered that McCallum might be connected to his wife. He'd had McCallum dead to rights twice, and twice McCallum had escaped. He looked around at the bare cinderblock walls and metal-covered door and window. There was no escape for him this time.

Three people threatened his livelihood, so he had to kill them. They were all here, and now that he had all three contained, he saw no need to rush. He still had the better part of three days until Glen returned, and he would know all of his wife's and McCallum's secrets before they died. He looked forward to torturing them to destruction to get those secrets.

*****

Jake's consciousness swam slowly up through the darkness. He kept his eyes closed as he tried to understand what had happened to him. He remembered going into the basement to free Billy and his mother. He'd found a door that was strongly secured against egress but not ingress, and he remembered thinking how easy this would be. He would just remove the bar and let them out. He clearly remembered opening the door, but his memory became a jumbled series of confusing images after that.

He hadn't seen Billy, but he'd seen a vision of Sarah standing in the middle of the brightly lit room. He remembered grappling for some explanation when everything went dark. The last thing he remembered was looking up through a veil of darkness and recognizing a hated enemy.

Jake cautiously opened his eyes and vaguely recognized the room. It was now illuminated only by a lamp on a bedside table, but he knew it was still the same room. He was lying on a bed, and a woman was sitting beside him on the edge of the bed, presenting him with only a profile of her face.

"Sarah?" he whispered in awe.

She turned her head to look at him and said in the same awed whisper, "Jake?"

Jake tried to rise, but a jagged bolt of lightning shot through his head. She was wiping his face with a damp cloth when he opened his eyes again. He must have blacked out because his head was back on the pillow.

"Take it easy," she said, adding, in a hushed whisper, "You've got a nasty knot on the back of your head."

This was the girl he'd met at the San Francisco Airport and with whom he'd spent one unforgettable night in a motel room. This was the girl he'd loved to the exclusion of all others. This was the girl whose father had said was dead.

"Your father's lawyer wrote me that you were killed in an accident at the airport on the same day I left," Jake whispered, matching her quiet tone. The total silence that surrounded them seemed to require whispering.

Her face clouded with concentration and confusion as she remembered that period of her life. "I don't understand," she said. "How did my father even know about the airport? And how could he know how to write to you?"

"There was an accident the day I got back to South Korea. I was falsely reported as killed in the line of duty," he said. "I couldn't take the chance that you might think I was dead, so I wrote you a letter. I expected to get a letter back from you, but I got a letter from your father's lawyer instead."

She was silent for another moment, remembering. "He showed

me an article in the newspaper that listed soldiers killed in a helicopter accident," she said. "Your name was among them. I never saw your letter, and I've always wondered how he knew that particular article would interest me." A sneer crossed her face as the truth dawned on her. "That vile, evil man," she said. "He purposely lied to both of us to keep us apart."

Jake remembered the threats the lawyer had made, and now he knew why the cops had never come for him. He was thinking about the circumstances that kept them apart for all those years, and he suddenly remembered the unlikely circumstances that brought them back together.

"Billy!" Jake said too loudly, trying to rise again.

"Shhhh," Connie/Sarah shushed him, gently forcing him back down. "You shouldn't try to get up yet – Billy's fine. I just got him to sleep. He was worried about you. He seemed to think you needed to give him an order."

Jake fought the darkness that tried to envelop him again. "He's your son?" he asked, but he knew the answer as soon as he said it.

Sarah was the familiarity he saw in Billy's face, and it was his likeness to her that inspired instant love. She was the phantom countenance, and it was her presence in him, combined with his certainty of her death, that had produced the dark sensation of communing with the dead.

"Yes," Sarah said with a proud smile, and then she asked, "How did you ..." She hesitated before finishing with, "meet each other?"

Waves of blackness washed over Jake, and he didn't surrender to the darkness as much as he was taken prisoner. He tried to respond to her, but it became too difficult to move his lips. Hours later, he awoke to a pressing need to urinate. The lamp was off, and the only light in the room came through a partially open door. He sincerely hoped it was a bathroom.

He sat up slowly, and his head began to pound. He wanted to lay back down, but the pressure in his bladder could not be ignored. He was going to use the bathroom, and he just hoped he was *in* a bathroom when that happened. He managed to get to his feet, but he had to stand still and wait for the dizziness to subside. He moved slowly, deliberately, and when he reached the door, he was delighted it *was* a bathroom.

He managed to relieve himself and felt steadier on his feet afterward. The pain in his bladder was gone, and the pounding in his head became localized, confined to a sensitive area at the back of his head. Fortunately, the skin hadn't been broken.

As he left the bathroom, he opened the door wide to survey the rest of the room beyond the rectangle of light on the floor. The room had no other light source, and darkness held sway over everything not directly touched by the light. He could see the bed and the lamp on the little table, but nothing else was immediately identifiable.

A slight movement of a shape on the floor near the wall drew his attention, and he stared at it for several seconds before he realized what it was: the sleeping forms of Billy and his mother covered by a blanket. Sarah, Jake reminded himself. Sarah was alive, and she was Billy's mother.

He looked at his watch. It was a few minutes past nine. Had he slept through the whole day? He didn't think so. He looked around the room and, remembering where he was, realized why there was a total absence of light. They were in a basement with either no windows or covered windows. He was sure it must be daytime, and they were probably still sleeping because they had been up most of the previous night.

He considered waking them to give them the bed but decided against it. If he disturbed them now, they might not get back to sleep. They needed more rest, and so did he. What lay ahead was uncertain, but reason dictated that they would need to be as rested and strong as possible.

He left the door partially open like he'd found it. Sarah and Billy would need that light when they woke up. He went slowly back to the bed, as much by memory as by the meager light the nearly closed door allowed. He sat on the bed and stared into the darkness where he knew Sarah lay. There wasn't even enough light to outline her sleeping form.

Apparently, her father had maliciously kept them apart. Jake imagined how different their lives could have been. Her father had denied them what might have been a wonderful life together. He tried to work up a hatred for the man but couldn't. If he hadn't been so despicable that Sarah wanted to run away from him, Jake would never have met her in the first place.

And then there was Billy. He had already realized the familiarity that had inspired instant love was Billy's likeness to Sarah, and now, that realization led to another inescapable conclusion. There was no way Billy could be an incarnation of the Holy Ghost because he was not born of a virgin. In telling him about the obscene birthday present Stanley had wanted to give him, Billy told him his birthday had been only a few months ago. Since Billy was eight years old, simple math proved Billy must have been conceived at least a year after he and Sarah had spent the unforgettable night together in the motel room. She had been a virgin until that night.

The thought of the odious birthday present and the man named Stanley produced an image of the man's face he'd seen while lying on the floor. He'd dismissed that hateful face as the product of a confused mind trying to make sense of the impossible, but now that he knew the living Sarah was possible, he had to reconsider that man. Was it possible that his assassin-want-to-be and Stanley were the same person?

He had easily recognized the man because he had seen his face twice, and both times, the man had been looking at him through the passenger window of a car. If he was a prisoner of such a cold-blooded killer, then death was the only thing waiting for him at the end of this confinement, and being locked in with him augured a similar fate for Sarah and Billy.

Jake hadn't realized he'd fallen back to sleep until he heard a small voice speaking to him from the darkness, and he realized that his eyes were closed. He didn't know what that voice had said, but he heard another voice farther away.

"Billy, don't bother him."

Jake opened his eyes to see Billy standing beside the bed, wringing his hands and staring worriedly at him. The lamp was on, and he could hear Sarah moving around, evidently folding the bedding she and Billy had recently vacated. Billy's expression brightened, and the tension left his face when he realized Jake had opened his eyes.

"What am I supposed to do?" Billy asked.

"Billy!" Sarah scolded. "I told you ..." she stopped when she saw Jake was awake.

"It's okay," Jake assured her. "He's just following orders."

Billy's worried expression turned into a satisfied smile, and Sarah looked from one to the other.

"Just give me a minute," Jake said as he cautiously raised himself up on the bed.

Sarah and Billy stepped back to give him more room. He reached a sitting position on the edge of the bed before he realized there had been no pain. He explored the back of his head with a hand, and although he felt a sensitive bump under his hair, it was painful only when touched. He was about to stand up when the overhead light came on, followed by abrasive noises at the door. Obviously, a light switch outside the door controlled the brighter overhead light in here, and it was turned on in advance of someone about to enter the room.

Jake was as close to panic-stricken as he'd ever been. It was too late now to do what he should have already done. He should have awakened Billy and retrieved the gun when he got up to use the bathroom. Now, he was caught defenseless.

"Remember how to work the slide," Jake urgently whispered to Billy, "and do exactly what I ordered you to do."

Sarah hugged Billy tightly as they all watched the door open.

A man came through the door carrying two chairs, one in each hand. Sarah knew him as Carl, and Jake and Billy knew him as the man who brought Billy into the house. The Uzi was hanging at his waist. Another man entered behind him, carrying the same kind of weapon as Carl, but he held his Uzi with both hands at the ready position. Neither man spoke.

Carl put the chairs beside a small table against the wall opposite the bed. The table already had one chair. He went back out the door and quickly returned with two large bags and drinks wearing the McDonald's logo. After setting them on the table, he turned and left the room.

The other man had stood stoically by the door with his weapon pointed at them, making it plain he was ready to unleash a deadly volley of lead at the slightest provocation. He backed out of the room and closed the door but didn't turn the overhead light off.

Although the threat of impending violence might be new to Sarah, food delivery was not. "We should try to eat something," she said, prodding Billy toward the table.

"I'm not hungry," Billy protested, resisting her prodding before they were halfway to the table.

"Billy!" Jake said, "Plan B."

Jake looked toward the bathroom but decided it wouldn't be necessary for them to enter that tight space. He stood up and shakily went to the table.

"We can do it right here," he said, directing Billy to the nearest chair.

Sarah was watching with great interest.

"Would you stand over here, please?" Jake asked Sarah, his request more formal than he'd intended.

He positioned Sarah between Billy and the door, mainly to inform her and keep her involved but also to guard against the unlikely possibility that the door might be opened abruptly enough to discover their activity.

Billy unfastened and unzipped his pants. He was about to pull them down when he hesitated, looking first at his mother and then at Jake.

At that moment, Jake could read Billy's mind. He was sure the boy had been in his underwear in front of his mother many times, but there had never been a witness before.

"Don't worry about it, pal," Jake said.

Billy dropped his pants to his ankles and sat down on the chair. He cocked his left leg and pulled the leg of his boxer shorts tightly against his crotch to fully expose a gray band of duct tape around his upper thigh.

Jake got down on one knee before Billy and extricated the little .25 automatic held in place by the duct tape. He had wrapped a piece of paper around the gun to protect it from the sticky residue. The makeshift holster fit snugly in Billy's crotch, keeping the little gun from slipping out the top or bottom.

Jake had represented "Plan B" to Billy as a backup precaution. He'd told Billy that just in case he was somehow caught and disarmed, the best way to get another weapon into the house was to conceal it on him. Nobody would suspect a kid of hiding a gun in such a manner.

Of course, there was no way Jake could have anticipated their current predicament. What he told Billy had been a valid consideration but that hadn't been his primary concern. He'd been worried that he might be delivering the boy into the maw of an animal. He feared Billy might be taken directly to Stanley instead of his mother. For that reason, he had spent the last hours of their time in the Walmart parking lot instructing Billy on how to work the slide and handle the gun.

Fearing that Stanley might pick up where Billy's mother had stopped him, Jake had given Billy one clear, unambiguous order. If he had another pants-down incident with Stanley, Billy was to pull the gun out, work the slide, point the gun at Stanley, and pull the trigger as many times as he could.

"If you have to pull the gun out," Jake had emphatically ordered, "DO NOT try to scare him. DO NOT try to bargain with him. SHOOT him!"

Now, however, "Plan B" turned out to be precisely what he had represented it to be. The .25 was the only thing that stood between them and whatever violence their captors might visit upon them. It was pitifully small compared to the big automatic weapons it must defend against, but it was a gun nevertheless and very much preferable to nothing at all.

It took only seconds for Jake to have the little gun in his hand. He pointed it at the floor, deftly worked the slide, and thumbed the safety on. He hadn't shown the safety to Billy because he hadn't wanted to complicate the instructions. Billy was to only inject a shell into the chamber immediately before pulling the trigger. Jake stood up, dropped the little gun into his pocket, and then unwound the band of tape from Billy's leg.

The tape came off Billy's hairless leg easily and painlessly. Jake held the skin taut with one hand and peeled the tape with the other. He was nearly finished when he heard a sob behind him. He turned to see Sarah holding her hands to her face, trying to stifle her crying.

"It's okay, Mom," Billy said. "Jake knows what he's doing."

That assurance seemed to have the opposite effect of its intent. Sarah turned her back to them and began sobbing in earnest.

Jake wanted to rush to her, wrap his arms around her, and drive all her tears away. He wanted to do that, but he couldn't. Her son was right here, and elsewhere in the house, she had a husband. He was an evil man and an estranged husband, to be sure, but a husband, nonetheless.

"Are you okay?" he asked.

The sobs turned to sniffles, and she picked up a napkin from the table and blew her nose. "I'm okay," she said.

"The gun was necessary," Jake said, "but it wasn't dangerous to Billy. It was the only way we could get it in here."

"I know," she said, drying her eyes. "I'm sorry." After an awkward pause, she added, "You know how girls can be."

Jake watched as Sarah took the food and drinks out of the bags. The three sandwiches, fries, and drinks were alike, so she divided them into three place settings. When they were all seated, Billy took Jake's hand and then took his mother's hand. His intent was clear to Jake. Before their last meal together on their way here, he had taken Billy's hand and encouraged him to say the blessing, and with a little prompting, Billy had pulled a prayer from his memory. Now, he seemed eager to repeat that prayer in his mother's presence.

"I think he wants to say the blessing," Jake said, offering his hand to Sarah.

"I'm surprised he remembered," Sarah said. "Stanley had permitted blessings over the food at first, but he soon became so belligerent to any invocation of God that we had to stop. She glanced at Billy with a raised brow.

Billy bowed his head, and without any prompting from Jake, he recited, "God is great, God is good. Let us thank Him for this food. By His hand, we must be fed. Give us now our daily bread. Amen."

Sarah's eyes were closed. A tear escaped from her left eye, and she didn't release their hands.

"Mom?" Billy said after several moments, a hint of concern in his tone.

"Amen," she finally said, opening her eyes and releasing their hands. "How long have you two known each other?" she asked.

"We met about a week ago," Jake volunteered when he saw that Billy was busy taking a drink.

"I'm glad you did," she said, smiling lovingly and approvingly at Billy.

It was the understatement of the year, Jake hoped.

"What does this Stanley look like?" Jake asked, energized by the food.

"I thought you knew him," Sarah said. "You seemed to

recognize him, and he certainly recognized you."

No longer needing a description of Stanley, Jake asked, "The man who stood by the door holding the gun when they brought the food in," he said, "Was that Wayne?" Jake had seen three men, but now he needed to know if a fourth existed. Billy had seemed content to listen, but now he spoke up.

"Those were the two men who were with Stanley when they got Mom," Billy said. Seeing the look on his mother's face, he briefly explained how he'd been going out the bedroom window to explore the streets when he ran into Jake. "I was coming home from Jake's when I saw them coming out of the building with you, and I went back to get Jake."

Letting Billy's explanation go by without comment, Sarah said, "Those two who brought the food were Carl and George. It was George pointing the gun at us." After a brief pause, she added, "I asked Carl about Wayne. He said he'd heard George and Stanley talking, and he was pretty sure Wayne was killed in a car wreck. George and Carl are brothers, but Carl seems to be mildly retarded, so you can sometimes get information out of him."

The name associated with a car wreck brought it back to Jake. Wayne Parsley. That was the name of the driver who had been killed in the car that had tried to run him down. That was definite confirmation that Stanley was the man who had tried to kill him twice. Stanley had been using the same weapon the other two men were carrying.

After eating, Jake scanned the room. The only objects that might provide cover were the table and the mattress, but he knew that even combining those two things wouldn't stop bullets. He checked the bathroom and noted the heavy, old-fashioned, claw-footed bathtub. It would provide the best protection, but even that had a flaw. Because it was sitting low on the floor, a bullet fired from a high angle could go inside, ricochet around, and prove devastating to anybody concealed within.

Jake had intended to protect Sarah and Billy from the danger of flying lead, but none of the options seemed right. He could put them in the bathtub and pile the table and mattress on top of it, but the bathtub could too easily turn into their coffin. Besides that, the radical displacement of people and furniture would immediately arouse suspicion and put the men on guard. The little .25 by itself would be insufficient against three well-armed men, but coupled with the element of surprise, he might stand a chance. He explained the options to Sarah and Billy and waited for their reaction.

"I'm not hiding," Billy declared, interpreting their glances at him as meaning that protecting him was their primary concern. "I want whatever happens to you to happen to me, too," he reaffirmed, looking up at Jake.

"Billy's right," Sarah said, staring at her son with unbounded love and approval. Then, looking at Jake, she surprised him with her own sentiment of togetherness. She said, "We stand together. I'd rather chance a quick bullet with you than to hide and then face death alone."

CHAPTER 29

S tanley waited impatiently for George to remove the crossbar. He wasn't trying be a good host when he sent the extra chairs down here. He only meant for each to have a chair in which to be chained. The food had been a sudden inspiration, intended only to strengthen them so the torture could last longer.

After removing the crossbar, George stepped back so Stanley could open the door and let him go in first. George held his Uzi with both hands, prepared to dole out death if the prisoners rushed them. Carl brought up the rear, his hands occupied with lengths of chain and several sets of handcuffs.

When he pulled the door open, the first sound that assaulted Stanley's ears was the word that lately enraged him beyond all reason. That word was "God," and it infuriated him even more that it came from his wife's lips. He had broken her of that years ago, and now she dared to bring God into his house again. Stanley didn't wait for George to go first. His rage and fury suppressed all rational thought of the necessity for caution.

"Shut up!" he screamed as he went through the door, "shut the hell up!"

The three stood beside the bed, holding hands with their heads bowed, and their eyes closed. They were oblivious to his presence, and Stanley seethed with hate and anger. He had expected them to be crying and cringing in fear. He pulled the revolver – Jake's .357 Magnum – from his belt, ready to fire on his wife when McCallum started making the closing appeal.

Jake finished, "In the name of the Father, the Son, and the Holy Ghost, Amen."

"You son-of-a-bitch!" Stanley screamed. He was tempted to fire on McCallum, but even through his madness, his need for answers and the anticipation of torture stayed his hand. Because it had all started going wrong with him, he saw McCallum as the root cause of all his failures. A bullet now would be unsatisfying for him and much too fast and easy for McCallum. When he finished with him, McCallum would be begging for a bullet.

He intended to dismiss George and Carl after the prisoners were secured in the chairs with chains and handcuffs. Then, he would have time to indulge in fun at his leisure. He would begin with McCallum, but he'd make the kid suffer instead of McCallum whenever he refused to cooperate. He'd hurt Connie next, saving McCallum for last. McCallum had been an honest cop, and making him watch helplessly as the others suffered and died would destroy him more thoroughly than would his own pain.

When the three raised their heads and opened their eyes, they became aware of his presence. Stanley lowered the gun, releasing a stream of curses that would make a sailor blush. He cursed God in general, and in response to Jake's closing prayer, he specifically cursed each Entity of the Holy Trinity to whom Jake had appealed, including the Holy Ghost.

After his diatribe, Stanley ordered, "Put the handcuffs on them."

Carl had placed the chains on the floor and was holding the wad of handcuffs, totally unfocused, absentmindedly ratcheting them closed. When Stanley saw the handcuffs, he redirected his anger at Carl and cursed his stupidity. Carl's fidgeting with the handcuffs had locked them together, making them useless until they were unlocked and separated. Stanley put the .357 back in his belt and searched his pockets for the key.

"The key must be on my desk," Stanley said after checking all his pockets. "Go get it," he spat the words at Carl, taking the wad of useless handcuffs from him.

Carl ran up the stairs to the den, and after a couple of minutes, his plaintive, anxious voice called from the top of the stairs, "It's not on the desk."

Stanley shook his head and stepped to the doorway. He yelled, "Check the middle drawer!" After another long silence, Stanley turned to George and said, "I'll have to go find it. Come outside and lock the door."

George took a step backward, dropping the muzzle of the Uzi

toward the floor. He started to turn to follow Stanley out of the room but stopped in mid-turn when he heard his brother.

"I found it," came the excited yell from upstairs.

Stanley stopped in the doorway, facing the stairs. In response to Carl's news, he turned back to face the room. George had stopped where he was several feet inside the room with his Uzi pointed at the floor, standing in profile to the room's occupants.

*****

As soon as George lowered the muzzle of the Uzi, Jake started making his move. He wasn't likely to get a better opportunity. He slipped the .25 out of his pocket and thumbed the safety off just as Carl called from upstairs that he'd found the key. When George turned to face the prisoners, Jake fired the little automatic twice. Stanley had started to take a step forward just as the small caliber bullets struck George in the chest.

George stiffened, and his finger reflexively tightened, sending a volley of lead into the carpet-covered, wood planking of the floor. His eyes widened as Jake charged and, with the little gun just two feet away from George's head, fired again. The bullet entered his forehead just above his right eye, and he dropped. Contact with the floor tore the Uzi from his hand, and the cacophony ceased as abruptly as it had started.

From the first shot to the last, the shooting was over in seconds. Stanley was caught flat-footed, cradling the tangled mass of handcuffs in both hands.

George fell, and Jake turned his attention to Stanley. Stanley tossed the loose mass of metal he was holding at Jake. As soon as the handcuffs left his hands, Stanley turned on his heels and bolted toward the stairs.

Jake easily side-stepped the flying handcuffs. There hadn't been any real force behind them. Stanley had only tossed them to give himself a chance to run.

"Stay here!" Jake shouted as he went through the door in pursuit of Stanley. He saw Stanley starting up the stairs. When he approached the bottom of the stairs, he saw Stanley pass Carl about midway. Carl was descending, holding his Uzi at the ready in a two-handed grip.

"They killed George," he heard Stanley say as he passed Carl. "Kill them all."

Jake raced back toward the room and grabbed the crossbar that was leaning against the outside wall. As he entered the room, he pulled the door behind him. His little .25 was no match for the Uzi. He brought the crossbar with him so that it couldn't be put back in the brackets, making them just as much prisoners as ever.

Tossing the crossbar farther into the room, he stopped beside the body that lay sprawled just inside the door. He thumbed the safety on and returned the little automatic to his pocket. He picked up the Uzi that lay near the fallen man and hurriedly stripped the lanyard from the man's right shoulder. He took several more steps to his left, going farther into the room.

"Get in the bathroom and lie in the bathtub!" he ordered, adjusting to the new circumstances.

He popped the magazine into his hand. He didn't know how many rounds remained, but it was slightly top-heavy, so there must be a few more rounds besides the two he could see. He slid the magazine back in and tapped it sharply. He wished he could conserve ammo by switching it to semi-automatic, but he couldn't spare the time to study the weapon.

The door suddenly jerked open about a foot, and a head poked through. Carl looked at Jake, looked at the body on the floor, and withdrew his head.

Jake was so surprised by the bizarre action that he didn't fire a shot. The act was startlingly unpredictable because no normal man would have done such a stupid thing, but then he remembered Carl wasn't entirely normal.

"Throw down your gun, and you won't be hurt!" Jake promised, instinctively backing up and dropping into a prone shooter's position after speaking.

In answer to his offer, the Uzi poked through the opening, turned its muzzle toward where Jake had been standing, and started spitting lead.

Ordinarily, the man's diminished capacity would make him less culpable for his actions. Still, that same limited mental capacity and his environment turned Carl into a vicious killer, comparable to a mad dog. A dog didn't choose to contract rabies, but if its environment caused it to become infected, it would become an instrument of death and would have to be put down.

The deadly barrage that Carl was spraying into the room must be stopped. The first rounds passed harmlessly overhead, aimed at his last standing position. However, Carl was a competent killer, and it would only be a matter of moments before he lowered his aim and systematically swept the room.

Jake judged the door was standing open less than a foot, and it swung outward. Although he didn't have a straight-line shot at Carl, his knowledge of a quirk of physics should serve him well in this situation. Carl was standing behind the door frame, his body filling the gap between the open door and the jamb. Since the inside of the door was reinforced with sheet metal, Jake raised the Uzi and fired at the door, aiming just to the left of the center. He knew from experience that bullets fired at an obtuse angle would ricochet off the metal, raise only an inch or two above the surface, and then travel parallel to that surface.

The first bullet struck the door waist-high, and Jake let the natural recoil of the weapon raise the muzzle a little higher with each succeeding round. The last rounds were about chest high when his weapon abruptly stopped chattering.

The muzzle of the Uzi slowly dropped straight down the doorframe, still spitting lead that drew a jagged line on the carpeted floor in front of where Jake lay. The last several rounds went straight into the wooden ramp, and the weapon went silent. A moment later, Jake heard a muffled thump.

Jake sprang up, rising into a smoky haze and a pungent smell of burned gunpowder. He had to hurry. Stanley had escaped, and if he became aware that both of his men were down, he might lock and barricade the door at the top of the stairs.

He pushed the door open and saw Carl sprawled on the floor. The many spots of blood dotting his clothes made it clear that every bullet that came through the gap had struck him. Jake dropped his useless weapon and picked up the one Carl had used. He quickly popped the magazine and found that it, too, was empty. At least one of the two dead men might have an extra loaded magazine on him, but he couldn't spare the time to search. He dropped Carl's Uzi, withdrew the .25 from his pocket, and thumbed the safety off.

"Give me a couple of minutes," Jake said to Sarah as she exited the bathroom. "I'll clear the path. Let Billy lead you to the car. He knows where to go and what to do."

Without waiting for a response, he turned and dashed for the stairs. Away from the carpeted flooring, his soft-soled shoes clapped on the cement, but by the time he reached the stairs, he was moving so fast that he silently sailed up the wooden steps two at a time. When he came through the open door, he saw Stanley standing at the far corner of his desk, his back to the basement door, holding a phone to his ear with his left hand.

"Hang it up," Jake commanded in a low, even tone.

He stopped behind Stanley and glanced swiftly around the room for any other danger. Stanley's right hand was in front of him, hidden from view. Stanley pulled the phone away from his ear, but he hesitated before placing it on the hook. His body language telegraphed his indecision.

"Go for it," Jake said, remembering his revolver in Stanley's belt. Part of him hoped Stanley would give him no other choice so that he could end this, here and now.

Stanley finally made his decision. Before turning around, he raised his right hand above his shoulder to show it was empty. He placed the receiver on the hook and turned to face Jake. The .357 was still in his belt.

"Take the gun out with your left hand and lay it on the desk," Jake ordered. "Slow and careful."

Stanley moved cautiously. He took the gun out with his left hand and placed it on the desk as far away from him as he could reach. He jerked his hands back like the desk was hot, slowly straightened up, and stepped backward.

"I'm not trying anything," Stanley said. "I know you can't shoot unless I give you good reason."

Jake heard an urgent whisper of conversation between Billy and his mother on the stairs, and he called to them to come on up. He moved closer to Stanley to give them plenty of room to pass without coming between them. Billy was obviously taking his job in the most literal sense. He had his mother by the hand and was leading her, but after they'd crossed half of the room, he dropped her hand and froze.

"Come on, honey," Sarah urged.

She went around Billy and took his other hand, trying to coax him into following her. He let her pull him a couple of steps, his eyes leaving Stanley just long enough to glance at the gun on the desk. They had passed the desk and were near the door when Billy suddenly tore his hand from his mother's. He ran back, grabbed the .357 off the corner of the desk, and pointed it at Stanley. Billy's face was flushed with anger and determination. The gun was almost too big for his small hands to hold.

"Billy, no!" Sarah screamed.

"He'll come after us, Mom," Billy said through clenched teeth. "He'll keep coming until he gets us again."

Stanley didn't move and kept his eyes down, cowardly refusing to challenge Billy by meeting his eyes.

"Billy," Jake said with a quiet intensity, "put the gun down, that's an order."

Since he'd set the tone of their relationship back in North Carolina by refusing Billy's demand to immediately chase after his mother, Billy had taken his orders well. Jake could only hope he would continue to do so. Even though Billy had valid reasons for wanting to shoot Stanley, he was much too young to have to live with taking a human life. Last night, he had given Billy an unambiguous order to shoot Stanley, but that order had been predicated on entirely different circumstances.

"But I have to," Billy said with less conviction, beads of sweat forming on his upper lip.

"No, you don't," Jake said, his tone making his authority absolute. "You promised to take my orders. Put the gun down now! You do your job, and I'll do mine."

Reminding Billy they each had a job to do had the desired impact. It was his job to get his mother out, and Jake's job was to stay behind and ensure there was no pursuit. Billy's mask of rage dissolved, and he placed the gun back in its original position on the desk. He pivoted around his mother, retook her hand, and led her from the room without a backward glance.

Stanley breathed an audible sigh of relief.

"You should have let the kid do it," he said, chuckling with only the slightest nervousness over his close brush with death. Instead of being appreciative that Jake had just saved his life, he contemptuously added, "You know you can't do it."

Jake didn't say anything. He was taking his time. The most

important thing was that Sarah and Billy were safe, and he wanted to give them plenty of time to get over the wall.

"I called the cops," Stanley said, obviously emboldened by Jake's silence. "They'll be here any minute."

Jake saw Stanley glance down at the .357 on the desk. "Go ahead," he encouraged the fiend. Jake was holding the .25 straight down, but as he spoke, he put it behind his back to give Stanley an added incentive.

Stanley seemed to consider it for just a split second, but when he looked at Jake, his mouth broadened in a humorless grin.

"I don't have to," he said with conviction. "You can't shoot me unless I give you no other choice, so I'm giving you other choices. You can leave now or wait and turn me over to the cops."

"You mean, turn you over to your brother?" Jake corrected him.

He was momentarily surprised that Jake knew about his brother but then remembered his wife's involvement. His smile faltered but came back broader than before.

"Since you know that," Stanley said, "you must already know you can't win. You serve a weak judicial system and an even weaker God."

Jake considered the situation. Cursing the Holy Ghost was the only unforgivable sin in the Bible, so Hell was Stanley's only possible destination. He had forever removed himself from any chance of being in God's presence in the next world. Ultimately, Jake concluded that Stanley couldn't remain in this world for Sarah's and Billy's sake.

"You're wrong on both counts," Jake said. "Thanks to you and your brother, I no longer serve the judicial system, and my God isn't weak. But you're right about the other thing. As long as you're alive, we can't win. My God will have a day of judgment in which He'll destroy His enemies." Bringing the .25 back around to point it at Stanley's head, he concluded, "Welcome to my day of judgment."

The smile vanished from Stanley's face. Death was in Jake's tone, and death was in his body language. He grabbed the gun off the desk and raised it toward Jake.

Jake calmly held his aim at Stanley's head from only three feet away, waiting for the instant when Stanley would stop moving. He was aware that Stanley had picked the gun up from the desk, but a preternatural calm gripped him, and he didn't hurry his last shots. He knew only two rounds remained in the .25.

As Stanley raised the gun, his lips twitched with the beginning of a smile. His success was beginning to look probable. He'd been right. Jake couldn't fire. Stanley paused for a split second when the gun was pointing at Jake's chest, and Jake fired. The two reports were no louder than large books slamming onto a hardwood floor. Two small dark dots appeared on Stanley's forehead, just a few millimeters left and right of center.

Jake examined Stanley's body and quickly confirmed he was dead. His eyes were still open, and although Stanley appeared to be staring out of two extra eyes in his forehead, eyes that were each shedding a single red teardrop, Jake knew that none of his eyes were seeing anything in this world. He returned the now empty little weapon to his pocket.

Jake had to assume Stanley's brother was on his way, or he might be sending other cohorts if he was too far away. Time was suddenly a factor. He snatched his .357 from the floor and shoved it into his belt. He pulled the desk drawers open, looking for his .380. Finally, he jerked the middle drawer out, and the gun "thunked" against the front of the drawer as it slid forward. He quickly shoved it into his belt at the small of his back and was about to turn away when a yellow glint caught his eye. He quickly dug it out and put it in his pocket.

Jake took a final glance around the room. He knew there was evidence here that would incriminate Stanley and his associates, like the books Sarah told him Stanley had taken back from her. He also knew plenty of evidence here could be used to incriminate him. However, he had neither the time nor inclination to search for the former or eradicate the latter. His attitude toward this world had changed dramatically over the past several months. He had once considered the judicial system to be the final arbiter of man's conduct, but now, he had more faith in the law of Christ than in the law of man.

He turned his back on the destruction of flesh wrought by his own hands and walked out of the den. As he opened the front door, he thought he heard a noise from the back of the house. After several seconds of silence, he went out the door. As he pulled the door closed behind him, movement at the far corner of the house caught his attention, and he froze. A man who had just stepped around the corner of the house also froze. Apparently, he was just as surprised to see Jake as Jake was to see him. They faced each other like gunfighters in an old Western, each waiting for the other to make the first move.

There was only one memorable thing about the man Jake had seen on the other rooftop watching this house. He was wearing a dark, obviously expensive, tailored suit. Other than the suit, this man was nondescript. He was of average height and weight; his brown hair and ruddy complexion were unremarkable. If he'd been dressed differently either then or now, it might not have occurred to Jake that this was the same man.

Jake was no gunslinger, but he was conscious of the revolver in his belt. He waited for the other man to make a move, but when he did move, it was in a non-threatening manner. The man stepped backward, slowly raised his left arm straight out from his side, and flipped the hand up in a "stop" gesture. He was apparently stopping someone who had been following him around the house. The man did this without taking his eyes off Jake. Then, he slowly and deliberately nodded his head.

Not a single word had been exchanged, but the communication was clear. Jake nodded his head once in return and began backing away, only briefly glancing down when he transitioned from concrete to grass. After a few more steps, seeing the man continue to hold his unseen companions at bay, Jake turned and sprinted toward the wall. He reached the wall and pulled himself up and over without looking back.

Jake straightened his shirt to cover the guns when he reached the sidewalk and began jogging toward the car. He was in a hurry but held to a jogger's pace so he wouldn't draw too much attention. When he neared the car, he slowed to a walk. Billy was in the passenger seat, and Sarah was in the driver's seat. They must have seen him coming because Billy started climbing between the seats to the back, and Sarah was sliding over the console into the passenger seat. Jake casually got into the car, calmly put the car in gear, and pulled away from the curb.

When he saw Billy look apprehensively through the gate as they passed, Jake said, "You don't have to worry about Stanley anymore. You'll never see him again – I guarantee it."

"Is he dead?" Billy asked.

"Yes," Jake said.

"Are you sure?" Billy said, not doubtfully but needing absolute confirmation since he'd once believed Stanley dead and had been devastated when he found out differently.

"Absolutely," Jake confirmed.

Remembering the yellow-handled knife he'd taken from the drawer, Jake took it out and held it up in his right palm.

"You want this back?" he asked Billy.

"I sure do," Billy said, enthusiastically snatching it from his hand.

When Billy grabbed the proffered knife, Jake glanced at Sarah and saw an enigmatic look on her face. "I'm sorry," he said apologetically, "I should have asked you before I gave that back to him."

"No," Sarah said, and then her enigmatic look was compounded by a bewildering tone. "You don't need permission."

Jake looked at her again. Her tone was even more puzzling than her facial expression.

"You think he's old enough to have it?" Sarah asked in response to Jake's continued glances.

"Sure," Jake said. "He's old enough, responsible enough, and he proved courageous enough."

Jake glanced through the rear-view mirror. Before Billy turned his head to look out the window, Jake saw that he was smiling from ear to ear.

CHAPTER 30

Jake drove out of the community and turned north. He had no specific destination in mind. The mysterious man from the other rooftop remained a wild card. The man had allowed him to leave the house peacefully, but that might only mean he wasn't a close ally to Stanley. He was likely not a rival drug dealer either, staging a war against his competition. If that were the case, Jake would likely have become collateral damage instead of being given a free pass. Although the expensive suit argued against an honest government employee, it was still the only reasonable explanation he could think of.

He thought about going home, but his hollow could too easily be put under siege like Waco, Texas, and Ruby Ridge, Idaho. His little hollow could be fortified against an assault, but it could also become an Alamo, limiting his options to surrender or fight. He couldn't win a gunfight against the government.

There had been very little conversation in the car for miles, but Billy spoke up soon after passing his turnoff. Obviously, he had been paying attention to the landmarks, both now and during his previous trip through this area.

"Aren't we going to your house, Jake?" Billy asked, leaning forward between the seats.

"It might not be safe right now," Jake said. "We've still got Stanley's brother to worry about." He didn't go into the details of the murder charges Stanley's brother was likely to bring against him for the dead bodies in the house.

Billy seemed to accept that answer, but something more must have been on his mind because he didn't move from his perch between the seats.

"We'll find a hotel in Charleston," Jake further explained. "We can get some rest and then decide where to go from there."

Apparently satisfied with that plan, Billy sat back in the seat and returned to the passing scenery.

From time to time, Jake glanced over at Sarah. She didn't look like she was in a comfortable position, but her face was turned away from him. Was it possible she could still love him, he wondered? According to Billy, she had married at least twice. He glanced at Billy through the rear-view mirror, and although he could easily see Billy inherited her good looks, he saw nothing else to indicate his heritage. Had she loved another man enough to want to bear his child, or had Billy been a mistake?

Jake admitted to himself that he still loved her. Even now, he wanted to reach out and touch her, but that feeling sent a nasty little doubt worming through his mind, reminding him of the story of King David in the Bible. King David had wanted another man's wife, and to free her from her marriage, he'd sent her husband to the most dangerous place on the battlefield, where he was sure to be killed. Had he rationalized the killing of Stanley so he could possess his wife?

The car crossed Oakwood Road and crawled down the last hill on Corridor G before Jake realized they had arrived in Charleston. The traffic was as heavy as usual for that time of day. Now, he had a specific destination in mind. He decided on the Holiday Inn across from the Town Center Mall. It was near the access ramps to the interstate and close to several restaurants. It was also within easy walking distance of mall shopping. He and Billy had a few changes of clothes with them, but Sarah had nothing except the clothes on her back.

A little after five in the afternoon, Jake pulled into the parking lot. Knowing that cops routinely look for secretive behavior, like cars hidden in hotel back lots, he intentionally hid his car in plain sight. He backed into the first available space.

"How about dinner before we check in?" Jake suggested as he got out and looked at his watch.

They left the car at the hotel and walked over to the Shoney's on the opposite corner of the next block. It was crowded, and they had a long wait for a table, but it only improved their spirits and appetites. Watching families come and go, hearing snatches of their mundane conversations, and being completely ignored by everybody was detoxifying. After a leisurely meal, they walked back toward the hotel, embracing their freedom and more in step with the pace of ordinary life.

"I think I feel like doing some shopping now," Sarah said as they approached the hotel.

The interactions with the calm, ordinary world had revitalized her more than the food or the naps in the car. While eating, Jake informed her of the mall across the street and suggested she go shopping as soon as she felt like it. He told her that he and Billy already had suitcases in the car.

"While you're doing that," Jake said, "I'll get the rooms. Do you need some money?"

"No thanks," Sarah said. "Amazingly," she added, "I somehow made it out of the basement with this," indicating her purse.

"Everything happens for a reason," Jake declared. "Billy can come with me if he wants."

"I'll need help carrying everything," she said. "Besides, he likes to go shopping."

"No, I don't," Billy said, looking hopefully at Jake.

"How about if Billy and I get the rooms, and then we meet you over there and carry your purchases?" Jake asked.

"How would you find me?" Sarah asked.

"Don't worry," Jake said, winking at Billy. "We found you once, and we can find you again."

"Sure, we can," Billy agreed wholeheartedly.

Sarah happily acquiesced. "I'll be in one of the clothing stores," she said as she headed for the mall.

Jake and Billy went into the hotel. At the front desk, Jake asked for two connected double rooms. He paid cash for the rooms for two days. He didn't know how long they might stay, but he didn't want to have to rush to leave by the eleven o'clock check-out time the following morning. He and Billy put their luggage in one of the rooms, but they didn't unlock the connecting doors.

"Just in time," Sarah said when they found her at the check-out in J.C. Penney.

Sarah already had more boxes and bags than she could easily manage, and she wasn't finished. Jake and Billy took possession of her purchases and freed her to complete her shopping. Jake found a saleslady in the luggage department and arranged to buy their most expensive set, provided she packed the luggage with the contents from the bags and boxes he and Billy were carrying.

It was after eight by the time they returned to the hotel. Jake and Billy carried Sarah's luggage into the same room where they left their own. After an awkward pause, Jake picked up his suitcases and excused himself to the other room.

"If you need me," Jake said, "I'll be next door."

As soon as he entered the other room, even before the pneumatic door closer allowed the door to click shut, Jake felt a powerful wave of loneliness wash over him. Looking at the empty room, he wondered how he had ever thought being alone was what he wanted. Time and distance became vague and indefinite, each seeming to mutate from well-defined measurements into an uncertain, ill-defined continuum. Had it only been minutes since he left Sarah and Billy, or had it been millennia? Were they nearby, or were they light-years away?

He wished he hadn't left their room, but what else could he do? Neither of them had objected or tried to delay his leaving. Maybe they didn't need him as much as he needed them. He dropped to the nearest bed, the loneliness in his heart amplifying the fatigue in his muscles. He was daydreaming about Sarah when a soft rap on the door that separated the two rooms brought him back to full alertness.

Sarah, he thought. The doors between the rooms were always locked unless the current occupants unlocked them. He bounded off the bed and quickly unlocked his side of the door. He pulled it open, but Sarah wasn't standing on the other side. It was Billy. He realized he still loved this boy, even if he wasn't the incarnation of the Holy Ghost and even if he had come from the union of the love of his life and some other man.

"Can I sleep in your room?" Billy asked.

Billy had already showered and was dressed for bed. Jake smiled and opened the door wide to welcome him in before he remembered the proprieties of the situation. Now that Billy's mother was present, he should get her permission before allowing Billy to do anything. He glanced around the room beyond Billy but didn't see her.

"Mom's getting ready to shower," Billy said in response to

Jake's visual inspection of the room.

"Did you clear it with her that you're sleeping over here?"

"She said it was okay with her if it's okay with you," Billy said, adding, "Is it okay with you?"

"Mi casa es su casa," Jake said with an elaborate bow and sweep of his arm.

Jake didn't know many Spanish phrases, but he was pretty sure those words meant, my house is your house. It was unlikely that Billy understood those words, but he laughed happily as he came through the door.

"Take your pick," Jake said, indicating the beds.

As Billy settled into the first bed he came to, Jake unpacked a few things before showering. While in the shower, he hummed happily, letting the water massage the fatigue out of his muscles, even as Billy's presence salved his loneliness. He felt vital again, as though he was a full-fledged member of the trio instead of an unnecessary third wheel.

When he came out of the shower, the first thing he noticed was that both doors between the rooms were standing wide open. The heavy curtains had been pulled together in both rooms, and the only source of light was a dim lamp between Billy's bed and the bed that would be his own.

He paused to stare into the silent darkness of the other room. Was the open door an invitation? He and Sarah certainly had a lot to talk about – nearly ten years of personal experiences to share. But it wasn't the lure of conversation that caused the saliva to thicken in his mouth, his groin to throb with an exquisite ache, and his heart to race wildly in his chest.

"Jake?" Billy whispered from his bed, "When are we going to your house?"

Jake jumped guiltily at the sound of Billy's voice as though caught with his hand in the cookie jar. He'd thought Billy was asleep. He went over and sat on the edge of his bed.

"I don't know, pal," Jake said. "We'll sleep on it and decide tomorrow."

"Do you like my mom?" Billy asked, lowering the volume of his whisper to make it more confidential.

"Yes, I like your mom," Jake said, lowering his head and matching Billy's air of confidentiality.

"Can she stay with us?" Billy asked with a quick smile, obviously pleased by Jake's response.

"We won't go anywhere without her," Jake promised.

He expected Billy to be pleased by his commitment to keep his mother with them. Still, Billy's smooth forehead wrinkled, and his eyes narrowed in concentration as though Jake spoke a foreign language again.

"Can she stay with us?" Billy repeated his question and added, "She can sleep in my bed if you don't want her in yours."

Jake smiled broadly as he realized what Billy was offering. He'd forgotten how naïve, innocent minds worked.

"She's probably already sleeping," Jake said, guiltily wondering if Billy had read his mind and knew what he'd been thinking just a few minutes ago. "It would be best if you were sleeping, too," he added. Before Billy could ask any more questions, he tucked the sheet under his chin, kissed him lightly on the forehead, and said, "Now shut up and go to sleep, and that's an order."

Jake got into the other bed and turned the lamp off. He and Sarah certainly needed to talk, but not tonight and not alone in a hotel room. As he surrendered to sleep, Billy's presence in the other bed and his mother in the other room resurrected Jake's fantasy of an instant family.

*****

When Billy entered Jake's room, although he didn't understand what Jake said, he was beginning to appreciate Jake's sense of humor. He didn't know exactly how, but he could tell more by the way Jake acted than by what he said. It was reassuring that Jake's attitude toward him hadn't changed.

When they were in the car, he'd been watching the scenery since leaving Stanley's house and became concerned when they passed the turnoff to Jake's house. Jake might intend to leave him and his mother somewhere else before going home alone. When he asked Jake about it, he was happy that Jake had a good reason for not going home, but he was even happier when he learned Jake had no immediate plans of leaving them.

He would have preferred that his mother be in the same room with them, but knowing she was close and safe was good, too. He hadn't understood what happened between her and Jake when they first saw each other in the basement, but he perceived they liked each other a lot. He was a little disappointed that they weren't sharing a bed, though. It seemed to him that when a man liked his mother and vice versa, she shared his bed. He never liked Stanley, but it had only been when his mother moved into another bedroom that things started getting bad between them. But Jake was nothing like Stanley, he reminded himself.

Billy lay in bed, reluctant to surrender to sleep. His fantasy of Jake becoming his dad seemed like it might be coming true. He and his mother might soon live with Jake in his big house. He was awake because he was concerned that it might all disappear if he went to sleep. The day had been so fantastic that the events already seemed like a dream. He finally drifted off to sleep with visions of a big house, dogs, and horses dancing in his head.

*****

Sarah intentionally left the connecting door open, hoping Jake would come over to talk. She sat on the edge of the bed in the dark for a long time, every fiber of her being wanting Jake to make the first move. Simultaneously, she feared what might happen if he did because she was so uncertain of what to tell him. Everything was her fault, from her father to Stanley. How could she expect Jake to forgive her?

After shopping, She felt normal and hopeful for the first time in a long time. George had searched her pocketbook when she was forced into the car, but he lost interest in it after finding a pay stub with her address and the apartment key. She was surprised they hadn't taken the couple thousand dollars that was in it. It was all she had left of the money she'd taken from Stanley's safe. She'd been even more surprised when she got out of the house earlier that day and found her pocketbook hanging on her arm. Even now, she couldn't remember picking it up before she and Billy left that room in the basement.

She had heard Billy and Jake talking in the car, but she hadn't attempted to join in. She had been happy to hear that Jake had no immediate plans to leave them. She was exhausted, but her mind was too active to allow her to sleep. The fact that Jake was alive made her checkered past seem coarse and vulgar. How much should she tell him? Did she have the right to tell him a secret that might keep him with them? And what about Jake's rights? Did he have a right to know? Every time she dozed off, one question or another pestered her back to full wakefulness.

She heard Jake and Billy whispering in the other room before they went to sleep. She was still amazed at how they had found each other and how such a trusting bond had grown so quickly between them. Back in the basement, when she'd been watching Jake remove the gun from Billy, it wasn't fear for Billy's safety at the sight of the gun that caused her to cry. She had seen the weapons they took from Jake, and she was sure he must have some proficiency with firearms.

What had caused her to cry back then was watching Jake and Billy together. Seeing Billy responding to a man, especially Jake, had made her so happy. After what two men had done to him, she had feared that Billy would never trust another man as long as he lived. The fact that he'd let Jake conceal the gun in so intimate a place on his body spoke volumes. Jake had somehow earned his absolute trust.

She knew she failed Jake as spectacularly as she failed Billy. As depression was finally letting sleep claim her, she was sadly wondering if she should avoid a confrontation and just slip away and quietly disappear.

CHAPTER 31

Jake awoke to the sound of a commercial blaring from the TV. When he opened his eyes, he saw Billy sitting on the other bed, grinning at him.

"Mom said there was something on the news you should see if you're awake," Billy said. "Are you awake?"

Jake pulled the pillow from under his head and slung it at Billy. Billy just embraced the pillow and rolled back on the bed with it, laughing.

Jake saw it was still gloomy in the room, but there was enough light around the edges of the heavy curtains to inform him that it was well past dawn. The time and temperature at the bottom of the screen said it was 8:35 and 75 degrees. He threw the covers back and was preparing to launch himself at Billy when he heard a familiar name on the TV. He settled back on the bed and propped his head on one elbow to watch.

The picture on the TV shifted from the anchorperson in the studio to a "live shot" of an older woman being interviewed by a much younger woman on a familiar street corner.

"That's Mrs. Zimmerman!" Billy excitedly volunteered.

Jake instantly recognized the wall in the distance. The camera zoomed in on a smoldering heap of ashes that had once been a big house. It was above a small house behind the wall. Jake sat up, the TV now commanding his full attention. The woman talked about coming home from an overnight visit with her sister in Virginia yesterday afternoon. She'd seen two black cars leaving the house. She said that later, she noticed smoke coming from the house and called the Fire Department.

By the time the firemen arrived, the whole house was fully

engulfed in flames. A fireman told her the fire burned so hot that it even destroyed a metal wall safe. This morning, nothing was left but a smoldering heap. When the woman started talking about the husband's separation from his wife and son, who no longer lived in the house, the interview was abruptly cut off, and the feed was returned to the studio.

The anchorperson recapped the story and added that nobody appeared to have been home at the time of the blaze. She further reported that the woman and her son had apparently not been living there for several months.

God works in mysterious ways, Jake thought as the newscast switched to another story. The man he'd met at the front of the house, presumably the same man he'd seen on the other rooftop, had become his accomplice. For whatever reason, the man had removed the dead bodies and then used fire to erase all evidence that crime, violence, and death had occurred there. From what Mrs. Zimmerman said, there was no reason to believe Sarah and Billy had been anywhere near the house for months.

Jake stood up to get dressed, but another news story caught his attention. Yesterday afternoon, around the same time as the house fire, a commuter plane bound for Atlantic City carrying several prominent law enforcement officials crashed. Now, a complete list of passengers could be released. Jake sat back down, shocked as he listened to the names. There were no survivors, and he recognized all but two names from the list of eleven. The list included U.S. Attorney Daniel Sullivan, West Virginia State Police Sergeant G.R. Stillwell, and Deputy Sheriff T. M. Mennis.

Dead, Jake thought. Talk about mysterious ways! Sarah and Billy were free of Stanley and Stanley's brother, and he was free of several of his old enemies. Jake leaped off the bed with a whoop. He grabbed Billy off the other bed and swung him around and around. He felt as ecstatic as the characters in *The Wizard of OZ* when the Wicked Witch was dead.

"It's over," Jake said, laughing. "We're free!"

Billy laughed gleefully as Jake whirled him around the room.

"Mom!" Billy shouted during one of the dizzying turns when he apparently saw his mother standing in the doorway.

When Jake turned to face the doorway again, he stopped so abruptly that he nearly upended them both.

"Did you see the news?" Jake asked, lowering Billy to the floor.

"I saw it," Sarah said, laughing while holding her hand over her mouth.

"This calls for a celebration. Let's go out on the town," Jake said, but when he looked at the bed and remembered he'd just gotten up, he amended, "Or at least, we can go out for breakfast."

"Okay," Sarah said, snickering through her hand, "but don't you think it might be a good idea to put on some pants first?"

Jake looked down at himself and, in an exaggerated gesture of modesty, pulled the covers down the bed and drew them around himself like a toga.

Billy, sitting on the edge of the other bed, giggled.

Jake picked up a pillow that had come down the bed on top of the covers and swung it at Billy. Billy didn't see it coming this time, but he rolled with the blow and came up on his knees in the middle of the bed. He grabbed one of the pillows from that bed and came back swinging. Jake had dropped his pillow, and he took several blows before letting go of the covers, retrieving his pillow, and the battle was on.

An hour later, they sat at a table in Bob Evans, situated in the next block, across from the Shoney's. It might not have qualified as being out on the town to the more serious party animal, but for Jake, the sheer pleasure of being here with Sarah and Billy was intoxicating. All through the meal, one question was uppermost in his mind. *Where do we go from here?* But he was reluctant to bring up the future for fear that it might shatter the togetherness of the present.

"They'll be looking for us, won't they?" Sarah finally broached the subject when they were finished eating. "Me and Billy, I mean," she added.

"I suppose so," Jake had to admit. "However," he added in a more encouraging tone, "I'm sure that since there likely won't be any criminal charges filed, they won't look very hard. When they don't find you or Stanley, they'll just wait for somebody to come forward to claim the property."

"What would happen if I came forward to claim Stanley's estate?" Sarah asked.

"You'd have questions to answer, like what do you know about Stanley's business," Jake said. If you told the whole truth, you and

I could end up in prison, and they'd seize all of Stanley's assets. If you don't tell the whole truth, they could trip you up, catch you in a lie, and still send you to prison.

"I can't take that risk," she said. After a few seconds, she asked, "What happens when I don't claim the estate?"

"Nothing," Jake said. "It would eventually be seized and auctioned off for back taxes by the County Sheriff."

Staring down at the table, Sarah quietly confessed, "I killed a man in California about five years ago."

Billy already knew about Richard, so she guiltily glanced around. Fortunately, nobody else paid them any attention.

"Billy's father?" Jake asked.

"Where did you ..." she started to ask, but one glance at Billy and the answer was obvious.

"I can help you if you'll let me," Jake volunteered. When she returned her attention to him, he continued, "I can find out if you're wanted, and if necessary, I can go to California with you to get it straightened out."

"That's a generous offer, but I can't ask you to do that."

"You didn't ask," Jake said, "I volunteered." When she offered no further objection, he asked, "What was your last name when it happened?"

"Sanchez," she said, frowning as though her mind's eye was looking into a place she didn't want to see. "His name was Richard Sanchez."

Billy excused himself to go to the bathroom.

Sarah pulled every detail of the incident from a place she'd never wanted to visit again. She described the drudgery of life with Richard, from her being the only one working to support the family to his drinking and gambling. She described the origin of the scars on Billy's back and every gory detail of what she did to Richard. She'd stripped him and took him out into the desert behind the house in an old wheelbarrow and dumped his naked body. She finished the story with her job in a restaurant in Cleveland, where she met Stanley.

Jake hadn't said anything as he listened to her story, but when he saw Billy returning from the bathroom, he hurriedly whispered, "Sarah, I'd like to know. Was Sanchez Billy's father?"

"No," Sarah said emphatically, drying her tears. When Billy

took his seat at the table, she confessed, "I owe you both an explanation."

"Excuse me," a young waitress interrupted.

Jake looked up with obvious impatience and annoyance.

"Will there be anything else?" she politely asked.

"No, thank you," Jake said loudly and curtly. When the waitress turned away, Jake realized how rude he'd been. "Maybe we should go back to the hotel to talk," he suggested, wondering at Sarah's agitated look.

He left a very generous tip on the table, both as compensation for having tied up the table for so long and as an apology for his rudeness.

Jake would call a friend at the Sheriff's Department in Beecham County. His friend could access the National Criminal Information Center (NCIC) and check Sarah's criminal history, automatically generating a national search for any crimes for which she might be wanted. He'd have to contact Dennis through the Sheriff's Office since he would most likely be out in the field. Accessing that information would take only minutes, but it might take hours for his friend to get into the office.

He was thinking as they walked back to the hotel. This might not be over, so he wasn't comfortable with letting the world know where they were. It wasn't Deputy Dennis Dingess he mistrusted. He mistrusted the current Sheriff, the man appointed to fill his friend's position, the former Sheriff. *Better safe than sorry*, he thought. He would make the phone call from someplace other than their hotel rooms. Another hotel was just a few blocks away, and it might be better if he walked over there.

When they returned to the hotel, Jake told Sarah what he would do before going inside. He explained that it might take a couple of hours, but they needed the information sooner rather than later to decide where to go from there. Sarah understood and agreed that she and Billy would wait for him in their rooms.

"One more thing," Jake said before they separated. "When you married Stanley, did you use Sanchez, or did you use your maiden name, Ramella, for the marriage license?" He had to know if a paper trail would link her to Stanley.

"Neither," she said. I was afraid they might be looking for me, so I made up a name when we got to Cleveland. I don't know how, but the restaurant owner paid me without documentation. I made up the name Connie Jones."

*****

Sarah waited anxiously while Jake was making the phone call, wishing she'd already told him the truth. He might learn some bad things about her before she could explain. She felt frustrated that when she finally dared to tell the whole truth, Jake stopped her, suggesting she wait and talk at the hotel. She would tell him and Billy everything as soon as he came back.

A good night's sleep had done wonders for her psyche; she awakened in much higher spirits this morning. Billy and Jake were the only two people in this world who mattered to her. She decided she wouldn't walk away until she found out how they felt about the secret she was keeping from them.

When Billy got up this morning, he came over from the other room and turned the TV on. When she heard the preview of the story about the house fire, she sent Billy over to alert Jake. She was sure it was something he needed to see. She stayed and watched the news report alone and was stunned that there'd been no mention of dead bodies in the house.

She continued staring at the screen while waiting for a reaction from the other room. The story of the airplane crash made no impression on her until she heard a name she recognized. She'd only begun to realize the impact of that news when she heard Jake's reaction. She stepped into the doorway and watched with amusement as Jake, still clad in boxer shorts and a T-shirt, swung Billy around the room.

When the pillow fight started, she backed out of the doorway to let the boys have their fun. As she listened to the rambunctious laughter coming from the other room, the tears that filled her eyes were a mixture of joy and regret. A pillow fight was only one of the many simple pleasures denied to Billy. She made one concrete promise to herself. Regardless of what happened to her, she would not take Billy away from Jake.

She had started talking at the breakfast table and intended to be completely truthful with both Jake and Billy. She was surprised when she found out Jake already knew something about Richard

Sanchez, but when she looked at Billy, the look on his face told her all she needed to know. She and Billy had never talked about that incident. It never occurred to her until Jake asked about Billy's father that she'd never told Billy some basic facts about himself. She never told him that Richard was not his real father. Billy had never mentioned it, and she'd thought he must have been too young to remember Richard until she realized he had those scars on his back for a constant reminder.

She was surprised by how much Billy had confided in Jake, but she was even more surprised that Billy didn't confide his actual age. That would have led Jake to a simple deduction when he discovered she was Billy's mother. It might have also relieved her of the guilt for keeping it secret from them both. More importantly, it might have helped explain some of the bad things Jake might learn about her.

*****

Jake strolled to the Elk River Lodge in high spirits. It was four blocks away. When he entered the hotel, he saw a house phone on the counter in the lobby, but he would likely have to wait hours for the information he needed. Any legal trouble for him seemed doubtful, but it was still necessary to safeguard Sarah's connection to Stanley. He duplicated his registration from the other hotel just to add confusion to her paper trail.

When he entered the room, he called the Sheriff's Office and was surprised when Dennis answered the phone. "You must be tight with the new sheriff to be hanging around the office," he greeted his friend.

"Jake," Dennis happily greeted him. "You wouldn't believe how much things have changed around here."

After they talked for a few minutes, Jake explained what he needed. He gave Dennis the names Sarah Sanchez, Connie Jones and Connie Gunther to run through NCIC. He was about to hang up when he hesitated and impulsively added her maiden name, Sarah Ramella. He gave Dennis his phone number and stretched out on the bed to wait. He thought he might nap, but it was only a little more than ten minutes before Dennis called back.

"Got it," Dennis said when Jake picked up the phone.

"That was fast," Jake said.

It had taken him longer to register for this room than to use the phone. If he had used the house phone in the lobby, he could already be finished and back with Sarah and Billy.

"Things are running pretty smooth today," Dennis replied. "By the way, the Sheriff sends his best."

"Best what?" Jake quipped, not entirely joking.

Soon after Eugene Wilkerson had been appointed sheriff to replace Jake's old school chum, he had seemed to take perverse pleasure in firing Jake when Jake's federal indictment was made public.

"I know what you mean," Dennis said, laughing. "But you'd be surprised at how much he changed overnight. Ready for the information?"

"Ready," Jake said.

"Sarah Sanchez, Connie Jones, and Connie Gunther," Dennis read the names from the responses. "All of them have no wants, no warrants, and no record NCIC."

Jake was surprised to feel a stab of disappointment along with that news. Had he wanted bad news for Sarah? He realized that the answer was both yes and no. He was convinced that because Sarah was the only witness, any charge against her could be beaten. He'd been looking forward to traveling to California with them, hiring the best lawyers, and sparing no expense to be her champion. He wanted her and Billy to need him because he wanted to continue to be a full-fledged member of the trio.

"The other name, Sarah C. Ramella," Dennis said, "no wants or warrants, but there is a short criminal history. Do you need that?"

"Yes," Jake said, curious but not concerned. He was familiar with criminal histories and the many pedestrian charges that many people have on their records.

"Prostitution," Dennis read from the short list, "pandering, shoplifting two counts, and prostitution, again." Then, he read off the conviction dates.

Jake was too stunned to reply, feeling like he'd been hit by a freight train. Prostitution? The love of his life had become a prostitute. The fact that she had married twice had been a bitter pill to swallow, but prostitution struck him as downright traitorous.

According to the dates, every one of those convictions had

occurred during a twelve-month period that began less than a year after they consummated their impromptu wedding. It was a simple deduction that since Billy was eight years old, it would have been right after the date of that first prostitution charge that Billy had been conceived.

He fell back onto the bed and thought about the last thing she'd said at the restaurant: I owe you both an explanation. She'd seemed displeased at his suggestion that they return to the room to talk. Had she wanted her confessions to be in a public place to blunt their reactions? Had she been about to tell him she was a whore, and her affections could be bought with either money or a wedding ring? And what explanation did she owe Billy? Jake's suspicious mind was in overdrive now. Was she going to tell him that Richard Sanchez wasn't his father and that his real father was a "john," whose name she didn't bother to get or couldn't remember? He closed his eyes.

There came a soft rap on the door. He turned the TV down as he slipped out of the warm bed. He was utterly mystified as to who it could be. He knew only one person in San Francisco; she had gone home hours ago. When he opened the door, he found that she had returned. Sarah stood in the doorway.

Jake was in another time and place. He had been surprised when she asked him to marry her. Thoughts of neither money nor a wedding ring corrupted his heartfelt declaration of love. All his senses argued that what he was experiencing was new and exciting. After the wedding ceremony, they were entwined in each other's arms in the hotel room bed, and he was about to enter her when he was snapped awake by the ringing phone.

"Jake?" a concerned voice asked.

The only sound that came out of Jake's mouth was a hoarse, raspy growl.

"Jake, are you all right?" the voice asked.

"Dennis?" Jake finally managed to say.

"What happened?" Dennis asked. "I was beginning to worry. I lost you ten minutes ago. When I finally got through, it rang five or six times before you picked up."

"I don't know," Jake said. "There must be something wrong with the phones."

Truthfully, Jake didn't know what it was, but he knew it hadn't been the phones. It must have been some combination of a fugue state and a dream.

After expressing his appreciation to Dennis and each pledging to stay in touch, Jake hung up the phone.

He'd had the now familiar dream again, but for the first time, it ended before he and Sarah could consummate their love. It left him with a need and a fierce craving for female companionship. He had hard feelings for Sarah, but they weren't the same kind of hard feelings as before.

He looked at his watch and was surprised it had been less than an hour since he'd left Sarah and Billy. He continued to lie on the bed, thinking. He couldn't deny he loved Sarah, but there was still the prostitution and the question of Billy's father.

Finally, he decided a cold shower might clear his head. He hadn't brought clean clothes with him, but it wasn't physical filth that he needed to wash away. As he walked back to the Holliday Inn, his heart still pumping hot blood, he realized there was only one acceptable course of action.

Jake entered his hotel room singing an old Waylon Jennings song, *You Ask Me To*. He was feeling vibrant and alive. He loved Sarah and Billy, so let the world call him a fool, but nothing else mattered if things were right between him and Sarah, as the song advocated. He saw the connecting doors open and could hear the TV in the other room. They must have heard him coming because the TV went silent. When he stepped into the doorway, they stared expectantly at him.

"Good news," he said, "you don't have to go to California." After a brief pause, he stared directly into Sarah's eyes and announced, "You're not wanted for anything anywhere."

Relief was written all over Sarah's face.

"Does that mean we can go back to your house?" Billy asked, hopefully.

"I need to talk to your mom first. He gave Billy a conspiratorial wink and asked, "Would you excuse us?"

"Sure," Billy said with a grin, "you're excused."

CHAPTER 32

"I'll excuse you," Jake said as he grabbed Billy, lifted him over his head, and roughly twisted him around and around. Finally, he set him down, propelled him toward the door, and said, "Get out!"

Still giggling, Billy stopped in the doorway and asked, "Want me to close the door?"

"You don't have to," Jake said, "but you could turn the TV on. It'll give you something to do."

How could anybody not love that kid, Jake wondered, *no matter who his father might be?* He turned to Sarah, who was sitting on the edge of the bed, smiling and looking beautiful as ever.

"I want to ask you something," Jake said, slowly pacing back and forth in front of her. "Sarah," he said, "I've loved you from the moment I helped you up off that airport floor. We've missed a lot of years we could have had together. I don't want to miss another minute." Stopping in front of her, dropping to one knee, and taking both of her hands in his, he said, "Sarah, I love you. Would you do me the honor of being my wife?"

"Jake, you don't ..." she stammered, "there's so much ..." Finally stringing three words together that made a complete thought, she said, "We should talk."

Jake wasn't about to be so easily dissuaded from the only course of action that would give his life meaning.

"You can say no, and I'll walk away," Jake gently responded, "but I'll do that only because I love you enough to let you go, not because it's what I want."

"I don't want to say no," she said, "but there are things you should know."

"Unimportant details," Jake said. "Just say yes, and we'll have the rest of our lives together for details."

"But there are some things, some bad things, you don't know about me," she insisted. Lowering her head, she added, "You might not love me anymore when you know."

Jake wasn't so naïve as to believe the spurt of criminal offenses years ago was the only "bad things" to which she was referring, but according to the Bible, there is a season for everything. He also believed everything happened for a reason, and he couldn't discount that God had led him to Sarah. Whatever she did, she did it while believing he was dead.

He released one hand so he could lift her chin. He looked into her eyes and spoke words that came spontaneously to his lips. He didn't know if the words were his own or if he'd heard them in a movie or a song, but they expressed his feelings exactly.

"Sarah," he said with grave sincerity, "I can't promise that I'll love you for the rest of your life, but I can promise that I'll love you for the rest of mine. Please say yes."

"Yes," she breathlessly whispered.

Jake had been looking into her liquid blue eyes when a swollen teardrop escaped from her left eye, ran down the hollow beside her nose, and hung on her upper lip, shimmering like a jewel. He pulled her up with him as he stood. He took her in his arms and kissed her, the salty teardrop acting like a superconductor to further electrify the intimacy of the contact. It was the kind of kiss that would usually lead to more amorous activities, but by mutual consent, they breathlessly separated.

"Billy," Sarah whispered.

"Billy," Jake echoed his name. "Let me tell him," he pleaded. "I think it'll make him as happy as it made me."

"There's something you should know," Sarah insisted.

Jake kissed the pad of his right index finger and placed it against her lips.

"Unimportant details," he reminded her.

If Billy had become an issue, he had been prepared to tell her that he loved the kid no matter who his father was, and he would work hard to be the best father any child could want. He started toward the other room but then stopped and turned in the doorway as he thought of something amusing Billy had said.

"Did you know you come highly recommended?" he asked. "I have it on excellent authority that you're a really good cook and hardly ever snore." He chuckled as he went through the door without waiting for a response.

Billy reacted enthusiastically to the news. He threw his arms around Jake's neck, and Jake hugged him tightly.

"Wait a minute. I want to ask you a question," Jake said, pulling him back from his shoulder so he could see his face. "You know that when I marry your mother, that will automatically make you my stepson, right?"

"Right," Billy said, still grinning.

"Well, the thing is," Jake continued with a straight face, "I don't really want you to be my stepson."

Billy's grin faltered, but it didn't entirely disappear.

"You see," Jake said, "what I want most of all is a real son, and out of all the boys in the world I could choose from, I choose you." With a broad grin, he said, "So my question is, would you be my real son, let me adopt you, and give you my name?"

Tears rolled down Billy's cheeks as he bounded off the bed and threw his arms around Jake's neck again. "Whoa," Jake said happily, "it's not official until we get your mother's permission."

The words were barely out of Jake's mouth before Billy excitedly asked, "Can he, Mom? Can Jake adopt me?"

Realizing that Sarah must be behind them, Jake wrapped his right arm around Billy's shoulders and swiveled so they both faced her. She didn't immediately answer Billy, so Jake added his plea to Billy's question.

"Can I?" Jake pleaded. "I love this kid."

"No," Sarah said.

"Aw, Mom," Billy objected immediately, "how come?"

"Yeah, Mom," Jake parroted Billy, "how come?"

"For one thing," she said, barely keeping a straight face, "it's not necessary."

"I know it's not necessary," Jake said, "but I want to."

"For another thing," she said, "it would probably be against the law."

She stepped forward and handed Jake the folded document hanging unobtrusively from her left hand. Jake wasn't as familiar with civil law as criminal law, but he was sure adoptions were a simple matter when nobody objected. Disheartened, he unfolded the document and saw the bold title, BIRTH CERTIFICATE. *Billy's father must be the problem*, he thought. All the other parties were here, so only Billy's father could object.

"Is it Billy's father?" Jake asked. "Will Billy's father stop me from adopting Billy?"

"In a manner of speaking," Sarah said with a broad smile. "Look at the names."

"William Jacob McCallum, Jr.," Jake read aloud. Skipping down the document to the father, he read, "William Jacob McCallum, Sr." Jake's eyes widened as he gave Sarah a questioning look.

"Is this mine?" Billy asked.

"Yes," Sarah said, answering both Jake and Billy. Then, her smile faltered and became tentative and uncertain.

Jake and Billy stared at each other as though they were seeing each other for the first time.

"That's what might make it against the law," she said. "It would be double … something or other. I doubt that a father can legally adopt his own son."

"According to this," Jake said, looking at the date of birth and quickly doing the math, "Billy would be nine years old."

"He is," Sarah said, explaining the new identification.

"Yeah," Billy said, looking at Jake. "I didn't want to tell you I was eight years old because I was afraid you might not give me the knife, but Mom told me I had to, no matter who asked. You never treated me like a stupid little kid, so I forgot about it."

"William – Billy, Jacob – Jake," Jake mused to himself.

Sarah buried her face in her hands and sobbed silently, just as she had done in that basement room eons ago.

Jake looked at Billy, and Billy looked at Jake. Having been instantly cast into the roles of father and son wasn't as dazzling as it might have been if a strong bond didn't already exist between them. As it was, their relationship was affected very little by the news. It was as though, subconsciously, they'd somehow intuited the truth from the first moment they'd seen each other. With a sidelong nod to indicate Sarah, Jake got up and went to her. Billy followed, and Jake put an arm under his armpit and lifted him to shoulder level so they both could put an arm around Sarah.

"I'm sorry," Sarah said, her voice squeaky. "I shouldn't have kept that a secret for so long." She sniffled and added, "From either of you."

"Sh, sh," Jake said, trying to comfort her. "I don't think it made any difference. Billy agreed to be my real son anyway."

Taking his cue from Jake, Billy exclaimed, "Yeah, Mom, we're okay. Jake *wanted* to be my dad."

After a minute, Sarah dropped her hands from her face and put her arms around them. "That was one of those unimportant details," she said, trying to smile through the tears.

"Let's not wait," Jake said after another minute, breaking the silence. "Let's get married right now."

"No objections," Sarah said, "but where would we go for that?"

"Let's go to Las Vegas." Jake said. "That's where we originally planned to get married. Let's do it."

"Back then, it was on our way," Sarah said, and just being practical, asked, "Wouldn't it be a long, hard trip from here?"

"Not if we charter a jet," Jake said.

Still being practical, she said, "That sounds great, but wouldn't that be much too extravagant?"

"We can afford it," Jake said, and with a playful smile, he added, "I guess that's one of my unimportant details. We've got a few million dollars."

*****

Sarah was stunned by Jake's proposal. She'd been prepared to answer all his questions, but that one hadn't even occurred to her. There were so many things to discuss, but Jake made such a strong case for love that her heart rushed to accept the proposal before her mind could argue a delay.

When Jake had gone into the other room to tell Billy, she started to follow but stopped when she remembered she had proof of what she would tell them. She grabbed her pocketbook and dug to the bottom until she found papers that had been undisturbed for so long that they were stuck together. She quickly separated them and removed the official copy of Billy's birth certificate. It hadn't been moved except when she changed pocketbooks. Nobody had ever seen it, not even Billy.

When she stepped into the room, it was evident that Jake had already given Billy the news. Jake sat on the first bed with his back to her, and Billy's arms were wrapped around Jake's neck, his chin resting on Jake's shoulder. His smile was evidence that Jake's prediction had been accurate. Billy was obviously happy with the news, but she hadn't doubted it. She'd witnessed how the two of them responded to each other.

Billy saw her and was about to say something when Jake pulled him off his shoulder to ask him a question. She watched as Billy sat back down on the bed, his face blocked from her view by Jake, and she waited for Jake to finish. However, the next thing she heard from Jake made her heart skip a beat. Could Jake have told Billy he didn't want him for a stepson? She couldn't see Billy's face, but he must be crushed.

However, the next thing she'd heard Jake say made her heart skip another beat, but this time, it was accompanied by a lump in her throat. When she saw Billy's chin on Jake's shoulder again, happy tears were in his eyes, and his face was radiant with joy. By making the fact that Billy would automatically become his stepson sound undesirable, Jake had made the fruit of his question all the sweeter. Sarah decided that her news might benefit from that same misdirection.

She didn't smile when she said no to their questions, but when she had to explain the necessity of changing Billy's age, her "no" was exposed as a secret she'd deliberately kept from them. She was disappointed that it had been necessary to explain the new identities and discomfited that her news hadn't been received with the joy she had imagined only minutes ago. Thankfully, Jake and Billy came to her rescue again.

*****

After nearly an hour on the phone with the people at the Executive Jet Management office at Yeager Airport, Jake came away mildly disappointed. He had unrealistically imagined jetting to Las Vegas, getting married, and flying home – all in only a few hours. As it turned out, money could be a shortcut to many things, but it couldn't change the natural laws, physically shorten distances, or alter the flow of time.

"It'll be easier if we just plan on spending the night in Las Vegas," Jake explained to Sarah and Billy when he finally got off the phone. "They can rush the paperwork and prep time but can't do anything about the distance. It takes nearly four-and-a-half hours of flight time each way, and then there's getting to and from the plane. There could also be a problem with getting a marriage license."

Jake explained that when he'd told the lady at the Executive Jet office the purpose of their trip, she offered to make all the arrangements on the Las Vegas end. What surprised him most was that a man and a woman couldn't just wander into any Wedding Chapel on a whim and get legally married. There was no waiting period, but for the marriage to be legal, every couple must first obtain a marriage license. The most expeditious way to get that license was to appear in person with a photo ID at the Clark County Marriage License Bureau.

"Do you have a photo ID?" Jake asked Sarah.

"I think I have three different driver's licenses," Sarah said. "I've got one with the last name Sanchez that's expired, one with Gunther, and the fake one from Cleveland."

"You can't use Sanchez or Gunther because they would tie you to your past. Let me see the fake one." When he looked at the license and saw the name Connie S. Horton, he asked, "What does the 'S' stand for?"

Sarah pulled out her Social Security card and Birth Certificate. They both had the same name.

"That's all there is," she said. "Everything else was destroyed with Stanley's papers."

"That's great," Jake said. "The 'S' can stand for whatever you say it stands for. If I call them back right now," Jake said, "the earliest we can lift off is around four. We would arrive in Vegas a little before nine. It'll be around six local time, and the Courthouse closes at five. We'll have to wait until tomorrow morning to get the license and get married."

"We've waited ten years," Sarah said, "I'm sure we can wait one more day. I don't care what we do so long as we can all be together."

"Amen to that," Jake said, embracing Sarah.

"I know what we can do," Billy piped up. "We can find a hotel with a swimming pool."

They boarded the jet and traveled west, crossing three time zones. During the flight, Jake and Sarah talked about a honeymoon and decided more travel didn't appeal to either of them. They could go to Paris or anywhere in the world, but home and hearth were their fondest desires for now.

In Las Vegas, Jake and Billy surprised Sarah with their unique swimwear and Billy's talent for swimming. The Executive Air people got them a reservation at the Circus Circus Hotel on Las Vegas Boulevard, which had two swimming pools. The specialized swimwear reminded Jake of his promise to Billy.

The scars were most vivid after successive submersions in cold and hot water, so Jake took pictures of Billy's back immediately after swimming and a hot shower. Billy resisted the pictures but relented after Jake explained he could show the images instead of dragging him from one doctor to another.

The next morning, they got the license and were back in the air just over an hour after getting married. Jake called his brother from the plane and, considering the time zones, told him what time he expected to be back home. He told Nick he was bringing home his new wife, Sarah, and son, Billy, the latter of whom Nick had met at Jake's house. He told Nick that his wife was the fiancée he thought had died ten years ago. He suggested that Walker could fill them in about that.

An hour and a half after landing in Charleston, Jake turned up the hollow to his house. The gate was open, and a "Welcome Home" banner hung over the road. Jake turned into the first driveway, intending to say "hello" to his brother and make introductions before they went home.

"That's Uncle Nick's house," Billy declared from the back seat, proud to display his prior knowledge of the place. "He's got dogs and horses."

"This is where Nick, Jenny, and Jimmy live," Jake explained to Sarah, having already spoken of them on the plane.

Nick and Jenny both worked, so each had a vehicle. However, when Jake started up the driveway to the back of the house, he saw that both cars were gone.

"No vehicles," Jake said. "Maybe they're already up at our house." *Our house,* he thought. That had a nice ring to it.

When they rounded the last curve to his house, Jake recognized the three vehicles parked there. Two belonged to his brother and sister-in-law, and the third belonged to Walker. Jake pulled into the space near the front steps that had apparently been left open for him. Another "Welcome Home" banner was strung across the banister of the porch. As they exited the car, greeters came streaming out the front door.

After introductions to the adults, Jake took particular pleasure in introducing his son to Jimmy and his "honorary" kids. The crowd waited for Jake to enter the house with his new family. As they started through the door, Jake swept Sarah into his arms, and the adults stepped back to give them a wide berth. The kids laughed gleefully, responding more to Sarah's surprised reaction than the old-fashioned tradition of carrying a bride across the threshold.

The house was decorated suitably for a wedding reception. There was a feast on the kitchen table, and there was even a three-tiered wedding cake. Now, Jake understood the necessity of three vehicles. To have accomplished so many arrangements so quickly, each driver must have gone in a different direction.

After eating and the customary cutting of the wedding cake, the kitchen table was cleared to provide a playing area for the kids. While the kids played a game on the kitchen table, the adults took their coffee in the living room, where they could hear the fantastic details of Jake's discovery of an "undead" fiancée and a half-grown son. It had been part of the plan, and possibly even the impetus, for the impromptu wedding reception.

"This is your home," Jake told Billy before leaving the kids sitting around a game on the table. "You're the host, and you're only obligated to treat Sarah and her brothers like guests, but I would greatly appreciate it if you treated them like family."

Nick, Jenny, and Jimmy had heard the basic details of Jake's "lost love" from Walker, so they were all anxious to hear the rest of the story. Jake and Sarah took turns telling the story. Jake left out only the things that must be kept secret or were highly personal, like the dead men at Stanley's house and the scars on Billy's back. Still, despite the adjustments for propriety's sake, everybody listened to the fantastic tale with rapt attention. Jake encouraged Sarah's participation because he wanted her to feel comfortable with this group.

Sarah told them about her father's deceits, her mother's death from cancer, her pregnancy, running away from home before the baby was born, and some of her hardships with Billy. She told them about her first ill-fated marriage. She'd been forced to accept the first marriage proposal after having been threatened by Child Welfare that she could lose custody of Billy. Like Jake, she left out painful and sensitive personal details, like her two dead husbands and her criminal convictions.

Sarah had told Jake those "unimportant details" during their flight to Las Vegas while Billy was given a VIP cockpit tour. Jake was so glad he hadn't let his injured pride keep him from Sarah and Billy. As Sarah was wrapping up the story, Jake excused himself to check on the kids.

When he stopped in the doorway and looked at the kids, he was pleased they were getting along splendidly. All four children were hunched over the table, a board game at the center of their attention. They had their knees in the chairs and leaned over with their elbows on the table. Billy and little Sarah were on the same side of the table with their backs to him.

He was about to turn away when the kids started laughing at something in the game. He froze when he saw little Sarah put her hand on Billy's back, right where the scars were most prominent. It was such an innocent, spontaneous gesture that it should have brought a smile to his lips, but instead, he cringed. He was sure the party would be over. He waited, sure that Billy would explode and refuse to associate further with the other kids.

However, just as spontaneously as little Sarah put her hand on Billy's back, she withdrew it. Jake hesitated, waiting to make sure the danger of an outburst from Billy had passed. As he turned away from the kitchen, his heart swelled with love and pride in those two kids. Billy had apparently taken his request seriously and accepted the other kids as family. And little Sarah, being the wonderfully sensitive child she was, would never point out anybody's physical deformity. He resolved to make it a priority to find a plastic surgeon.

It was nearly midnight before the party ended, and both Nick and Walker came to Jake privately to offer to keep Billy for a few days. Jake graciously refused their offers and assured them the house was big enough that privacy shouldn't become an issue.

However, after everybody was gone and Billy was given his choice of bedrooms, Jake was a bit disappointed that he chose the same bedroom as before and not one of the four upstairs.

While Billy showered in the bathroom down the hall, Jake used the shower off his – or now, his and Sarah's – bedroom. It wasn't like the last time he and Billy stayed here. This time, Sarah was humming, unpacking Billy's clothes in the other bedroom, and instead of thoughts of freeing Billy's mother, Jake was occupied with thoughts of the night ahead with Sarah.

By the time he got out of the shower, he could think of only one solution to Billy being in the next bedroom. He had often gone to sleep listening to music, and now, music could be played loud enough to mask his and Sarah's intimacies. Besides, he would soon need to have the sex talk with Billy. Billy's sheltered naivete was cute, but soon, he would have to learn there was more to a woman sharing a man's bed than sleeping.

He was searching through his music collection when Sarah screamed. He instantly dropped what he was doing to rush to her side. He pulled up abruptly, scanned the room, and couldn't identify any threat. He saw only Sarah and Billy.

"Look!" Sarah exclaimed as she turned Billy around. She held his pajama top in her hand.

"What?" Jake asked, looking from Sarah to Billy. He still saw no threat but was beginning to understand that Sarah was more excited than alarmed.

"Look!" Sarah repeated, rubbing her hand over Billy's back.

Jake suddenly understood the cause of her excitement. It wasn't what was there – it was what wasn't. He stepped forward and placed his hand on Billy's back, sliding it up, down, and all around. No blemish was visible to the eyes, and no trace of the scars was discernible to the touch.

Jake recalled that he thought Billy might be the Holy Ghost incarnate when he first met him. However, after hearing his age of eight and discovering Sarah was his mother, he discounted that possibility. Now, knowing Billy's actual age, he had to reconsider. She had been a virgin and could have experienced an immaculate conception before their "wedding night."

Since sex between Joseph and Mary would not have been inherently sinful within the confines of their marriage, the only reason Joseph abstained from sex with Mary until after the birth of Jesus was that he was explicitly commanded to do so. In that time period, verifiable proof that Mary was a virgin before Jesus was born depended considerably on Mary having an unbroken hymen.

Jake was sure he and Sarah had been married in the eyes of God at the time they'd had sex in that hotel room. To the best of his knowledge, neither he nor Sarah were commanded not to have sex, and as he recalled, every fiber of his being was in favor of it.

Comparing the date on Billy's birth certificate with the date of their physical union, which was indelibly etched in his mind, Jake calculated that Billy was born approximately one week short of a nine-month gestation period. That amount of time was statistically irrelevant, but it did provide a narrow window of opportunity in which Billy could have been divinely conceived. It was possible Sarah could have already been pregnant with Billy when they consummated their "wedding."

It was deeply unsettling when he remembered that only minutes ago, he had been looking ahead to a time when he would need to have the sex talk with Billy. Because of who Billy might be, talking about sex to him, even in the context of societal norms, might be blasphemous. The Bible didn't say so, but the worldly pleasure of sex might have been one of the temptations the devil used against Jesus.

Fortunately, according to the preacher, you can't accidentally blaspheme the Holy Ghost any more than you can accidentally commit murder. Causing death is an intended consequence of murder, so murder can't be unintentional. If there is no murder without the intent to kill, then logically, no sin is imputed without the intent to blaspheme the Holy Ghost.

As his hand sailed over smooth, supple skin, a familiar phrase reverberated through Jake's mind: *physician, heal thyself.*

CHAPTER 33

J ake returned to selecting the music to mask the sounds coming from this bedroom. After finding a few old albums he deemed appropriate, he moved the antique stereo speakers against the wall separating the two bedrooms.

When Sarah got out of the shower, she came to Jake and kissed him passionately, but then she pulled away and got dressed. "Wait a minute," she said, "I want this to be perfect."

She went back into the bathroom, and Jake heard the shower. A few minutes later, Sarah knocked on the bathroom door. After only a slight hesitation, Jake opened the door. There stood Sarah, her hair plastered to her head and her clothes clinging to her body like they were painted on. Jake wrapped his arms around her and pulled her into the room. She quickly undressed, toweled off, and slid into bed, holding back the corner of the covers for Jake.

When Jake started the music and climbed into bed, their first coupling was urgent and demanding, fueled by need. In their subsequent unions, they rocked in each other's arms, their passion driven by love, fusing their souls together. They cuddled for a long time, and Jake held her until her slow, rhythmic breathing told him she was asleep.

He closed his eyes, reflecting on his happiness and thanking God for Sarah and Billy. He'd never felt like this. It was as though parts of him had been absent, and he hadn't even realized they'd been missing. One missing part had been this female half he held in his arms, and the other was the child sleeping in the next bedroom. As he drifted off, his feeling of completeness subconsciously connected free-floating associations. *God is one, but God is Three. I am one, but I am three.*

The next morning, Jake was awakened by a rap on the bedroom door. The degree of light filtering through the curtains told him it must be near mid-morning.

"Dad," Billy called through the door, "Mom says breakfast will be ready in about ten minutes."

"Okay," Jake responded, smiling at how appropriate, natural, and fulfilling it had sounded to hear Billy address him as Dad for the very first time.

He hadn't awakened when Sarah got out of bed, but considering the intensity of his dream, he wasn't surprised. After he fell asleep, he'd entered a realm so awesomely captivating that if anybody had checked him, they might have concluded he was in a coma. This morning, he woke up with a clear mind, the memories of another lifetime, and a new clarity of purpose. He had the lifetimes of two distinct people within him, but he knew it wasn't a multiple personality disorder. It was reincarnation.

As he washed up and dressed for breakfast, he thought about what he needed to do. First, he needed to call the preacher and get him here for a meeting this weekend. In addition to the preacher, he also needed to get Nick, Walker, and their wives and children here. He would reveal a truth to them about the nature of existence that was more awesome than any of them had imagined. Thanks to last night's dream, he could answer many puzzling questions. Now, existence made perfect sense to him, and the identity of the Holy Ghost incarnate was clear. They would also need to make plans for what will be a fantastic future.

When he got to the kitchen, breakfast was on the table. Jake warmly greeted his wife and son before they sat down to their first private meal together as a family in their own home. They held hands while Billy said the blessing, and Jake hoped to make that a family tradition for as long as possible. Soon after they started eating – and the food was as good as Billy had advertised – Billy asked a question.

"Dad," Billy asked, "can I have a pup? Aunt Jenny said I could have one of Rocky's pups if it's all right with you and Mom."

Jake looked at Sarah, expecting this subject to require a family discussion, but she refused to acknowledge his stare. Instead, she looked at the food on her plate as though it required her undivided attention. Being somewhat practiced with reading guilty reactions, he deduced that she had already been asked this question and had already given Billy her approval.

"What did your mom say about it?" Jake asked, noticing the quick look Sarah gave Billy, confirming his deduction.

"She said it was fine with her, but I'd have to ask you," Billy said, oblivious to his mother's glance.

"I see," Jake said, pretending it was a serious decision. "You know, Rocky's of a short-haired breed accustomed to living in the house. How does your mom feel about pets in the house?"

"It's okay with her," Billy exclaimed, excited by the possibility that the declaration would get him a puppy.

Even though Sarah had focused her attention on her plate again, Jake saw a hint of a smile at the corners of her mouth. He liked the idea of having dogs in the house.

"Tell you what," Jake said, "I'll agree with your mom under one condition."

Rocky and Apollo were males, and Jenny sometimes let the dogs provide stud service. She usually didn't charge anything, but she sometimes accepted one of the pups if somebody she knew wanted one.

"I'll feed him every day and take real good care of him," Billy promised.

"That's good," Jake said, "but that's not the condition."

He stared at Sarah, patiently waiting for her to raise her head to acknowledge his stare.

"The condition is," he said, looking into Sarah's eyes, "you can have one of Rocky's pups if I can have one of Apollo's pups."

Sarah burst into laughter and asked, "What am I going to do with you two?"

"You can do anything you want to do *with* us," Jake said with a broad smile, "so long as you never try to do without us."

While they finished eating, Jake told them about how Rocky and Apollo had saved him from the rattlesnakes. When Jake and Billy started talking about horses and Nick's barn, Sarah got up and began clearing the table.

"How about I help you with the dishes?" Jake offered.

He got up and playfully goosed her, making her squeal like a little girl. She slapped him with a dishtowel and then placed the dishtowel in his hands.

"I'll wash, and you dry," she said sternly.

"Your command is my wish," Jake bantered, bowing deeply.

They happily giggled and laughed as they moved around each other, performing like a comedy team, but each performing only for the other's amusement.

When Jake noticed Billy watching them from the table, he picked up a second dish towel and tossed it at him.

"I volunteered," he said to Billy, "but you're drafted. You can help me dry and put away."

"Wait a minute," Sarah complained happily, "I didn't know that job would get a helper. I want to change jobs."

"Sorry, lady," Jake said, "but all positions have been filled."

"Yeah, Mom," Billy said as he joined them, "you picked your job, and now you have to do it."

"So, that's how it's going to be, huh," she said through barely suppressed giggles, "two against one."

"Not always," Jake said, meaningfully grinning and winking.

"Yeah, Mom," Billy agreed, "just when it's stuff we don't like."

They were still laughing when the phone rang.

Jake flipped the phone off the wall hook, caught it mid-air, and said, "It's your nickel."

That brought a renewed round of laughter.

"Sounds like a party going on," said the voice on the phone.

"Nah," Jake said, recognizing Donna's voice, "we're just doing the dishes."

"Sarah has got to let me in on her secret," Donna said. "If I could make doing the dishes that much fun, I might get some help around here."

They laughed and talked about the kids for a few minutes, and Donna said, "Walker doesn't have to work on Friday. We were thinking about coming down if you guys are going to be home."

Jake had planned to call Walker and invite him to the meeting he needed to have with the preacher. Their intention to come down on Friday was perfect timing.

"Sure," Jake said. Then, remembering that he hadn't mentioned it to Sarah yet, he said, "Hold on a second."

Covering the mouthpiece, he asked Sarah and Billy, "Would it be okay if Walker and Donna came down on Friday and stayed for the weekend? I know we're just getting settled, but something important has come up. I'll explain when I get off the phone."

He was sure of what Sarah would say, but he never wanted her to feel he was taking her for granted. He'd included Billy in the question because the gathering he was planning would bring children into the house, and he hoped Billy would help entertain them. He expected to have Nick's son, Walker's three children, and the preacher's two kids.

"I don't mind at all," Sarah said agreeably.

"I like Sarah and her little brothers," Billy said with a shrug in response to Jake's questioning look.

"Sorry about that," Jake said when he uncovered the mouthpiece. "Do you guys have plans for this weekend?"

"I don't think so," Donna said. "Walker said something about barbecuing in the backyard on Saturday if it doesn't rain."

"Perfect. How about coming down Friday afternoon and staying for the weekend?" Jake said. Then he added, "It'll give Walker a chance to try out the repairs he made on my grill. He can be the chief cook on Saturday."

After he got off the phone and they finished the dishes, Jake explained his search for the Holy Ghost incarnate and his promise to a preacher. Without going into a lot of detail, he told them about his dream last night and the need to invite the preacher to come there. He needed to keep his promise because that preacher would play a prominent role in their futures.

Still sitting at the table after their conversation, Jake called Nick and secured his agreement to be available over the weekend. Then, he used the phone again to call the preacher. This would be the first time he had talked to him since that day in the visitors' center. He had intended to call him soon after finding Billy in that town in North Carolina, but he'd kept putting it off until circumstances made it unnecessary.

Those circumstances had changed repeatedly, but he was now sure of the facts. He was surprised when the phone was picked up after the first ring. When he identified himself, the preacher put him on hold so he could conclude another call. When the preacher came back on the line, he told Jake to call him Eli, explaining that he was known as Preacher only at the prison camp. Then, he immediately asked the most relevant question.

"You found him?" Eli asked. "You found the Holy Ghost

incarnate?"

"I found the boy I was meant to find," Jake said.

"Who is he?" Eli asked.

"I could give you a name, but the name would only invite more questions than answers," Jake explained. "I'm having a small gathering at my house to discuss the Holy Ghost and make plans for the future. I was hoping you could come Friday afternoon and stay for the weekend."

"Thank you for the invitation," Eli said hesitantly, "but I'm afraid I already have plans for the weekend."

"Change your plans," Jake said sharply. "This is important. I need you here."

"I'm not sure I can," Eli said. "I've got a business meeting Friday evening, and my wife's been looking forward to a family getaway this weekend. I already canceled the service at the prison camp, and she'd kill me if I backed out again."

"That's perfect," Jake said. "If your wife wants a family outing, bring her and your kids here for the weekend."

The preacher's silence lasted so long that Jake was about to ask if he was still on the line. When Eli did speak, Jake was surprised by the reason for his reluctance.

"I don't mean to offend you," Eli finally said, "but I don't know if my family would be comfortable spending that much time at a bachelor's home. The kids get bored easily."

"That's not a problem," Jake said, taking no offense because the preacher had no way of knowing his new circumstances. "I have a wife and son now. Besides that, there'll be two other couples here with kids."

"Sounds interesting," the preacher said, obviously more seriously considering the invitation, "but I'll need to check with my wife."

This was the same man who'd delayed joining his family in Texas to come to the prison camp. Jake knew the lure that was sure to bring him there.

"If you can't come, you can't come," he said nonchalantly. "I just thought you'd want to meet the Holy Ghost in the flesh, so to speak," he added.

It was both a pun and a fantastic reality. He suspected the preacher's silence this time was because he was speechless. When he spoke again, Jake knew he had him.

"He'll be at your house," the preacher said, breathlessly adding, "And I could meet him?"

After getting the preacher's commitment to be there, Jake sent Sarah and Billy to Walmart to pick up additional supplies for the guests and toys to occupy the kids over the coming weekend. He needed to go to the hospital to get some medical records that would prove what he intended to tell his visitors. He already knew the truth, but he wanted to show them proof.

He went to the hospital and found the Chief of Security, an old friend, and just as he'd hoped, the security officer could help him get copies of the desired records. Next, taking the records with him, Jake found a doctor he'd once helped out of a jam. He offered a generous donation to the hospital for help, but the doctor assured him that a donation wasn't required. The doctor confirmed that he could do a comparative analysis of the medical records, give his best guess at the child's paternity, and have it ready by Friday. Jake guaranteed each that no legal entanglements would arise from their assistance.

On Friday morning, Jake picked up the package of records from the doctor's office. Jenny and Jimmy came up to help put the finishing touches to all the bedrooms, and Nick joined them when he got out of bed. Walker and Donna arrived about an hour later. When Eli and his wife and kids arrived just after four o'clock, the four ladies introduced themselves and got acquainted while preparing the evening meal.

After assuring the preacher that the "Honored Guest" was present, Jake found it highly entertaining to watch him continually assessing each of the boys, trying to determine for himself which one was the Holy Ghost incarnate.

CHAPTER 34

Alexander Mason Rotterdam sat behind a mahogany desk in his penthouse in New York City, reading a private report from his personal assistant titled *The Dissolution of a Drug Organization in West Virginia*. It was a comprehensive report on the greedy bureaucrats in West Virginia who had to be eliminated with extreme prejudice. It contained the details of a plane crash, a house fire, a hostile takeover and breakup of a major law firm, and a payoff to a deputy sheriff. The extreme actions ensured that every trace of Rotterdam's participation in the illegal drug trade was eradicated.

Alexander could be in any of his more than a dozen residences, including several palatial estates in foreign countries. However, this was where he most often resided because it was closest to the seat of world power. He was sometimes called "the boss" or "Alexander the Great." He approved of those monikers because he'd earned them, and they bolstered his self-image.

He had enemies, but none declared themselves as such because his brutality was legendary. His business tactics often had more in common with a mob boss than a hard-nosed businessman. He was a self-made billionaire, much like H. Ross Perot, except he stepped on people instead of over them.

Decades ago, he watched Ross Perot's unsuccessful bid for the Presidency of the United States and toyed with the idea of seeking that office for himself. He was an egotist and harbored visions of world conquest, but he was also a realist. If he permitted his past to come under public scrutiny, something that was sure to happen if he entered the political arena, the risk of disaster was far too great. He was pragmatic enough to know that, at least for the time being, he operated best behind the scenes, tweaking power while limiting his own exposure. However, he was optimistic enough to believe that he could tweak power to the extent that, eventually, public scrutiny would no longer be of consequence.

Even when he was sixty-eight, Alexander still envisioned dominating the world through deception, manipulation, and covert violent seizure. He had worked with Vladimir Putin to install a lackey con man into the Presidency of the United States, and even though the lackey failed to win reelection, Alexander secured him a second term four years later. During those intervening years, Alexander's situation changed, and his new ambition was to pave the way for his young son.

Alexander was a Republican by nature and the architect of his own success. He felt no compassion or empathy toward poor people. If they failed to get what they needed for themselves, they didn't deserve to have it handed to them. He believed that if you gave a man a fish, the only thing you've done was encouraged him to become a *"set ass,"* but if you turned him into a slave, then you've created an *"asset."* Money and power were the only things that really mattered in his world.

Alexander married for the first time at nineteen, and his first wife was the only child of a widower real estate developer. He could have gone on working for his father-in-law for decades, but he couldn't wait for his wife to acquire her inheritance through the natural course of events. An unfortunate accident made her an orphan and him the head of the company before his twenty-fifth birthday. At thirty-three, after he had tripled the company's value, his first marriage ended, childless and bitter. His wife had wanted half of the fortune, but what she got was the same fate and misfortune as her father.

Three years later, at thirty-six, he remarried, and his second wife fared much better. She had given him two daughters and had been with him as his ruthlessness and wealth multiplied. During that time, he became a card-carrying member of the privileged billionaires. After twenty-eight years of mediocre family life, at the age of sixty-five, he ended his second marriage with a divorce. He gave his second wife and each grown daughter a very generous settlement in exchange for quitclaim agreements to any further entitlement to his estate.

He married his current third wife four years after his second marriage ended. She had been a child bride of sixteen and the daughter of Romanian royalty. His bride hadn't wanted to relocate to America, so he had allowed her to continue to live at his palatial estate in Romania, and he became a commuter between Romania and New York City. Six months later, his young wife became pregnant. After learning it was a boy growing in her womb, he'd cajoled and coerced her into moving into his estate in Hawaii two weeks before her delivery date. He had wanted his son to be born on American soil.

He'd promised she could return to Romania after the boy was born, but that was only one of many false promises. He found true love when he looked into his son's eyes. He hadn't known how powerful love could be until he gazed into the face of the most beautiful baby ever born. He grew weary of the frequent trips to Hawaii to see his son and could no longer bear to have him so far away. He forced his young wife to move into his estate in the Hamptons, and from there, it was only a short move to his penthouse apartment.

Even as a newborn, his son displayed a natural charisma that drew people to him. Later, taking the boy out in public became a pure pleasure. Almost everybody who saw the little Prince fell in love with him, fawned over him, and was reluctant to leave him. There had been only one exception to that kind of reaction. It had happened when he'd taken his son to the Archbishop of Boston for a christening ceremony.

He wasn't Catholic and had never had any use or respect for religious affiliations. His only motivation for having the ceremony performed was the calculation that it might benefit the boy later in life. Many regular church members were at the service, and he immediately noticed that an excessive number of them seemed oblivious to his son's charm. When the old Archbishop took his son in his arms, the old goat feigned illness and the service was abruptly canceled.

He overheard whispers of words like blasphemy and unholy presence, and once, he even heard the word Antichrist. He rationalized that those church members must have been referring to a previous service or a movie because there was no way any of those words could be connected to his son. Since then, Alexander studiously avoided churches, whether his son was with him or not. Those self-righteous hypocrites were undeserving of the presence of his beautiful boy.

His son, Herodias Nathan Rotterdam, proved exceptional in many ways. He learned to walk and talk early and displayed an amazing talent for communicating with anybody. At age four, he did tricks nobody could explain, and he was already computer-literate. He had been special at birth, but his beauty and charm continued to increase daily.

Although he could see how his son affected others, Alexander never realized how much his son affected him. His dreams of conquering the world had been so slowly and subtly altered that he didn't realize his ambitions for himself had been transferred to his son. In his new reality, his son, not him, was destined to become the ruler of the world.

Eight months ago, in accordance with his new ambitions and objectives, he instituted "Operation Clean Sweep." He started severing all of his associations with criminal enterprises, intending for his son to have billions with which to conquer the world, and those billions would be untainted by even a hint that they were the product of ill-gotten gains.

He had become masterful at handling politicians, so he switched to managing public funds, which had become the most lucrative trade in the world. Now, he had his sights set on the Social Security Trust Fund, and with his lackey con man back in the White House, the most significant coup of his career was within reach. It could nearly double his already enormous wealth; more importantly, it was perfectly legal.

He wanted his son to have so much wealth that he wouldn't need to forcefully seize power. His son would be so charismatic, wealthy, and squeaky clean that leadership of the world would be thrust upon him.

The report he was reading contained details of the end of his illicit activities in West Virginia. Of all his connections worldwide, that greedy bunch of bureaucrats had required the most extreme actions. Even as he was terminating his involvement in activities in other parts of the world, trouble with a sheriff who could not be persuaded to redirect the drug investigations of his department had kept him entangled with a particular U.S. Attorney. When the sheriff was finally removed, a new problem with a deputy sheriff emerged. The former deputy won a reversal of his conviction from the Court of Appeals and was about to file lawsuits. He had to be dealt with, but the deputy had survived several attempts on his life, so killing him didn't seem to be a viable solution.

One of Alexander's greatest strengths was his ability to switch horses mid-stream. He never became irrevocably tethered to any single course of action. When one course of action failed, he quickly switched to another that had a better chance of success. Consequently, when it appeared the ex-deputy must have nine lives, he decided to use his wealth more directly. He'd learned the name of the law firm the ex-deputy went to for representation, bought the firm, arranged for a highly generous settlement, and then disposed of the firm at a profit.

After giving him ten million dollars, Alexander was confident the ex-deputy would no longer be a problem. However, he had no such confidence in the greedy bureaucrats. Their corruption had served him well, but their greed and tenacity had become a liability. He sent his assistant down there to eliminate the problem. His assistant arranged a chartered flight to Atlantic City with a prearranged appointment with disaster. The brother of one of those associates had collected evidence that might prove troublesome. So, scheduled to occur at the same time as the air disaster, that brother would disappear, and every trace of the house itself would be completely erased.

His man had put a twenty-four-hour watch on the house the day before, so he knew the ex-deputy and a kid had entered the house. The ex-deputy might have caused the assistant's plan to fail if he'd still been inside the house at the scheduled time of its destruction. Fortunately, his assistant had had a surprise encounter with the ex-deputy and wisely avoided a confrontation. The man had escaped the house, leaving three men dead in his wake.

A wry smile creased Alexander's face as he read that detail. He was delighted that his decision – his horse-swapping – to buy the former deputy off rather than killing him had been the most practical solution. Now, the matter was permanently closed.

Alexander looked at the former deputy's name: William Jacob McCallum. He expected never to hear that name again. After all, the guy was a small fish in a small pond, notwithstanding that he'd made him a slightly bigger fish by giving him ten million dollars. But the big pond was still a long way from the backwaters of West Virginia, and it took a lot more than a few million dollars to become a player on the world stage.

He scanned the four-page report into his computer system before shredding the hard copy. He allowed only himself and his young son access to those files, and his system had more layers of protection than Fort Knox. Although he was an old man and might never have any use for much of the information he stored, his five-year-old son might. Alexander was thrilled that he would soon turn over his entire empire to his little Prince.

CHAPTER 35

After they finished eating, Nick and Walker went out to help the kids set up some of the toys and games Sarah and Billy had picked up at Walmart, and Jake took the preacher into his new den. He told Jenny to wait thirty or forty minutes before she asked Nick and Walker to join them there. Jake didn't miss the prison camp, but he missed having discussions with the preacher, and he wanted some time alone with him to fulfill his promise to let him be the first to know.

When Nick supervised the work on the house, he remodeled and furnished the den so there would be a place for the security system. He'd put the security hardware behind the modest wooden desk that held a personal computer so that a swivel chair on wheels could easily turn from one to the other. The remainder of the small room was filled with four plush leather chairs that Jake had arranged in a cluster around a glass coffee table.

From the moment he arrived, the preacher had been eager to learn which boy was the Holy Ghost incarnate. Jake had intended to tell him before they sat down to eat, but watching the preacher try to figure it out on his own had become so amusing that he let it continue. He watched the preacher evaluate each boy in turn. He would look from Billy to Walker's two boys. Then he'd look from Nick's boy to his own boy, but each time, his eyes would go back to linger on Billy. Jake was prepared to tell him as soon as they entered the den, but when he glanced out the window, he saw a more entertaining way of doing it.

"If you look out this window," Jake said, "you'll see the Holy Ghost incarnate."

Jake stepped back to give the preacher more room and himself a better angle from which to watch. Eli stared out the window, and Jake patiently waited for him to realize the enormity of what he was seeing. After a few minutes, the preacher finally reacted, but not as Jake expected.

With a broad smile, the preacher said, "I'm not surprised. I had already guessed. Your son was really the only possible choice. Your brother's son is a little too old, and my son and your friend's two sons all have older siblings."

Jake stepped over and looked out the window. He couldn't help but smile when he saw Billy comfortably dressed in shorts and a tank top. He was standing beside the picnic table.

"I'm sorry," he said, "but my son wasn't there a moment ago. I was referring to the one *sitting on* the picnic table."

Jake stepped back again to watch. This time, he was rewarded with what he'd expected: a vastly more entertaining reaction. The preacher's face went through a full spectrum of expressions, flashing from shock to disbelief, disbelief to awe, and finally, from awe to skeptical acceptance.

"Are you sure?" the preacher said without turning his head.

"Allow me to answer that question with a question," Jake said. "Have you ever considered the relationships among the Entities of the Holy Trinity?"

Eli glanced at Jake and returned his attention to the window.

"God the Father and God the Son share a common familial bond to which we can easily relate," Jake said, "but what about God the Holy Ghost? What relationship does the Holy Ghost share with the Father and the Son? A Brother and Uncle, respectively. Or a First and Second Cousin? Surely, the Holy Ghost couldn't be a nonfamilial Acquaintance or, God forbid, a Perfect Stranger. Given the logic of established patterns, shouldn't the fact that Two share a common familial bond tell us there must be a conventional familial bond with the Third?"

"Yes, yes," the preacher whispered, staring out the window.

"While you're thinking about that," Jake said, "let me give you something else to ponder. Which came first, the chicken or the egg?"

This time, the preacher tore his gaze from the window and gave Jake a mildly annoyed look.

"No, really, I'm not joking," Jake said. "Seriously."

"Creation dictates the chicken, of course," Eli replied.

With what at first seemed to be a digression, Jake said, "The conceit of male superiority is just that: conceit. The idea that God created the male and then created the female to be subservient to the male is nothing more than male chauvinism. It comes from men, not from the Bible. The male and the female were created simultaneously as a single creature. The male isn't more suited for leadership because his gender is the same as God the Father's, and the male isn't entitled to special considerations based on his seniority of creation because he has no seniority.

"God is so often referred to as the Father, but not the Mother," Jake said, explaining the harsh treatment of Frankie by his father and the loving indulgence from his mother. "The Bible contains many references to the person, character, and work of the Holy Ghost, and not one of those references is inconsistent with a mother's love. It appeals to my sense of constancy that the Holy Trinity is so in harmony with our concept of family that it also includes the Personality of a Mother. The family unit has always existed in Heaven as the Holy Trinity.

"No creature was ever created by God as strictly male. They were all created in God's image as trinity beings. *Let US make man in OUR image,* the Bible says. Adam was placed in the garden and then separated into male and female, each entity possessing half of a yet-to-be-expressed third entity. Family wasn't a brand-new concept freshly minted by God for humanity. God was working from the perfect template: the Holy Trinity. Heaven wasn't based upon what existed on Earth. What exists on Earth was based on what first existed in Heaven."

"Yes, yes," the preacher said again, getting more excited. "The chicken had to be separated into the rooster and the hen to make its offspring, the fertilized egg, possible," Eli said. "Amazing. The fact that all of God's earthly creatures were created as trinity beings like Himself before being separated into male, female, and offspring proves a logical, natural progression from God to the physical world and mankind."

Jake said, "When I invited you here, Eli, you were reluctant to bring your family into my home because you believed my home was a male-only household. Your reluctance was somewhat mollified when I assured you I now have a wife and son. Considering how you're looking forward to spending eternity in Heaven with your family, how much more pleasing is it to know that Heaven is not a Male-only Household?"

Nick and Walker were at the door sooner than expected. His and Eli's alone-time had flown by.

"Sorry to interrupt," Nick said from the doorway. "Mind if we join you?"

"Come in, come in, and welcome," Jake called to his brother. "We've been discussing the Holy Ghost coming into the world in the flesh. I know you guys don't see things exactly like we do, so I beg your indulgence."

Jake brought Nick and Walker up to speed in their discussion. He told them about the significance of God being a Trinity Being, the family nature of the Holy Trinity, and how all earthly fauna were created as trinity beings. Then, Jake explained his purpose for inviting everybody there for the weekend.

"Discussing The Holy Ghost was the primary reason for this gathering, but I also brought you here to warn you. A new, more deadly pandemic is coming relatively soon, but a more immediate concern will come from the disintegration of law and order and the presence of demons in the world. Demons have become more active in this natural world, and their presence will be a danger affecting all our families."

After explaining how a new alliance would be made between America and Russia, Jake told them about his experiences with demons, including details of the incident with the prison guard that he'd not previously revealed to Nick.

"We can fight those dangers separately or face them together," Jake said. "I propose we circle the wagons. Contingent upon Nick's approval, I propose everybody here moves into this hollow. This house, Nick's house, that empty house, and this entire hollow needs to be consecrated against Satan and his demons."

"That would solve only part of the problem," Eli said. "Demons can still gain entrance, even upon hallowed ground, if they find a suitable host, like one did at a synagogue where Jesus was teaching."

"Yes," Jake agreed. "And consecrated ground wouldn't have stopped that prison guard and won't stop the coming lawlessness and plague from being brought among us. That's why this hollow must also be protected against human intrusion."

"Are you talking about an armed compound?" Nick asked.

"More like a restricted community," Jake said, "but I do plan to hire armed security guards. Nick, since you've already improved the security of this hollow, I was hoping you'd take the position of chief of security."

Jake knew by Nick's reaction that he wasn't outright rejecting the idea, so he expanded on the subject.

"In fact," Jake said, "I propose we expand our community and bring in whoever we want. I have a friend and his family I met in North Carolina in mind. We could build over a dozen homes and still have plenty of room. We could even build ten times that many and still not be as crowded as the coal camps were in the early part of the last century."

"Eli, Walker," Jake continued, "if Nick has no objections, I invite both of you to move into this hollow with your families. You could stay in this house until we build more houses, or we could bring in mobile homes, temporary or permanent, whichever you prefer. There's also that fairly nice, empty house on that third property that Nick bought."

Eli said, "That's very generous, but ..."

"Excuse me," Jake interrupted, "but I'm not looking for an immediate decision. Eli, I chose this weekend because something will happen to you that will give you a whole new perspective on this world. Before making any decisions, we'll need multiple meetings that include the ladies."

"This is kind of far from my job," Walker interjected.

"We'll need more security personnel," Jake said. "The more positions we can fill from within, the better. I hoped you would take one of those security positions and work with Nick."

"I don't understand what you meant by something happening, but I'm afraid I don't know the first thing about security," Eli said, "and I have no experience with guns."

"That's not a problem," Jake said. "Our community will need a church and a pastor. I know Nick is qualified, but again, if he has no objections, I hope you will fill that position."

"I have no objections," Nick said. "In fact, I offer my services in any capacity that might be helpful."

"Thank you, Nick," Jake said. "I didn't doubt you for a minute, brother. I would not have proposed any of these plans otherwise." Turning to the preacher, he said, "If you become our resident prophet, you could start a TV ministry, preaching and teaching to the world from right here."

"Amazing," the preacher said, laughing. "Do you know what that meeting was about that I skipped to come here? It was an exploratory meeting to start a TV ministry."

"If you broadcast from here," Jake said, "I guarantee you would have complete autonomy. I can cover the start-up costs," he added, confident that he'd found the true purpose for his money. "If you become our resident prophet and preach the Bible like you did at the prison camp, you can save a whole new crop of souls."

"That's very gracious," the preacher said, "but it seems to me that you have more of a claim to the title of prophet than I do."

"But that will change, and besides, my name isn't Elijah," Jake said. "And I wasn't commissioned to preach to the world."

"Could you be more specific," Eli said. "I don't understand."

"The last two verses in the Old Testament," Jake said, "speak of Elijah, one of only two men who ascended to heaven without dying. Those two men, Elijah and Enoch, will be the preachers at the Wailing Wall during the tribulation period. The Antichrist will kill them. Since it was decreed that man was appointed once to die, these two men were prevented from suffering death for the express purpose of preaching at the Wailing Wall.

"You're the reincarnation of that Elijah," Jake continued. "First, you'll preach to the world, and then you'll be killed at the Wailing Wall and lie in the street for three days. You came back into the world as the Holy Trinity did but without the necessity of a virgin birth. You reentered the world by God performing what science might call artificial insemination."

The preacher opened his mouth to speak but was momentarily at a loss for words.

"We'll have plenty of time to talk about that later," Jake said. "Besides, there's another job for me. The supernatural community is becoming much more active. With the help of the Holy Ghost working through me, I must focus on the unnatural world and the Antichrist, who has already come into the world."

After a brief pause, speaking directly to Nick and Walker, Jake said, "You guys know I went on a trip to try to find the boy who is the Holy Ghost incarnate. I found my son, thank God, but I didn't find the Holy Ghost incarnate until I got back home because the Holy Ghost wasn't a boy; He's a girl."

"Then," Eli interjected, "It's proper to refer to the Holy Ghost as He, even though He is a girl?"

"Absolutely," Jake said. "The female gender exists only among mortal beings. God set the standard that all trinity beings, including Himself, are referred to in the masculine gender. Before God separated Adam into male and female, the Bible referred to that trinity being with the masculine pronouns *him, his, and he*. When God put the trinity being to sleep to separate Eve from Adam, the Bible refers to that trinity being by saying, '*He* slept.'"

Jake continued, "There are no female Angels in the Bible because Angels are immortal and weren't separated into male and female because, like Adam and Eve in the garden, they could never give expression to an offspring. Angels are trinity beings and are therefore always referred to in the masculine gender."

Looking at Nick and Walker, Jake said, "I expected you guys to be hard to convince about this, but that's okay. Fortunately, this isn't a Heaven or Hell issue, so it doesn't pose any danger to your salvation, but something will happen tonight that will stand witness to everything I've said. However, I am surprised that you guys aren't curious. We're talking about God having been born into the world as a girl, and neither of you have asked, or even commented, about the identity of that female."

"I assumed you must be talking about your new wife," Nick said, "and by the way, I agree that this is not a Heaven or Hell issue. Believing or not believing that God is come into the world again can't condemn anybody."

"Walker," Jake said, noticing how uncomfortable he'd become, "who do you think we've been talking about?"

"It must be the preacher's girl," Walker said argumentatively, refusing to lift his eyes from the floor.

"I've already shown the preacher who she is," Jake said, bewildered and disappointed by Walker's reaction. "Now, I'll just tell you guys."

CHAPTER 36

E li Cavenaugh's reaction to the identity of the Holy Ghost incarnate was predictable and entertaining. Given that he wasn't aware of the age limitation, Nick's response was understandable, but Walker Davidson's reaction to the name was alarming and inexplicable. His eyes were closed, he sat in a dejected slump, and the color was drained from his face.

"You don't look good, Walker," Jake said, breaking the silence that followed the name Sarah Davidson, Walker's daughter. "Can I get you something? Maybe a cold drink?"

"I think I have to leave," Walker said weakly, but he didn't immediately open his eyes. Then, instead of getting up to leave, his eyes popped open, and he said, "It can't be Sarah. She would have died if you hadn't saved her."

Walker sounded miserable, as though he'd been told his little girl was demon-possessed instead of God incarnate. He acted like his life depended on Jake being wrong.

"I didn't save her," Jake said gently, but Walker flinched as though he'd screamed it. "If you're well enough to continue, I can prove it."

"Just get it over with," Walker said with ambivalence, clearly torn between a desire to resolve the issue quickly and dreading the outcome.

"I'll be as brief as possible," Jake promised. "I'll only mention two of these things little Sarah knew that should have been beyond her knowledge and maturity."

He had a list of nearly a dozen of the most apparent instances of insights he attributed to Sarah. To save time, he only went into the details of the first and last. The list began with the "I love you, I

341

know" game little Sarah invented as soon as she could talk. The list ended with the "you'll see Sarah soon" prediction that referred to big Sarah, but he'd mistakenly thought little Sarah was referring to herself in the third person.

"We can talk more about the others later," Jake said. "Since he was around her a lot more than I was, I'm sure when Walker's feeling better, he'll remember many more formerly misunderstood instances of her very smart, mature behavior."

He glanced at Walker, and what he saw was alarming. Walker looked wild-eyed as though his grip on reality was tenuous at best. Jake couldn't understand it, but the more he talked about little Sarah, the more troubled Walker became.

"Let's move on to the miracles," Jake said, hoping the miracles would give Walker a better perspective and an appreciation for the rare honor of his position. "There were numerous miracles," he continued. "The dogs that saved me from the rattlesnakes, the mysterious window that turned out to be the only glass in the prison camp, the incident of that car wreck while my Jeep was stuck in the ditch, and several others, but in the interest of time, I'll talk about only two. I'll start with the most recent."

"This is a picture of my son's back," Jake said as he produced a print from his camera phone. "The injuries that caused those scars were inflicted on Billy at an early age. The first night we arrived here, his mother discovered all those scars were gone, and I took another picture."

He produced a second picture and passed them both around.

"I mistakenly decided Billy was the Holy Ghost incarnate and that he had drawn me to himself," Jake continued, "but now I realize that if I hadn't had an irresistible urge to stop and call little Sarah, I would never have laid eyes on him. Later, I assumed that Billy had healed himself, but now I realize the healing touch came from little Sarah. Billy had always been sensitive about anybody touching those scars, but I saw Sarah casually lay her hand on the most disfigured area, and Billy didn't react at all."

When they came to him, Walker glanced at the snapshots and returned them to Jake. He seemed more connected to the world; some color had returned to his face.

"We'll move on to the miracle to which Walker referred," Jake said. "A little over a month ago, little Sarah had a brain tumor, and she almost died. It was one of the encounters with demons that I mentioned earlier."

"You saved her," Walker insisted. "I had no choice," he added, closing his eyes again, "I was just trying to save my family."

Jake had no idea what Walker was talking about, but he appeared to be retreating into his own private hell again. His whole attitude seemed off-kilter, as though he was being persecuted instead of being allowed to follow in the footsteps of Joseph. Jake continued by describing the brain tumors that afflicted little Sarah and many other little girls of the same approximate age.

"Sarah described her tumor to me as 'bad people,' and now I understand why," Jake said. "I know the tumor was demons. She knew I would come, and she knew I would make the bad people go away. She knew I would be a willing vessel into which she could push them."

Walker moaned, but Jake ignored it and added, "I have no personal power over sickness or demons. I could neither take the sickness from a woman I met on the road trip nor the scars from Billy's back. I didn't pull the demons from Sarah. She pushed them out. But if Sarah had pushed those demons into animals, she would have destroyed those animals."

Jake briefly digressed to explain how unnatural laws govern the unnatural world, illustrating a few examples of animals destroying themselves rather than accepting demonic possession.

Jake continued. "The tumors disappeared in those other little girls because when Sarah didn't die, Satan knew he'd found the Holy Ghost incarnate. The other demons would have been recalled. It's another unnatural law; Satan is not in the business of sending little girls straight into the lap of God. I didn't know it then, but I know it now; I was inoculated against the effects of the demons. We'll talk more about that later, but suffice it to say, Eli and I share a past far beyond this natural world."

Ignoring for the moment Jake's remark about a shared past, the preacher said, "Saving the best for last, I presume. The definitive proof. The virgin birth."

"Exactly," Jake said.

He retrieved the package he'd gotten from the doctor and ripped the wrapping off. On top of three medical files, he found a short, two-page report. He'd asked the doctor to review these files and, based on the information they contained, give his best guess as to the little girl's paternity. While unwrapping the package, Jake noticed Walker had regained his composure, and he hoped his friend could stay that way.

"By the way, Walker," Jake said, "I took the liberty of getting yours and little Sarah's medical records along with mine."

"What?" Walker nearly screamed. "You can't do that. I'll sue the hospital."

A flush of anger colored Walker's face, and the outburst took Jake aback. He hadn't expected a hostile reaction. He'd guaranteed there would be no legal problems, and he was sure Walker wouldn't go to court, but he would do whatever was necessary to keep his promise.

"I'm sorry, but I'm the only one to blame," Jake said. "I borrowed these records without the hospital's knowledge. If you sue anybody, you'll have to sue me. I got these records because they'll prove what you and I already know."

"Why are you doing this to me?" Walker cried angrily.

Jake was reminded of his own anger when Walker accused him of sleeping with Donna, but this anger seemed counterfeit. After a moment, he concluded that it wasn't anger at all. It was the natural response of a cornered animal.

"Easy," Jake said, "this is necessary to get at the truth. I must ask you a question; you don't have to fear the answer. What made you think I had slept with Donna?"

Walker seemed to accept that question with more equanimity, as though it was less threatening. He explained the circumstances that had caused him to make that accusation.

"It started with a guy calling me and telling me things about you and Donna," Walker said. "I hung up the first time, but a different guy called the next day. I believed him because he told me things he shouldn't have known. He said he would send me pictures to prove what he said, and a few days later, I found an envelope on my windshield when I got off work. I kept the envelope in the car's glovebox and thought about it for a week before I came to Nick's to confront you. I intended to show you the pictures, but you walked away before I could get them out of the glovebox."

When Walker started wrapping up his explanation, he was almost back to his usual self.

"It wasn't until you took an oath on the Bible that I had to believe you. It hadn't occurred to me until then that I should have the pictures authenticated. When I had them analyzed, it turned out they were photoshopped. When I found out the guy lied, I couldn't believe anything he'd said. I considered apologizing to you again, but I remembered how awkward that first apology was and hoped we could just forget it."

"Thank you," Jake said, "I didn't know that part, and now I can at least understand what motivated you. But that's not the whole story, is it? Isn't it true that little Sarah was born just seven months after you married Donna?" Jake continued, "Although there was no logical explanation for Sarah's early birth, you believed Donna's claim of fidelity right up until the day that guy called you? He must have told you I had been having an affair with Donna before you married her and that I was little Sarah's father. For the record," Jake added, "it would be easy for anybody to calculate Sarah's early birth. However, truthfully, her birth didn't happen early. Anybody who looked at her perfect, fully formed body could tell that Donna had carried her to full term. An immaculate conception is the only explanation."

Just as in Billy's case, simple math was all it took to reveal the truth. Jake had been present the day little Sarah was born, and she had been born fully formed and perfect. She had not been a preemie. He had also been at their wedding, and Walker confided in him that both he and Donna were virgins on their wedding night. These days, the birth of a baby isn't necessarily tied to a wedding, and Jake hadn't even noted little Sarah's arrival just seven months after the wedding until time and circumstance required him to examine the dates.

"I haven't read it yet," Jake said, indicating the report from the package of medical records, but I'm confident it will confirm that I couldn't be little Sarah's father. I doubt it will prove God is the father, but in the immortal words of Sherlock Holmes: when you've eliminated all possibilities, whatever is left, regardless of how improbable it might seem, must be the truth."

Walker leaned forward as huge, racking sobs escaped his throat. Tears flowed from his eyes, and his hands came up to cover the uncontrollable contortions of his face. After several seconds, he managed to choke off the sobs.

"I'm sorry, I'm sorry," Walker whispered.

"It's okay," Jake said, "you don't have to be sorry."

That only drew a renewed series of loud, racking sobs from Walker. Jake had expected this part of the discussion to be a breeze, but Walker's despondency and lack of cooperation were an unexpected hindrance. He couldn't understand his reaction. He'd thought that seeing proof that his best friend had not betrayed him would be cause for joy rather than misery.

Not knowing what to do for Walker, Jake began reading the report. Since he had only asked the doctor for his best guess based on their medical records, he didn't expect to find any conclusive evidence to establish paternity. Still, he expected to be eliminated based on a blood comparison alone. Because he had worn military dog tags, he knew he had a relatively rare blood type. When Jake was a few paragraphs into the report, Walker's crying abated, and his blubbering words became less distorted. A few words were even understandable.

"... unforgivable sin," Walker said, the two recognizable words coming at the end of a long, indecipherable string of sounds. "I denied her," he continued, and after a series of racking sobs, added, "I gave them permission to kill her."

After making those declarations, Walker regressed deeper into his private hell again, his words running together and becoming incoherent but filled with regret and misery.

Jake found something totally unexpected in the report. It did indeed contain conclusive evidence of paternity. It also contained a perfectly understandable explanation for Walker's odd, sorrowful behavior.

Jake got up and took the report with him. He went to Walker's chair and absently handed the report to Eli as he considered how to proceed. Finally, he knelt in front of Walker.

Walker was quieter, but his hands still covered his face, and he seemed totally unaware of Jake's nearness.

"Walker," Jake said gently, "Walker, you're wrong."

Walker remained locked inside his world of misery, completely unresponsive.

From what Walker said and what Jake read, he discovered that Walker must have realized that little Sarah was the Holy Ghost incarnate early on. Walker wasn't suffering from being the center of attention and fearing the responsibility of his position. His pain went much deeper. Because of his lifelong commitment to God, he was fearful that he'd committed the unforgivable sin. He had denied the Holy Ghost in the person of his daughter.

Jake hadn't connected Walker's reactions to each stimulus until he'd finished reading the report. Walker had become agitated at the first indication that the Holy Ghost had been born into the flesh of a girl. He'd become positively miserable when little Sarah was identified by name, and finally, he'd completely lost control of his emotions when he found out Jake had his medical records. Walker knew his medical file would reveal the paternity test that proved he'd questioned the legitimacy of his daughter just before he'd given her up to die.

"Walker?" Jake said, shaking the arm of the chair, but there was no response. He shook the arm of the chair harder, and when there was still no response, he raised his hand high and forcefully slapped the arm of the padded, leather chair.

Walker jumped, and his hands came away from his face. His hands and cheeks were wet with tears, and his nose was runny, but for the moment, he was startled out of his misery.

Handing him a box of tissues from the desk, Jake gently said, "Listen to me. You're wrong. You can't accidentally or unintentionally commit the unforgivable sin."

Walker's eyes widened, and he sat up straighter in the chair. For the first time, he appeared hopeful.

When the doctor agreed to study the three medical records, Jake did not suspect what might be in Walker's file. As it turned out, his and Sarah's medical files were superfluous. According to the report, soon after his daughter was confined to the hospital, Walker ordered a DNA paternity test. The hospital sent the samples to an independent lab, but the results were posted to Walker's file.

The paternity test itself was inconclusive. Jake couldn't be eliminated as the father, but neither could Walker. In fact, 99.9 percent of the world's male population could not be eliminated. The report explained that the only reason the figure wasn't 100 percent was that an exhaustive study would be required to reach that determination. There were extra markers in little Sarah's DNA that made neither race, blood type, nor the combination of any other traits adequate eliminating factors.

The lab concluded that there could be only one explanation for those impossible results: the child's blood must have been contaminated. The lab recommended that the child be brought in for further testing. There was no record of a second test, possibly due to the child's immobility.

"The paternity test's inconclusive nature is itself the conclusive evidence," Jake said. "If DNA analysis were a known science two thousand years ago, the same claim of a 'contaminant' would have been found in Jesus's blood.

"Everything happens for a reason, Walker," Jake continued. "God won't put more on us than we can bear. Maybe you needed to believe another man fathered Sarah to give you enough strength to give her up so that what must happen could happen." Jake compassionately reminded his friend, "If you'd intended for her to die, you could have refused to call me. Besides, unintended consequences result from accidents, not from purposeful actions. You can't accidentally commit the unforgivable sin any more than you can accidentally commit murder."

Walker regained more control over his emotions as he wiped his face with a wad of tissues.

"God will judge you by your heart," Jake said, "and He knows better than I that you didn't blaspheme the Holy Ghost. Like you said, you only did what you thought was best. Even if you were sure you weren't her father, I know you still wouldn't have wanted her to die." He finally drew a tenuous smile from Walker when he added, "Sometimes your brain might go AWOL, but your heart has always been in the right place."

When Eli finished reading the report, he got up and handed it to Nick. He then came over and joined Jake, kneeling at the right side of Walker's chair.

"I don't know all the details," Eli said, "but I've heard enough to agree with Jake. You must have had reason to be suspicious of that birth so soon after your wedding, but you didn't put your wife away. Even Joseph had intended to put Mary away until an Angel visited him." Standing up, the preacher added, "I do not doubt that God in His infinite wisdom chose the right man and woman to care for His Holy Entity."

"Amen," Jake said, standing up and taking a step backward to give Walker room to stand up.

When Nick joined them, they shook hands in fellowship and committed themselves to each other to become a small community where all their children could grow up safely.

Eli returned to Jake a second time and, while shaking his hand again, said, "I've got to ask. What did you mean when you said that you and I shared a past beyond this natural world, and how do you know everything you've been saying, like how I'll die?"

"Classic Elijah," Jake said with a chuckle. "Patience was never your greatest virtue, my friend. You are my witness to everything I've said. I was born a few days before you, but I'm confident that your edification of your past life will occur tonight. The difference in the gestation periods of our mothers was the only reason for our slight age difference. I can't do justice to explaining your past life, so we should wait until tomorrow to talk about it. That's why I needed you here this weekend."

"I'm still confused," Eli insisted.

"You'll indeed die at the wailing wall, but you won't die alone," Jake said. "After tonight, you'll know everything. You'll also understand why you and I were chosen to return to the world like this." Jake assured him.

"Me and you?" Eli asked. "How do you know that?"

Still amused, Jake chuckled again, "Because I was with you in Heaven, and I'll be with you at the Wailing Wall. I'm the reincarnation of Enoch."

ABOUT THE AUTHOR

Russell Marcum, Jr. grew up in the mountains of Wild, Wonderful West Virginia. He graduated from Logan High School in Logan, West Virginia, and received two associate degrees from Southern West Virginia Community College.

Marcum had practical experience in various fields, including law enforcement, coal mining, store clerking, insurance salesman, and over-the-road truck driving, before becoming an aspiring novelist and publishing his debut novel, *Incarnate: The Third Entity*.

Russell is a Christian, a U.S. Army veteran, and a retired Logan County, West Virginia resident.

www.ingramcontent.com/pod-product-compliance
Lightning Source LLC
Chambersburg PA
CBHW071215250626
47159CB00001B/312